Also by Peggy Schimmelman

Whippoorwills
Crazytown
Tick-Tock
Long Stories Short (a Wild Vine Writers' Anthology)
Two Truths and a Lie (a Wild Vine Writers' Anthology)

INSOMNIACS, INC.

PEGGY SCHIMMELMAN

Russian Hill Press Book
United States • United Kingdom • Australia

Russian Hill Press

The publisher bears no responsibility for the quality of information provided through author or third party websites and does not have any control over, nor assumes any responsibility for, information contained in these sites.

Cover design by Paul Schimmelman

ISBN: 978-1-7378246-2-6
Library of Congress Control Number: 2022901717

For the many insomniacs among us. May your wakeful
hours be productive if not peaceful, and may sleep find
you long before dawn.

Acknowledgments

The idea for this book sprang from a writing prompt, "peanut curry," suggested by my fellow Wild Vine Writer Carla Hanson. Other Wild Vine members, Linda Milanese and Julie Orvis, donated months of proofreading and insightful critique. Danielle Cunningham and Loretta Willoughby contributed moral support and advice. Via Zoom, texts, and emails, Wild Vine Writers have kept each other writing and laughing throughout the pandemic. We even completed and published our second anthology, *Two Truths and a Lie,* a collection of short stories, poems, and essays available at Amazon.com.

Kelsey Schimmelman, my talented and perceptive daughter, proofread and critiqued the book as it developed and provided feedback on query letters and synopses.

My editor and friend, Kelly Essary, with insight and an eagle eye, nudged the book into its final form. Cathy Brabec provided input as a beta reader, and Paula Chinick of Russian Hill Press expertly transformed the manuscript into a published novel.

Finally, I'm grateful to my husband, Paul, for the many hours spent designing the awesome cover and for his patience during those times when I "disappeared" during the creative process. I cherish his love and support.

1

The year 2020, with its political hijinks and confounding, life-altering plague, was still six months in the future as Jack and I sipped Sauvignon Blanc on the back patio while FaceTiming with our two daughters. Chloe and Natalie had just finished a jovial, off-key rendition of "Happy 63rd Birthday to Dad" when the customary peace of our suburban neighborhood was shattered by the shrieking of sirens.

Jack cocked an ear toward the end of the block. "Probably Greg Patchett's blood sugar again," he predicted before turning back to the girls. "We'll run down later and check."

But this time the sirens were not for our neighborhood's eldest resident. Within the hour, when we hurried down to the Patchetts to find out if Greg was still among the living, we learned that Michael Redding, the disagreeable young musician who lived on the corner (and had once advised Jack to "get a life, old man"), had been found face down on the kitchen floor, clutching his cell phone following a frantic 911 call. Greg and Brenda shared with us the horrifying experience of watching the sheet-covered body being carried from the house on a stretcher and loaded into the ambulance.

"Of course we stayed inside," Brenda explained from their doorway, clutching the back of Greg's wheelchair for support. "We couldn't hear everything, but I swear one of the policemen used the word 'murder.' I heard him clearly."

"Uh-huh." Jack gave me a sideways glance.

Brenda hadn't heard anything clearly for ten years or more, even when she inserted the new high-tech hearing aids her kids had forced upon her, and the idea of a murder in our quiet neighborhood seemed about as likely as the drought-busting rainstorm we so desperately needed.

Greg said, "But you know, Nancy Abbot's new tenant, the Korean with the twin toddlers,"—he waved a bony arm toward the house across the street— "she overheard one cop say it was something Redding ate. He was allergic to peanuts, you know."

"Oh, that's true," I said, remembering the musician's snarling response to a well-intentioned platter of cookies that was meant to welcome him to the neighborhood. (How was I to know?)

"If he called 911 himself, he must have swallowed something with nuts in it by accident," Jack speculated.

Brenda verified, "Oh yes, he did make that call himself. We both heard that part for sure. Right, Greg?"

Greg concurred, and we held onto the best possible scenario of the death being an accident until the young detective assigned to the case visited our home the following evening to set us straight.

"Andrew Thacker. Call me Andy." The detective flashed an amiable grin as he brandished his badge and pressed a card into Jack's palm. Jack reached for it, pulling himself up to his full five foot seven and throwing out his chest, rooster-like, as men will do when they find themselves eyeball to chin with a taller person.

Despite the identification, it was hard to reconcile his appearance with his profession—although admittedly, my exposure to homicide investigators had been restricted to movies, TV, and mystery novels—an African American man with a stylish buzz cut, black-framed rectangular glasses, and a spiffy wardrobe that complimented his skin tones while de-emphasizing his portly build, which (we would soon learn) reflected his habit of forking mooched food into his mouth at every opportunity. Jack, an enthusiastic bestower of sobriquets, would soon be referring to him as "Detective Lumpy." Also "Detective Dumbass" and "Officer Chunkybutt." Just between him and me, of course. Jack is sly but not cruel.

"Say, Marilyn, my mom is a redhead," the detective said as Jack led him into the dining room. "Hers is a salon job, but I'm thinking yours is real. Am I right?

What a thing to ask a sixty-two-year-old woman. No doubt they trained him in detective school to win over suspects and potential witnesses with a compliment.

"This is my natural color," I informed him.

"These days, she gives it a little help now and then," said Jack for no good reason other than his tongue's inability to lie immobile in his mouth for more than a few seconds at a time.

The detective eased himself into a chair at the table and opened his laptop. "Go ahead and finish your dinner. We can talk while you eat."

Jack swallowed his last bite of pork loin, but my appetite was adversely affected by the unfamiliar police presence at our table, so I collected our plates and walked them over to the sink while the detective readied his computer for our testimony.

"This is my first homicide case," he told us, as if it were something to boast about instead of cause for concern.

"Homicide? But we thought it was an accident," Jack said, and we exchanged dismayed glances as I returned to my chair. "He was allergic to peanuts, you know."

"It could've been an accident," Thacker conceded. "There was evidence that pointed to that, certainly. But other factors suggest the possibility of murder, so we have to investigate it as such."

After that unsettling news, he returned to the process of boasting about his credentials. He had just finished an extensive training program after a solid year of police work on the streets of Oakland and another two in San Diego.

I did the math in my head. Twenty-three, twenty-four? Younger than both my daughters, which is a comparison I tended to make out of habit. Not that either Natalie or Chloe was looking for a husband, and not that I was yearning for grandchildren. It was reflexive, is all.

"I'm thirty-one," he said, and chuckled at my obvious surprise. "There were a few lost years between high school and college." He shook his head, smiling at the memories.

"Your mother must be proud," Jack told him. "So much responsibility at such a young age. And I'm sure you're well qualified."

The "let's get on with it" went unspoken, but I kicked him under the table anyway.

Thacker smiled. "Yes, I do believe she's proud. And thrilled to have me living with her here in Las Oliviñas. I was most fortunate the police department had an open slot."

"Moved here from Oakland, did she?" asked Jack. "That seems to be a trend."

I cringed, but the detective chuckled. "Oakland? No, not Oakland. She lived most of her life in San Francisco, where I grew up as well. I know it's more affordable out here in the East Bay, but the big draw for Mom is her sister. She bought a little bungalow on the north side of town, same neighborhood as Aunt Maddie."

"That's nice," I said. "Family is so important."

I did find it interesting that a man in his thirties was

living with his mother, and I was mildly curious about the circumstances of the situation. But a neighbor was dead—possibly murdered! —his body only one day cold. Perhaps we should get down to business. What did Thacker's mother's downsizing have to do with anything? We didn't even know the woman. Or the detective either, for that matter.

His smile faded, and for a moment I thought he was about to share more irrelevant personal information. But then he brightened.

"What's for dessert, if I might ask? Do I smell cookies?"

I did the polite thing and brought out coffee and a plate of brownies. He reached for one with a childlike eagerness.

"Mmm, tasty. You bake these yourself? I guess marrying a home economics teacher has its benefits, huh Jack?" He had done some research. Not entirely inept, we could hope.

After savoring a bite and dabbing his mouth with the cloth napkin I'd provided, he positioned his hands above the computer keys, ready to record our comments. Or so we thought. As it turned out, his laptop sat useless throughout the interrogation while he savored his dessert, too engrossed by our conversation to bother taking notes.

"So, what do y'all do with yourselves now that you're retired? Keeping busy?"

Jack's eyes met mine: *Seriously? This is his idea of an investigation?*

"It's been less than a year," said Jack. "We took an RV trip up the coast last fall."

Our little road trip being too boring to pursue, Detective Thacker pressed on. "What else? Any hobbies, either of you?" He winked at me. "Besides baking, I mean."

As if baking shouldn't count as a hobby.

"She's really good at it," said Jack, offended on my behalf. "She bakes every day. She's like an *artiste* in the kitchen." He closed his eyes and kissed his fingertips for effect.

"Not every day," I clarified. "A few times a week."

"Yes, I can see she's quite the expert. Anything else you do for fun?"

"We're still exploring new interests," I said. "I read a lot and do crosswords. Jack has taken up woodworking and plays golf at least twice a month."

"I work in the yard," Jack contributed. And we take a long walk every day."

I hadn't thought of us as a boring old retired couple, but darned if I could come up with anything more. Even woodworking was more of a goal for Jack than a hobby. Filling up the garage with equipment and supplies was the extent of his progress so far.

A new possibility occurred to me. "Jack's a CPA. He might work part-time during tax season."

Jack sniffed. "That's not my idea of retirement."

From hobbies, we progressed to family matters. Our two daughters: teachers, were they? Took after Mom, huh? Not married? He bet we were eager to get some grandkids. Ever since he'd found steady work, his mother was on him all the time to find a wife, one that was eager to start a family. He was in no hurry, himself. Plenty of time for that.

Then, out of the blue: "What did y'all think of Mr. Redding? Did you know him well?"

Jack bit into his brownie, leaving the response to me. Smart move—confessing animosity towards a recent murder victim was a sure way to land oneself on a suspect list.

I groped for something positive to say about our surly, inconsiderate, and sometimes downright provocative neighbor, but then decided to stick to the facts.

"We only spoke to him a couple of times. Right after he moved in, we went down to welcome him to the neighborhood. It was a short visit—he didn't invite us in. And two other times we had to ask him—Jack asked him— to keep his dog from doing its business in our yard."

"So you weren't friendly, I take it?" I hoped his grin meant we weren't being seriously interrogated as suspects.

"No," I said. If he heard Jack mutter "Hardly," he didn't let on.

"Any idea what the other neighbors thought of him?"

Jack grunted. "You'll have to ask them."

Andy Thacker raised not so much as one eyebrow and his smile never wavered. "You can bet I will, Jack. But I hope you won't hesitate to share anything that might be helpful—we are treating this as a homicide, as I said."

Jack could restrain himself no longer. "If you must know—and again, this is just my opinion—Michael Redding was an immature, inconsiderate asshole."

"Jack! Language, please."

Under my withering gaze, he shrugged and clammed up again.

To avoid a rant about the rosebush encounter, which I had already heard multiple times and which I knew might reflect as poorly on Jack as on Michael Redding—even though Jack had been completely within his rights to point out that dog pee can hinder bloom production—I said to Thacker, "We have no idea how well he got along with the other neighbors. Speaking only for ourselves, we found him rather abrasive. But as I said, we hardly knew him."

"Fair enough." He sipped his coffee. "Woodworking, huh, Jack? Any particular projects in mind?"

While Jack, caught off guard, tried to muster enthusiasm about chopping blocks and storage cabinets, I reflected on what little I did know about Michael Redding—surely nothing the detective hadn't already uncovered.

Redding had been a professional drummer, or as he preferred to call himself, a percussionist. At any rate, from the racket that assaulted our ears at all hours through his open windows, he must have had a houseful of cymbals, tom-toms, bongos or what have you. He was a surly fellow, but handsome in a dangerous sort of way, if you could get past the aggressive tattoos, piercings, and shaved head. Which I could not, but presumably younger women were attracted to tongue studs and that sort of thing.

When the woodworking discussion had run its course, the detective said, "I may take it up one day myself," and then suddenly remembered why he had come.

"Before I forget, where were you both between 2:30 and 3:00 yesterday afternoon?" He looked from one of us to the other, then chuckled at our obvious shock. "I'm sure you can vouch for each other, am I right?"

"Of course," we both said at once, and I explained about Jack's birthday and our phone conversation with the girls.

"Well then, happy belated birthday!" He scrutinized Jack in a way that suggested he was about to take a stab at guessing his age. Instead, he asked, "And prior to that?"

"I was replacing sprinkler heads in the backyard, and Marilyn went grocery shopping," Jack said. "You can't possibly think—"

"No, no." He gave us a reassuring smile. "I have to ask. It's procedure."

But you don't have to record our answers? Yes, the man was a straight-up amateur.

Jack asked, "Can you tell us why you think Redding might have been murdered? All we know is that he called 911, and something was said at the crime scene about an allergic reaction. That suggests an accident, doesn't it?"

"You think so, do you?" the Detective teased, sounding smug even as he ogled the plate of brownies that sat within his reach. "Do you mind? These are delicious, and I have a wicked sweet tooth."

"Help yourself," I said. "But isn't there something more you could share with us? I mean, Jack is right—an allergic reaction could hardly be classified as murder, could it?"

"Not ordinarily, no. It was the transcript of the 911 call that raised the possibility of homicide."

After dangling that tidbit, he dug into his second brownie and finished it off in three bites, savoring each before swallowing—and savoring our anticipation as well, I imagined. Finally, he wiped his lips and placed the napkin on his plate. And then he stunned us with the shocking details.

Redding hadn't been one to share much, at least not with Jack and me, but one of the few things he had made certain we knew about him was that he had a deadly peanut allergy. Mr. Manners had all but slammed the door in our faces when we went over to welcome him with a tin of assorted goodies that included peanut butter cookies. (Again, how was I to know?)

So we, the Patchetts, and I assume any other neighbor he had ever spoken with, had been aware that peanuts were his kryptonite. And yet there it was (Thacker revealed as we listened in rapt silence), waiting for the cops in plain sight on his kitchen table: a plate of chicken and rice with Thai peanut curry sauce, only a bite or two left uneaten. No fingerprints except his on the utensils, no signs of a disturbance or injuries to the body.

"And yet," the detective continued, "there is the mystery of that 911 call."

And he proceeded to share with us Michael Redding's baffling and incriminating final words: "Help ... allergic... neighbor knows ..."

While we were still struggling to make sense of it, Thatcher got up and zipped the unused laptop into a bag that I gathered was the modern equivalent of a briefcase.

"Thanks for the dessert and coffee," he said, shaking first my hand and then Jack's. "You'll have to tell me more about Mr. Redding's dog and your yard next time we talk."

"Wait a second," Jack said. "Speaking of the hound, where was he yesterday afternoon between, what did you say, 2:30 and 3 o'clock? Not much of a guard dog, huh?"

The detective smiled. "I'm impressed, Jack. That's a

darn good question. He has an alibi, though. Seems he was in the backyard the whole time. Locked out of the house when the police arrived."

When Jack returned to the kitchen after seeing Thacker to the door, he speculated, "Maybe it really was suicide, and the 911 call was revenge on us for asking him to control that blasted bloodhound. Or on any one of the other neighbors for God knows what."

"Could be," I said. But privately I had to agree with Thacker that Redding's 911 message pointed to murder—and to one of the neighbors, maybe even Jack or me, as either perpetrator or what I believed was called a "party of interest."

"He's probably smirking in Hell right now," Jack grumbled, "pounding away on his bongos, tormenting the other sinners."

"Don't speak ill of the dead," I scolded him. But I had to admit that his theory didn't seem all that farfetched.

2

Excuse me for indulging in stereotypes, but let's be candid: how often does your everyday suburban retired couple commit murder? A tax accountant and a home economics teacher, for God's sake. As if more likely candidates didn't live in nearly every house on the block. Not that the detective ever got around to accusing us of anything outright, mind you. Merely following procedure, he assured us.

Yet he kept returning.

In the first eight days following the death of Michael Redding, Detective Andy Thacker made himself at home in our kitchen on three separate occasions, having timed his arrival to coincide with coffee and dessert. You might think that after the autopsy report listed uniphasic anaphylaxis—severe allergic reaction—as the sole cause of death, he would move on to another case. But no.

"There's more to this story," he insisted, and continued to fire question after question at us, as if hoping that with enough random shots, sooner or later one was bound to hit the bullseye.

On his second visit, he probed for details about our

neighbors' circumstances and habits— "just your impressions"—and for lack of any useful information that I could think of, I found myself relating our encounter with the young Mexican woman who had recently moved into the rental across the street. The relevance of this encounter was dubious, since Michael Redding had been alive in all his inconsiderate, nose-thumbing glory at the time, and his name had never come up during our short visit with the new neighbor.

Relevant or not, I recounted our meeting with this neighbor as best I could remember. Of course, some details were unnecessary, so I left those out in the interest of saving time—and also to avoid the passing of unfair judgment on Jack and me, which could happen if some of my comments were misinterpreted, depending on the Detective's political and social outlooks, which were yet to be revealed.

Jack and I had met Alejandra Stevens (the detective prompted me twice regarding her name—Jack had dubbed her "Pigpen" and the snide but apt moniker kept overriding her real name in my memory) on an evening in early May, almost a month before the murder, as we set off on our habitual pre-dinner walk around the block.

The last shower of the season had saturated the air with the scent of lavender, which merged oddly but not unpleasantly with the dinnertime smell of Chinese something-or-other coming from the house next door, courtesy of old Mrs. Chang. Or was it Chung? I couldn't remember.

"Mmm. Nice." I lifted my head to breathe in the air. But Jack emitted one of the low growls that foreshadowed either a reflux emission or a complaint.

"Great God almighty," he said. "More damn junk every day."

While my husband was practiced at inserting his nose where some might say it didn't belong, this time his disgust was justified. It was aimed at the front porch and yard across the street and their contents, which within a few weeks had come to include a rusty tricycle, a faded, tattered seventies era sofa-bed, a floor lamp with no shade, and a rickety end table, along with a number of overflowing cardboard boxes and various scattered items that I supposed were purchases from the local thrift shops and rummage sales. A cheap acoustic guitar with no strings, tacky lawn ornaments, that kind of junk.

While I had never shared Jack's interest in neighborhood oversight, it was true that one shabby property could make the whole street look like a white trash enclave. Not that we were planning to move anytime soon, but it did pay to keep an eye on property values.

Back when the kids still lived at home and the street bubbled with the energy of families demographically similar to our own, we knew everyone on the block and we all got along swimmingly: block parties, carpooling and what have you, and many of us went to the same church. For years, we had welcomed each new neighbor with a small gathering in our own kitchen, serving them lemonade and sweet treats I had made myself from recipes perfected through years of classroom trial and error.

But more recently, as I explained to Thacker, with the tech boom flushing all but the rich out of San Francisco and Oakland and dumping the overflow onto our own suburban streets, Jack and I had become more inclined to keep to ourselves. Dropping off a plate of cookies and exchanging introductions was about as far as it went anymore, sad to say. By the time this new neighbor arrived, more than half of the houses were owned by investors whose tenants came and went like fireflies, so that it was hardly worth the trouble to learn to pronounce their odd names.

At this point, Jack contributed an elaboration that I might have withheld, considering our audience. "I mean, we're talking all shapes, colors, religions, and sexual orientations here. Hijabs and do-rags, turbans and cowboy hats. Around dinnertime the neighborhood smells like one of those international food courts."

Hurrying things along, I explained to Thacker how we had been allowing our newest neighbor, the one with the junkyard in progress, time to settle in. But since she seemed in no hurry to do so, I told Jack it was time we stopped by to introduce ourselves. The next afternoon, I whipped up a batch of chocolate mint cookies and arranged them on a paper plate, covered with saran wrap and tied with a ribbon, to deliver before we embarked on our walk. She peeked through the drawn curtains before opening the door and stepped outside so fast we couldn't get so much as a peek at the interior.

Before then, I had only caught glimpses from across the street, not registering much more than her outline. Up close, she was quite pretty, with round, curious, deep brown eyes, a sweet smile and thick, glossy black hair that might be stunning if she wore it down around her shoulders instead of in a ponytail poking out the back of a Raiders cap. A shame about all that extra weight—a good twenty pounds over, I guessed, similar build to Chloe, my youngest.

It was hard to guess her age: I might have thought mid-twenties, but we would soon learn that she had a twelve-year-old son, so she must have been at least thirty—or maybe not. I reminded myself that heavy women didn't show their age like the rest of us, even without makeup. And her sense of style gave nothing away, as women of all ages could be seen in public sporting rolled-up jeans, sneakers, and too-tight t-shirts—myself included, although my jeans were creased and rip-free and I preferred t-shirts in my actual size.

(Again, some of these observations and exchanges I elected to withhold, not wanting to clutter my statement with unnecessary details such as mine and Jack's personal impressions that had nothing to do with the Redding case.)

I told Thacker how I had delivered the usual spiel. "We're Marilyn and Jack Middleton from the house across the street, just stopping by to say welcome to the neighborhood, let us know if you need anything, and if you don't have a church, Fifth Street Methodist welcomes newcomers," and so forth.

"I'm Alejandra Stevens. Thank you so much." She accepted the cookie platter and placed it on top of a nearby cardboard box, then wiped her hands on her shirt and let them rest there, fumbling with the fabric, waiting for one of us to initiate a handshake. Jack failed to step up, so it was all on me. It would have been impolite not to do so, despite my long-held view of handshaking as an overrated, meaningless, unsanitary tradition, like casual hugs outside of the immediate family.

We had assumed she was Mexican, possibly undocumented like many in town. Her ex-husband, with the surname "Stevens," could have been the color of our esteemed former president for all we knew. But that was neither here nor there. Despite my girls' often-stated opinions to the contrary, Jack and I were not racists. We might have voted for Obama in the spirit of historical significance, had he been a little less invested in giving undocumented immigrants free college, encouraging abortion as birth control, disarming the military, and raising taxes on people like us.

(Of course, our political convictions were irrelevant to the murder case and therefore were left unspoken.)

Alejandra had wanted to stay in Oakland after the divorce, she told us with only the slightest trace of an accent, but her ex had kept their house in the hills, as well as their son, Kyle.

"I couldn't afford the rent on a decent place by myself.

Nowhere in Oakland, not anymore."

I knew we were supposed to say, "What a shame." But honestly, Jack and I had been flirting with the idea of investing in a rental property in Oakland ourselves, now that the city was being spiffed up. Now there would be more people like us—an observation that was pronounced "racist" by our daughters, who did not buy my explanation that nobody wants to live in a neighborhood where you feel like an outsider and run the risk of being mowed down in your own front yard by a stray bullet or one of those sideshows gone wrong.

(Again, none of Thacker's business, no need to make it part of my testimony—if that's what this was. He was not taking notes anyway.)

"Kyle visits sometimes," Alejandra continued. "But not as much as I'd like him to."

"I know how that feels," I said, surprising myself as well as Jack, whose grimace told me I'd shared too much. But it was the sad truth, although my two daughters were adults with apparently busy lives, and they lived out of state, so circumstances were entirely different. Thank God for modern technology: Sunday night FaceTime and sporadic texts were a poor substitute for their physical presence, but more than my own foster mother had gotten for a few years after I left the nest.

"This is so far from Kyle, but it's the nicest neighborhood I can afford on the money his dad gives me. I'm looking for work, but—" Her eyes flicked away from us. "I married young. I've never actually had a job."

We said our goodbyes, and when we were out of earshot, Jack sniped, "No wonder her son never visits. He'd have to sleep on top of the boxes."

Instead of rewarding this malice with the chuckle he expected, I said, "It would've killed me at her age, to be apart from the girls." That shut him up until I asked, "Do you think she's illegal?" Then remembering a scolding from

Chloe, I corrected myself: "Undocumented, I mean?"

"Wouldn't surprise me. Not much of an accent—but she did say she'd lived in Oakland for twelve years. And her husband can't be Mexican, with a name like Stevens."

A hopeful possibility occurred to me. "Maybe she's gearing up for a yard sale."

But no such event was forthcoming, and soon the mess had spilled off the porch, out of the yard, and into the driveway, while her dusty gray or possibly white van was relegated to the street—directly in Jack's line of vision when he peered out from what was his home office before he retired and which now served as his observation point for monitoring street activity.

At that point, Michael Redding's murder was a few weeks in the future. Murder! On our own peaceful street, in one of the safest neighborhoods in one of the safest cities in the county—or at least that had been true in the past. By the time Alejandra landed in the neighborhood, it was no longer the same atmosphere we used to enjoy, but we all tolerated each other. And except for Michael Redding, rest his soul, no one ever went out of their way to aggravate someone else.

And that is the story I related to Detective Thacker, with a few necessary omissions. What did I say that might justify his continued hounding of us? Was there some shred of evidence in my statement that threw light on the investigation? Did I sound like I was I accusing our neighbor of murder? Best I could tell, there was nothing to suggest that she killed Redding, and I said so to Thacker.

"I'm sure you're right," he said.

In the days that followed, Detective Thatcher continued to dart like a thirsty mosquito from Alejandra's house to the lesbian's house to ours, inviting himself for dessert and asking "just a couple more questions."

Near the beginning of his third visit, Thacker was interrogating us about the neighbors again, when he trailed off mid-sentence. I blinked, startled to discover that he was studying my face.

"Have you been sleeping okay, Marilyn? I wouldn't be at all surprised if Mr. Redding's death was causing you some restless nights."

"She's up and down all night long, every night," Jack complained. "Mostly up."

I frowned at him. What business was it of Thacker's, whether I slept like a baby or wandered the house all night like an agitated ghost?

"I'm sorry to hear that," said Thacker. "You looked exhausted."

His concern seemed so genuine that instead of chafing at the unflattering reference to my appearance, I teared up and began to babble about the insomnia with which I'd been afflicted shortly after that first encounter with Alejandra Stevens (whose name had to be provided again by Thacker, to my embarrassment— but I blamed the recurring memory lapses on lack of sleep, and he seemed to find that plausible).

"The condition of Ms. Stevens' premises are keeping you awake nights?" He seemed surprised by this, although I had seen him leaving her house at least twice since the investigation began, so he must have been aware of the mess.

I nodded. Why mention that his continuing presence in our dining room wasn't helping the situation any, with its implication that either we or one of our neighbors might be the killer he was searching for?

"And the thing is," I said, "none of the other neighbors seem concerned about it. Not even the woman next door to her. Rachel, I think her name is."

He opened his laptop and pecked at the keys. "Rachel Van Buren," he provided.

"Yes, that's her. And before you ask, I don't know her at all. She keeps to herself, especially since her—her partner, or wife, or whatever you call her—died a while back. I've only had one real conversation with her, up at the CVS pharmaceutical counter a few weeks ago."

That piqued his curiosity, and he began to press for details—the tiniest of details such as what time of day it was and what she wore, whether I thought she was depressed.

"Do I look like a psychiatrist?" I asked.

"Sort of, yes," he said with that silly chortle before shoveling another spoonful of tapioca pudding into his mouth.

Perhaps Rachel the Fox (nickname courtesy of Jack, naturally) was a suspect. Not surprising, considering her neurotic behavior and disheveled appearance, along with her obvious attachment to wine and whatever else it was that made her forget to change out of her pajamas.

So I told him how my anxiety over Alejandra's untidy premises had led to an unpleasant encounter with Rachel, our widowed young lesbian neighbor, at CVS. But of course, when relating the incident to Thacker, I left out some irrelevant facts in the interest of saving time and avoiding misconceptions on his part.

A few weeks before Michael Redding's murder, when it had become clear that the junkyard across the street wasn't meant to be a temporary art installation, I began to lie awake nights pondering the situation. What makes a person collect useless, unsightly crap? I hoped to God that our neighbor wasn't one of those hoarders I had seen on TV, but the evidence was stacking up, so to speak, day by day.

I knew it wasn't a cultural thing. Our other Hispanics, scattered here and there throughout the neighborhood, displayed no such clutter-bug tendencies. Quite the opposite. The nearest to us were the Menendez family, two blocks over, who despite the lively presence of three school-age kids, kept their premises spotless. Mrs. Menendez or the oldest girl could sometimes be seen scouring their driveway and even the sidewalk in front of their house.

In search of an explanation, I turned to the internet. Among other potential causes, Google revealed that hoarders were sometimes loath to part with an item for fear they would need it later (a rusty tricycle?) and others were trying to compensate for a devastating loss in their lives by holding onto whatever they could, junk or what have you.

"Maybe she misses her family in Mexico," I said to Jack one morning as we started out on a walk.

"Easy fix for that."

"There's the boy to think about," I reminded him.

When sleep did finally come, it brought with it hellish images of chaos and clutter: greasy casserole dishes and battered pots and pans piled on my otherwise immaculate countertops; Jack and me navigating the mess to get from kitchen to living room, settling in among piles of thrift store clothing to watch TV. If I escaped outdoors, I'd find myself ankle deep in lawn ornaments, boxes waiting to be unpacked, and scatterings of miscellaneous thrift store treasures.

In the worst dream, a Fox News crew showed up to interview us—rare examples of Bay Area voters who had voted Republican in the last election, and I was eager to voice my frustration with my fellow citizens who thought undocumented immigrants shouldn't be deported—as if they weren't breaking a law just by being here.

"You don't let thieves go on stealing, murderers go on murdering. Why have laws at all?"

That's what I planned to say to the reporter. But in this horrid dream, there was no direction they could aim the camera without capturing an unsightly mess in the background. (I saw no need to share this dream with

Thacker: nothing to do with the investigation, and why run the risk of having to defend my political views should he turn out to be yet another liberal?)

Such dreams, which were soon coming more than once a night, would have been unsettling for anyone who cared about the tidiness of her home, and I found myself awakening from them with a galloping heartbeat and the compulsion to walk through the house to reassure myself that everything was in its rightful place.

I had always taken pride in my housekeeping, and since retiring, there was no excuse for the place to be anything but spotless, especially since it was just the two of us. My friend Sue Ellen, rest her soul, used to chide me that when I departed this world, no one was going to exclaim about what a clean house I'd kept, but I argued that this was only convenient justification on the part of those with an aversion to housework.

So as I told Thacker, after a week of losing sleep over my new neighbor's disorderly surroundings, worrying that a health hazard was in the making—mold, rats and what have you—I had driven up to CVS to investigate mild sleeping aids.

Lo and behold, there was Rachel standing in line for a pharmacist's consultation. She was wearing flannel pajamas, I kid you not—a fashion trend for teenagers, yes, but I judged her to be in her early thirties, about the age of Chloe, my youngest. Jack was right, I had to admit: she was a beauty, in a careless, unkempt kind of way—those messy dirty blond curls just begging for a hairbrush. Not that I monitored her premises, but I'd seen her climb in and out of her Prius enough times to know that since the other one's death, her appearance had done a downhill slide from fashionably casual to slovenly.

With a line of customers ahead of her, I figured she wouldn't mind a distraction. True, she had never shown any inclination toward friendship and even less so since the other one died. Still, in my troubled state I longed for commiseration, so although she never met my eyes for more than a split second and did in fact yawn once right in my face, I confided my worries about the junkyard developing next door to her house.

When I suggested she might contact the city herself about the possible health hazards, instead of waiting like the rest of the neighborhood for Jack to put on his sheriff of the block hat, she murmured "huh" and turned her back on me without so much as a nod.

The woman was on something, I would've sworn—something more than the alcohol I smelled on her breath. Pain pills or what have you. I could have stuck around to overhear the consultation with the pharmacist, but it was none of my business if she wanted to medicate herself into a stupor.

At this point, Thacker spoke up. "Ms. Van Buren never contacted the city. But you must've made an impression because she did discuss the situation with Michael Redding. She's the reason he offered to use his van to haul some of Alejandra's, um, accumulations, to the dump."

"That might have pissed her off, don't you think?" said Jack, self-appointed member of the investigative team. "Maybe she flew into a rage when he threatened to take her junk."

"Interesting theory," said Thacker, his tone suggesting it was anything but.

Another juicy revelation by Thacker, who seemed to find nothing unethical or unprofessional about filling us all in on what the others among us were saying: Rachael and Michael had been acquainted from the Coal Bin, a club downtown where Michael's band sometimes performed and where Rachel tended bar whenever she bothered to go to work. Which was none too often anymore, Jack interjected, judging by how her car was always in the driveway, day or night.

As we walked Thacker to the door that evening, he thanked us politely for the dessert and coffee. "And I hope you start getting some sleep, Marilyn. Insomnia can cause all sorts of health problems." He gave me a reassuring smile. "Don't worry. We'll find Mr. Redding's killer."

"I'm sure you will," I lied. "Thanks."

I locked the door behind him, and Jack said, "Let's hope he won't be back. How much more could we tell him, anyway?"

I couldn't think of a thing. But in the weeks that followed, the frequency of Detective Thacker's visits to our home would continue to puzzle, irk, and even alarm us.

And with each of his visits, the insomnia with which I'd been suffering for several weeks prior to the murder intensified. Had I known that certain of my neighbors were similarly afflicted, sleepless and wrestling with their own anxieties at 3:00 a.m., I might have felt less alone and frightened.

But that discovery was yet to come.

3

Five days later, there was a development in the Michael Redding case. As a result, the neighborhood went into sort of a self-imposed lockdown: nobody out walking after dark, blinds drawn and doors locked in the middle of the day—except for Rachel, who sat on the porch and wandered her yard in pajamas at all hours, according to Jack. We learned of this new development during Detective Thacker's fourth dinnertime visit to our kitchen.

"Sorry to drop by unannounced, Marilyn." He brushed by me to pull up a chair at the table where Jack and I had just started on our macaroons and coffee. "You weren't answering the phone, and I have a few more questions."

Jack dabbed his mustache with a napkin, although any stray crumbs were invisible among the salt-and-pepper bristles. "Have a seat. Don't mind us. We're just finishing dinner."

Judging by his chuckle, Thacker found the sarcasm amusing. I frowned at Jack, and he forced an upward turn to his lips. "Fourth time we've had the pleasure of your company at dinnertime. Are we suspects in this case, or is it the dessert you're after?"

The joke fell flat, foiled by Jack's impatient delivery. I

worried that his irascibility might throw further suspicion on us—assuming we really were suspects, which was a ludicrous idea, and yet the man did keep returning.

But Thacker assured us that although all the neighbors were suspects of a sort because of Redding's 911 message, and the macaroons were certainly above average (as were the brownies, cheesecake, and tapioca pudding I had served during his previous visits), he had other motives for gracing us with his presence.

"Have either of you ever seen this before?"

The photo he pulled from his satchel was of a dull gray ceramic dinner plate with a faded floral pattern that might once have represented a bouquet of geraniums. There were two small chips in the rim, one above and one to the right of the pattern.

"Looks like something from the Salvation Army store," Jack commented.

"Actually, they don't accept chipped dinnerware," I said.

Jack snorted, but Thacker said, "Hmm. Is that right?"

He scrutinized the photo from several angles, as if my remark might have raised some mysterious new possibility. Then he tucked it back into his satchel. "Well, anyway. Do y'all ever go over to Oakland?"

"Why? Do they have a less finicky thrift store there?" Jack chuckled at his own wit.

"No, no." The detective smiled just enough to acknowledge the attempted humor. "This is a different matter. That plate is the one Michael Redding was eating from when he died."

I stopped chewing and Jack put down his coffee cup.

"Did he cook the curry himself?" Jack asked, "Or was it takeout?"

Thatcher looked startled to find himself on the other end of the interrogation, and I smiled inwardly. Move over, Columbo.

"Because if it was takeout, you could trace it, right?"

"Possibly. Unfortunately, it did not appear to be takeout. No containers or receipts found anywhere on the premises."

"Too bad," said Jack. "You think he whipped it up himself? I wouldn't have figured him for a chef."

"There aren't any fingerprints to suggest someone else was involved. But we're considering other possibilities."

"Unlikely," pronounced Jack. "Seems pretty clear it was suicide."

"Huh," said Thacker. "Well, we hope to find out."

"I take it you don't think it's Michael's plate?" I asked.

"We don't know for sure. Like I said, no fingerprints on it except for his, but it doesn't match any of the other plates he had in his cabinets. Except for this one, there was only a set of inexpensive bright red dishes purchased at Target. His mother said she gave those to him last Christmas." He was punching keys on his laptop, distracted. "Poor woman. She's heartbroken, as you can imagine."

"His mother?" It had not occurred to me to wonder who might be grieving for Michael Redding. He seemed the sort who would be estranged from his family. I felt a pang of pity for the woman and started to ask if Michael had other close family, but Jack interrupted me.

"So if you think it's not his plate, shouldn't you be searching people's cabinets for matching dishes?" He put down his macaroon. "Oh, I see. Is that why you're here?"

"One of the reasons, yes." Thacker let us absorb that. "But it can wait a few minutes."

The main thing he had come to talk to us about, he said, was an anonymous tip texted from a stolen phone that had been recovered that morning from the top of a trash can in Oakland.

"Well, that figures," said Jack. "Let me guess. The murderer is from Oakland, somebody Redding knew from one of the sleazy joints he played at over there, am I right? Maybe a drug deal gone wrong?"

Detective Thatcher beamed his approval. "That's pretty much exactly what the message said. Maybe I should hire you to give me a hand, Jack. You're quite the sleuth."

Uh-oh, I thought, intuiting the next question before he posed it.

"How did you guess, Jack? I mean that's incredible, really. You pretty much repeated what the text said, verbatim: 'Check out Jenny Ho's and Redding's sleazy friends. Drug deal gone bad.'" He shook his head. "You nailed it, right down to the word 'sleazy.' Amazing."

Unable to process that coincidence, I moved on. "Jenny Ho's? Sounds like a strip club."

He pointed his index finger at me. "Bam! Man, you two are good. It's a bar that features exotic dancers, but on Friday nights they also offer live metal music." He grinned. "A warm-up act, if you will."

Jack and I glanced at each other, both afraid to open our mouths lest we give the impression of knowing too much. Which we absolutely did not.

After a few tense moments, Jack took the plunge. "So the murderer is someone who hangs out at this Jenny Ho's club? Or worked there?"

"Would you mind if I had just one more of these?" The detective gestured toward the plate of cookies, then leaned in to claim one before I finished nodding.

After savoring a bite and washing it down, he said, "Could be. That's what our mystery tip implies, but ..." He paused, looking from Jack to me. "You ever been to Jenny Ho's, either of you?"

"Of course not!" I said. "We don't frequent that sort of place. I never heard of it until you said the name just now."

He shifted his gaze. "How about you, Jack? Had you heard of Jenny Ho's before tonight?"

"Of course he hasn't. He—" Then I saw that Jack's face

and nearly hairless pate were the color of a tablecloth at Christmastime. He coughed.

"I'd heard of it, yes."

"Huh. But you've never been there?" the detective asked in a casual voice, as if inquiring about a restaurant or a new church that had popped up on the outskirts of town, nibbling on his macaroon while he waited for Jack's response—which took a few seconds too long, I thought. The detective might read hesitation as guilt, while I knew Jack was simply embarrassed to admit he was aware that such places existed. The idea that he would set foot in a strip club was laughable. But Jack didn't see the humor, and I was having a little trouble with it myself.

"No." Jack cleared his throat. "As Marilyn said, we don't frequent those kinds of places. I've seen their ads in the paper, is all. In the so-called 'Arts' section."

"They advertise, do they?"

"Well, I—I guess they must have at some point. I've seen an ad somewhere, and I thought it was in the newspaper."

"Huh."

I wanted to slap the macaroon right out from between his lips. And those innocent eyes, as if he hadn't just accused a fine man of immoral behavior, right in front of his wife at their own kitchen table. Where he sat uninvited, mooching dessert.

"Well anyway. The last part of the text, despite the Jenny Ho tip, gives us reason to think the murderer lives nearby—very close by, in fact."

"Oh? What did that last part say?"

"Sorry Marilyn, but I'm not at liberty to tell you the exact words," he said with an air of importance. "Some things are confidential."

"How about unexact words then," Jack prodded. We both knew already that keeping information to himself was not the detective's strong suit.

He barely hesitated. "Well, I can tell you this: it was a suggestion that the killer lives here in the neighborhood. And of course, Mr. Redding's final words also pointed to a neighbor's involvement on some level."

He looked from Jack to me and back again, as if waiting for one of us to blurt out a confession. When that didn't happen, he continued, "So we're patrolling the neighborhood 24-7 and advising everyone to be careful."

We were struck dumb for a few seconds, during which he pulled a cloth from his shirt pocket and began wiping his glasses, remarking on the heat on this side of the Bay compared to the city, as if he hadn't just warned us that a killer really might be lurking in the house next door, across the street, or on the corner. We had been clinging to the hope that the 911 message was a final burst of malice aimed at us or at one of the other neighbors, choked out just before Redding forked the final bite of deadly peanut curry into his own mouth.

After examining the eyeglasses and finding them acceptable, he returned them to his face and blinked as our shocked faces fell into view, reminding him of the reason for his visit. "So anyway, I need to ask just a couple more questions about—"

"Whoa whoa whoa," Jack said. "You mean to tell me you guys honestly believe that someone in this neighborhood killed Michael Redding? With his lifestyle and that hateful attitude, he must have had enemies all over the place. Why, he trained his bloodhound to piss on our roses just because we asked him to keep it from doing its business on the sidewalk."

The detective's ears almost visibly flapped. "Is that right? Pretty vindictive, was he? That must have really steamed you when he set the hound loose on your roses."

"Jack, good grief." The man baffled me with his lack of tongue control. "That has nothing to do with anything."

Fortunately, the detective seemed to agree. "So

anyway, I do need to ask a few questions about street activity. You've told me you saw nothing suspicious around the time of the murder, but I'd like your impressions about the routines and habits of some of the residents."

"Like whether or not they frequent strip clubs?" I was still miffed about the accusation—or implication, at least—that he had directed at Jack. "How would we know such a thing?"

"I'm guessing you wouldn't. But I'm wondering if you've ever noticed any signs of overt drunkenness or drug abuse among the neighbors. Do any of them fight with their spouses, or show other signs of a short fuse? Any suspicious visitors to any of the homes?"

"Other than what I've already shared with you about the depressed woman across the street and her possible alcohol or drug habits, I haven't seen anything, but it's not like we go around sticking our noses in other people's business," I said.

He grinned as if to say, "Yeah, sure. What a joker." That's when he shared with us "some of the neighbors'" opinion that we were a pair of Nosy Nellies. Those were his words, and he chortled at our drop-jawed reactions.

"Now, I'm sure that's not true," he said. "But they did seem to think that if anyone is inclined to notice suspicious activity on the block, it would be you two."

I was speechless, but Jacked huffed, "Nosy Nellies? Who would say such a thing?" He narrowed his eyes at Thatcher. "You're kidding us, right?"

The detective winked at him. "Maybe I am, and maybe I'm not."

After a cursory peek into the cabinets, he seemed satisfied that we didn't possess any ancient, gray, once floral dinner plates. We thought we'd be rid of him then, but instead he returned to the table.

"One more thing." He opened his notebook. "I nearly forgot. Did either of your kids go to Maple Avenue

Elementary School, or do you know anyone who works there?"

"Both girls spent first through sixth grades there," I said. "But what's this about?"

He ignored the question. "You know some of the employees there, do you?"

"Not anymore. I imagine the staff has turned over a few times since our girls were there."

"Ah. Okay then." He circled some items in his notebook and scooted it toward us, leaving it closer to Jack than to me. "Either one of you familiar with these two websites?"

After we stared for a few seconds in silence, he closed the notebook and pulled it away from us. "I had to ask. They were among the texted clues we got."

"Oh dear god," I said, when I finally made sense of the odd names: *getyerroxoff.com* and *chicksonchicks.com.*

Jack's face radiated an interesting mix of alarm, embarrassment, and disgust. Detective Thacker didn't seem to notice. "Ok then," he repeated.

On his way out, he paused. "Say, do you have a recommendation for a good gym here in town? I intend to start working out if I ever find time. Any thoughts about Twenty-four Hour Fitness?"

"Sorry. No idea," I said, eager to hasten his exit. It was true: I worked out on my elliptical machine upstairs and Jack's routine was limited to our daily walks, puttering around in the backyard, and whatever exercise he got on the golf course when not riding the cart from one hole to the next.

When he was finally gone, Jack grumbled, "I wonder if he's got a trace of the Asperger's. No filters, seems like. Nosy Nellies? Why would he repeat such a thing to us? And who would say it in the first place?"

"He might have made it up. But if not, it had to be either the lesbian or the Mexican. Those are the two he keeps talking to, besides us." This knowledge, too, had come from Jack's office window reconnaissance. "My money is on Rachel. She obviously dislikes us, God knows why."

The next afternoon, I caught Jack frowning out the window at Rachel's front porch, where she sat looking like an overmedicated mental patient, still in pajamas, clutching a wine glass and gazing into space, an unopened magazine on her lap.

"Drinking in the middle of the afternoon. How long has it been now since her girlfriend died? Three months or more?"

"I can't remember for sure. She could probably use some therapy. Or AA, maybe both. But she doesn't exactly invite helpful suggestions." I reminded him about how she had rebuffed me at CVS.

"A terrible waste," he said, turning away from the window.

I didn't think he was referring to her mental condition, but I bit my tongue. We had already hashed out the homosexuality issue many times with no clear resolution. The Bible told us one thing, but I figured what they did with each other under their own roof was none of my business, so long as they didn't expect us to change the Constitution and the rules of the church on their behalf.

Jack, on the other hand, insisted that homosexuality was a threat to the future of our species, and he and our girls butted heads, holiday dinner be damned, whenever the subject was brought up. Thank God both Chloe and Natalie turned out to be straight. I'm not sure if Jack could have survived the trauma.

It was bad enough they had sworn never to provide us with grandchildren, having swallowed the left-wing overcrowded earth and global warming doom-and-gloom propaganda. I prayed they would miraculously end up with sensible husbands who understood that as far as nature was concerned, procreation was the sole purpose of all that hot sex I overheard them giggling about in the kitchen last Christmas. High school English teachers up in Portland, both of them. Chloe thirty-one and Natalie turning thirty-four in November. Tick-tock, ladies.

4

The next morning, despite Rachel's obvious lack of interest in getting to know me, I let Jack goad me into wandering across the street to find out if Detective Thacker had shared anything with her on his most recent visit, something he might have neglected to tell us. We were both anxious about his newest line of questioning, which seemed too personal and almost accusatory. We felt like real suspects, although the very idea boggled the mind.

"Yeah, he was here," she said in that distracted manner, twirling a thick strand of unbrushed hair. "He stopped by yesterday, but ..." Her eyes, which showed signs of a poor night's sleep despite whatever it was the pharmacist was giving her, had been flitting here and there like hyperactive grasshoppers since the conversation began. Now they widened and abruptly locked with mine, and I correctly guessed that the conversation was about to take a turn for the weird.

"There must be a CB radio somewhere in the neighborhood," she said.

"I don't think anyone uses those things anymore, except for truck drivers, and—" I stopped as I remembered that the other one had been a trucker. Dear god, might she be hoping to communicate with her dead partner? Jack would love this.

Why?" I asked. "Do you need a CB for something?"

"No, I just once in a while think I hear one, is all."

"Huh."

No doubt I seemed wary, so she hurried to explain. "My cousin told me once that her television was picking up a CB radio conversation at random times, even when it was turned off. It totally freaked her out the first time she heard it. It was the middle of the night."

After a few moments of silence while I processed this, she added, "So that's a possible explanation" and nodded in agreement with herself, her tone suggesting I was dimwitted if I didn't buy this harebrained theory.

"Maybe," I said. "How often do you hear these transmissions?"

A look of "Oops, I've said too much" crossed her face. "Oh, not often. But no, I really don't know anything more about the investigation."

She stood to go inside, dismissing me just like that, but changed her mind when Pigpen—oh, why could I never remember her real name? —pulled up in her van. Such a clunky space waster, considering that she lived alone and didn't even have a job to drive to. It was probably handy for hauling her purchases home, though.

Sure enough, she opened the hatch and pulled out an enormous black plastic garbage bag filled with God knows what and two throw pillows that actually sort of matched the worn sofa bed on the porch. She called hello as she walked into her own yard next door, looking a little sheepish.

"Say, uh ..." Her real name hovered just out of my grasp, so I looked at Rachel for help. She turned away with something just short of a smirk, so after an awkward pause, I went on: "We were just talking about the murder case. Have you heard anything from Detective Thacker?"

She nodded, sat the bags and pillows at the edge of her cluttered porch and walked over to join us.

"He came by again last night. He has so many questions. We talked for nearly an hour." Her smile was puzzled. "He seems very interested in all of us. And your husband too, Mrs. Middleton."

So it turns out Thacker had gone so far as to grill her about our walks around the neighborhood: how regular were they? Jack's tendency to monitor the neighbors' activity: did they resent it? What did she know about Rachel's deceased partner, Deb? He had heard rumors of "trouble in paradise" unrelated to the illness. Had there been another woman involved, or possibly even a man? How close had Rachel been to Michael Redding? As for Pigpen (damn Jack and his nicknames), how had she felt when Michael offered to haul some things to the dump for her? How pushy had he been? Why did he make the offer, in her opinion?

She looked accusingly at Rachel and me when she said that last part. I said "Huh" and waited for Rachel to defend herself. But she had stopped listening after the remarks about Deb and her.

Showing a temper that surprised me—the woman had some life left in her after all—she growled, "That son-of-a-bitch. This is no investigation. He's just fucking nosy! Alejandra, did you tell him those things I said—"

"Of course not!" interrupted Alejandra (whose name I now knew, thanks to Rachel). "But you told me yourself how you vented on Facebook, so maybe he found out about it online somehow."

I waited, hoping to hear more without having to ask. No one likes a Nosy Nellie.

But Alejandra chose to move on. "Anyway, he seems totally focused on our street, not on that nightclub in Oakland."

"Hold on," I said. "Jack and I have accounted for our

whereabouts during the time of the murder. I assume you've done the same?"

"Fuh," said Rachel (or something to that effect). "I was taking a nap, and I told him that."

"I was shopping," said Alejandra. "By myself."

Silence ensued as we assessed each other's responses. I was inclined to accept the innocence of them both. The affronted glint in Rachel's eyes, the anxiety in Alejandra's, seemed genuine.

"But that's stupid, limiting his search that way," I said. "And worse, it means the real murderer isn't even a suspect. He's running around loose somewhere."

"Or she," Rachel pointed out. "And why us, anyway? It could just as well be someone he met at one of his gigs. If not in Oakland, then somewhere else. His band played all over the Bay Area."

"Although he did say something about a neighbor on his 911 call," I reminded them.

We all glanced up and down the street.

"You've been here the longest, Mrs. Middleton," said Alejandra. "What do you think of the other neighbors?"

Although I'd brought welcome platters to each new household, I couldn't come up with a single surname other than Chung, or possibly Chang, from next door. And of course the Patchetts, who had been on the street for fifty years and could hardly be considered suspects. A collection of faces swam in front of me, and I knew which of them belonged with which house, of course—one could not help but observe some of their comings and goings. But what did I think of them? Good question.

"None of them seem like obvious murderers, but I've had little contact. We like to mind our own business," I said. Amusement made a brief appearance on Rachel's face, and Alejandra looked away. Then something a little more useful occurred to me.

"Maybe Jack can help. He's head of the Neighborhood

Watch committee and keeps an eye on that community website. Nextdoor, it's called."

I had always begged off the Watch meetings myself, a decision that, considering current circumstances, now seemed both unfriendly and irresponsible. But Jack had complained of low attendance anyway, and from the few who did show up, a lot of fretting about nothing. In the thirty-four years we had lived here, there had been two burglaries, a spate of package-swiping from front porches last Christmas, and only one instance of a smashed windshield. And poor Michael Redding had the distinction of being the neighborhood's first homicide.

"I'll see if Jack has any ideas," I offered. "But maybe Michael said 'Neighbor knows' because the murderer was an employee or customer from that bar where you work, Rachel, since Michael's band sometimes played there. He might have said it because he thought you could point the police toward the murderer." I felt a rush of excitement. It was fun coming up with my own theory.

But Rachel shook her head. "I've told Thacker everything I know. I can't think of anyone who might have wanted to kill him. Maybe some chick he picked up, or a jealous boyfriend." Regret crept into her voice. "I'm not employed there anymore, but I'll give the owner a call and pick her brain."

"My friend Daniela hangs out at that bar sometimes, too," said Alejandra. "I'll see if she can think of anyone who—"

Shhh!" Rachel hissed, fingers to her lips. "Listen!"

We absorbed the silence for a moment, Alejandra and I exchanging silent question marks while Rachel cocked her head in various directions, eyes narrowed in concentration.

"Did you hear that?" It was more of a command than a question. "That voice. The radio."

We shook our heads.

"Dammit. It always stops whenever I ask someone else to listen."

In an instant, she had zipped to the top of the list I planned to make of suspects in Michael's murder. So far, she and the victim himself were the only ones on it, but I hoped that would change. She clearly didn't like me, and neither one of those two sad sacks was my cup of tea anyway, and not just because one was probably undocumented and the other unbalanced—but I rather relished this common goal of proving our collective innocence.

The next morning at breakfast, after enduring my grousing about another wakeful night, Jack commented, "You really need to call Dr. Randall."

"Maybe," I said.

My brain was still in overdrive from recent events, and the sleeplessness and stress dreams continued to plague me in defiance of the melatonin I had picked up at CVS two weeks before. And the previous night, after the detective's baffling insinuations, there had been a new arrival to the insomnia party: an image of Jack's flustered, crimson face had suddenly floated before me, protesting any knowledge of strip clubs and porn websites.

Jack was right—I was muddle-headed from lack of sleep. But almost certainly Dr. Randall would prescribe caffeine withdrawal, increased exercise, anti-anxiety pills, and yet another round of therapy, just as he had done during Chloe's regrettable freshman year of college and again a year and a half ago when my best friend, Sue Ellen, had died from a sudden bout of pneumonia.

But already I was half-caffing my coffee and had doubled my elliptical machine workout. And anyway, the pills I had taken on those previous occasions hadn't brought back my friend, nor had they stopped Chloe from partying away her scholarship and landing temporarily back home to consider her options while simultaneously sneaking out of the house at night to run with a bunch of underachievers from the local community college.

Later, on the way home from church, during which I had stayed alert by the force of sheer will, Jack's voice interrupted the fog-like trance I had fallen into.

"Let's pack a lunch and go to the lake—" He stopped short when he saw me struggling to focus. "I'll make sandwiches," he said. "We'll eat on the patio."

After lunch, at his insistence, I sank into a restorative two-hour nap. Instead of going downstairs when I awoke, I shut the bedroom door and dialed Chloe, our youngest. Usually I waited until evening and initiated a FaceTime call that included Jack, but today I was in the mood for a private chat. His response to my announcement of the investigative partnership I had formed with the women he still called Pigpen and the Fox had bordered on ridicule, and I was hoping for a more encouraging response from the girls.

"Stop moving the phone up and down, Mom," ordered Chloe. "You're making me dizzy. Nobody looks gorgeous on FaceTime calls anyway."

"So I've wasted my time putting on mascara and brushing my hair?"

I continued bringing her up to date on the murder investigation and my recent foray into crime-solving with two unlikely partners. "So that was yesterday. We agreed to do some of our own snooping around and meet again soon."

"Oh that's interesting," she kept repeating. "Awesome ... Wow ... Huh."

"Is something wrong?" I finally asked. "You seem distracted, and you look tired. Are you sleeping okay?"

"You don't look so great yourself," she snapped. After reminding me yet again that to suggest a person looks tired is an insult, she added, "If you recall what I told you last week, tomorrow is the last day of classes. I'm still grading papers that have to be returned, and I don't even want to think about all the grades I still have to submit. That's all."

"Okay. I'll let you get back to it then." I forced a more cheerful tone. "Call me when things settle down. Oh, one more thing."

"Are you going to ask me if I'll be home for a visit now that school is out? The answer is maybe, after I spend a week or so decompressing. And only if you agree to no fat-shaming and no politics at mealtime."

"I do not 'fat-shame'! I think you're gorgeous as you are. I just worry that you aren't getting enough exercise—"

"Asking me if I'm sure I want seconds on dessert? That's not fat-shaming?"

"I don't intend it as such. I'm concerned for your health, is all. And anyway, can't you decompress just as well here? Your room is still—"

"Mom? I really need to get these papers graded."

After a similarly brief conversation with Natalie, I was left with no one to talk to. Jack was glued to the TV learning about our president's latest tweets and what he really meant versus what the left-wing media wanted us to believe he meant. As usual, Jack was aggravating himself by switching back and forth between Fox News and MSNBC, which one might think would be a good thing, exposure to the perspective of both sides, but his grumbling and frequent cries of disgust compelled me to suggest he do a self-check on his blood pressure.

"I'm fine," he snapped. Then under his breath, "Jesus Christ, what is wrong with that woman?" Meaning the smirking news anchor, I hoped, and not me.

I considered joining him but the sniping and sneers and general incivility (on his part as well as the talking heads') tended to sour my disposition. Instead, I perused the Sunday paper until Jack clicked off the TV and announced he was going to Home Depot to pick up nails and a can of stain to repair a section of the fence in back. Then, feeling more human after the nap and stimulated by the conversation with my daughters, mostly one-sided though it was, I was struck by an idea: I would tackle the issue of our neighbor's clutter head-on. I would call on Alejandra—fortunately, Jack had remembered her name—and invite her to my house for tea or coffee.

Now that we were unofficially working together to solve a murder, maybe she would lend me a sympathetic ear about the clutter if I steered the conversation just right, using the investigation as a segue. Jack had given me a list of names and addresses of everyone who had been to a Neighborhood Watch meeting during the past two years and clued me in about a few regulars on Nextdoor. It was something to share, an excuse to go calling.

5

lejandra's van was in its usual spot, but the doorbell went unanswered. Probably saw me coming, I thought. Honestly, a person could get a complex from exposure to these two unneighborly neighbors. Then I heard voices coming from Alejandra's backyard, so I walked in that direction, pausing halfway to call out "Hello?"

After a silence that felt intentional, Alejandra appeared from behind the house. When I asked if she had a few minutes to talk, she scrunched her eyebrows and glanced over her shoulder before saying, "Umm... sure. Come on back. We're having iced tea on my patio."

Rachel looked dazed and bedraggled, although at least she had switched from pajamas to yoga pants and a tube top. Her eyes were pink, puffy slits. A box of Kleenex was on her lap, and a few discarded tissues had been tossed onto the ground beside the lawn chair in which she lounged like a wounded mermaid among the flotsam on the back porch.

Alejandra waded through an assortment of wind chimes yet to be hung and lawn ornaments awaiting installation, to a far corner of the yard where she retrieved a matching chair. She pulled a Kleenex from the box perched on Rachel's lap, brushed off the cobwebs and motioned for me to sit down.

"I'll get you some tea."

She disappeared through the back door, thighs swishing beneath jeans that had probably fit well enough five pounds ago. While we waited, Rachel blew her nose a few times and I sneezed once, which is what passed for conversation between us until Alejandra brought a glass for me from the kitchen and settled herself into the lap of a vinyl beanbag chair that might have graced some hippie's living room back in the seventies.

The two of them did not jump back into their previous conversation. Perhaps Rachel had gotten the worst of it out of her system. They both looked at me as if waiting for me to state my business—which I was unable to do, as the mood wasn't exactly receptive.

The effects of awkward silence, temperature in the nineties, and several sheet-wrestling nights in a row merged into a simmering stew of self-pity. I unexpectedly thought of Sue Ellen, how we used to sit on her front porch or out back on my patio, catching up on family news and gossip over coffee after dropping off the kids at school.

"Now, get a load of this, hon," she would say in a Scarlett O'Hara drawl untempered by two decades on the West Coast. A nurse by training, she had opted, like me, for a stay-at-home mom position until the kids left the nest. While I would eventually slip back into my teacher's shoes, she never got another crack at what no doubt would have been a successful nursing career.

Smart, fun, generous, thoughtful Sue Ellen. After she had died, my book club dissolved, Sue Ellen having been the glue that held us together—the one who could sweetly insist, "Now that's enough politics, girls," without incurring the wrath of the left-wing faction of the club, which included everyone but Sue Ellen and me.

The parents of my kids' friends had all moved on as

well, in one way or another. And only one set of neighbors from the old days was left on the block: the Patchetts, octogenarians whose kids hadn't yet succeeded in herding them into a geriatric warehousing situation. The others had either downsized, died, or cashed in on the housing spike and were living off the profits in rural Nevada or some other godforsaken place.

Memories brought an ache to my throat. When Sue Ellen died, she had lived for twenty-six years in a three-bedroom ranch-style home on the northwestern corner of our street. The current owners were investors from San Francisco, and a young Pakistani family now occupied the space.

And now here I was, friendless old me, having a glass of iced tea with two depressed women who were waiting for me to leave so they could get on with their pity party. Was it our age difference that made them unable to relate to me? At sixty-two, I was probably twice Rachel's age, and Alejandra looked even younger. And did they really think of Jack and me as grumpy old busybodies?

Why would they bother to befriend me? And why should I care if they didn't? It wasn't as if I had anything in common with an undocumented hoarder or a gay crazy woman. (During our brief conversation earlier, I had been chastised by Chloe for using the antiquated term "lesbian" instead of "gay," and in fact, why should I refer to her sexual preference anyway? Was it any of my business? Chloe thought not.) But we were neighbors, after all. And I had imagined us working together to find Michael Redding's murderer. *Dream on, Marilyn.* I was once again that chubby, friendless, pathetic little girl on the playground.

"Oh my ..." Alejandra lifted herself out of the chair and pulled another Kleenex from the box. As she thrust it toward me, I watched curiosity replace disdain on Rachel's face.

Alejandra laid a hand on my shoulder. "Is something wrong, Mrs. Middleton? What did you come to talk to me about?"

The Neighborhood Watch roster now seemed like a lame excuse to stop by uninvited. I was no doubt getting dotty. Why would they want to explore the murder case with me, old Nosy Nellie? One of them could barely stand being near me, for unknown reasons, and the other was too preoccupied with parental and legality issues to give me any thought at all.

"It doesn't matter. Sorry. I'm fine, really."

Good grief. Thank God I hadn't broken all the way down. A few tears were embarrassing enough, in front of these two non-friends. "I'm tired, I guess. I've had trouble sleeping."

"Huh. Join the party," said Rachel, about as sympathetic as I would have expected.

"Me too." Alejandra patted my shoulder again. "Maybe we should start a middle-of-the-night club."

This weak humor dissolved the tension. Alejandra returned to her chair and threw Rachel a questioning look, but she just shrugged and focused her gaze on her fingernails—the most attention she had paid to them for some time, judging from appearances.

Alejandra said, "We were just talking about Michael's band and whether the detective has—"

"Oh please," Rachel interrupted. "We weren't talking about Michael at all. I was venting again about how my ex cheated on me before she died." My appalled expression seemed to please her. "Poor Alejandra, she's heard it all before, but I just can't stop myself from giving an earful to anyone who'll listen."

"Well," I said. "I haven't heard any of it. And believe it or not, I can keep a secret as well as the next person."

I heard the sharpness in my own voice and expected a sneer or even a snicker, but she just held my gaze for a moment and then said, "Well, if you insist. Where was I, Alejandra?"

"You should probably start at the beginning, I suppose." Her reluctance went unnoticed by Rachel, who took another swallow of tea before commencing to unload.

"Okay," she began. "So about two weeks before last Christmas, only minutes before running out the door to a doctor's appointment, Deb sat me down at the kitchen table and told me she wanted a divorce."

And maybe your snarly attitude and attachment to the wine bottle contributed to that decision, I thought.

Then I remembered how Sue Ellen had once offered an unsolicited critique of my listening skills: I was too quick to judge, she said, and "not terribly empathetic, hon." Stung, and not wanting to lose my best friend, I had devoured several books about how to be the sort of compassionate person that others want to confide in. A lot of it was shallow pop psychology crap, but Sue Ellen claimed to be proud of me. She had noticed improvement, she said.

"How awful," I said to Rachel. "I'm so sorry that happened."

Alejandra stood up. "I think I'll bring out the tea pitcher and some ice. And I need to make a phone call." She hurried into the house again. I wondered how many times she had let Rachel bend her ear over this betrayal.

"Betrayal" was the word Sue Ellen had used each time she caught Phil in an affair. The third time, when she returned home after visiting their new grandchild and found him naked on the sofa with his fitness trainer, she finally threw the ass out of the house. Six months later, she called him to her deathbed, forgave him and died clutching his hand. I sensed that Rachel had not embraced the grace of forgiveness, as the Bible insists we must do. Lee Houston's drunken, sneering face popped into my vision: *Who are you to talk?*

Rachel's right knee bobbed up and down, driven by caffeine and nerves. When she stilled it, the left knee took over without missing a bounce.

"She claimed our constant bickering was making her ill. She'd been to the doctor three times already and gone through a buttload of tests, but her doctor suspected the problem was irritable bowels aggravated by stress."

Constant bickering? And yet you were blind-sided? I swallowed the questions.

"Well, you guessed it. Her so-called unhappiness had driven her into the arms of someone else. She was forty-four years old, life was short, I was too young to understand, and blah blah blah."

She punctuated the monologue with a vindictive snort. "When she got back from the doctor's office, she was singing a different tune: the one called poor pitiful me, why now, when I was just getting my shit together?"

While I was still absorbing the snort and the caustic tone—this was a deceased person she was ridiculing, remember—she went on: "I tried to be sad about the cancer in her pancreas, but—" She shrugged. "Hell hath no fury, as they say."

"Well, I can certainly understand your anger." I did understand it, but I was a bit put off by the oversharing. She barely knew me—by her own choice, mostly. And had she really disparaged a dying woman on Facebook, as Alejandra had implied the day before?

Betrayal notwithstanding, Rachel's behavior didn't sound normal to me. She had chosen to stay with her dying partner—which would have been a noble decision had she not then devoted herself to making Deb's remaining months a Hell on Earth. That was cruel and unchristian, to say the least.

Furthermore, if Rachel was feeling that vicious, might her malice be extended to someone else who crossed her— someone like Michael Redding, whom she knew from the bar? All kinds of nasty encounters happened in those places; my deceased birth mother could attest to that.

Rachel's eyes welled up. "It all happened so fast. Three months from diagnosis, she was gone."

After gnawing at her lip for a bit, she watched my face closely as she added, "Two days later, I heard that woman's voice for the first time. That CB radio transmission. At first, I thought it might be inside my head." Her defiant eyes held mine. "But it's not."

None of the books on effective listening had covered how to respond to comments that suggested the speaker was delusional. What should I say? I had never been driven nuts to the point of hearing voices, nor did I have any experience listening to someone who had. Sue Ellen had been troubled at times, but she had stayed on the sane side of the border.

Rachel was silent, her contemptuous gaze daring me to recommend a good therapist. I knew of an excellent one in fact, and I was tempted.

"That must be very troubling," I said. "I can see why you aren't sleeping well."

She relaxed a little. "Yeah, no shit, right?"

As much as I had ridiculed those books at the time, Sue Ellen had done me a real favor.

I hoped Rachel would reveal, without my having to ask, what those voices were saying. But just then Alejandra returned with the tea pitcher, a bowl of ice cubes, and apple slices in a bowl. She placed a bath towel on a small plastic table beside Rachel's chair, arranged the tea and fruit on top of it, and then scooted the table to the center of our little triangle.

"So, where are we now?" she asked, after refilling all our glasses and plopping back down into the beanbag.

"Rachel was telling me about the voices." Maybe this sounded too eager, so I hurried to add, "But I'm curious. You stayed with—I'm sorry, I've forgotten her name—Deb, wasn't it? You stayed despite all this anger you were feeling? Rightfully feeling, of course."

She took a long swallow of tea. "Yep, I sure did. She was dying, so it didn't seem right to ditch her—or to slice off her tits while she slept."

My grimace amused her. "Sorry. I don't mean to shock you. I'll bet you've never been so pissed that you fantasized about jamming a butcher knife into someone's gut." She and Alejandra exchanged grins and knowing looks. Maybe that was what passed for humor among younger people raised on too much violent TV and the internet.

"I sure have," said Alejandra. "When I found out Brian was cheating, I wanted to cut off his *cojones* and mail them to the *puta*—excuse me, Mrs. Middleton. The witch, I meant."

They both tittered again. Were they laughing at me? I would never get the whole story from Rachel if they couldn't trust me to listen with an open mind.

"Oh, it takes a lot to shock me," I said.

"Well, that's a good thing," said Alejandra, "if you are going to hang around us two. Right, Rachel?"

A noncommittal half-smile told me Rachel doubted that I would be hanging around the two of them for much longer, but she continued her tale of woe anyway. As she had admitted earlier, she didn't seem to be able to stop herself.

She must have forgotten that we'd been talking about the voices.

"Besides, when they told her she would have six months if she was lucky—which she wasn't—she decided what the hell, what's the point in ruining my life? She broke it off with the bitch, a fellow driver she met at a truck stop diner. Liliana—that was the bitch's name—the slut had tried to convince Deb to spend those last months with her, but finally she understood Deb's obligation to me as the grieving widow-to-be and backed the hell off."

"Well, that's a good thing, at least. I mean, if that's what you wanted."

Instead of answering, she chose an apple slice, frowned at it, and tossed it back onto the plate. Such manners, but hardly a surprise. "She kept insisting that our relationship was already in the dumpster before she met this bitch, but I wasn't having that shit. I told her, 'It's a midlife crisis, you dumbass. Classic symptom, falling for a coworker, which in your case is another driver. Don't lay this on me. I'm the victim here.'"

Unable to think of a way to steer conversation back to the CB radio lunacy without seeming to pry, I could only listen and hope she would eventually find her own way back.

"Is it five o'clock yet? I hear a bottle of Chardonnay calling my name."

Alejandra frowned. "No, Rachel. It's not quite 3:30."

"Oh." Rachel settled back, disappointed. "I'll wait, then." As if she didn't drink at all hours of the day, according to Jack.

She may have read my eyes. "I joined a twelve-step program on the internet yesterday."

I was about to offer congratulations when she added, "I'm not ready to go on the wagon, but it can't hurt to get started a little later in the day."

"Maybe we should talk about the murder," said Alejandra. "Mrs. Middleton, you were going to ask your husband. Did he have any ideas?"

I held up the roster. Maybe bringing it hadn't been foolish after all.

"Jack gave me names and addresses of everyone in the neighborhood who has been to a Watch meeting for the past two years. I'm not sure what to do with it, though."

Encouraged by Alejandra's nod of approval and Rachel's "Huh," I continued. "And he showed me how to use the Nextdoor website. People on there are talking about the murder, everyone shocked and scared just like us, but I don't recognize any of the names, although many of them match those on the Neighborhood Watch list."

I didn't add that Jack had suggested I step back and let the detective do his job, instead of reimagining myself as some sort of geriatric crime solver from a mystery novel. "That's not going to help you sleep at night," he had said. "It'll only get your brain more riled up."

"Other than names and addresses, he couldn't really think of anything," I said. "And anyway, he thinks we'd get more information on Nextdoor than by ringing doorbells."

"Makes sense," Alejandra agreed. "So I guess we sign up for Nextdoor then, and start asking questions?"

So the Neighborhood Watch list was useless. Disappointed, I folded it and was stashing it in my pocket when Rachel said, "Hold on a minute. What about that bug-eyed bitch with the bird-slashing cats? Laura or Lisa or something? She lives right back there." She pointed to a house with a hedge that straddled both hers and Alejandra's property lines. "Two killer cats she refuses to keep inside. Is she on that list? What's her last name? I want to call Wildlife Protection on her."

I scanned the list, since she obviously felt strongly about it, although not controlling one's cats wasn't the crime we were supposed to be investigating. "No Laura at the meetings. Oh, here's a Lisa."

Alejandra frowned. "Come on, Rachel. Just because her cats are killers, that doesn't mean she's one. The list is meant to give us names of people to talk to about Michael Redding."

"Let me see that." Rachel tore the list from my hands and ran her finger down the page until she came to the offensive name. "Ha! That's her alright. Lisa Cardwell. 3316 Helena Street." She turned and pointed again. "Right over there. Give me something to write with."

Alejandra rolled her eyes but obediently trudged into

the kitchen and returned with a pen. While Rachel copied the phone number and address, Alejandra prodded her: "Have you talked to anyone down at the bar yet?"

"I talked to Jackie this morning. My former boss, manager of the Coal Bin. The one who fired me." Her eyes darted in my direction, and I tried not to look curious. Sometimes it felt as if she were baiting me. "For my own good, of course. She checks in every few days, out of guilt."

I bit. "For your own good, you say?"

"Yep. Jackie decided the bar was an unhealthy environment for me in my current state. She thought I wasn't ready to be back at work."

"I see. Well, she may have been right about that. You are grieving."

"Right. And it's also true that by the end of every night I was too shitfaced to drive home."

Smirking, she searched my face for disapproval, but I wouldn't give her the satisfaction.

"I'm sorry to hear that," I said. "It must be so difficult for you."

She reached for another apple slice. This one was a keeper, so she took a minute to finish it off before continuing. "I needed more time to heal, Jackie said when she canned me, and she reminded me that in my hammered state the night before, I'd revealed the details of my finances to anyone who would listen." With a smug smile, she added, "Between Deb's savings, life insurance money, and her share of her parents' estate, I'll never have to work again unless I want to."

Well, la-di-dah. She was sober, but it struck me that some of this inappropriate oversharing might be due to the caffeine. Her windfall was none of my business, surely.

Alejandra interrupted, sounding annoyed. No doubt this was another story she'd heard a few times before. "So did you ask Jackie if she had thought of anything worth telling the police?"

"I asked, sure. She said Thacker has been in there almost every night since it happened and has interviewed the staff and every customer that she could point him toward. Other than that, she just reminded me how Michael would hit on anything with a pussy and rarely went home alone." She took a swallow of tea. "He even chatted me up, poor fool, even though I'm ten years older than most of the women he hooks up with. Even after I told him about Deb, he didn't stop trying. Some guys just can't resist that challenge."

This was not a direction I wanted to travel in, so I blurted out, "You didn't finish telling me about the voices you're hearing. The CB radio, I mean."

It was as if I hadn't spoken.

"But anyway, I guess it's possible that one of those bar chicks did find herself in Michael's kitchen offering up a plate of Thai peanut curry, either to impress him or to do him in. Or maybe one of them had a jealous boyfriend who worked at Nam Thai downtown or something. Seems far-fetched, though. Why not just stab him one night as he left the Coal Bin, loaded down with drums and cymbals?" She stood and stretched. "That's what I would have done. Anyone else for a cold glass of chardonnay?"

"Too early for me," said Alejandra. She looked at her phone. "Barely past four. You ought to—"

We were interrupted by a familiar, mournful braying that came from the other side of Alejandra's back door. She got up and released the exuberant floppy-eared creature into the yard.

"There you are, sweetie," she cooed. "Your nap is over now, huh?"

Michael Redding's liver-colored bloodhound lurched at Rachel's chair and covered her face with slobbers while she scratched his ears and told him repeatedly that he was a good doggie, yes he was. When he finally got enough of that, he turned to me, crouched, bared his teeth, and growled. Sweet God in heaven. I had assumed that one of Michael's band friends would take him in, or that he would go to the shelter.

"Now Boondoggles, you stop that!" Alejandra waggled her finger at him, and he ceased growling. "This is Mrs. Middleton, your neighbor. Be nice to her."

He whimpered and headed to a corner of the yard to do his business. So much for Jack's renewed hope for the roses and the lawn. I said my goodbyes and went home to deliver the news to my husband, but not before we had exchanged numbers and agreed to go the Nextdoor route to glean information from the neighbors.

6

"Now what?" Jack grumbled.

I slid the apple polenta cake into the oven, set the timer, and joined him at his office window. Peering over his shoulder, I saw that a silver Mercedes had just pulled into Alejandra's driveway. A man of early middle age with a miniature Schwarzenegger build and a corporate blond haircut, clad in gym shorts, tank top, and sunglasses, emerged from the car and stood frowning, arms akimbo, at the mess that was Alejandra's yard.

I stepped back. "Jack, really. They can see you from over there."

"So what?" But he closed the blinds. Then, to improve the audio, he reached under the blind to crank open the window and lifted a slat to peek through.

"They can still see you." But after a few seconds, I rejoined him. The detective had told us to be vigilant, after all.

Alejandra stalked toward the man from Rachel's front porch. She had spiffed herself up in a red sleeveless blouse and cropped jeans that fit, and she appeared to be wearing makeup, although perhaps not for the benefit of this particular visitor. Her fists were clenched as if she was planning to use them.

"Where's my son?" she demanded. "You promised he would visit this weekend."

The man was surveying the neighborhood as if he had just landed his spaceship on a strange and obviously inferior planet. "Yeah, that was before the dude on the corner got iced." He smirked. "Maybe your pal Daniela's old man got wise."

Daniela? At first, I couldn't place the name. Then I remembered something Alejandra had said that afternoon in Rachel's front yard, when we had first decided to put our heads together regarding the murder: her friend Daniela sometimes hung out at the Coal Bin, where Michael's band had sometimes played and Rachel had tended bar before she was canned.

Alejandra drew back. "What are you talking about? Daniela—there was nothing between her and Michael. And where is Kyle? Why isn't he here, like you promised?"

"Because I'm not sure your new digs are safe for my son to visit. Another bad choice on your part." He looked around at the porch and yard, shaking his head. "I'll never understand what in God's name you need with all this shit. How do you find a place to sit down?"

"What business is that of yours? I have a clean bed for Kyle, and books and games. I want to see my son!"

Brian's eyes wandered next door. He gave Rachel the once-over as she got up without looking their way and walked into her house. "Making friends with the neighbors? Looks like that one just crawled out of the sack."

"Where is he?" Alejandra was shrieking now. "Where's Kyle?"

He gestured toward the front porch. "I believe what I said was, 'Clean up this dump to provide a healthy environment for Kyle, and then I'll let him visit again.' And you promised to do so." He sighed. "But I figured you couldn't pull it off, so I didn't bother making him come."

"*Making* him come! You are—you are—" Her voice was choked with fury. "You can't keep him from me. I'm his mother. You can't do it! You can't!"

He smiled. "Watch that temper, babe. Tut tut. What will the neighbors say?"

Alejandra glanced in our direction and Jack closed the slat for a few seconds. But if she saw us, she was too agitated to care.

"I don't give one damn what the neighbors say." She spoke even louder. "I will go to the police or—or I will find my own lawyer. An honest one, not an evil *hijo de puta* like you.

Sensing she'd gone too far, she took a step back. But it was too late. As his fingers closed around her upper arm, I sucked in my breath. Jack whispered, "You okay?" I nodded, forcing myself to exhale.

"Let's go inside," the man said in a cold voice that Jack and I strained to hear. "We need to talk this over, and I want to see if you've done anything to clean up the mess inside like you promised. If you did, maybe I'll bring Kyle out later tonight."

"That's a lie! No way would you make another trip from Oakland today. I'm surprised you drove out here at all. Did you come just to piss me off, or what?"

Tugging at her arm, he took a step toward the door.

"I'm not going inside with you!" She planted her feet and struggled to twist free. His next words were no surprise, but Jack growled anyway, and I swallowed my disappointment. At some point I had started to hope we were wrong.

"You want to go back to Mexico, huh? Would you like that?" He grabbed a fistful of hair and started to drag her toward the house. I whispered "Oh," and Jack laid a hand on my shoulder.

"No! Leave me alone, Brian. Go home and bring me

Kyle, like you promised."

"I told you to keep your voice down. If you want to see Kyle, then—"

"Take your fucking hands off me!"

"You ought to try being nicer to me when you want something. Now let's—what the *fuck*? Call that thing off!"

Boondoggles had burst out from behind the front screen door to greet them with the donkey call that made him sound less ferocious than sad. Alejandra glanced nervously at Brian, who still had a grip on her hair and upper arm.

"Sit! Boondoggles, sit!" she said.

Miraculously, he did. Instead of attacking or even growling at the son-of-a-bitch, the bloodhound sat at Alejandra's feet, thumping his tail on the grass and awaiting further instructions, or possibly a treat. Evidently, some training had taken place within the past few days.

"He's a good dog," she told her astounded ex-husband. She was still scared, but defiant. "He likes people. He—"

"Oh no. No, no, no. I won't have Kyle exposed to a strange dog or moose or whatever this is, on top of the filth in your house and the dangerous neighborhood. Now get that thing on a leash, and let's go inside to talk about how soon you can dump it off at the pound."

He tugged her toward the door while she dug in her heels and pulled back. Boondoggles growled, then cowered under the man's glare.

I backed away from the window and leaned against Jack's desk, feeling queasy. "Should we do something? I mean, maybe he's going to—"

"Boondoggles! Here boy!"

We hurried back to the window. Rachel had reappeared on her front porch, almost unrecognizable in full makeup, hip-hugger gauchos, ankle boots, and a spaghetti-strap crop top that exposed several inches of sun-bronzed skin above her belly button. Her unruly mass of curls had been transformed into a casual updo secured by a kerchief-style bandana. Jack emitted a grunt of approval that turned into a quiet cough when I gave him a look.

Startled, Brian released his grasp on Alejandra. With a joyful bray, Boondoggles bounded toward Rachel as she stepped into the yard.

"Alejandra, I'm so sorry." She took hold of the bloodhound's collar. "Sit!" And he did, his entire body vibrating with joy. He had forgotten the trespasser, and clearly, he wasn't missing his previous master much.

Rachel said, "I didn't know you were expecting company, Alejandra." She extended her hand to Brian with a confident smile. "Hi. I'm Rachel Van Buren."

After a moment, he accepted the handshake. "Brian Stevens." He waited, calculating his next move.

"So, thanks for offering to watch him, Alejandra, but I'll just take Boondoggles home," Rachel said. "He'll be okay alone for the two hours it'll take to get my hair done. I don't want him interfering with your visit."

"No need," said Alejandra, whose fury still shone on her face, although Rachel pretended not to see it. "Brian was just leaving. Right, Brian?"

He twisted his scowl into a sour smile. "Right. Nice to meet you, Rachel." He gave Alejandra a curt nod. "See you next time."

Boondoggles managed a low growl at his retreating back, then whimpered and looked from Rachel to Alejandra for approval.

Alejandra patted his head with a half-hearted "Good boy," and all of us watched as Brian climbed into the Mercedes, rolled down his window and threw an exaggerated wave at Jack's office window before driving away. Jack let the slat fall shut and I stepped back.

"I told you he could see us."

"Nah," said Jack. "Lucky guess, that's all."

Later, over a dinner consisting of leftovers from the past two days, Jack said, "I wonder if Thacker knows about Pigpen's friend Daniela."

I was wondering the same thing. Alejandra had said that Daniela sometimes hung out at the bar, but she had seemed shocked when Brian suggested there might be something between her friend and Michael.

"No surprise she's illegal," Jack went on. "Thacker might be interested in knowing that, too, if he doesn't already."

"We don't know for sure. The bully never said that."

He looked at me in a way that reminded me of our daughters, and not in a good way. It was a look that said, "Exactly how clueless are you?" But aloud he said, "Um, let's see. He asked if she wanted to go back to Mexico. What do you think he meant by that, Marilyn?"

"We don't know for sure, is all I'm saying. Maybe he meant he would pay for a trip to see her family, if she was— you know, nice to him, like he said."

He shook his head, but I hurried on: "I doubt Detective Thacker has time to go sniffing out undocumented immigrants. He's got a murder to solve, after all."

Jack reacted to the sting in my voice by putting down his fork. Experience had taught him to expect a follow-up, and I didn't let him down.

"And now that we've remembered her real name, let's use it, okay? I'm a little tired of this 'Pigpen' business. It's the kind of things kids do, giving each other hateful nicknames."

He raised his eyebrows. "Sure." We ate in silence for a few minutes before he returned the fork to his plate. "Are you mad at me about something?"

"Why would you ask that?" I stabbed a chunk of

braised paprika chicken with my fork, not meeting his eyes. "I just think she's a nice enough person. We don't need to make fun of her. That's all."

He cleared his throat. "Are you sure that's it? Because ..."

At the sight of his flushed face, I put down my own fork and waited.

He continued, "I thought it might be what that dumbass detective said about the bar—that strip club—asking how I knew about it, and all."

"Well, that certainly was an eye-opener." The sharp words flew off my tongue. "You never mentioned such a place to me, even jokingly."

"Because it didn't seem important. It's not like I ever went there. I just remembered their ads, that's all."

"Huh. If you say so."

"Oh my God, Marilyn. I swear I've never been in the place. And those websites—I mean, come on. You believe me, don't you?"

I did believe him. Sort of. It was only in the worrisome dark hours that doubts nagged at me. In the light of day, the thought of Jack hanging out in a strip club and viewing porn on the internet was inconceivable. Laughable. That's exactly what we should be doing, I thought. Laughing that whole thing off.

Instead, I sniffed. "Of course. You've never given me any reason to doubt your word about such things." I held his gaze. "And I certainly hope you never will."

He dropped his eyes and picked up his fork. "I'm glad. I was afraid you might take his questions the wrong way."

"Nope."

And then it hit me: a delayed reaction, the first attack in eight years. Cold sweat, thundering heartbeat, dizziness. In the past, these episodes had been triggered by a violent scene in a movie or on TV, a too graphic description in the newspaper. In the grocery store parking lot, once, when some asshole shoved his wife into the car while calling her a dumb bitch for overloading the shopping cart with "junk" for the kids.

Jack jumped up to stand behind my chair and rub my shoulders. "It's okay, sweetheart," he soothed. "I'm sorry, Marilyn."

"He might have beaten her senseless," I whispered. "We did nothing."

"Marilyn, please honey. I'm sorry. I should have warned you to step back, just in case he did do something—"

"So you thought he might punch her, or drag her inside by the hair? Rape her?" I turned to glare at him through my tears. "And all you could do was watch?"

After a moment, he said, "You're right. We could have called the police. Should have. Although ..."

"Although what?"

"Although seeing as how she's illegal—I mean, if in fact she is, that might not be the thing she would want us to do, either."

"We don't know that she's undocumented," I reminded him.

When I was feeling close to normal again, we decided to skip dessert and cleared the table together in silence, after which Jack checked his phone messages and groaned. "Dick Tracy's parked outside. Says he has a few more questions. If you're not up to it—"

I reached for the cake knife. "No. Might as well invite him in. Maybe he's got news."

"We'll have to let him know about that little scene across the street, you know. He told us to watch out for signs of anyone with a hot temper. I think that Brian guy qualifies."

I hesitated. "Let's wait. Let me talk to Alejandra first."

"Why? We don't have to mention that we know—that we think she might be undocumented. But what if he asks us outright about any unusual street activity? We can't just pretend we didn't hear the man suggest that Pigpen's—Alejandra's—friend, whatever her name is, might have been screwing around with Redding."

"That was most likely just a jab at Alejandra. I really would like to talk to her, or maybe Rachel, before we say anything to the police."

He grumbled something under his breath before returning Thacker's call. I was surprised at how easily he had caved, but then he usually walked on eggshells for a short while after one of my anxiety attacks.

"If he asks us outright," I conceded, "we'll tell him. But otherwise, let's wait."

Once seated, the first words out of the detective's mouth (after "Don't mind if I do" as he accepted the generous slice of apple polenta cake drizzled with crème Anglaise) were "So it seems your neighbor across the street had a visitor earlier today. Did you see or hear anything?"

Jack nodded. "Well yes, in fact—"

I said, "If it's already been reported, then why ask us about it? Why don't you just talk to Alejandra?" I was starting to think Rachel's assessment of Thacker was correct. A little too eager for the juicy details, whether relevant or not.

The detective flashed his pleasant grin. "Some reason you don't want to discuss it, Marilyn?" He was a perceptive young man, I would give him that.

I bit my lip. "Of course not. Just asking a simple question. But by all means, Jack, tell the man everything you saw and heard while spying on Alejandra through your office window."

I got up without excusing myself and went into the bathroom, where I dawdled for the next ten minutes, giving him time to spill the beans on Alejandra without my having to witness it. When I returned, entering the room from behind Jack's chair, to my horror he was saying, "... so it's hard for her to watch that kind of thing ..."

He trailed off, reading in the detective's eyes that I was within earshot. Fighting the urge to bark "How dare you?" and make another dramatic exit, I returned to my seat at the table and settled for a piercing "How dare you?" glare instead. Jack squirmed in his chair.

"So anyway, that's all we heard. He drove away after Rachel came out and pretended the dog was hers."

"I see," said Thatcher. "He didn't threaten Mrs. Stevens, as far as you heard?"

"I'm not sure," I said at the same time that Jack said, "Not physically, no."

"Pardon me?"

"Well, like I said, he asked if she wanted to go back to Mexico, whatever he meant by that." Jack glanced at me to see how much hot water he was in.

Unfazed, the detective smiled. "Well, we can't arrest him for that, unfortunately."

"Arrest him? Is Alejandra the one who called you? Does she want him arrested?" I was worried that we were saying all the wrong things.

"Nope. I'm not at liberty to say who tipped us off, but it wasn't Mrs. Stevens. This cake is superb, Marilyn. What's this white cream called?"

I ignored the compliment as well as the question. "Rachel notified you, then?"

Oh, why hadn't I called him myself? When had Jack and I become such cowards? Nosy Nellies instead of concerned neighbors. But then, I'd been worried about Alejandra's legal status. Surely Rachel was, too. Someone else must have called. Mrs. Chang, maybe. Or Chung. She was an elderly widow with lots of free time to spend at the window, although admittedly I had never noticed her there. I'd only ever seen her out front tending her herb garden, so tiny and wrinkled she could pass for a garden gnome.

"He just said he couldn't tell us that, Marilyn," Jack reminded me. "I doubt anything has changed in the last three seconds." Then he remembered the eggshells and added, "Honey."

Detective Thacker had been hunched over his laptop, transcribing some unknown segment of our conversation. When he snapped it shut and looked up, something in my face elicited a sympathetic smile. "Don't worry, Marilyn. There's not much in your report that we didn't know already. I was hoping to verify something that was mentioned by the person who called in the report this evening."

"What's that?" Why had he closed the computer if there was still information left to verify. Our neighborhood's first murder, and they had to assign the case to a bumbling beginner.

He finished his coffee before answering. "This is decaf, right?"

I snapped, "Yes, of course. Is that relevant?" Impatience and stress were having a negative effect on my manners. Jack looked worried, as if wondering what he was in for later.

Thacker laughed. "Relevant to my sleep, is all. It's hard enough, with this job, to nod off at night."

Oh brother. Mr. Self-important. When we didn't offer the expected sympathy and admiration, he got on with it.

"Did either of you see anyone on Mrs. Stevens property this afternoon after the gentleman left and the ladies went inside their houses? Did you notice any activity at all?"

"We stopped watching after he left. Just them and the dog, that's all we saw," said Jack.

"You're certain."

"Of course," I said. "Did whoever called in the report mention another person?"

He scratched his chin and nodded. "She saw a figure in dark clothes, long pants and a hoodie, sneaking out from behind Mrs. Stevens' house not long after Mr. Stevens departed. The person ran across the front yard, turned right at the corner, and disappeared, she said."

She? I didn't point out this slip of his tongue. What an amateur. But what did it matter who had called? It could have been Mrs. Chang or any one of the other neighbor women.

"Just what we needed," I said. "Something new to worry about."

When Thacker had finally left, we collected dishes and loaded the dishwasher in tense silence. Jack escaped into the family room for an episode of "Longmire" while I tried to lose myself in a new novel that had made its way onto the bestseller list despite a myriad cast of dull characters that had me flipping back and forth to remind myself of their connection to each other.

I plowed through to the end of the book and fell into bed exhausted at 11 o'clock—then awoke at 3:00 a.m. as usual. Between then and dawn, I obsessed—as one will do during those witchy hours—but not about the possibility of a murderer in the neighborhood or the unsightly state of Alejandra's property. I wasn't thinking about her bully of an ex-husband, either, or the report of a mysterious figure racing across her lawn after she and Rachel went inside. And while I was peeved that Jack had ratted out Alejandra on the citizenship issue and blabbed to Thacker certain secrets from my past that had nothing to do with the investigation, those things weren't weighing on my mind either.

No, what I could not stop thinking about was Jack's concern that I might be suspicious of him because of the detective's strip club and porn sites questions. Why would he be so anxious unless he were guilty of something? Was it possible he had been inside that sleazy joint, perhaps during one of my trips to visit my foster mom in St. Louis before she succumbed to Parkinson's last year?

What other secrets might he be keeping from me? Had he really not recognized those two porn websites? Our sex life was, well, not exactly over, but not exactly spicy either. Which was normal at our age, according to Google.

Over and over, I told myself to stop it and go back to sleep. But I lay awake, fretting, until the sunlight through the curtains gave me permission to concede defeat. Then I climbed out of bed and trudged into the kitchen, where I opened my laptop and googled "dangers of insomnia."

On the web I learned that chronic sleep loss had been linked to cancer, dementia, and obesity. My genetic predispositions were unknown, my birth mother having died of alcohol poisoning in her mid-twenties without ever revealing the identity of my father. She had been estranged from her family, and after her death, none of them surfaced. Anyway, while cancer and dementia were frightful to contemplate, I was almost equally disturbed at the prospect of obesity.

Starting at the age of thirteen, ever since my metabolism went from zero to ninety and melted away the baby fat like magic, I had shown my gratitude by managing my diet and staying in shape—although admittedly since that time I hadn't had to work very hard to keep the pounds off. Still, the idea of turning into a walking wad of Playdough with toothpick limbs, like so many women my age, was distressing—and preventable. I would remain on guard.

I went back upstairs to shower, and then stepped on the scales to find myself three pounds heavier than on my previous weigh-in one week prior. No wonder my capris now felt snug around the waistline. I was eating more than normal—lack of sleep caused me to crave energy boosts throughout the day—and exercising a little less due to fatigue. I had to start getting some sleep or I'd be forced to order a new wardrobe in a size I would immediately start working like hell to diet myself out of.

Prayer was having no effect—apparently Jesus had more pressing problems to worry about—so I tackled my insomnia directly. I resolved to pack the daytime hours with stress-free activities such as reading, puzzles of every variety, and exercise.

So after forty minutes on the elliptical machine, I invited Jack to go for a stroll around the neighborhood just before lunch, during which I managed to avoid any talk of Alejandra's hodgepodge of junk or the murder investigation. When Jack wondered aloud when we might have another visit from Detective Dumbass, I answered with a lighthearted quip about us opening a dessert restaurant. Maybe by keeping the day as relaxing as possible, I could avoid another night of wrestling with the sheets until dawn.

It might have worked, had I not made a spontaneous decision at bedtime to kill a little more time before turning in. Jack and I had just laughed out loud several times while watching an old Eddie Murphy movie on Netflix. The internet had suggested that laughing was good for overall health in addition to combating insomnia. It was 11:45, but I had yawned only twice so far, so I decided to aim for midnight.

I didn't want to start a new book until the one I'd ordered on Amazon had arrived, and I had mastered today's crossword and Sudoku puzzles earlier. So I turned to something I had given up months ago in the interest of reduced aggravation (it was appalling and even frightening how uncivil, snide, and downright mean-spirited so-called friends could be when seated before a screen with their fingers on a keyboard): I logged onto Facebook.

I soon saw that not much had changed, as far as the overall tone. Too much politics. No new posts by Natalie or Chloe in the past several weeks. Disappointed, I continued scrolling until a familiar face jumped out at me: Kate Murphy, an old book club friend—or rather, acquaintance.

Sue Ellen had brought me into the Rabid Readers book club eight months before her death and had remained my only real friend among the seven ladies. The books we read and dissected were interesting enough, but I wasn't always comfortable with the social interactions. Before and after our book discussions, and sometimes right in the darn middle, Kate and the others were strident in expressing their left-wing political views. Debate was not encouraged; it was more of an "Amen, sister" kind of situation. I put up with it because of Sue Ellen, who was an unaffiliated voter but seemed to think highly of these ladies, whom she knew through her kids' athletic activities and Girl Scouts.

A month after my friend's death, I'd received Kate's email telling me the book club was going on hiatus, since no one had the heart to meet without Sue Ellen. Not yet, anyway.

Kate's profile picture hadn't changed. It was a photo suitable for the back of a book jacket, although to my knowledge Kate, a recently retired dental assistant, had no aspirations of the writerly sort. I had to admit that the photo showed Kate in the best possible light, considering that expensive salon visits can only do so much to compensate for a scrawny neck, thin lips, and a weak jawline.

So what was Kate up to these days?

Above a photo of eight women seated around what I recognized as Carla Oldman's back patio, Kate had posted: "Fun times with book club friends! The Rabid Readers, together again. Thanks, Carla Oldman, for hosting!"

I glared at the photo, my stomach lurching. And before I could talk myself down, I had posted a "Wow" emoji and a comment: "Looks like fun!"

And then I slammed the laptop shut. It took a while for my brain to settle enough to allow sleep, as one might expect after such a discovery. But just before I drifted off, I reminded myself that Sue Ellen had considered me to be her best friend. *Me*, not Yertle (Jack's name for Kate, which I had once thought too cruel but could now thoroughly embrace), or any of the other women.

It was unfortunate that I had let other old friendships die through the years, but there was no reason I couldn't attract new friends if I put my mind to it. Anyway, these days I had more pressing matters with which to occupy myself. A murder in the neighborhood. A Peeping Tom. A possible hoarder across the street. Porn sites and strip clubs. All of these continued to drift in and out of my dreams.

7

Three days had passed since the detective's last visit, with no news and no further suspicious or alarming street activity. Rachel still sat on her porch in pajamas much of the time and Alejandra came and went with carloads of crap, not even bothering to unload half of it anymore. That evening, complaining of his arthritic hip, Jack begged off our pre-dinner walk. It flared up just now and then, and I had never given much thought to how quickly he seemed to recover.

"That's how it goes," is the way he explained it. "That's why they call it a flare-up."

But now, for the first time I wondered: *What does he do with that alone time? Should I sneak onto his computer and check his search history?* Such thoughts had never occurred to me before. Damn that detective.

Jack's absence turned out to be for the best, though, as Alejandra would almost certainly have been less forthcoming in his presence. And it's possible I wouldn't have met her friend Daniela, an encounter which led to Alejandra's spewing a fount of useful information—and not only about Daniela.

Preoccupied with Jack's flare-up, I was in no mood to socialize. So, when I saw Alejandra in her driveway, engaged in a hushed, emphatic conversation with a woman who was sleek and stylish, the opposite of Alejandra except for the similar dark eyes, I considered walking in the opposite direction despite my curiosity. But Alejandra waved me over, thereby saving me from what might have been an unnecessary fifteen-minute seething session followed by a stealthy entry through the back door, which would have been hard to explain had I found Jack setting the table for dinner.

Up close, the woman was even more striking. All those various shades of blond highlights must have cost more than I would spend in a year's worth of salon visits. She appeared dressed for a party in a thigh-high floral dress and stiletto heels, although her demeanor suggested she wasn't in a party mood. She forced an impatient smile as Alejandra introduced us.

"I'd like you to meet my best friend, Daniela. Daniela, this is Mrs. Meddleson."

"Middleton," I corrected, taken aback. Was this an innocent slip of the lip? Or another private neighborhood joke on Jack and me? Nosy Nellies wasn't enough? I would insist on an explanation next time I was alone with Alejandra. Meanwhile, I accepted the manicured hand Daniela extended. Despite the smile, her "Hello" was curt and the handshake mercifully quick, as if she wished to get it over with. Perhaps she shared my aversion to the practice.

"I won't interrupt your visit," I said. "I'm just off on a short walk."

"Oh," said Alejandra. "Would you mind if Boonie and I tag along? I'm training him to walk properly on a leash. Michael was a little too—well you know, easy with him."

The two friends hugged rather coolly as they said their farewells, and Alejandra said "Let's talk soon" in a tone that suggested there was something that needed more discussion. And yet it was as if she had intentionally cut the conversation short by inviting herself on my walk.

I doubted we would achieve any real exercise, having observed Michael Redding strolling behind an unleashed Boondoggles, head buried in his phone while the bloodhound loped through the neighborhood, his snout in every bush, shrub and flowerbed, his powerful stream of urine not far behind. Leash training was sure to be quite the project. Sure enough, my usual fifteen-minute walk turned into thirty, but it was well worth it, seeing as how I got the scoop that secured Daniela's spot on my suspect list.

"I sure hope Brian won't find out that Boondoggles doesn't really belong to Rachel."

I thought it best to play dumb. "What do you mean?"

She related the details of Brian's visit, which of course I had witnessed, ending with "He's just such a mean son-of-a-bitch. I can't believe I was married to that prick for thirteen years."

I barely winced at the foul language. A little more time with my two neighbors and I'd be having to wash out my own mouth with soap.

The conversation took a sudden turn. "Daniela is beautiful, isn't she?"

"Why yes," I said. "But then, so are you." She shook her head modestly, but it was true that she was pretty, although her weight might have been up a pound or two since the week before, and the ponytail prevailed. I wondered if Daniela ever tried to give her beauty advice.

"She's the only friend who has stood by me. Boonie, *no!* Not there!"

She tugged on the leash, dragging him spraddle-legged into the street to empty his bowels and saturate a good square yard of pavement with stinky urine. From the pocket of her jeans, she produced a baggie and scooped up the excrement, so of course the foul odor plagued us for the rest of the walk.

I didn't relish being thought of as a snoop. But our neighbor was dead, and it seemed as though the police still had no real leads. Maybe I could learn something useful to share with Detective Thacker. I pushed my tone toward concern and away from nosy.

"It sounds as if you're afraid of Brian. Have you told that to the police?"

"Detective Thacker came to the house after Brian's visit because somebody called him, but I played the whole thing down. It's complicated, Mrs. Middleton."

At least she had the name right this time. I decided her "Meddleson" slip of the tongue could be addressed later. "Please call me Marilyn."

I sensed her reluctance to trust me. Who could blame her, with so much at stake? It was hard enough for me, seeing my girls only a few times a year. But they were grown women now. As a young mother, losing them would have destroyed me—just as losing me had destroyed my own mother, or contributed to her downfall, certainly. Not that she hadn't brought it on herself. Alcohol and abusive men, her poisons of choice.

So my concern was sincere when I said in a low voice, "I heard him threaten to deport you. It must be terrifying, the possibility of being taken so far from your son." I was outing myself as an eavesdropper, but so what? Almost certainly, she already knew.

"I was afraid you might have heard that."

"I can keep a secret, my dear."

My husband was another matter, but it was best not to mention that. Anyway, Detective Thacker had assured me that Jack hadn't spilled anything the police weren't already aware of. Still, I was glad I wasn't in the room when he blabbed. I was a little less guilty, or so I liked to think.

Deciding to trust me since I knew the worst of it anyway, Alejandra blurted out the whole disturbing story.

"When I met Brian, he was a dream come true: a sexy,

smart, older boyfriend with money. I thanked God for him every night, until God let the government send my parents and my little brother back to Mexico without me."

Deported, of course. Although not without sympathy, this was something I couldn't understand about all these undocumented immigrants, thousands of them crossing the border each month: didn't any of them consider the possibility that their families might end up divided and heartbroken? Why risk putting yourself and your kids through that nightmare?

She continued, "Brian convinced my parents that I was better off in the States. He would take care of me, he promised. Send me to college. Ha."

"You had been here most of your life?"

"No. I was fourteen when Papi paid a coyote to smuggle us across the border, and sixteen when my family was deported. Brian got me fake documentation and married me to get me on the fast track for citizenship—supposedly, but later he reminded me that my papers claimed I was already a citizen, and he didn't want to 'blow my cover.' It was all a trick."

"What a horrible man! And he has custody of your son?"

"I was afraid to fight him. He's an immigration lawyer with connections in all the right places, including the INS."

"An immigration lawyer! How did you meet him, if you don't mind telling me?"

"My father had been working with him to make us all legal, since by that time Papi had a growing landscaping business with clients willing to give him references, but something went wrong. Daniela says Brian probably set Papi up—because Papi was using a social security number sold to him by some connection of Brian's—"

I all but gasped, and she broke off to defend her father. "Yes, I know. It's not right. But all too common as you probably know, and sometimes people have no choice."

I wasn't about to debate this sensitive issue. "I imagine that's true."

"So anyway, Daniela says Brian likely wanted my family out of the picture so he could have me all to himself, his own shabby little Mexican doll that he could transform into Model Immigrant Barbie, the lawyer's wife. But I was only sixteen, and he was twice my age." She shook her head. "It was a terrible match."

Sixteen years old, and her parents had seen fit to leave her in the hands of a thirty-two- year-old pedophile. I would have throttled such a man if he had come sniffing around one of my daughters.

"Smart as he was, he didn't see that I was the wrong choice until it was too late. We had Kyle, then he was afraid to divorce me. He thought I might figure out how to smuggle his son to Guadalajara."

Before I could ask what had changed his mind about the divorce, she took a step backwards. "He bought me nice clothes and paid for salon visits and English lessons. He wanted to show me off, but other than looking pretty, I couldn't meet his standards." Her tone shifted from bitter to rueful. "I gained ten pounds the year after Kyle was born and another eight the next year. Dieting and exercise didn't work. I was a disappointment and he made sure I knew it."

"A little extra weight is certainly no reason for a divorce," I said.

"I tried to please him, Marilyn. I really did. I spoke only English, except on the Sunday phone calls he let me make to my family in Mexico. I practiced with a tutor to try to lose my accent. I refused translators at school conferences —oh my god no, it always had to be English, English, English."

I was about to comment on the importance of practicing a new language at every opportunity but thought better of it. My two semesters of college French, much of it forgotten, wouldn't give me much credibility.

"Your English is excellent," I said truthfully. "And your accent is nearly unnoticeable."

She mumbled "Thanks" and continued, "I dropped my old friends from high school and began hanging out with women Brian approved of: gringas or second or third generation Latinas, wives of his friends from work or the gym. If I forgot and dropped a word or two in Spanish over coffee at Starbucks, they'd scold me and say, 'Speak English!'"

This brought to mind Jack's complaint that "Immigrants in this country have always learned English and dropped their native language, but not this new batch. La Raza and that bunch has decided we should all learn Spanish for their benefit, not the other way around."

This reflection, of course, would be kept to myself for now. Alejandra had fallen silent while my mind was wandering in a direction that no doubt would have offended her, so I jumped in with a prompt.

"Is that where you met Daniela? At Starbucks?"

"No, we met at the gym. But yes, we used to go to Starbucks with the others. She's the only one of that group who became a real friend. The others were—well, how close can you be to someone who doesn't know you're undocumented or that your husband sometimes turns the color of a tomato and slams his fist into the wall or your arm, whichever is closest?"

Oh dear. No surprise, after what we'd seen. I shuddered anyway.

"Our sick marriage lasted thirteen miserable years before Brian took up with some *puta* he met at the gym."

I did some quick math. Ah yes, the old midlife crisis story. Brian would be in his forties now, about the right age for it. No wonder Alejandra and Rachel were drawn to each other.

"I found out from Daniela, who thought I deserved to know."

"So did you confront Brian about the other woman?"

"No, I was afraid to. And not just scared he would beat me. I couldn't imagine being on my own, divorced and undocumented."

"But if you have papers, you're okay to find employment, right?"

"My papers are fake, remember? I couldn't risk someone finding out, especially since the last election. Before, I could have come clean and maybe been protected under the DREAM Act. But he wouldn't let me do it when we were married, and now it would just be stupid to out myself."

Ah yes. The DREAM Act. Obama's plan to give citizens' rights to children brought here illegally by their parents. Punish the parents, not the kids, said Obama—over the objections of Congress. Not so fast, said Trump. A president can't just wave his hand every time he doesn't get his way. That's why we have the legislative branch. Checks and balances. Jack and I spent half an hour over Christmas dinner with the girls, debating the issue until Natalie was so frustrated she cried, and Chloe threatened to leave the table if we didn't change the subject.

None of that particular family drama should, or would, be shared with Alejandra.

"So I bit my tongue and let him rave. I gave up exercising altogether and packed on another five pounds. I spent all my free time at thrift stores and yard sales."

So that explained the junkyard, at least partially. Maybe her shopping habit was a way to keep her mind off her misfortune. If so, between Rachel and me, perhaps we could come up with some healthier ways for her to distract herself.

Alejandra continued, "He started to obsess over it, asking me over and over, 'Jesus, why do you need all this shit?'"

A darn good question, so I risked alienating her by

pursuing it: "And why *do* you need it? Does it make you feel better?"

Her voice rose. "I don't need it. I just want it, okay? I might have a little shopping problem, that's all. And I wish people would leave me alone about it. Since it's my house and yard, why does everyone else think their opinion counts? Even Rachel, as if she doesn't have enough of her own shit to worry about, offered to have Michael Redding help me get rid of some stuff." She threw me a huffy look that said, "Can you believe that?"

"Gosh," I said.

We had learned of Redding's offer from Thacker already, but I hoped Alejandra would reveal more—specifically, just how furious had it made her? But try as I might, I was unable to envision Alejandra poisoning a cockroach, much less a human. Pursuit of that angle would be a waste of time.

Before I could apologize for prying, she resumed venting about her ex. "But that was much later. In the beginning, it was only Brian who noticed, and his nagging was constant."

"That must have been hard to take."

For both of you, I was thinking. Brian was despicable, sure, but living in a house crammed with junk would not be a picnic for anyone.

"He offered to pay for therapy, but when I agreed to go, he changed his mind."

Although I was hesitant to admit it, therapy is a subject on which I did in fact have some credibility. "That's too bad. Therapy can be useful if it's done right."

I might have said more, but she rushed ahead, growing ever more agitated as she spoke, her voice quivering at times. "I guess he was afraid of how much I might tell the therapist, and anyway, he had zero interest in saving the marriage, so why should he care about my mental health? If he could prove I was *loca*, it would be even easier for him to take Kyle from me."

We paused to let Boondoggle pee in the street again. He led the way there this time, after regretfully turning away from a tempting lilac bush. Maybe he was trainable after all.

"I'm sorry for laying all this on you, Marilyn. These days, between Michael's murder and Brian's asshole behavior, I'm always on the verge of falling apart. Last Saturday, after that scene with Brian, I couldn't find my keys and spent the afternoon in a panic, ransacking the house and the van before I remembered using them that morning to unlock the little shed in the corner of the backyard. When I saw them sticking out of the door lock, I was so relieved that I burst into tears. Can you believe that?"

"I believe it," I assured her. "Crying is sometimes good stress relief." I gave her a verbal nudge: "Speaking of Brian, you were telling me about your divorce. All this happened in Oakland, right? How did you and Daniela both end up in Las Oliviñas?"

"Her husband grew up here and it's close to his new job, so they moved about a year ago. When Brian dumped me and I was looking for something affordable, Daniela helped me to check out some places here in town."

"He left you even though you hadn't confronted him about that business with the other woman?"

"Yep. One night he said, 'You're sick, girl. You're gonna take this junk and move your ass somewhere else. Kyle stays with me.' No amount of begging would sway him. Daniela said I should just let him go. Her first marriage ended in a similar way, she said. But in no time at all she had met Eric, her second husband, so it was a blessing that Ray had left her."

"In no time at all, you say? I guess some of us are more resilient than others."

"Well, with her first husband, she had no kids to think

about. And she was born in California. If Eric ever leaves, she has rights. He'd have a hard time taking their two kids."

As interesting as all this was, I was eager to know more about Daniela's relationship with Michael Redding. There was no easy segue that I could think of, and since I was unwilling to remind her that we had been eavesdropping on her conversation with Brian when he dropped his snide accusation about Daniela and Michael, I just blurted out the question accompanied by a tiny white lie.

"I recall you mentioning something in the backyard last week—or maybe it was before that, when you, Rachel and I were talking in your front yard, about Daniela being friends with Michael Redding. How did they know each other?"

Her response was curt. "I don't remember saying that."

Okay then, I would stick to the facts. "Now that I think about it, maybe what you said was that Daniela goes to the bar sometimes and you would ask her if she had any ideas about who might have had it in for Michael."

"I said she has been to the bar a few times, that's all."

"So she didn't know Michael, then?"

After a pause followed by an "oh what's the use" sigh, she said, "Sure, she knew him. Eric travels a lot on business, so sometimes she goes with friends down to the Coal Bin when he's out of town on a Friday night. She met Michael there."

I waited. Now we were getting somewhere. A married woman who hung out in bars while her husband worked out of town. A woman with small children at home, no less.

As if reading my mind, she leapt to her friend's defense: "Daniela's kind of a wild one, but good-hearted."

"I'm sure she is," I said. "Good-hearted, I mean."

"Truthfully, I do think she had kind of a crush on Michael. One morning, she came over to help me unpack some boxes, and when she saw him passing by with Boondoggles, she called out 'Hey there!' in what was kind of a flirty voice for a married woman, but that's Daniela."

I had begun to mistrust Daniela. Young kids, and what was the woman thinking? By the grace of God, a heaven-sent foster mom, and intermittent therapy, I survived an alcoholic barfly, loser-magnet mother, but not all kids are that strong or that lucky.

"She said she was surprised, yes."

Which didn't exactly answer my question, but I let her continue.

"By then, Rachel had already introduced me to Michael when she invited him over to talk about hauling some boxes to the dump for me. From what Rachel had told me about how he hooked up with different women at the bar, I wasn't eager to get close to him."

"Yes, she did say he was quite the Romeo. In his own mind, anyway."

"I can't say I didn't find him attractive in a certain way, but he made me self-conscious. Even with those dark glasses he wore indoors or out, I felt his eyes crawling over me like fingers. He had one of those smiles that was more sexy than friendly. Know what I mean?"

"Sure," I said. "Somewhere in the deep recesses of my memory, I think I can recall being leered at."

She laughed, and the conversation went in a lighter direction. "I'm sure you still get plenty of leers, with that figure. You must work out a lot, huh?"

"Well, I do the elliptical machine every day, plus a good walk. And some ten-pound weights." Sucked in by the compliments, I had let the conversation get off track. "So anyway, you were saying that Daniela used to go to the Coal Bin to hear Michael's band play?"

"Yeah. Other bands too. But his band, Crocodile Lips, was her favorite. She would sit with all the musicians when they were on break, flirt with them I guess, but I'm sure that's all."

She didn't sound sure. And the more she talked, the

less certain she sounded. "She was always after me to go with her when Eric was away and she could get her mom to babysit. But I thought, what if Brian found out I was in a bar hanging out with what he calls the lowlife? And I also asked her if Eric knew she went to the bar and chatted up the band."

"What did she say to that?"

"She said, 'A girl needs a few secrets. I always come home alone. That's all that matters.'"

Appalled, I persisted. "What if the kids told him? Or her mother let it slip?"

"Julia's three, but she's severely autistic and doesn't talk. Carlos is still a baby, not even two."

Just as I was feeling a twinge of sympathy, she added, "She tells her mom she's having dinner and a movie with me or one of her other friends."

"That's too bad, about the autistic child. And a toddler to boot. I can see where she needs to get out of the house sometimes." *But hanging out in bars and flirting with musicians is not the answer,* is what I didn't say. And lying to her mother?

"So have you told Thacker about this? The fact that she frequented the Coal Bin when Michael played might be reason for him to question her. Just to see if she has any ideas for suspects, I mean."

She threw me a suspicious glance. "He interviewed her over the phone already. Someone told him what Brian said to me that night, about Daniela's old man getting wise."

She waited for a confession. After a moment, I said, "That might have been Jack. I tried to keep him quiet, but he thought it was important. And you have to admit ..."

"I know," she said, tugging Boondoggles to a halt. We both stopped walking as she turned to look at me. "She lied to the detective, Marilyn. She told him she'd been to the Coal Bin only three times, to celebrate her friends' engagements and birthdays. She said she'd never talked to

Michael or to anyone else in the bar except for her girlfriends."

Aghast, I said, "But he'll find out she lied and then she'll be in hot water for sure. She needs to come clean, and the sooner the better."

"Marilyn, I know I should tell him, but I'm not sure what Eric would do if he found out. He's not a wife-beater, and I doubt he would divorce her. But if she wants to keep her visits to the bar a secret, I don't want to be the one to rat her out. She's my best friend, remember?"

I could appreciate her position. During Phil's second affair, Sue Ellen had become attracted to her therapist. As any good Christian would, she found a new counselor and focused on saving her marriage. But what if, instead, she had indulged her crush and then the therapist had been murdered? Would I have talked to the police about her affair, even if she had begged me not to?

Aha. So that's what Alejandra and Daniela had been discussing when I interrupted them earlier. Even if Daniela wasn't having an affair with Michael, she would of course have asked Alejandra not to expose her lies and reckless behavior.

"Here's a thought," I said. "What if you tell Thacker what you told me and ask him to interview Daniela at the police station or at your house? Or even on the phone again, in a private conversastion?"

"She would kill me. But maybe if I talk to her first, get her permission—"

We both pulled up short, although Boondoggles gave a joyful bray and strained at the leash, when half a block ahead we saw Rachel standing in front of a neighbor's house—the neighbor whose backyard abutted her own—waving a wine glass as she ranted at a middle-aged woman with a gray-streaked bun, who stood with her scrawny arms stuffed in the pockets of her cargo shorts as she peered up at Rachel with owl-like eyes.

I began walking toward them in a hurry, thinking it might be necessary to intervene. Rachel was confronting her neighbor from across the back fence: "the bug-eyed bitch with the bird-slashing cats."

8

Jack and I had said hello to this neighbor in passing and even introduced ourselves at some point, after which Jack had dubbed her "Bird Legs." (No matter the temperature, shorts are an inadvisable fashion choice for some women.) I searched my memory for her real name and found it: Lisa, a widow who had moved into the neighborhood several months ago and lived alone with her two cats.

Until now, I had not connected the melancholic new neighbor to Rachel's across-the-fence nemesis. I wondered if Rachel had called Wildlife Protection on the poor widow after culling her phone number from the Neighborhood Watch list I'd provided.

Lisa appeared wary but not intimidated by Rachel, who towered over her by several inches. As we came closer, I noted that "bug-eyed" had been an unkind exaggeration on Rachel's part—which is not to say the peepers weren't quite large. But while those eyes could have been an asset in the cliched emerald green, chocolate brown, or sparkling violet of romance novels, they were of an indistinct shade with a total lack of brilliance that only added to the aura of sadness that surrounded the woman.

Judging by Rachel's antagonistic tone, I suspected one

mutilated goldfinch too many had been deposited on the back patio. But as we came closer, we heard her complain, "My god, how could you not have heard it? It's been going on for at least half an hour, and this isn't the first time." She cocked her head. "I guess it stopped again. But still, unless you're deaf, you could not have missed it."

With a dramatic flourish, she swallowed the remaining contents of the wine glass and then turned and stalked past us—headed home for a refill, I presumed, without so much as a glance at Alejandra or me, or even Boondoggles, who whimpered as his sad eyes followed her down the sidewalk.

We were left standing with poor, perplexed Lisa who after a moment said, "What on earth is with that woman?"

I opened my mouth to say, "We've been wondering the same thing," but Alejandra cut me off.

"Why do you ask?"

"She was babbling about some radio transmission that she keeps hearing. She said it was coming from my backyard and that I'd have to be stone deaf not to hear it. When I told her the truth, that I was sitting on my back porch reading and hadn't heard any such thing, she all but called me a liar."

"Huh," Alejandra and I both said.

"Well, that's strange." Alejandra shrugged. "Who knows? But anyway, we'd best get going so you can get dinner started, Marilyn."

As soon as we were out of earshot, I said, "So she's still hearing those voices. Do you think she's—you know—mentally ill, or what?"

"I don't know what to think." She lowered her voice. "Please don't let her know I told you this, but I need to share it with someone. It's making me really anxious."

"Of course."

"Promise you won't repeat it to anyone. Not Detective Thacker and not even Mr. Middleton."

"Of course," I repeated, seeing no way to avoid it. I wasn't in the habit of keeping secrets from my husband. But then again, did I really know all of Jack's secrets?

"Okay, then." She was almost whispering now. "You've heard her ask about the CB radio before, right? Well, she has it in her head that she's hearing a conversation between Deb and the woman she was having an affair with before she died." She waited for this to sink in. "Except she only hears the other woman's end of the conversation, not Deb's. It sounds like they're flirting over the radio while out on the highway in their trucks."

"And she thinks—wait, that makes no sense. Deb is dead."

"Right? Rachel knows it's crazy. That's why at first, she was hoping it was two other truckers, so she started searching for a CB radio in the neighborhood. To prove to herself that she wasn't losing her mind."

"You said, 'at first'? What does she believe now?"

"Ever since the day you and I told her we didn't hear anything, after she had just claimed to have heard it herself, she's grasping at other explanations. Some days she thinks the woman is taunting her. That's she's planted a CB radio nearby, close enough for Rachel to hear."

"Yikes," I said.

"Yes. And now the woman is trying to hurt Rachel by flirting with whoever she's talking to on the CB—which could be nobody, if it's just a nasty trick she's playing—calling her 'sugar' which was Rachel's pet name for Deb. And she makes snide remarks about 'your old lady, the barmaid,' and—" she looked at me as if wondering whether to go on. "And she somehow knows embarrassing details about Rachel and Deb's sex life."

"You said 'on some days' she thinks that. What about other days?"

"Yeah, so sometimes she's afraid this is some kind of, you know, psychic experience. That she's picking up transmissions from another time or dimension. From back when Deb was still on the road and cheating on her. That's when it really freaks her out."

Oh dear god. Why had I promised not to tell?

"Alejandra, you've got to tell Thacker about this. It's just—I mean, you have to admit—"

"But Rachel couldn't have murdered Michael, Marilyn. Why would she? She didn't kill Deb, who cheated on her, even though she was plainly furious. Michael never did anything at all to her except flirt a little bit down at the bar. And she just laughed about that."

Good point. But still. "Insanity is sometimes motive enough," I suggested.

She shook her head. "She's innocent."

Before I could think of an effective rebuttal, she moved on. "The other day, I asked if she'd considered seeing a therapist. She blew up and said I'm the pot calling the kettle, with all this 'junk' in my yard, as she put it. Then I yelled at her. 'I can't afford a damn psychiatrist, but you certainly can, with that big inheritance you love to talk about!'"

Low blows on both sides. "Good point."

"So of course it was me who apologized, after a whole day went by without us speaking. I hate it when people I care about are mad at me."

She turned to me. "Please, Marilyn. We don't need to tell Detective Thacker about this. Rachel has enough problems right now. She needs her friends, and we both know she couldn't have poisoned Michael, right?"

"Well, I doubt she thinks of me as a friend, but..."

"Sure she does. All her old friends are abandoning her, just like mine did. You and me, we have to support her."

Oh boy. So now I'd been sworn to two secrets involving potential suspects in a crime I was trying to help solve. And one of my two co-solvers is the one swearing me to secrecy.

"I won't say anything for now, but don't you think the

more information Thacker has, the better? Even if both Rachel and Daniela are innocent—and I'm sure they are—he might learn something useful that could lead to the real killer."

"Maybe."

We were now standing on the sidewalk in front of Rachel's house, but thankfully she was nowhere in sight. Probably passed out on the kitchen floor at six o'clock in the evening, I thought. Then I scolded myself: to be fair, she might also be on the internet, spilling her guts to the AA people.

Across the street, Jack was standing on Mrs. Chung/Chang/Ching's lawn talking with her and a man I'd never seen before. An attractive enough Asian gentleman if you like that type. Tall enough to tower over Jack, he was thin with no sign of a pot belly and no trace of gray in his hair, although from his lined face I guessed him to be around my age and Jack's.

Turning her back to the gathering, Alejandra whispered, "See? He didn't exactly leer at you, but did you see how his eyes smiled when he noticed you?"

"Oh please. He was probably looking at you."

I left Alejandra in a lighter mood than when we had started out, and my own mind was whirling with new possibilities regarding the investigation as I joined the gathering on the lawn, questioning Jack with my eyes.

"It was Mrs. Chang who saw the guy run across Rachel's front yard last week," he told me, before remembering his manners. "Marilyn, this is Zhang Wei, or"—he turned to the man, who was eyeing me in a way that was kind and thoughtful, definitely not a leer—"Wei Zhang, is it? Forgive my geriatric memory." He chuckled. I cringed.

"Call me Wei." Unfazed by Jack's questionable social skills, he inclined his head ever so slightly in my direction.

"Wei here is Mrs. Chang's son. He lives on the west

side of town, but he's decided to come and stay with his mother for a while," Jack further informed me. "To make her feel safer, what with the murder and all."

"Me too—Zhang," the miniature old woman said, sounding miffed as she poked herself in the chest with the blunt end of a pair of hedge clippers. She craned her neck and teetered on the toes of her gardener's boots in a futile attempt to raise herself to the level of Jack's face, as she swept off her sunhat and slapped it against her thigh for emphasis. "Not *Chang*. Zhang."

"Got it." Jack turned to me. "Don't you have your phone with you? Our new buddy plans to stop by for dessert. I've already got water on for spaghetti."

We gobbled our dinner ahead of Detective Thacker's visit. Between forkfuls, Jack said, "Touchy old thing. What's the big deal? Chang or Zhang? The names sound practically the same."

I got up and collected the dishes. "I don't know. Maybe it would be like someone calling us 'Meddleson' instead of 'Middleton.' Can you dry this pot while I whip some cream?"

"Sure," he said, accepting the towel I thrust at him. "Meddleson, you say? That's not even a real name, far as I know."

Our visit from the detective was a disappointment in that he had "nothing new to report, just keeping all the neighbors posted, making sure you're all staying safe."

Despite my assumption that he had come for dessert—which was a bowl of mixed fruit with a dollop of whipped cream since I had not baked today, and Jack had snarfed the leftover lava cake at lunchtime—I was touched by his concern for our well-being.

"Have you had any luck finding the source of that dinner plate?" I asked. Lately all the plates on the cluttered countertops of my dreams had two small chips and a faded geranium pattern.

"Not yet. We've checked out everyone's cabinets in the neighborhood, and now we're looking in all the thrift stores in the East Bay."

Jack asked about the hooded stranger Mrs. Zhang had seen loping across Alejandra's lawn after that incident with her horrible ex-husband.

"What? Oh yes. Well, other than the three earlier reports, and now this possible sighting, we haven't had any further complaints, but I wouldn't worry too much about that guy. Or gal."

Jacks brows shot up. "Gal?"

"Sure. Tall person, athletic looking. Probably young-ish, since he was moving right along. Or she. Looking for an uncovered bathroom window to check out, maybe."

He chuckled and went on to reassure us that Peeping Toms are usually harmless. "He'll get caught eventually. Meanwhile, another reason to keep the shades down. Right, Marilyn?"

I wasn't amused by his cavalier attitude. "How do you know this person who ran across Alejandra's lawn is the Peeping Tom? Anyway, I'll bet not all Peeping Toms are harmless. Who knows why he was peeping? And even if they happen to be two different people, isn't it possible that one of them killed Redding?"

He lost the grin. "Of course, there is a chance of that. But other reports of the Peeping Tom's appearance, his size, the hoodie, and all that are consistent with the reported description of the guy Mrs. Zhang saw crossing Rachel's lawn. Or gal. And as I said, Peeping Toms are usually harmless."

"Usually" I started to say, but he cut me off.

"Yes, yes, not always, but a big percentage of the time. Regardless, I don't want you to worry. We're checking out every possibility."

"I'm sure you are," I lied.

I walked him to the door, biting my lip all the way, sorely tempted to steer him toward either Alejandra's buddy Daniela or Rachel. Or both. But one thing I had learned from the gang of bullies I briefly ran with in middle school is that rats don't have friends. And since I had lost Sue Ellen, friends were in short supply.

My two neighbors were unlikely prospects for BFFs, as Sue Ellen had called us, but what if both Rachel and Daniela were innocent? In that case, once Redding's murder was solved, if I didn't alienate both Rachel and Alejandra during the investigation, I could be two friends richer. Not BFFs maybe, but friends.

Anyway, Jack had a point: it was Detective Thacker's job, not mine, to find Michael Redding's killer. But meanwhile, I would continue investigating in my own way. Thacker's lackadaisical attitude about the Peeping Tom was disturbing. Nice kid, but gosh. What an amateur.

9

This was not about friendship, I told myself as I settled in at the dining room table with my laptop and retyped Rachel's name onto my suspect list. This was about finding the killer, or at least getting Detective Thacker pointed in the right direction.

Honestly, it was like playing pin-the-tail-on-the-donkey with an uncoordinated two-hundred-and-thirty-pound adult. You wanted to point him toward the target, but at the same time you were inclined to stay out of his way. One never knew when a new bizarre, anxiety-producing clue might be revealed: strip clubs, porn sites, Peeping Tom. What next?

In the family room, the TV went silent, and I reflexively started to shut down the computer. But why should I do that? I had barely begun, although there was little more to add or amend at this point. I studied my list, undecided, as Jack approached.

"About ready for bed?" He leaned over my shoulder. "What's this one for? You'll need a list for your lists pretty soon."

I made a mental note to add the purchase of a desk for myself to the home projects list; a little privacy now and then wouldn't hurt. In fact, either of the girls' rooms might make a fine office space for me. Considering how seldom we were graced with their company, they could learn to double up.

"Just jotting down names of suspects. I keep adding people and taking them off."

I braced myself for "Go get 'em, Miss Marple" after which he would walk away chuckling at his own wit. It was a nice surprise when he finished reading the list before commenting. While he read, I scolded myself for expecting the worst from Jack. Why was I so ready to be cross with him? He was being consistently himself, the same husband I had been happy enough with for over thirty years, since we met at a Young Republicans function back in college— a slice of family history that tickled my girls' funny bones every time they heard it.

I answered my own question: an unsolved murder in the neighborhood, a Peeping Tom, a junkyard across the street, three to four hours of sleep every night, bruise-colored bags under my eyes, three stubborn extra pounds, and an incompetent detective's insinuating interrogation about a strip club and computer porn. Who wouldn't be cranky?

"Hmm. I thought Rachel was your buddy now."

"I keep adding her name and then deleting it. There's that thing about the CB radio she claims to hear. Too weird to ignore."

I had already told him about Rachel's revelation that day in Alejandra's backyard, and how she had cut short any further discussion of the voices. I should now lay on him the shocking details provided by Alejandra on our walk earlier, but I couldn't because Alejandra had sworn me to secrecy. A promise is a promise. And a rat is a rat, as Dannie Shumaker said back in seventh grade, just before ordering the other girls to shun me.

Then Jack further surprised me. "Not bad sleuthing. Looks like you've got more than Detective Useless."

After he went upstairs, I looked over my list again and added some notes.

Suspects (in no particular order)
1. Daniela Morrison, Alejandra's friend. (Motive: romantically involved with victim? Lover's quarrel?)
2. Eric Morrison, Daniela's husband. (Motive: jealousy?)
3. Rachel Van Buren, depressed neighbor. (Motive: delusional? Anger issues over partner's cheating?)
4. Brian Stevens, Alejandra's ex-husband and hot-tempered bully. (Motive: unknown)
5. Hooded stranger—assuming he/she was not one of the above-named suspects. Presumably male, although possibly a tall, athletic woman. Detective Thacker says he/she could be Peeping Tom, <u>usually</u> harmless. (Motive: unknown)

I silently congratulated myself. It felt good to be taking action when, let's face it, Detective Andy Thacker—who I had to admit was starting to grow on me the way a liberal but financially stable, fertile son-in-law might, if I ever got so lucky as to acquire such a thing as a son-in-law—the young man might have been prematurely assigned to a task he wasn't ready for, due to diversity quotas or a lack of qualified candidates.

I powered down the laptop and went upstairs to bed, hoping for but not expecting a solid night's sleep for a change. I prayed for one anyway, out of habit.

At some point, Jack nudged me. "Would you settle down, for Christ's sake?"

I tried, but even I was annoyed by my sighs and the repeated lighting up of the cell phone as I checked the time. At 3:30 a.m., I climbed out of bed with the intention of swallowing a slice of turkey on a saltine, hoping a tryptophan fix would calm me. With my phone tucked into my robe pocket, I shuffled downstairs to the kitchen.

Next thing I knew, I was in Jack's office, my heart racing as I stood at his desk with one hand on his closed laptop. There was only one way to prove his innocence, I told myself, after which our marriage would return to its previously healthy state. I would no longer wonder if there was something the detective knew about my husband that I wasn't aware of, regarding his taste in websites. Between my neighbor's unsolved murder, a Peeping Tom, secrets I shouldn't be keeping, and Alejandra's unsightly porch and yard, I already had plenty to lose sleep over. I needed my marriage to be the safe harbor it had always been. I deserved that, right?

I closed the office door and switched on the lamp. On the corner of the desk was a book, *Native Garden Plants of California*, which I flipped open and placed next to the laptop to be used as a prop in the unlikely event of footsteps sounding on the stairs. Whatever excuse I would use for reading it in Jack's office would have to be improvised, but Jack was a heavy sleeper. I wouldn't borrow trouble.

I opened the laptop. The password had been easy to memorize from the list he kept hidden (for the benefit of the girls in the event of our untimely deaths) on page 76 of *The Art of the Deal*. And having consulted Google the day before, I knew how to check the search history.

Fingers on the keyboard, I told myself to calm down; Jack would never know, and my snooping was in the interest of marital health. Then I closed the laptop and wandered over to the window to distract myself. My hands were too shaky, my heartbeat too erratic. I wasn't equipped for this level of subterfuge.

In my keyed-up state, I hadn't noticed that Jack had left the blinds partially open, and as I reached for the cord to close them, I saw that lights were on inside of both Alejandra's and Rachel's houses. Between the drawn curtains on Alejandra's living room window, a face peeked out at me. So someone else was up and about: the Middle-of-the-Night Club, Alejandra had called us.

My phone buzzed, startling me. I had forgotten to set the "do not disturb," something I did every night at Jack's insistence, despite my concerns that one of the girls would call with an emergency that I might be invited to help with. His grousing about my restless checking of the phone at all hours was the price he paid for not being awakened by the phone itself.

The phone hummed again. Having left my reading glasses on the bedside table, I squinted at the text messages while holding the phone at various angles and distances from my face, while two more messages buzzed their way onto the screen. Then I remembered that Jack kept a pair of readers in his desk drawer.

The texts were from Rachel. When we had exchanged numbers that afternoon in Alejandra's backyard, I had hardly expected her to be drunk-texting me in the middle of the night.

The messages continued to fly onto the screen faster than I could read them:

> Whacha lookin for in there? Is that ur old man's laptop?
>
> U shud close ur blinds at nite!
>
> Try covering one eye, Mrs. Magoo. It will help you focus.
>
> The middle-of-the-night club is now in session.
>
> Free wine and chips. Or not, if ur no fun like some people. (sad face emoji)
>
> But seriously folks we might solve the murder this very night!

The texting paused as Rachel waited for my response. Did I dare? Did I want to? It was nearly 4:00 a.m. What would Jack say?

The phone hummed again:

(two entire rows of chicken emojis)

Oh, what the heck. If nothing else, I could offer them a viable excuse for opening Jack's laptop. I would claim that when he had realized my insomnia was leading me downstairs, he had asked me to make sure he had shut it down. They might buy it. I typed:

Give me a minute.

I scribbled a quick note to Jack: "Don't worry, I'm across the street. Couldn't sleep and they asked me over. Back soon." I placed it on the kitchen counter next to the coffee pot, one of the first places he would look.

And shut ur blinds girlfriend there's
a pipping Tom lurking about and also a
murderer!

emojis: birthday cake, balloons, a row
of wine glasses, a cat in sunglasses)

As I slipped through the front door, my heartbeat ticked up. *What am I doing? Who goes outside at this time of the morning, with a killer on the loose?* I turned on my phone flashlight and aimed it up and down the street, but its range was insufficient to provide much reassurance.

Rachel met me at Alejandra's open door, phone in one hand and wineglass in the other.

"Nice robe, Mrs. M." She stepped aside with a sweeping gesture to let me enter. "Lightweight and elegant, ideal for those balmy summer nights in northern California."

It was probably fifty degrees outside, but I ignored the sarcasm and thanked her anyway. I couldn't very well return the compliment, as she wore no robe at all, just a hot pink zip-up sweatshirt over thin summer pajamas.

"So is it someone's birthday?" I asked, in reference to the emojis.

The response was a blank look from Alejandra, who was sitting primly on the sofa in a fuzzy blue robe that someone's grandma had no doubt dumped at the thrift store, and a "Not unless it's yours" from Rachel, who pushed the door shut behind me with her foot, sloshing wine onto the already stained carpet in the process. She giggled. "Oopsie."

Masking my distaste at the sight of the over-stuffed cardboard boxes that crowded the visible living area, I joined Alejandra on the sofa. The only other choices were a recliner stacked with magazines and a Bentwood rocker that was a little too close to where Rachel stood with a precarious grip on her wineglass.

"What's going on, then? You mentioned solving the murder this very night. Have you gotten wind of some new clues?"

"Maybe we have," said Rachel with a sly grin, "and maybe we haven't." She pointed to a glass of red wine on the coffee table. "That's for you, Mrs. Magoo. Drink up!"

Alejandra smiled at me while shaking her head at Rachel's nonsense. To my relief, she was holding a water glass and appeared to be sober, or at least substantially less inebriated than Rachel. The tortilla chips Rachel had mentioned were history, with only a few crumbs and a smattering of salsa left on the plate. At least they hadn't been drinking on empty stomachs.

"We thought it was time we talked some more about the investigation," Alejandra said. "Before you came over, we were checking out those websites the detective asked about."

"Websites?"

Relief flooded through me, followed by guilt. Why had I assumed that Thacker's questions about the strip club and porn sites were directed only at Jack? Of course he would have asked the others as well! I was processing this when Rachel chimed in.

"You wanna see some girl-on-girl, Mrs. Magoo? Or did you already check out the websites?" She waggled her little finger at me, tilting her glass at a dangerous angle. "Maybe you and Mr. Magoo already knew about those porn sites, huh?"

Alejandra spoke up. "Please, Rachel. Settle down, will you?" But then she commented, "You do look surprised, Marilyn. Didn't Detective Thacker ask you about those two websites—what are the names again, Rachel?"

"Never mind," I said, denying Rachel the thrill of uttering the offensive words. "Yes, he asked us." Then stupidly, I added, "I just didn't know he had asked everyone else."

The alcohol hadn't numbed Rachel's perception much, and if anything, it accentuated her smirk. "Is there some reason he might specifically ask you—or Mr. Magoo—about the websites and not ask all the rest of us? Come on, girlfriend, spill. You two watch porn to spice things up now and then, right? It's okay, you can tell us."

"No, I—"

"Aha! The plot thickens!" She plunked down her glass, clasped her hands behind her back and began pacing the room, brows furrowed. Sherlock Holmes in a hot pink, wine-stained sweatshirt. "The question is, how did Detective Thacker know you two were into porn, and what does that have to do with the case?"

"We're not into porn! Can we talk about something else? He asked us the same questions as everyone else. Get it out of your head that we watch porn. Because we don't."

"Hmm." She seemed nearly sober now as she stood looking down at me. "So, what's up, then? Why were you surprised that Thacker asked all of us about the porn links? You thought it was just you and Jack. Or maybe you thought he was accusing Jack of being involved in the murder. Is that it?"

"Rachel," said Alejandra. But she was looking at me, too. Waiting.

"I don't know." I picked up the glass and took a long swallow. Other than a taste with dinner now and then, I rarely imbibed. But I did know how to pace myself, so why not?

The truth flew off my tongue against my will, propelled by—anger? Confusion? "I don't know why I thought he was aiming an accusation at Jack, but I did."

There, I had betrayed my husband by revealing my suspicion to strangers. Unjustified suspicion, at that.

Light bulbs flared in Rachel's eyes. "Ha! I knew that was his laptop you were sneaking around on. Am I right?"

"Stop, Rachel." Alejandra was looking at me with such kindness that I wanted to cry. Instead, I picked up the bottle and topped off my glass. I took a slow sip, hoping Rachel would get distracted by a sudden CB radio broadcast.

"Yep. I had a feeling—"

"I said, 'Stop it!'" Alejandra glared at her.

Rachel threw up both hands and settled into the rocking chair, leaving her glass on the coffee table. Her eyes were still probing, but she fell silent. Thank God.

Alejandra touched my arm. "Do you want to talk about this, Marilyn?"

I glanced at Rachel. *Not with her,* I wanted to say. But her gaze had lost its meanness and now fell somewhere between curious and sympathetic.

Possibly Alejandra gave her a signal, because Rachel blurted out: "So okay, I'm an asshole. But listen, Mrs. M. We've been around, me and Alejandra. We know marriages aren't always perfect." She was suddenly teary-eyed, probably thanks to the Merlot. "Even the ones that seem good from the outside—and even from the inside. I mean, look at me, blindsided."

I was in no mood for her "poor little victimized me" routine, but it was better than being interrogated, so I withheld comment.

She reached for her empty wine glass, then thought better of it. Maybe she had finally remembered the internet

AA group. Ha. Some program. I'd have liked to read the Yelp reviews on that one.

"Anyway," she went on, "there are a lot worse things than porn. I mean, do you suspect him of cheating? Or sneaking out to strip clubs or seeing hookers behind your back?"

"Of course not. He's always home, and when he's not, we're together or I know where he is." What was I doing, having such a discussion with these two unstable women? "Look, I don't know what's got into me. I'm fine, Jack is fine, there is no problem with our marriage."

"So why don't you trust him, then?" She suppressed a yawn, as if the answer didn't really matter much to her.

"Rachel, stop. Maybe we should call it a night. We can meet to discuss the murder another time." Alejandra moved to get up, but I put my hand on her arm.

"I do trust him," I insisted. "Can we please talk about the investigation just a bit? That's why I came over here, after all."

Rachel yawned again. "Bullshit. You came over to show off that awesome robe. Where'd you get that? Nordstrom, I'll bet."

"I made it myself. Now can we please—"

"Holy shit. That's impressive." And she immediately lost interest. "I think I'll write a book. Maybe a whole series, along the lines of Sue Grafton's alphabet novels. Instead of letters, I'll use, let's see, numbers. The first one could be 'One Cheater Dead Already,' followed by"—she grinned at Alejandra—"'Two Cojones and a Butcher Knife.' What do you think, Mrs. M?"

Could it be that this possibly psychotic woman and I had at least one thing in common? Perhaps we could start a new book club focused on mystery novels.

"I'm afraid Janet Evanovich beat you to it. The numbers thing, I mean."

"Oh, right. That bounty hunter lady. Wow, that was a

long time ago. I'll have to think of some other gimmick."

"You'll need a protagonist, like Louise Penny's Inspector Gamache. Maybe you could model him after Detective Thacker." Anything to get her off the topic of my marriage.

She squealed. "I love Louise Penny. I've read the whole series so far." She was eyeing me with new appreciation. "Do you read Tana French? I just bought—"

"Oooh-kay," said Alejandra, suddenly taking charge—which was fine with me: better her than Rachel. "We were all visited by Detective Thacker last night. Let's compare notes."

I shrugged. "He didn't have anything new to report, at least not to Jack and me. Just that the lawn-loper could have been a woman, and that Peeping Toms are 'usually' innocent."

"Same here," said Alejandra. "Nothing new. So let's just review what we know."

"Lawn-loper," Rachel tittered. "I like the sound of it."

"For starters," I said, ignoring her and turning to Alejandra, "Michael implicated one of the neighbors with that confusing 911 call. Which might have been bogus, but who knows?"

"Bogus?" they repeated in unison.

"Oh please. Don't tell me you never wondered if he did himself in and tried to lay the blame on one of us, out of spite or—or just his idea of a parting prank?"

"Parting prank," Rachel marveled. "You're so poetic, Mrs. M. But really? Don't you think that's a bit of a stretch?"

"Maybe it is," Alejandra said, "but I'm writing it down anyway."

She had retrieved a notebook from the stacks of who-knows-what on the dining room table and sat poised on the edge of the sofa with her pen, like a secretary from the 1960s. A chunky secretary in a fuzzy robe, house slippers, and lopsided ponytail.

"Okay, then," she said. "Number one: 911 call says, 'neighbor knows.' Possible prank by Michael himself. What's number two?"

"Strip club," said Rachel. "Porn sites."

I grimaced, but she was right. There had to be a reason we had all been asked about them.

Alejandra added "strip club/porn sites" to the short list. "What do you suppose it means? Detective Thacker said a tip about the club was called in from that stolen phone they found. But has he given us any idea what the websites have to do with anything? They must have found them in the search history on Michael's computer, don't you think?"

"Or maybe Thacker digs porn himself and is looking for kindred spirits? He's single, you know." Rachel yawned, and yawns being contagious, Alejandra and I followed suit. Rachel's eyelids fluttered and closed. Just my luck to finally get a serious discussion going when all three of us were practically sleepwalking.

"What else, though?" Like me, Alejandra seemed to have had enough porn site discussion for the night.

Rachel pushed herself out of the rocker. "Time for water." She wandered toward the kitchen. "Always start the morning with a full eight ounces."

I glanced toward the window. Sure enough, the first dim light of dawn was filtering between the curtains. "I should go home. But please, let's just quickly finish the list. So we can feel like we've accomplished something."

"Peeping Tom," said Alejandra, scribbling in her notebook.

"You mean lawn-loper," Rachel corrected. On her way to the kitchen, she had been distracted by some boxes on the dining room table and was now fully awake and pulling CDs out of a carton.

"Gender uncertain," I prompted. "Thacker says probably harmless, but who knows?"

"Wow, these are cool." Rachel waved two CDs at us. "Mexican stuff." She then rescued a set of glass mixing bowls from another box and held one up for our approval. "My mom used to have a set of these. Where'd you get them, Alejandra?"

"Please, Rachel. Concentrate." She had reddened, probably from embarrassment. My own ire was steadily rising as Rachel continued to interrupt us with her drunken commentary.

"Thrift store. I'll bet. Hey, wait—"

Alejandra directed her question at me. "Anything else?"

I searched my memory. "Well, there was that photo he showed us of the chipped plate, the one he ransacked the cabinets looking for."

"But the question is," Rachel called from the dining room, "did he look through these boxes on the table, Alejandra?"

We turned to find her holding a cup in one hand and a dinner plate in another, both pale gray with a faded red geranium pattern. The dishes Andy Thacker had been searching for—dishes that matched the plate from which Michael Redding had eaten the Thai curry that killed him.

10

Alejandra sucked in her breath. "Oh my god. I've never even opened that box. It's been there for a while, I think. But—"

"But did Detective Thacker look inside it?" Rachel persisted.

"Not while I was in the room. But I went outside once or twice to take phone calls. Oh my god," she said again. "Do you think he'll suspect me? I can't believe this!"

She and I hurried to join Rachel at the table and the three of us set about sorting the dishes into place settings. Six salad plates. Six cups. Six saucers.

Five dinner plates.

"Oh Jesus. Shit," Alejandra moaned. "I swear, I've never seen these before."

"Calm down," I said. "Take a breath and think. A garage sale, maybe?"

She shook her head. "I go to garage sales all the time. But I never buy anything without looking at it first. And I would remember seeing these."

"Uh-huh," said Rachel.

"It's true." Alejandra insisted. "I don't just buy random crap."

"Uh-huh," Rachel said again, looking around her.

"There's just an awful lot to remember, that's all."

Her eyes glazed with fright, Alejandra murmured, "We have to tell Detective Thacker. Oh my god. What will he think?"

"But you're innocent!" Rachel said, as if the alternative had never occurred to her. Surprisingly, I too believed this, despite the newfound incriminating evidence, not that it mattered one whit how Rachel and I felt. The detective would still have to know. Anyway, he would be able to prove Alejandra's innocence—wouldn't he?

I surprised myself by saying, "Wait until morning to call him. Maybe you'll remember buying them somewhere: yard sale, Salvation Army, Craigslist?"

She shook her head, and Rachel began returning dishes to their cardboard carton.

"Stop!" I warned. "The police may want to look for fingerprints, and we've added enough tonight already."

"Right," she said, then continued tossing plates into the box, fingerprints be damned. If anything, she was trying to add more. She threw me a defiant look before saying to Alejandra, "You can't call the cops, and you know it."

When I opened my mouth to argue, she cut me off.

"You can't risk it, Alejandra. Think what Brian might do. Think of Kyle."

At the mention of her son, Alejandra's lowered herself onto the sofa. Rachel sat down beside her. "Don't worry, girlfriend. We've got your back. You're innocent. We'll figure out where the damn plates came from."

Innocent or not, this was too much.

"But we can't withhold evidence," I protested. "The detective could use these to track down the person who sold them. It's—"

Rachel pointed to the top of the box, where someone had scribbled in black marker, underlining it twice for emphasis: *Complete set.* The same words were written on all four sides of the carton.

"Their word against hers." She gestured at Alejandra. "Who will they believe?"

Oh dear god. What had I gotten myself into? This would teach me to traipse around in the middle of the night and align myself with people who were willing to lie to the cops. And had reason to do so.

Now what? Alejandra's surprise at the discovery of the plates on her own dining room table was genuine, I was sure of that. Rachel and I could attest to it, and surely Detective Thacker would believe the three of us. And it was our civic duty to call him.

Rachel's eyes never left mine as she wrapped Alejandra in a hug. "We're your friends, Alejandra. We'll help you to figure this out. Right, Marilyn?"

So now it was Marilyn. No more Mrs. Magoo. No more Mrs. M.

Rachel grew tired of waiting for my response. "It's been nearly a month. He needs to come up with a suspect. It's his first case, and he's struggling to make an impression. What would you do if you were him?"

Even drunk, she was no dummy. Thacker was no Inspector Gamache. Alejandra was no killer. And I was no lawbreaker, but neither was I a rat.

"Let's all get some sleep and talk tomorrow," I said. "You don't need to call him before then anyway." To satisfy Rachel, I added, "If you do at all."

In lieu of a hug, I patted Alejandra's arm. "Don't worry, honey."

We said good night, and I walked out into the dawn. As I crossed the street, a figure took shape on Mrs. Zhang's front porch. It was her son, Wei, watching my approach with polite curiosity. He was smoking, a vice I had never associated with Asians.

"You're up early," he commented.

"You too," I answered, for lack of a reasonable excuse.

"Watching the street," he said. "Murderers, Peeping Toms, you know."

Was he expecting a chuckle, or a "Thanks for your vigilance?" I smiled in a way I hoped would cover both bases. "Well, good night, Wei."

He returned the smile. "Good morning, Marilyn."

His warm voice and easy manner were a comforting distraction that held as I let myself into the house and started upstairs. Drowsiness set in as I felt the pull of my comfortable mattress. A few hours of catch-up sleep would clear my mind, leaving me better equipped to advise Alejandra about the missing plate.

I was five steps up the staircase before my anxiety returned with a vengeance. *My God, we're withholding evidence in a murder case!* I turned back and retrieved my laptop from the bookshelf. After a moment of hesitation, I added to my suspect list:

> 6. *Alejandra Stevens (Motive: fear of deportation? Maybe Redding knew about her fake papers.)*

Out of remorse for my disloyalty, I added:

> *Almost certainly innocent. Only question is her possession of dishes.*

I deleted her name and reentered it. This time it stayed, as did the sadness that trailed me upstairs, where I fell into two hours of heavy sleep, feigning unawareness when Jack jiggled my shoulder and asked if his snoring had driven me to sleep on the sofa again. Explaining would lead to interrogation, which would mean mounting a defense on my own behalf. The thought was exhausting. When I rolled over and burrowed under the comforter, Jack gave up and went down to breakfast on his own.

11

Only an hour after Jack left the bedroom, I awoke from a perturbing dream that fled as soon as my eyelids popped open. There was no point in closing them again: with my racing heartbeat, sweaty palms, and tense limbs it was if I'd chugged a double espresso. I climbed into the shower, dressed, and was on my way downstairs when the doorbell rang.

"Eight o'clock in the morning," Jack grumbled from the kitchen. "Must be one of your new insomniac buddies." He had found my note beside the coffee pot. In my exhaustion, I'd forgotten I'd left it.

Ignoring him, I opened the door. "Don't you ever look at your phone?" Rachel stepped aside so I could see across the street. Detective Andy Thacker was walking toward Alejandra's front yard accompanied by—oh dear god, a uniformed police officer.

"Rachel, I didn't call them, I swear!"

"Who said you did? Come on, she'll need us."

"But who—"

"Are you coming or not?"

I gestured for Jack to follow; better to not have him feeling left out. He shook his head, but out of loyalty or curiosity or both, he trotted across the street behind us.

At the sound of a screen door closing, I looked over my shoulder to see Wei placing a cigarette between his lips as he emerged from Mrs. Zhang's house. Jack noticed him too and mumbled a distracted "Good morning." Even in my agitated state, I met Wei's eyes and spent a split-second trying to remember if I had put on my makeup before coming downstairs. I wasted another second wondering why I should give a darn.

Detective Thacker and the officer turned and signaled for us to come no closer. Their expressions were friendly enough, but as I looked past them, Alejandra stepped out onto her front steps. It was unsettling to see her looking so weak and vulnerable, her eyes swollen and raw, although at least she had changed out of that shabby robe and straightened her ponytail.

Thacker turned to her while the officer kept an authoritative eye on us.

"Let's go inside and talk, Alejandra," said the Detective. He called over his shoulder to the rest of us. "You all can go on home now." It was not a suggestion. "I'll stop by later if there's anything you need to know."

Rachel trailed Jack and me home like a lost puppy and helped me to fill Jack in over coffee at the dining room table. The question was, if Rachel hadn't called about the plates, and I hadn't called, then who had? Alejandra herself, acting out of fright or some sense of civic responsibility? Could the Peeping Tom have been watching through a back window when we were inspecting the dishes? Or the real killer, assuming he wasn't the Peeping Tom?

While we talked, Rachel sprang up every few minutes to peer out of our living room window toward Alejandra's house.

"Oh, I forgot." Jack gestured toward the basket where we keep the mail. "Somebody left you a present."

Beside the basket was a large manila envelope.

"It was on the porch this morning," he said.

To distract myself from Rachel's impatient mutterings (*What the hell? … Jesus … What the hell?*), I picked up the envelope and was surprised to see that there was nothing written on the front except "MARILYN," in thick purple felt-tip marker.

As I picked up the letter opener, Rachel called out, "Here we go."

I went to the window just as Detective Thacker and the officer emerged—without Alejandra in tow, thank God. As they drove away, Rachel said "Come on." She was out the door before Jack finished saying, "Let's just wait for Thacker to fill us in."

I tossed the letter opener and envelope into the mail basket. "Suit yourself. I'll be back in a minute." I thought he might follow but didn't wait to see.

"Who called them?" Rachel demanded after bursting through Alejandra's door without knocking.

Alejandra was sprawled on the sofa and didn't get up. She looked exhausted, and no wonder. I was running on about three hours sleep myself, and she had probably had less than that. On the floor in front of her, Boondoggles lifted his head long enough to bray a friendly greeting to Rachel and me before yawning and resuming his nap.

"I did," Alejandra said flatly. "I called. It was me."

"*What the fuck*?" Rachel was personally insulted that Alejandra had made the decision on her own. "You couldn't wait for us to get a few hours of sleep to clear our minds so we could talk this over before you—"

"Never mind that," I interrupted. "It's done. Tell us what happened, Alejandra. You told him everything? About the plates?"

"What? Oh. Well no, not exactly." We were still standing, and she gestured again for us to sit, but we were struck motionless as well as speechless.

Finally, Rachel blurted out, "What do you mean, 'not exactly'? Did you blab about—"

The arm she raised toward the dining room table froze mid-gesture, along with her voice.

"Oh no," I said, frightened for Alejandra yet relieved at the same time. No more concealing evidence. "He took the dishes?"

"Um, no ... not exactly."

"Enough with the 'not exactly!'" Rachel snapped. "What the fuck happened to the dishes if he didn't take them?"

"Language, please," I said, momentarily back in the classroom. My own frustration had almost risen to a "What the hell?" level, but the F-word was a whole step up from there. Or down.

Rachel lowered the hysteria a notch. "Alejandra, where are the damn dishes?"

She jerked her head toward the back of the house. "Under the bed. He could've found them if he'd looked." Her voice was weak, defeated. "I almost wish he had."

Concealing evidence, back into play.

"But why call him, then?" Rachel was exasperated. "If you didn't mean to show him the plates?"

Alejandra pulled her phone from the pocket of her robe.

"Put that down!" Rachel demanded. "Tell us why you called the cops. On yourself. *Yourself.*"

Rachel fiddled with the phone. "I got another one," she said. "I showed all of them to Detective Thacker."

She handed the phone to Rachel, who took an excruciatingly long time to comment, other than quiet, unhelpful utterances such as "Yes, but ..." "Okay, I know, but ..."

"What's going on?" Clearly, I had been left out of the loop. So much for teamwork.

"Ah," said Rachel. "When did this new one come?"

"It was taped to the outside of my kitchen window this morning." Alejandra retrieved the phone from Rachel and handed it to me. "There are six altogether. Just slide right after you've looked at one."

"I know how to view photos on a cell phone," I snapped. Jeez.

"Oh dear god," were my only words for the next minute, repeated each time I viewed one of the photos.

I read them one by one, my stomach lurching by the time I'd finished. Six photos, each of an index card containing a single sentence, variations on a theme. Such filth. Vitriolic, racist, filth typed in large font, capital letters, peppered with words that were surely intentionally misspelled.

ILEGAL MEXIKUNTS DON'T BELONG HEAR.
HELLO, CHALUPA. I'M ALWAYS WATCHING ....
FENCE JUMPERS DON'T DESERVE WELFAIR.
I KNOW YOUR SECRET, WETBACK-HO.
GUESS WHO'S NEXT, CHALUPA?

And the most disturbing:

YOUR BOY WALKS ALL ALONE TO A PRETTY FANCY SCHOOL $$$$

I handed the camera to Alejandra. "Oh dear god," I said again.

She nodded. "Yes. Oh dear god."

"When did they start coming?" I asked.

"I found the first one two days after the murder. I've been writing down the dates and times I find them. They were all in different places: under my windshield wiper, taped to the welcome mat, on the back patio, never in the same place."

Rachel watched me absorb this. "Do you think it's related to the dishes? Whoever wrote them could have sneaked into the house after the murder and left the box on the table to set Alejandra up, not knowing Thacker would do a half-assed inspection. When he didn't find the dishes, they sent the notes knowing she would get spooked and call the cops."

Two sets of eyes begged me to jump all over this theory. It was promising, and I was a little envious that I hadn't thought of it myself. It took me a moment to figure out why I hadn't.

"Maybe," I said. "But those last two—at least they were the last two that I saw photos of—they threatened her and the boy. That implicates whoever wrote them, not Alejandra."

Rachel rubbed her head. I guessed the hangover was belatedly kicking in.

"So what was Detective Thacker's take on it?" I asked Alejandra.

"Same as what you just said: that it made whoever wrote the notes a suspect in Michael's murder. Especially the 'Guess Who's Next?' And he told me he would get the police to patrol more until the murder was solved. He said I'd done the right thing by reporting this, but ...."

Rachel and I sat down, reclaiming our spots from the night before, as each of us silently mulled it over. On the bright side, the notes would give Detective Thacker something new to investigate that could lead to the murderer. But what would that mean for Alejandra?

As for deportation, would Brian dare to raise the issue of her fake papers? Wouldn't that cause him trouble as well? It was true that undocumented foreigners were reportedly being rounded up now and deported on a more regular basis. Which was a good thing, regarding those who had knowingly broken the law by jumping the border, but I wouldn't want it to happen to Alejandra, or anyone else whose parents made the unwise choice to drag them across. But they weren't deporting those kids, the "dreamers." Or were they?

"Even if Brian squeals, they can't deport you for just being here," I said. "Can they?"

"Not yet, no. But if they suspect me of a crime? I mean,

it's happening to others. I see it in the news all the time."

"Fucking orange clown," muttered Rachel.

I bit my tongue. This was not the time. Thank God Jack hadn't followed us.

"Still, I had to tell him." Alejandra looked from Rachel to me, seeking agreement.

Rachel's response was an exasperated groan.

I said, "Well, of course you did. He threatened your boy. The police will notify your ex and probably the school, so they can watch over him closely."

She burst into tears. Rachel gave me a "Way to go, Einstein" look.

"I'm so sorry." I looked around. "Is there a box of Kleenex anywhere?"

Alejandra pulled an abused tissue from her pocket and blew her nose. "It's okay. Of course Brian will have to know. That's one reason I called Detective Thacker, so I wouldn't have to tell him myself. God only knows what he's going to do—"

"He won't do anything," I said. "Revealing your papers would cause him trouble, too. And he's not stupid. He knows the cops will be even more focused on our neighborhood now. Maybe he'll use it as an excuse to try to keep the boy from seeing you, but you can fight that with your own lawyer."

"I don't have a lawyer and can't afford one. Anyway, you don't know him." She shook her head. "You just don't know—"

"I know him better than you think."

I would have preferred leaving it at that, but their curious expressions told me it was unlikely.

"Uh ..." Rachel said. "Huh."

"Oh, not him personally," I clarified.

The malignant, threatening image of Lee Houston, his thick fingers pressing lightly against my mother's throat, the terror and shame in her eyes, swam in front of me. I shivered, although he was nothing now but a withered, demented, incontinent old man in a nursing home. I checked with the facility once a year, on my mother's birthday, but the old devil refused to die.

What was I thinking, opening up to these two women, practically strangers? Jack knew, of course, but Sue Ellen was the only other person I'd ever shared the sordid details with, and that was after a year or more of friendship. As I tried to think of a way to backpedal, Jack appeared in the open doorway.

"Thacker wants to talk to us ASAP. I guess you've given up checking your phone."

Midway across the street, he reached for my arm and tugged me to a stop. "Did they find the dishes?"

Without thinking it through, I whispered, "She hid them under the bed."

"Jesus Christ, Marilyn!"

I tried to keep walking, but he clutched at my arm. "You have to let Thacker know. If not, you're withholding evidence. I'm not going to be part of that, and neither should you."

"Did you mention to him that we had found them?" Oh god, why had Rachel and I let him in on this? And why had I just revealed that Alejandra had stowed the dishes under the bed.

"Of course not. That's your responsibility, not mine."

"Then stay out of it. Please. Just for now."

You would have thought I'd asked him to commit perjury.

"Are you kidding me? Marilyn, what has gotten into you? The woman is an illegal immigrant and, whether you want to believe it or not, she could even be a murderer." He paused for effect, but I resumed walking and refused to meet his eyes.

"She's innocent."

"Dear god, Marilyn. That may be, but at the very least,

she's hiding evidence in a homicide investigation."

"Just for now, please don't say anything. If there's trouble over withholding information, I'll pretend I never told you."

"Oh, now I feel much better! You would lie under oath, I guess, if it came to that."

We had reached our front door, and since it was ajar, I whispered, "No, you know I'd never do such a thing. Please just give us some time."

"'Us,'" He muttered.

"Hello, Detective Thacker," I said. "Do you mind if we have coffee and banana bread while we talk? I haven't had time for breakfast yet."

"That sounds marvelous, Marilyn. And I do wish you would call me Andy."

I smiled. "Sure, Andy."

He took his usual spot at the dining room table and opened his laptop, suddenly all business. "So Marilyn, I assume you know about the hate messages Alejandra has received."

"I wasn't aware of those until a few minutes ago."

I must have sounded defensive, because he said, "Of course not. But she filled you in after we spoke with her? You ladies being friends and all?"

"Friends? Well, I mean, we talk sometimes, She and Rachel and I. Over iced tea, and that kind of thing. More neighbors than friends, I'd say."

"Huh. Well, she told me you and Rachel were good friends of hers, and that she'd feel comfortable calling either of you if she felt threatened or frightened."

"Oh, did she?" From the corner of my eye, I watched Jack give his head an almost imperceptible shake. The detective's eyes flicked toward him, interested. Or maybe that was my imagination and guilty conscience at work.

"Indeed she did," said Andy.

"Well, she's alone, you know. And considering the

possibility of a killer in the neighborhood, it seems wise for all of us to look out for each other.”

“Does she confide in you? About her husband’s behavior, her legal situation, or other problems?”

“Not much.”

Oh, what a whopper. I backtracked: “Well, she did tell me yesterday, when we ran into each other and ended up taking a walk together, the circumstances of her being here and all. Is that what you mean?”

“So she told you her husband had sometimes abused her during their marriage?”

Was this a trap of some kind? Darn it, Jack had been right. I had no business withholding anything from a homicide detective, even an incompetent one—if he was in fact incompetent. I was never sure all his cards were on the table. I decided to switch tactics. No more lying if I could avoid it.

“Well, yes. She told me quite a bit about her husband, in fact. She needed to talk that afternoon, and apparently I’m a good listener.”

“I imagine that’s true. Has she spoken to you, then, about her fear of being deported?”

“Yes,” I answered. “But I assured her it can’t happen, since she was brought here by her parents and therefore, she herself has committed no crime. That’s true, isn’t it?”

“So far, yes. Although I wouldn’t call that fear irrational. The way things are going these days.”

Another liberal. Not willing to wade into that debate, I offered a weak, “Yes, well.”

“But although she confided in you about her ex and her legality issues, she never told you about those index cards.” He thrummed his fingertips on the keys, impatient for me to give him something worth noting.

At last, something I could be a hundred percent honest about. “That’s the absolute truth, I swear. I can’t tell you why she withheld—why she didn’t share that with me, although she apparently told Rachel—"

I mentally kicked myself as he typed that into his notes. But surely, when he interviewed Rachel, she wouldn't lie about having been aware of the threats. Or would she? She had been ready enough to advise Alejandra to withhold information about the plates. The plates! *Please dear God, don't let him ask if there's anything Alejandra might have told me that pertains to the murder investigation.*

"Is there anything else she may have confided in you, Marilyn, that might have to do with Mr. Redding's murder? For example, her friend—" he checked his notes— "Daniela Morrison. Has she spoken to you about Daniela?"

Oh boy. I had sworn not to reveal that Daniela had lied to him about the frequency of her visits to the bar and her crush on Michael, but wouldn't that be preferable to blabbing about the plates? Which would have to be blabbed about soon enough anyway—as soon as he left, I would run across the street and tell Alejandra I wouldn't keep that secret any longer. I'd convince her to make the call herself, but it was not my place to tell him. Not yet anyway.

"She told me Daniela had been to the bar a few times," I hedged. He already knew that much, supposedly.

He waited, but I was finished.

"Okay," he said. "Anything else you want to tell me?"

Hell no, I thought. "Not that I can think of at the moment."

He closed his laptop, then reopened it when Jack cleared his throat and said, "Marilyn, aren't you forgetting something?"

The detective's eyebrows went up and stayed there. Then, thank you Jesus, the front door flew open. Startled, we all turned toward it.

A cheery voice called "Surprise!"

And there stood Chloe.

12

"More banana bread?"

I waved the platter at all three—Detective Thacker as well as Chloe and Jack, since he had made no move to leave us alone to enjoy this rare, unannounced visit from our daughter, whom we hadn't seen since Christmas.

Despite my reservations about adding needless calories to her diet, I smiled encouragingly at Chloe, who had confessed to having stopped on the road for an early lunch at McDonald's. It wasn't my place to monitor her eating habits, but what kind of mother would I be if I weren't mindful of her health?

"Just a tiny slice more," she said. "It's too yummy to pass up." I thanked her while knowing it was less a compliment than a transfer of blame.

It's not that Chloe was obese—"plump" was a more apt description—but every pound counted when you were five-foot-two. Unlike Natalie, who like me had emerged from puberty as a tall, willowy redhead, Chloe had matured into a mirror image of my mother in the photo taken when I was five years old, shortly before I was removed from her care after the Lee Houston incident.

Chloe inherited the abundant dark mane with which

Jack was blessed in his youth, but now there was only about half an inch of it left, chopped into a youthful, fashionable (I assumed) style that accentuated her chubby cheeks, but far be it from me to point out the obvious. Such a pretty young lady, though. Sparkling blue eyes, dimples, long black lashes, infectious smile.

Introductions had been made— "Call me Andy," insisted the detective—and so far, I'd been able to steer the conversation toward Chloe: her spontaneous decision to visit, why she came by car instead of by plane, her stressful semester and plans for the summer. Then she abruptly took the wheel and drove us headlong into the very topic I had been hoping to avoid.

"So what's new with this murder investigation?"

She directed this at Thacker, who puffed up a bit, cleared his throat and dabbed stray crumbs from his lips in preparation for impressing this surprise visitor who was all smiles, cheerful dialogue, and polite curiosity— probably not at all what he had expected from a daughter of mine and Jack's. Too bad he couldn't have been a fly on the wall at Christmastime.

"You missed a crumb or two right here." I brushed my own left cheek to help him locate the spot. Chloe gave me the "Oh my god" look, but if I hadn't clued him in it would have distracted me for the rest of his visit. Which I was eager to see concluded.

"Well, let's see," he began. "What have your parents told you so far? No reason to waste your time repeating what you already know."

A moment's panic. Chloe didn't know we had found the box of dishes, because I hadn't spoken with her since they appeared. What other possibly incriminating evidence had I shared with her? Alejandra's legality issues and the abusive husband, yes, but Andy already knew about those. Rachel's drinking and the voices she claimed to hear? Daniela's lies?

It would be safer to keep Chloe in listening mode.

"I'm sure she would appreciate a retelling in your words," I said. "She was under a lot of work stress when I was filling her in, and who knows whether I got all the details correct?"

It worked even better than I had hoped. He first walked her through the perplexing details of the murder itself—"neighbor knows ..." etc. then moved on to the time-consuming search for matches to the chipped dinner plate, commenting on the number of thrift stores in the Bay Area and how difficult it was to thoroughly investigate each one.

He was devoting a tad too much time to this topic—not that Chloe didn't seem positively entranced—and Jack kept giving me pointed looks, silently reminding me of the question Andy had asked just before Chloe's timely arrival: *Anything else you want to tell me?*

"Withholding evidence," Jack's eyes said.

"Please don't blab," mine answered. "Not yet."

Chloe gave Andy her rapt attention as he told her about the Peeping Tom and the anonymous tips regarding Jenny Ho's, the strip club, and the kinky websites. She was showing a surprising amount of interest, considering her intermittent, distracted responses when I had shared the same information over the phone.

"That sounds like a lot to investigate," she said. "Gosh, you really have your hands full."

"Yes, and there's another promising clue that I'm not at liberty to discuss at this time." With an air of importance, he added, "Some things are confidential, you know."

Her eyes sparkled with admiration. "I would imagine so."

"But also," he continued, "there are the index cards Alejandra Stevens received, which I just learned about this morning. There's a possibility they're somehow connected with the murder. Although of course, we don't know that for sure yet."

"Wow. So fascinating." Not even a hint of boredom or sarcasm. "And I take it you haven't got any real suspects yet?"

Andy chuckled. "You're a curious one, aren't you? Take after your mom. But as I keep telling Marilyn, I can't share information about potential suspects." Then, with a mysterious smile, "Everyone's a suspect at this point, I'm afraid."

"Even me?" Chloe didn't go so far as to bat her eyelashes, but her coy smile and mischievous tone put a premature end to Jack's yawn, which settled into a gape. For my part, I was impressed with her tactics. Nothing could loosen a man's tongue like a little flirting and ego-stroking.

Detective Thacker was not exempt. He gave Chloe a sly wink. "I will say this: your mom and dad are not at the top of the list. Although—"

I stopped breathing for a moment. His next wink was for me. "I do get the feeling sometimes that Marilyn here is not telling me everything she knows."

Chloe laughed, just like she was supposed to. Jack grunted, and I twisted my mouth into some semblance of a grin.

"Yes, you know me," I said to Chloe. "So mysterious and inclined to commit murder or withhold evidence"—I actually uttered those words—"or something. But honey, you must be tired from the long drive. Nine hours, wasn't it? Andy, would you mind?"

"Of course not." He stood and picked up his satchel. "I should be going anyway."

"Actually, I stopped overnight—" Chloe began, then flinched as my foot poked her shin under the table. "I mean, I guess I could use a rest, if you say so, Mother."

"Well, it has certainly been a pleasure to make your acquaintance," said Detective Thacker to Chloe, ignoring Jack and me as we all walked him to the door. "Will you be staying for the rest of the summer?"

None of your business, I thought. But Chloe flashed a smile. "I'm not sure yet. I hadn't planned on it, but it might be hard to pull myself away from all the excitement. And maybe I should stick around just to help keep the old folks safe."

"Hey now," Jack said.

Chloe's tone had implied kidding, but I allowed myself to hope. Maybe she would be intrigued enough to stay and help my neighbors and me with our own informal investigation.

"Great idea," I said, matching her jocular tone. Nothing would scare her away sooner than a note of maternal yearning in my voice. "Your old room is waiting."

Jack carried her bag upstairs, and I followed.

"You should try to take a nap, I parented. "We can talk later."

"Good idea. She hugged me. "Great to see you, Mom."

"It's a wonderful surprise," I said. "The best kind."

I returned to my room for a nap of my own. When I walked past Chloe's room an hour later, her snoring told me she might be down for a while.

By now it was mid-afternoon, and the slice of banana bread I'd had for breakfast was a pleasant but distant memory. My stomach cried out for some real food. But on my way to the refrigerator, I remembered the manila envelope I'd tossed back into the basket that morning when Rachel demanded I follow her across the street. Curious, I picked up my reading glasses, slit open the envelope, and pulled out a single half-sheet of paper with a typed note. Waste of an envelope, was my first thought— a thought that lasted two seconds before shock pushed it aside.

Jenny Ho's
getyerrocksoff.com
chicksonchicks.com
Twenty-four Hour Fitness
Maple Avenue Elementary

The bottom line was in large, bold type:
HELP THE FOOL TO DO HIS JOB.

Just then, Jack entered through the kitchen door. Without a word, I thrust the note at him and fell into a chair at the table. His lips tightened as he scanned the list, after which he looked up at me and murmured, "What the *hell* ...?"

After reading it a second time, he waved the paper at me. "We need to call Thacker," he said. "The strip joint and websites—whoever wrote this could be the person who tipped the detective off in the first place, using the stolen cell phone."

My insides were churning. Had I been singled out, or had others received a similar message? Should I talk to Alejandra and Rachel?

"You call Thacker." I reached over and took the list from him. "And while you're doing that, I'll copy this before we hand it over. In case there's a new clue in there somewhere." I looked again at the note. "As a matter of fact, Twenty-four Hour Fitness—wasn't that one of the clues sent by that stolen phone?"

"He didn't say so, but he did ask us if we could recommend a good gym."

"Maple Avenue Elementary," I mused. "That rings a bell, too."

"He wanted to know if we knew any staff there, remember? But he didn't say why he was asking."

As I walked into the living room where I'd left my laptop, I heard him muttering something about meddling in police business and middle of the night craziness.

The detective managed to arrive just as we were cleaning up after dinner.

"Sorry I couldn't get back here sooner. Buried in phone calls and paperwork," he explained, directing the remark at Chloe, who seemed suitably impressed.

"I can only imagine," she said.

"No problem," said Jack. "Just too bad you missed dessert."

"There's some chocolate tart left," Chloe chirped. "Right, Mom?"

"Sure." Might as well stuff the man with sweets for the second time in one day. Keep him happy so he would keep coming back with more information for us to work with.

Between bites, Andy digested the contents of the message without commenting on the author's critique of his investigative skills.

"Huh," he said, surprisingly nonchalant. "I guess y'all have put your fingerprints all over this already."

"Well after all, it was addressed to me. I opened the envelope and was holding it before I had any idea what it was. And then I gave it to Jack without thinking—"

He shrugged. "No biggie."

No biggie. For god's sake.

He folded the paper in half and put it in his satchel. "The question is, who wrote it?"

Jack and I exchanged "No shit, Sherlock" glances.

"Intriguing," Chloe said. "What's the connection between the murder and those establishments, do you suppose? And I don't remember hearing anything about Maple Avenue Elementary or the Twenty-four-Hour Fitness. Are those new clues?"

"New to you, maybe." He grinned at her. "Some things are confidential. The bigger question is, why did they give this to your mom, and not to me."

Because they don't trust you to get to the bottom of it, I thought. *Isn't that obvious by the last sentence: "Help the fool to do his job."*

When Thacker had gone, the three of us lingered awhile at the table, rehashing the mysterious message before moving on to Chloe's intentions for the next school year, the pros and cons of teaching high school versus starting in pursuit of a master's degree, a longtime dream of hers that she seemed less attached to each time I saw her.

I refrained from asking about her love life, as did Jack. If she had one, she probably wouldn't be in Las Oliviñas, conversing with her parents at the dining room table without pausing to check her phone even once.

After Jack had turned in for the night, Chloe and I sat up watching "Stranger Things" on TV. A bit creepy for my taste, but she claimed to be hooked on it. I endured it, relishing her company.

When she yawned and clicked off the TV, I said, "So have I mentioned that my two neighbors and I have taken to meeting late at night to discuss the murder case?"

So what if there had been only one spontaneous middle-of-the-night meeting and we had made no definitive plans for another? It seemed obvious to me that after the events of last night and this morning, none of us would be sleeping well tonight, regardless of how tired we were. I could feel another rendezvous brewing.

"So you said. But why not meet in the daytime?"

"We're all insomniacs, for one reason or another. I'm thinking we may meet later tonight, after we all grab a few hours of sleep. Considering the anonymous note I got today, it should be an interesting discussion."

I thought she might volunteer without my asking, but she yawned and said, "Wish I could join you, but the hotel was noisy last night, so I barely slept at all. I'd best sack in."

She went up to bed, so I switched off the TV and was soon lying next to Jack, saying my prayers with my mind whirling:

Please God, let Chloe be content to stay here for a while. Don't let Jack or me say anything to set her off. And help me to discover why that note with the list was sent to me. And please, help my friends—neighbors, co-detectives, whatever they are—and me to figure out where those dishes came from before Andy realizes he missed a box when he did the initial search for the—

Wait just a minute. I stopped mid-prayer. Hold that thought, God.

Why were we assuming that Andy had missed a box? We had jumped to that conclusion because it would have taken at least an hour, maybe more, to do a thorough search of Alejandra's cluttered premises. She had reported that he and the officer helping him had looked for maybe thirty minutes, leading me to conclude he had bungled the search.

My perception of the detective as incompetent had led to the assumption that he had overlooked the box of dishes—which was sitting on the dining room table, clearly marked "complete set" on all four sides and the top. Sure, it was possible, depending on just how inept he and his assistant actually were. But what if the box hadn't been on the table when they did the search? Rachel and I had scoffed at Alejandra's insistence that she remembered everything she purchased, but what if it were true?

If she hadn't bought the dishes, someone else must have sneaked the box into her dining room. What a chilling thought! But wouldn't Alejandra lock all her doors and windows when she went out? Not everyone did, but surely after the murder, all of us in the neighborhood were taking precautions.

Sleep was not going to happen now. I polished off my prayer with a quick "Amen" and started downstairs with my phone and reading glasses in the pocket of my robe. As I paused in front of Chloe's bedroom door with my hand on the doorknob, her deep snoring ignited my motherly instinct. She needed her sleep. Maybe she would wake up on her own and decide to join us, in which case she could text me. Her snoring was even louder than Jack's, probably made worse by the extra pounds. Heaven forbid I should suggest such a possibility.

Rachel's compliments about my robe notwithstanding—or maybe because of the attention she had called to my wearing of it—I was suddenly self-conscious about being seen outside of my home in nightclothes. I might run into Wei again, and polite though he was, who knew what he might think about a woman calling on her neighbors in her robe, regardless of its flattering lines and impressive craftsmanship?

As I slipped into a blouse and capris I'd laid out on the kitchen table before turning in, I remembered that the temperature was predicted to drop into the 40's later, so I pulled a light jacket from the coat closet and threw it on over my clothes.

I checked the phone, but neither Rachel nor Alejandra had reached out. It was just past midnight, so probably they were still in bed, as I should have been. Our previous meeting had taken place after 3:00 a.m., but because of the mysterious envelope and my revelation about the dishes perhaps being placed on Alejandra's table after Andy's search, I was hoping for an earlier start tonight. If I didn't hear from Rachel or Alejandra within half an hour, I would take it upon myself to initiate a meeting.

I peeked through the living room curtain, but no lights were on across the street. Or was there a dim glow from behind Alejandra's curtains, possibly from the kitchen or one of the back rooms? But that could be meaningless. Poor thing was probably sleeping with a lamp on since those taunts and threats started coming.

My eyes swept the street, which was devoid of activity, as could be expected at that hour. The only movement was tree branches swaying in the wind, which had kicked up several notches, throwing dancing shadows across lawns and sidewalks. Then I saw a car come creeping up the street and turn into the driveway next door. Zhang Wei. Where had he been at this hour?

I listened for the sound of the garage door rising, but he parked his BMW in the driveway. Would he pause on the front steps, perhaps to smoke while he surveyed the street, watching out for any threats to his mother? It was touching that he had come for an extended stay so that Mrs. Zhang would feel safer. Remembering Chloe's joke about how she might do the same for us, I wondered why we had laughed. Families were supposed to look after each other.

I felt a warm surge of appreciation for Wei's tenderness toward his mother, and since I was wide awake with no one else to talk to, I might as well tell him so.

"Marilyn," he said as I climbed his mom's front steps. "You're up late again."

He offered me a cigarette and when I declined, he stubbed out the one he had just lit for himself and placed the butt in a soup can overflowing with other butts. A chain-smoker. Perhaps sensing my distaste, he said with a sheepish smile, "I'm planning to quit any day now."

I tried to remember what it was that had propelled me to his doorstep. Just as it came to me and I was about to convey my appreciation for his surveillance of the neighborhood on his mother's behalf, Rachels's living room light flicked on. I itched to check my phone, but that seemed rude. It hadn't pinged, but I wasn't sure that I had unmuted it.

"Wei, I just wanted to say that we all—the neighbors and me, and Jack—are all grateful for another pair of eyes in the neighborhood." Jack and the neighbors hadn't shared with me their feelings about Wei's presence, but I was sure they appreciated it whether they had said so or not. Why wouldn't they?

He smiled. "Thank you, Marilyn. I'm happy to be here. While I was still working, I tried to come visit my mom every weekend, but sometimes I just couldn't get away."

That's what they all say, I thought. Funny, I had never wondered about his job.

"I guess I'd assumed you were retired."

"I am now," he said with a smile that fell somewhere between wistful and relieved. "So I've got nothing but time."

Still no sign of life at Alejandra's house. I could risk getting tangled up in conversation for a few minutes.

"So, what did you do in your previous life as a working man?"

He laughed. "My mother hasn't told you a thousand times that her son is—was—a doctor?"

"A doctor! Well, no. She never mentioned that." No need to tell him I had never asked a single question about Mrs. Zhang's family, other than "do you live alone?" when we brought her the plate of cookies on our "welcome to the neighborhood" visit. Her response had been "Why do you need to know?"

"Did you have a specialty?"

"Yes. I was in Obstetrics and Gynecology. My partner and I had a private practice."

A gynecologist. Who would have thought it? Of course, he would have a lovely bedside manner, with that deep voice and those kind eyes. For a moment I involuntarily pictured his face peering into my privates as I lay on my back in a hospital gown with my feet in stirrups. The image was unnerving.

"That must have been … interesting?"

We both laughed. "Believe it or not, I loved my job. Rewarding, but lots of hours." Sadness crept into his voice. "No time for a family. I sometimes regret never having married. You and Jack are lucky to have each other. Especially in frightening times like these."

We were both startled when the front door opened behind us. Tiny Mrs. Zhang stood there in her robe, radiating disapproval. The elegant, embroidered housecoat, along with the silver braid that fell nearly to her waist, lent her a dignified air that surprised me. But her scowl was intact and her words predictable.

"You come inside," she told Wei. "You, Mrs. Middleton, go home now."

"Sure," I said. "I was just about to do that." I glanced across the street, but I wasn't rude enough to check my phone in front of Mrs. Zhang and her son.

"Too noisy," said her retreating figure as Wei followed her inside. "Too much talk."

"Good night, Marilyn. Get some sleep." Wei smiled as he shut the door behind him.

I pulled out my phone and found a single message from Rachel:

    Casa de Alejandra in 10.

As I looked up, she exited her own house and hurried across the lawn to Alejandra's. I started across the street, but as I crossed Mrs. Zhang's driveway, a ribbon of paper dimly illuminated by a streetlight dislodged itself from the privet that divided our front yards and blew past me on a gust of wind. Since neither Mrs. Zhang nor Wei seemed the type to intentionally litter, the wind must have swept it into the privet after one of them dropped it by accident. So I did them the favor of chasing it down.

It was too dark for me to make out details, but it appeared to be a receipt, possibly from the Asian market where a friend drove Mrs. Zhang to buy groceries every Sunday. Or it could belong to Wei. Either way, I would call on them tomorrow, just in case it was important.

I tucked the receipt into the pocket of my jacket and hurried across the street, pushing back the thought that maybe a happily married woman should not be looking for an excuse to drop in on the handsome son of the lady next door. Still, it could be an important receipt. They might be looking for it.

13

Rachel, seated in Alejandra's Bentwood rocker, was frowning into a mug and seemed sober. I hoped that would be a good thing.

Alejandra came in from the kitchen and handed me a steaming teacup. "I thought we might get more done if we have this instead of wine."

Her eyes were bloodshot and swollen, still wet from a recent crying jag. She looked away and sat down on the other end of the sofa from me. Boondoggles wandered in from the kitchen and folded himself into a lump at her feet. Even he looked concerned, casting doleful eyes on her before resting his head on his paws.

Rachel rocked slowly in the Bentwood, sipping her tea, oblivious. Possibly Alejandra had cried on her shoulder before I got there. I searched my mind for a remark that would express more concern than curiosity.

"Are you okay, Alejandra?"

"If I lose Kyle, I'll kill myself, but other than that, I'm fine." She forced a laugh. "But let's please not discuss that, if you don't mind."

"Whoa, now," said Rachel. "Let's not have any suicide talk, okay? You are not going to lose that boy. Brian has custody for now, but we'll get you a lawyer. I'll help. And meanwhile, he's got no right to withhold visitation. Safe neighborhood or not."

"Well he's managing to do it, though, isn't he? And now that he knows about those threats, it'll be easier." Her face crumpled. "Oh, I just miss Kyle so much, and the thought of him with Brian and that woman—I can't stand it!"

She sobbed into a tissue as I scooted closer and patted her arm. A new, horrible thought occurred to me. "Do you think—I mean, are you afraid he might hurt your boy?"

She shook her head. "No, no. He loves Kyle. I believe that. It's just that—who knows what he's telling my son about me? And I have no chance to deny whatever lies he's spouting."

Rachel suddenly stopped rocking. "Do you think Brian might have written those notes? Like you just said, the threats give him a good excuse to keep Kyle at home with him under close watch."

Alejandra shook her head. "I thought of that, sure. I even mentioned it to Andy. But it doesn't feel right to me. Brian is a bully, and he doesn't respect women, but believe it or not, he isn't a racist. In fact, although he doesn't talk much about it, one of his grandmothers was from Mexico. That's one reason he got into immigration law."

"No shit?" Rachel looked doubtful. "He looks a hundred percent Norwegian." She chuckled. "Except for his height, I guess."

Alejandra went on, "And anyway, I honestly don't think he would do something so serious as a hate crime. He would be in enough trouble if the business about my papers and other legal shenanigans in the past happened to come out. Since we married and had Kyle, he's been careful to play by the rules."

"He could have written those cards anyway," Rachel persisted. "Pretending to be a racist so the police would look in the wrong direction."

"I don't think so." Alejandra had recovered somewhat,

and now she blew her nose and said, "Please. You can help most by distracting me. Let's talk about the investigation."

Rachel gave me an exaggerated wave that told me I had the floor. Since Alejandra had asked us to move on, I pulled my typed copy of the list I'd received the evening before from my pocket and held it out to her.

"So this is new," I said. "It was left on my front porch last night, addressed to me."

Alejandra studied the list in silence, then got up and passed it to Rachel, who read it aloud in a disbelieving voice.

"Holy shit. This was addressed specifically to you? Not to Jack and you?"

"Why does that matter?" Alejandra wanted to know.

"Duh. It might mean someone knows about our own investigation. Have either of you told anyone about our meetings?"

"Not me," said Alejandra. "I mean, we've only met once before tonight. And there was that day we talked in my backyard. But no, I don't think I've mentioned it to anyone."

"Only Jack, Chloe, and Natalie," I said. "How about you, Rachel?"

"Not a soul."

"Anyway," I pointed out, "we don't know that whoever gave me this list knows we're discussing the investigation. Detective Thacker has been at my house a lot, so maybe whoever wrote this is one of the neighbors who noticed that, and—"

I broke off as an image of Wei, scrutinizing the street from his front porch at odd hours of the day and night, flashed before me.

Rachel read my mind. "What about that guy next door to you, Marilyn? Mr. Chang, Zhang, or whatever? He's out on the front porch most of the time. He would've seen Andy coming and going."

"But why feed the detective clues through me? If he

knew something important, he would go straight to Thacker, wouldn't he?"

"Good question," said Rachel. "In fact, why would anyone, not just him, go to you instead of to the police?"

"Makes no sense," I agreed. "Except the note did imply that Andy couldn't be trusted to get the job done."

"*Or...*" Rachel sat down her cup as she was stuck by a more intriguing possibility. "Or maybe the murderer wants to get caught, and Thacker isn't moving fast enough for him?"

I smiled at her enthusiasm. "It's at least a possibility. What do you think, Alejandra?"

"Why wouldn't whoever it is just turn themselves in?"

Neither of us had an answer for that. Rachel looked crestfallen, so I moved on. When I shared my revelation about the box of dishes possibly having been placed on the table after the detective's search, she perked up.

"Hmm. Never thought of that."

Alejandra said, "I don't see how anyone could have sneaked into the house while I was gone without breaking a lock on the door or a windowpane or something."

Rachel challenged her. "You've never gone out without closing a window? Or kept one open while you slept?"

"I've had the a.c. going, although I do turn it off at night when it cools off, and I open the windows a crack. But I put in a wooden rod so there's not enough space for anyone to crawl through." She held up her hands about five inches apart. "Just this much room."

Rachel pressed on. "But I know you don't always have your doors locked when you're home during the day. Could someone have sneaked in while you were napping on the sofa or out back in the yard?"

"How would they have known I was asleep or wasn't in the house? It's not like anyone is keeping tabs on my every move. As far as I know, anyway."

"Except maybe the person who's leaving you those hate

messages," Rachel pointed out, and Alejandra grimaced.

"Those have all been left on the outside of the house or on the car, not on the dining room table."

Though reluctant to let go of the theory I had been so proud of devising, I had to agree it was unlikely that someone had boldly delivered the box of dishes in broad daylight, nor could anyone have pushed themselves through a five-inch opening during the night, with or without a cardboard carton with fragile contents.

"So then we have to assume you purchased the dishes yourself and never got around to looking inside the box," Rachel said.

Alejandra shook her head. She had shot down my theory, while still refusing to accept the most likely alternative. I tried another approach.

"Is it possible you bought the dishes but didn't remember the pattern well enough to recognize it when Detective Thacker showed you the plate Michael was poisoned from? Or could you have bought them after the inspection and forgot?"

"If I had bought them, I'd remember," she insisted.

"Well if you didn't buy them, and nobody sneaked them in after the inspection, then we have to assume that Detective Thacker and his helper looked right past a pretty good-sized box of dishes marked 'Complete set' on all sides, which means he's even worse at his job than we thought."

Rachel looked at me curiously. "What do you mean by that?"

Alejandra was also surprised. "You think he's bad at his job? It's only been a month, and he seems to be doing everything he can. He told me he's checked out over thirty thrift stores in the Bay Area and talked to scads of people who had garage sales recently."

"That may be. But he did only a very casual check of our houses for the dishes. And he has no suspects, while I —"

They waited, Rachel's eyes narrowing while Alejandra's

widened. I decided to be as honest as I could be without admitting that I had a suspect list of my own and that both their names were on it.

"I mean, I think there are actually some characters he could be checking out. Your husband, for instance."

"What? Oh my god, no. Like I said, Brian's a bully, but he had no reason to kill Michael."

"Maybe," said Rachel. "Unless he hangs out at that strip club in Oakland where Michael's band played sometimes. Jenny Ho's. Maybe there was a squabble over a stripper."

Alejandra was incredulous. "Are you kidding me? Brian is all about his image and professional reputation. He wouldn't risk being seen in a place like that."

Rachel asked, "What if Michael knew you have fake documentation, and that Brian was responsible for that? Couldn't Brian lose his job? Maybe go to jail?"

The woman was certainly on her toes this evening. Not that she ever missed a trick when schnockered, either.

Alejandra thought it over. "Blackmail, you mean. But I never talked about what Brian did for me and my family, even to friends—until I told you two. And Daniela knows, but that's it. And she would never have had any reason to tell Michael, even if he asked her. And why would he do that?"

Rachel shrugged, and I moved on. "Speaking of Daniela."

Alejandra was already shaking her head. "No way."

"Just hear me out," I said.

Then we were all jolted by a knock on the front door. Boondoggles leapt up and stood staring in that direction but didn't make a sound. A watchdog this creature was not.

The knock came again. A normal knock, not too insistent, not too weak. But who came calling at this hour?

"Bark, Boonie," murmured Alejandra. He whimpered instead.

"Is it locked?" Rachel whispered, reaching for her phone.

Alejandra nodded. They both looked at me.

"Hold onto that phone," I said in a loud, businesslike voice and walked over to the door. Not that I wasn't scared, but somebody had to be the grown-up.

Standing a few feet from the door, I bellowed, "Who is it?"

"It's Chloe, Mom." She giggled. "I'm unarmed, I promise."

"For heaven's sake," I said, throwing open the door and breaking into a wide smile. "You should have texted me first!"

"I heard voices and looked out the window. You were talking to that spooky man next door, then I saw you crossing the street, so I figured your Middle-of-the-Night Club was about to convene."

Spooky? When had she even met the man? I filed the comment away to investigate later.

Boondoggles, seeing that she posed no threat, conjured up a belated, half-hearted growl, then yawned as he settled back down at Alejandra's feet.

I made the introductions, and Alejandra fetched tea for Chloe after directing her to sit on the sofa next to me. She emptied the contents of a dining room chair onto the floor and brought it into the living room for herself.

"But aren't you a few months early? It's not Christmas yet," Rachel joked.

Chloe reprimanded me: "Mom, really."

I made a mental note to reduce the amount of personal sharing, especially involving the girls.

Rachel embarrassed me further by asking, "Middle-of-the-night club?" as if she'd never heard of it. True, she had been soused when Alejandra referred to us as such on that day of our first gathering, and none of us had mentioned it since. Maybe it was time to make the suggestion and put it to a vote. But Alejandra was a step ahead of me.

"That's us, all right. The middle-of-the-night club.

Either that or Insomniacs, Incorporated."

"Middle-of-the-night club." Rachel raised her cup in a toast. "I like it."

We all lifted our teacups, even Chloe, although she was quick to say, "Here's to you all. I'm not an official member."

"Why not?" Rachel asked. "You're here, aren't you? And it's the middle of the night, so..." She hoisted her cup in Chloe's direction, and I reflexively flinched before remembering the vessel held tea, not wine, and was being hoisted by a steady hand. Alejandra's rug was temporarily safe from further ruin.

"It seems I'm a member at least temporarily," said Chloe. "So fill me in."

Alejandra's smile went south. "We're working our way down your mom's suspect list. We've eliminated my ex-husband and moved on to accusing my best friend."

"I don't think we've eliminated the asshole completely," said Rachel. "We'll probably come back to him later."

"So what about your best friend, then?" asked Chloe.

She listened attentively as Alejandra explained that Daniela sometimes visited the bar downtown where Michael's band had regularly performed, and that she had lied to the detective about the number of times she had gone to hear Michael play. She finished with, "But none of that means anything. Daniela is simply not capable of murdering anyone," and picked up her teacup. "So who else is on your list, Marilyn."

"Not so fast," I said. "You left out the part where Daniela lied to both her mother and her husband about where she was when she went to the bar, because her mother was watching her two little kids and Daniela was afraid her husband would find out."

Alejandra threw me a resentful look. Chloe asked, "What does that have to do with the murder?"

"She had a crush on Michael," I said. Might as well put all the facts on the table. "And also, it establishes that she's a person of questionable moral character."

Chloe, perhaps to smooth Alejandra's ruffled feathers, pretended to be shocked. "Heaven forbid! Next you'll be telling me she's a Democrat."

Instead of laughing, Rachel and Alejandra looked at me with "Oh my god, a Republican" written all over their faces.

Ever since inviting Chloe to join us, I'd been afraid this would happen. I wasn't ashamed of my political viewpoints—far from it—but those on the left were so resistant to opposing opinions that I had decided to avoid political discussion until our friendship had evolved a bit. Also, our club had been organized for the purpose of investigating a murder, not to discuss the pros and cons of abortion and open borders.

To her credit, Chloe accurately read my face and redirected the conversation. "What I mean is, lots of people commit adultery. Not that it's right, but it doesn't necessarily make her a horrible person, does it?"

"Well, it sure as hell doesn't make her a good person," said Rachel, suddenly taking my side.

To avoid her launching into the sordid story of her spouse's cheating and subsequent death, I hurried to say, "I just think we don't know for sure, exactly how good of a person she is. Can we agree on that?"

Alejandra frowned. "I never said she slept with Michael. I don't believe she did, in fact. This is ridiculous. Can we please move on to whoever's next on your list?"

"Daniela's husband. What's his name again? Eric?"

Rachel nodded her approval. "So he might have found out Michael was screwing his wife and killed him out of jealousy? Hmmm. Credible theory." One she related to personally, no doubt, having admittedly fantasized about slicing off her cheating wife's breasts while she slept.

With an annoyed shake of her head, Alejandra said, "Eric is the nicest man I know. Very gentle with Daniela and the kids."

"Unlike your own husband, who we aren't allowed to consider as a suspect either," Rachel pointed out.

"Anyone else on your list, Mom?" Chloe asked. Her eyes glittered with interest, and I was glad I'd invited her. For the moment at least. If we could only avoid politics.

I couldn't reveal that both Rachel and Alejandra had made my list, so who did that leave?

"The Peeping Tom," I said. "Or whoever it was that ran from behind Alejandra's house that evening after Brian had left."

Chloe said, "Peeping Tom? It's probably that guy who lives next door to you, Mom. He checked me over good when I got out of the car earlier."

I spooned an imaginary something out of my teacup, hoping to conceal my surprise and disappointment. So Wei was a gentleman with old ladies like me, but a lecher with the young ones. But then, Chloe had been tired from the trip. Maybe she was mistaken.

"Are you sure? He seems like such a nice, respectful man."

"Oooh," Rachel sang. "Somebody's jealous."

Alejandra grinned. "He definitely likes to look at your mom, too, Chloe."

Chloe said, "That's not what I meant. He wasn't checking me out in a sexual way. Just a little too curious, is how it felt."

"But really," Alejandra said. "I don't see Mr. Zhang as a suspect. He moved in after the murder. After the person was seen crossing my lawn, even. So we can assume he's neither the Peeping Tom nor the killer."

"And yet, the Peeping Tom could still be the killer," I said, relieved to have the conversation shift away from Wei.

"We know nothing about the Peeping Tom," said Rachel. "So how do we pursue that lead?"

"Maybe you can find out who has seen the guy—which windows he looked in, and so forth—and talk to the witnesses?" Chloe was making me proud.

"Nextdoor?" I suggested. "I haven't seen anything on there about it, but we could ask the question pointblank."

"Or better yet," said Rachel, "try to worm the information out of Thacker, aka Mr. Some-information-is-confidential."

Chloe piped up, "I'll ask him. He's coming for dinner tomorrow night. Right, Mom?"

"I don't believe he has been invited, no."

"Then that's your assignment. You'll invite him first thing tomorrow, okay?"

"Yes ma'am," I said in response to what sounded pretty much like an order.

Indulging in her first yawn of the night, or rather morning, Rachel looked at her phone. "Jesus, it's only 2:30, but I'm fading fast. Anything else we need to talk about?"

For God's sake. Regarding issues they wanted to avoid, those two were the queens of denial. Well, I had promised Jack to stop withholding evidence, and it was time to address a certain important matter.

"The dishes under Alejandra's bed, perhaps?"

They both winced but stayed quiet while I told Chloe about the box of dishes and our reasons for not turning them over to Detective Thacker.

"Oh my god," she said, when I'd finished. "So you all are sitting on evidence that could help crack the case?" She looked from one to the other of us, pronouncing us insane with her eyes. Rachel chuckled, while Alejandra started to tear up again.

"Yes," I said. "We certainly are doing just that."

"But not without good reason," Rachel insisted. "We'll turn them over to him as soon as Alejandra can remember where she got them. That way he'll have to investigate whoever sold them instead of tossing Alejandra in jail just to prove he can solve a case."

Alejandra was uncharacteristically surly. "I know I would remember buying those dishes. I admit I have a shopping habit—"she looked at Rachel, who was smirking—"but I don't randomly buy boxes without looking inside to see if it's something I need."

We all let it pass.

"Uh-huh," I said. "Then the only option is to turn the dishes over to Andy and let him do his job. Every minute we hang onto that box is another minute the killer goes free."

"Nope," said Rachel. "I won't let you do that to yourself, Alejandra."

Unbelievable. Why couldn't they see the importance of this box to the investigation? Even Chloe, instead of backing me up as I had hoped, looked uncertain.

"Oh dear God," I said. "We can't just hold onto them indefinitely."

"Wait," said Chloe. "Alejandra has good reason to be afraid. This is a real dilemma, but Rachel is yawning nonstop and the rest of us are sleep-deprived as well. I'm not sure we should make a decision tonight."

"Tomorrow, then?" I was not about to let this go on much longer.

They all murmured agreement.

"Anything else, then?" Rachel was already out of her chair, hands on her hips, stretching her back.

"No," I lied. I could fill Chloe in later about how the other half of our little investigation group had ended up being on the suspect list.

"We have our assignments, then?" Chloe looked from one of us to the other.

"You and I do." I turned to the others. "And what will you two be doing to contribute to the investigation?"

Rachel piped up, "Alejandra, I think you need to press Daniela to come clean with Detective Thacker. And if she won't, you have to fill him in."

"Even though I know she's innocent? What kind of friend does such a thing?"

"A friend who wants to stop a murderer before he kills again?" I suggested. "She may well be innocent, but maybe her husband isn't. Or someone she knows from the bar, who might have gotten sideways with Michael. She just needs to be honest about how often she went there, that's all."

"Sure," was Alejandra's sullen response. "I'll talk to her tomorrow. And how about you, Rachel? What's your assignment?"

Rachel shrugged. "Any ideas? All I can think about right now is sleep."

"You could go on Nextdoor and specifically ask for information about the Peeping Tom, just in case Andy won't cooperate," I suggested. "Someone may have gotten a closer look than the detective let on. Some things being confidential, and all."

My daughter got up and extended her hand to me. As we walked arm in arm across the street, she jerked her head in the direction of Mrs. Zhang's front porch. "There he is," she whispered. "What's he doing still up at this hour?"

Sure enough, the glow from a cigarette pulled my eye to a figure on the shadowy front porch. After obediently following his mother inside like a good son, he had returned to keep watch over the street. My goodness. Did the man never sleep?

14

After Chloe outed me as a Republican, I started to worry that it was only a matter of time before one of my two new friends asked me how in God's name, as an educated Christian woman, I could continue to defend the narcissistic, bigoted, lying bully in the oval office.

Okay, so he would not have been my first choice. And no, since he took office, I had not been impressed by his sometimes nonsensical and cringeworthy tweets and press conferences, which the media had continually and jubilantly dissected, twisted, and ridiculed. What I did approve of, though, was reduced unemployment, a reassuring stock market, and most of all, the rebalancing of the Supreme Court in the direction of wisdom and morality.

"Was it worth it?" they would ask, with eyes that insisted such a thing was impossible, and there would follow a lecture about the sacrificing of human dignity, putting kids in cages, and trampling on women's rights. They would half-listen to my response while silently composing their next round of attacks even as I spoke.

From having gone there with the girls a few times too many, the last debate taking place over Christmas dinner—Natalie's last visit and Chloe's too, up until now—I knew that I was unlikely to come away from such an encounter feeling good about my relationship with my fellow investigators.

And this was no time for dissension in the ranks. Such discussion could slow down our informal murder investigation—and that, I decided, would be my position should the subject arise before said investigation was concluded. There were more pressing matters at hand, starting with preparations for the evening meal to which I had invited detective Thacker, per Chloe's instructions, so that she could coax information from him about the Peeping Tom.

After sleeping for five hours upon my return home that morning, I spent the rest of the day planning dinner, grocery shopping, and cleaning the house. In the late afternoon, as I was setting out the ingredients for the lemon chicken piccata, Jack paused on his way to the backyard. "Is it genetic, this list-making compulsion?"

Chloe sat hunkered over a notebook at the dining room table, alternately writing and tapping her pen on her chin. She was a woman on a mission, compiling a list of questions to feed the detective—two whole pages of inquiries that suggested her curiosity was fired up over more than the mysterious Peeping Tom.

"She's not so unlike me after all. Right, sweetie?" I patted Chloe's shoulder. She grunted and waved her pen at me, eyes still glued to the list.

Jack walked to the back door, and with a jerk of his chin, summoned me to follow.

"What's up?" I asked. "You're okay with this dinner, right?"

I had cleared it with him earlier, filling him in on the late night/early morning meeting and our respective assignments. He had shrugged. "Sure. Anything in the interest of the investigation." It hadn't sounded like sarcasm, but now I wasn't so sure.

"I'm okay with it. More or less. I don't enjoy the man's company as much as you two apparently do, but I can see where it might be useful to grill him, if for no other reason than to plant some ideas he should have had on his own."

We stood on the patio in silence for a bit, looking out at the yard with its Japanese maple in one corner, palm tree in the other, various greenery and blossoms in between. I could never remember all their names, but all were thriving, thanks mostly to Jack's diligent care. I'd never had much of a green thumb.

"Beautiful day, wasn't it?"

I murmured agreement, wishing he would spit it out, whatever it was.

"I'd been hoping we could go out to the lake for a picnic lunch. The three of us. Remember how Chloe and Natalie used to love romping around in the water?"

So that was it: a guilt trip. I was annoyed enough to avoid climbing on board. "Then you should've woken me up earlier. You're right. It would've been fun."

"Oh come on. You would've fallen asleep in the car. Look, I'm not trying to lay a guilt trip on you."

Ha! Read my mind, did you?

"All I'm asking is if you might try to schedule your little get-togethers in the daytime. Is that possible?" He forced a lighter tone as he put an arm around my waist and pulled me closer. "I get lonely when I wake up at night and you're gone."

A reasonable request, right? Then why wasn't I feeling guilty, or even sympathetic? I reminded myself to listen. Make Sue Ellen proud, up there in Heaven.

And yet, "little get-togethers?" Sheesh.

"That's understandable," I said. "I can see where that wouldn't feel good at all, waking up alone during the night."

He waited for me to go on, but I reminded myself that

"Talking isn't listening." No kidding, right? But believe it or not, this was the title of a chapter in the book called *When It's Time to Shut up*. Following the author's advice, I'd figured something else out on my own: if you let someone keep yacking about whatever burr is up their behind, they will often chat themselves into a solution—or start feeling silly and back off completely. Jack went the latter route.

He cleared his throat. "I guess I'm being selfish. So never mind. I'm behind you in this investigation thing, believe me." He squeezed my waist. "Just wanted you to know I miss you."

I kissed his cheek. "I understand. I'll talk to the others about a regular daytime meeting, and I'll definitely stay at home tonight."

"Good. I'm not really comfortable with you going outside after dark, under the circumstances."

"I get it. But I'm not alone. There are two of us now."

He scoffed. "Oh, much better. Now I can worry about my daughter as well as my wife."

"You can always text me if you get worried when you wake up and I'm not there. But you're right. There's no reason we can't meet during the day sometimes."

I didn't remind him that there were two other people's preferences to consider—three if you counted Chloe. We would deal with the meeting schedule later.

The lemon chicken piccata was a hit with Andy, although I sensed that whatever I had served would have tickled his taste buds.

"So, Andy," asked Chloe. "Mom tells me you're living with your mother here in Las Oliviñas. She must love having you at home."

I feared we would have to listen again to the story of his mom's property values skyrocketing and her move to Las Oliviñas to be with her beloved sister, but this time he was even more forthcoming.

"Yes, she's happy I'm here." His smile faded, and he

paused in the process of slicing off a bite of chicken. His eyes locked with Chloe's as he explained, "Last year she started having some health issues. She was alone in Oakland, and my brother lives in Chicago, so that left me to deal. As I told your parents before, her sister is here in town, so she sold the house and moved into Aunt Maddie's neighborhood."

Chloe's listening skills had become top-notch in adulthood (an outcome that Jack and I would not have predicted and never failed to marvel at after each visit). She gazed at Andy with sympathetic interest and waited in silence. Jack and I were feeling like eavesdroppers at this point, so we were mum as well.

"And then I got transferred so that I could move in with her and see her through the treatments. Aunt Maddie helps some with Mom. But it's mostly just me."

"I'm so sorry to hear that," Chloe murmured. "Has her health improved, I hope?"

"Not much." He forked a bite of garlic mashed potatoes into his mouth and swallowed it. "Right now, she's finishing up a bout of chemo for thyroid cancer. It's taking a lot out of her. I wouldn't say she seems healthy, no."

"I'm so sorry," Chloe said again.

"That must be very painful for you," I said.

"Does she still cook for you, and all that?" asked Jack.

"Jesus, Dad." Chloe fired him a look that made him flinch.

But Andy laughed out loud. "Not much cooking going on, no." He raised his glass of Chardonnay and turned his smile on me. "This is delicious, Marilyn. My compliments to the chef."

So how might we get from the topic of his dying mother to the murder investigation? I could see that Chloe was mentally running down her list of questions, looking for a tactful segue. Luckily, he provided one for her.

"Did you sleep well last night, Chloe? I can see where

an unsolved murder in the neighborhood might lend itself to a little insomnia."

"Now that you mention it, I've had better nights. I kept wondering about that Peeping Tom, whether he's still around."

"Oh. Yes, well. We've had no reports since that possible sighting in Mrs. Stevens' yard on the afternoon of her ex-husband's visit. What's that been, Marilyn? About a week?"

"Six days," I said without missing a beat, and they all lifted their eyebrows.

Jack laughed. "Chloe, your mom is really on top of this investigation. She probably knows as much as the detective here. In fact," he said, pointing his fork at Andy and me in turn, "You two should compare notes. Suspect lists and such." He read my face and added, "What's wrong? Two heads are better than one, so they say."

Chloe gave him the "What is *wrong* with you?" look that we both knew all too well. This time it was justified, and I would've shot some eye-daggers in his direction myself, had I not been busy scrambling for the explanation that Andy, judging by his eyebrows, was waiting for.

The detective raised a finger to cut me off mid-stammer, his eyes abandoning mine as he swept his phone from his pocket. Then we heard it too. The wail of sirens—multiple sirens, screaming toward us. Chloe jumped up and hurried to the living room window.

"Got it," Andy said, after repeating an address that poked at my memory. "On my way."

And indeed he was already halfway to the door, with Jack and me at his heels. Chloe turned from the window. "Andy, what's happened? They've stopped on the next block over. I can see the revolving lights through Rachel's backyard."

"I'm not at liberty to tell you that," said Mr. Self-important, pausing in the doorway just long enough to caution us. "Please stay inside until you hear from me. There has been another—uh, another incident."

And without so much as a thank you for my culinary efforts, he ran past his car to the end of the block and disappeared around the corner. Surprisingly fleet-footed, considering his girth.

"What do you suppose—" Jack began.

"3316 Helena Street," I murmured, as the address found its place in my memory. "Oh my Lord."

The flashing lights and sirens had come to a sudden stop at 3316 Helena Street, one block over. The home of Lisa Cardwell, aka Bird Legs, aka "that bug-eyed bitch with the bird-slashing cats."

15

As I stepped outside at 2:00 a.m. in response to Rachel's summons, pushing aside my guilt over having promised Jack I'd stay put tonight, Zhang Wei was enjoying a cigarette next door on his mom's porch. I watched as he languidly inhaled, slowly lowered his arm as he savored the taste, then released the smoke in a leisurely, thoughtful manner. The scene would've been suitable for a television commercial back in the day when the industry was still promoting the sexy, manly aspects of smoking while downplaying the more disgusting effects such as off-putting breath, stained teeth, and a hacking cough. Not to mention lung cancer and emphysema.

Seduced by the image, I held off on closing my front door behind me, so as not to interrupt him until the last wisp of smoke had drifted into the night air and he had tapped the ashes into the soup can he held in his other hand. No wonder so many fell prey to the lure.

"Up late again," he observed, as I descended my front steps.

"You too," I said. Then "Ouch," as my left calf cramped up, hobbling me.

As I limped toward him, he ground out the cigarette, considerate as always. "Leg cramps?" he guessed.

"Yes, doctor," I said, "what would you prescribe?" Then appalled by my own flirtatious tone, I reined it in. "It happens a lot these days. I've been trying to eat more bananas."

"That won't hurt, but if it's a potassium deficiency, you'd do better with sweet potatoes or melons. Black beans are good, too. But if it happens often, you should talk to your doctor."

"I know," I said. "I've promised Jack that I'll do just that. I need to deal with this insomnia problem as well. Although I hate the idea of prescription sleeping aids."

"Best to sleep naturally if you can. But drug-induced sleep is healthier than none at all."

I wondered if he was reminding himself as well as me. He didn't look exhausted, but he sounded weary. And he certainly kept nocturnal hours.

"How about you?" I asked, at the risk of being labeled a Nosy Nellie by yet another neighbor. "You're up at night a lot. Are you losing sleep over Michael Redding's murder, too?"

"I've always had insomnia issues," he said. "It's worse now than before, and yes, I think that might have to do with the homicide investigation." He turned his eyes toward the street. "Among other things."

Those other things were none of my business. I knew that. And yet I heard myself say, "Nothing too serious, I hope."

He smiled with his eyes. "No. Nothing too serious."

Was he laughing at me? *Serves you right, Nosy Nellie.*

Embarrassed, I began to jabber, "Well then, I'm expected across the street. Rachel, Alejandra, and I have been getting together when we can't sleep, to help pass the time. My daughter Chloe, too, now that she's here visiting. She went over ahead of me while I was putting a snack together." I held out the sack I was clutching. "Carrot sticks and a low-cal snack dip. Some of the girls are dieting." This last part, in addition to being information he hadn't asked for and didn't need, was just wishful thinking on my part.

"Yes, I saw Chloe crossing the street," he said, suddenly concerned. He peered into my eyes. "I do hope you'll be careful, you and Chloe. I know you're only outdoors for a minute or two, but just remember, Mr. Redding's murder hasn't been solved yet. And those phone texts with the clues sent to Detective Thacker came from nearby."

"What? But he said they were sent from a stolen cell phone that was later found in a dumpster in Oakland."

"Yes, but they traced the origin of the texts back to this neighborhood. Two separate locations: the street in front of Harrison Park, and the front steps of the Presbyterian church on the corner of Purdue and Ninth."

"They can do that? Trace a call or a text to a specific location?"

"Sure. Modern technology. Amazing, isn't it?" His warm smile made me feel a bit less like a nitwit.

"I wonder why Thacker never told us that."

"Well," he said thoughtfully. "Some things are confidential, I hear."

We exchanged smiles, and as I crossed the street to Alejandra's house, I felt his eyes follow me. Or maybe I just imagined that. It was a nice sensation, regardless.

Chloe scolded me as I entered the room. "Where have you been, Mom? I was starting to worry. You said it would be ten minutes at most."

"She stopped to talk to her boyfriend, I bet," said Rachel. "Am I right, Mrs. M.?"

"I stopped to chat with Dr. Zhang, if that's what you mean. And I uncovered an interesting fact, by the way."

I shared with them what Andy had withheld: the reason he suspected the murderer might live among us (along with the mysterious 911 message, "Neighbor knows ...") was that they had traced the origin of the texted clues to our neighborhood.

I concluded, "We already knew he thinks the killer lives nearby, but this makes it even more likely. That's why the patrol cars are cruising by all night."

"Jeez, that's scary" said Chloe, and Alejandra shivered.

Only Rachel was unabashed. "Crazy stuff," she said with huge grin. She seemed in a jolly mood, although sober as far as I could tell. "But let's talk about the bug-eyed cat lady."

Lisa Cardwell was not dead. A great relief to all of us, even Rachel—especially Rachel, I assumed, considering the animosity she bore for the woman, which she had made little effort to hide, and which still might make her a suspect in whatever charges were to be filed against the vandal, once he or she was found.

Had Lisa been at home, God knows what might have happened. Fortunately, she had driven to Jack-in-the-Box after realizing her cupboard and refrigerator were bare of anything appetizing for dinner.

She had caused quite a kerfuffle, what with the ambulance, fire truck and police car sirens blasting away. But who could blame her for calling 911 instead of the non-emergency police number? Maybe the intruder was still in her house, for all she knew. I would've done the same thing, had I come home to find my back French door standing open with half its pane missing, a large rock lying amidst the shattered glass that covered the floor, and cat feces smeared all over the kitchen countertops, stove, and table.

"What a ditz." Rachel leaned forward in the rocker to reach for the teacup Alejandra offered. "Hilarious that they made her climb into the ambulance even after she dropped the whole heart attack charade. I hope they've made her stay up all night running the treadmill. I can hear her now: 'But I must get home to my babies, *Claw-dius* and *Catula*!'"

She cackled while Chloe frowned at this appalling display of insensitivity. I pursed my lips, and Alejandra made a "Tsk-tsk" sound.

Oblivious to our quiet reprimands, Rachel chortled, "I'll bet her eyes got even buggier when she saw that cat shit all over the countertops."

Alejandra chastised her. "But my God, Rachel. She probably did have chest pains when she saw the broken glass and cat poop everywhere in the kitchen. Wouldn't you be terrified?"

"Fttt." Rachel swallowed her glee, took a sip from her cup, grimaced (as if we didn't already know that tea wasn't her beverage of choice) and was suddenly all business. "So Chloe, did you get anywhere with Andy on the Peeping Tom situation?"

Chloe explained that our fact-finding dinner with the detective had been cut short by the sirens at Lisa's house. "We'll ask him over again soon," she said with a sideways glance at me. "Maybe just for dessert this time."

She then suggested that once Lisa had returned from the hospital, we might pick up a cheery bouquet at the florist downtown, and as a group of concerned neighbors, drop in on her.

"What a nice idea!" I said, pleased at my daughter's thoughtfulness.

Rachel grinned. "Just to check on her well-being, of course."

"Right," said Chloe. "But who knows, maybe she'll give us her take on Michael Redding, the Peeping Tom, or anything else pertaining to the investigation."

"Sounds good. Now, what else do we need to talk about?" Alejandra asked, pen poised above her notebook.

I stated the obvious. "The box of dishes. Alejandra, you really have to talk to Andy about those soon. Any revelations yet about where they came from?"

"Nope." Her jaw was set. "All I know is that I didn't buy

them. And I told you, I'll tell Andy about them as soon as we can all agree that I should." She looked at Rachel, begging with her eyes for the usual dissenting vote.

Rachel would not disappoint her. "I'm not there yet. We need a plan for finding out where they came from. Maybe we should call on the local thrift stores ourselves, take a plate with us—" She stopped rocking and her face lit up. "Hello! I just had a truly brilliant idea."

She leaned over and sat the cup on the floor beside her chair, her enthusiasm such that Chloe and Alejandra leaned forward as well. I too was curious, if somewhat leery. The way Rachel's mind worked, God only knew what shenanigans she might lead us into.

"Field trip!" she exclaimed. "Exploratory excursion! On-site investigation, whatever you want to call it."

"It's Andy's job to check with those stores." Chloe was less than impressed with Rachel's truly brilliant idea. "He's already doing that. We'd be wasting our time."

Rachel was jiggling in her chair from excitement. "Forget the thrift stores. I say we go straight to the scene of the crime."

I was both appalled and disappointed at this meritless idea. "Michael Redding's kitchen? The investigators have already—"

"No, of course I don't mean Michael's house." She dismissed the idea with an impatient wave of her hand. "I'm talking about the real scene of the crime, hinted at by the anonymous clues: 'a drug deal gone wrong, check out Redding's sleazy friends,' remember?"

"Oh no," I said emphatically. "No, I don't think so. Bad idea."

Chloe clapped her hands in glee, "I'm in!"

"No, you are not in," I said. "Nor am I. What would your father say?"

Alejandra looked worried. "Jenny Ho's? I don't know, Rachel. What if Brian found out?"

"He's already withholding visitation, so what have you got to lose?"

"A lot," Alejandra said. Then she giggled. "But you know, it does sound kind of fun."

"Wait, wait, wait," I said. Again, someone had to be the adult in the room. "You cannot be serious, Rachel. A strip club? In Oakland. Four unarmed women."

"Don't be a wimp, Marilyn. Talk to her, Chloe." Rachel said. "Here's the plan: we go there around say, eight o'clock, when there's nothing much going on yet, maybe a stripper or two, is all—"

"Is all?" I couldn't believe my ears. "And how do you know what the entertainment schedule is? Are you a regular customer?" And then I made the mistake of asking, "What would we do there anyway?"

"As I started to say before you rudely butted in, we take a table, order a beer—the wine in sleazy bars always sucks big time—then we chit-chat with the waiters and the clientele."

"Sure," I scoffed. "Just like they do on TV."

"It's not a crazy idea, Mom," said Chloe. "It might be fun."

"And dangerous," I said. "Jack will never agree to this." The very idea of telling him made my stomach turn a cartwheel. "And I refuse to go behind his back."

Chloe's eyes shone with mischief. "How about if we invite him to come along?"

"For protection!" Rachel said. "Men love that shit. Tell him the rest of us will go regardless, and you'd feel better if we all went. Safety in numbers."

"Would you?" I asked. "Go without me, I mean?"

"You bet!" said Rachel. "Right, girls?'

"I'm in," Chloe said again. "And Mom, I'm an adult, remember? I don't need permission."

Alejandra said, "I'm only going if Jack and Marilyn come, too."

"It's settled, then," said Chloe. "Mom, you tell Dad that Rachel and I are determined to check the place out, and that you want him and you to go along for protection."

A strip club. In Oakland. "He'll say no," I predicted. "But I guess I have no choice but to ask him."

Discussion ensued about when the field work was to take place. Rachel, the strip club expert, lobbied for the following night, pointing out that Tuesday would be a slow night in the place. I would've liked more time to find the right moment to discuss it with Jack, but I also wanted to get those dishes to Thacker, ASAP. If a visit to the strip club was standing in the way of that, it was best to get it over with.

"So tomorrow we call on Lisa the cat lady, and tomorrow night we hit Jenny Ho's?" Rachel looked around for consensus, and Chloe gave her a thumbs up. Alejandra and I nodded.

We then agreed—reluctantly on my part—to let the issue of the box of dishes ride for another night. I regretted telling Jack about our deception. I wasn't sure how long I could keep Mr. Law and Order from opening his yap, especially if Andy continued to show up at our house nearly every evening to interrogate us.

With nothing more to discuss, we adjourned for the night. Chloe and I watched Rachel sprint across the lawn to her own house next door and waited until she had unlocked her door and given us the thumbs up before we crossed the street. I glanced surreptitiously at Mrs. Zhang's porch, but Wei hadn't waited up to see us safely home.

"Just think," Chloe whispered, her eyes darting up and down the street. "The killer could live in one these houses. Or just around the corner."

"Or," I whispered back, "he might live in Oakland, or anywhere else. He could have come back to send those texts from the neighborhood where he killed Redding, trying to throw the investigators off track."

"I hope so. But I'm more nervous about being outside now, aren't you?"

I tried to be reassuring. "Here comes a patrol car now. They're watching us closely."

The two officers were, in fact, surveying us with incredulous eyes as they pulled the car to a stop in the street we had just crossed. The young man in the passenger seat, who looked like a teenager, rolled down his window and scrutinized us with alert, dark eyes, judging our potential guilt—or maybe our sanity. We exchanged brief "Good mornings."

"Ladies, you do know there was a murder down the street just a few weeks ago?"

"Yes, of course," I said. "And we sure do appreciate you guys patrolling the neighborhood to keep us safe."

"This hour of the morning is not generally considered the best time to be out and about. We've advised everyone in the neighborhood to be careful."

I said, "I'm sorry, Officer. We were visiting our neighbor across the street. It's a short walk, as you can see, and our friend is watching from the door to make sure we get safely inside. We're being careful, honest."

The officers turned their eyes to Alejandra's doorway, where sure enough, she stood peering at us with anxious eyes. Both officers nodded in her direction. "Just be careful, please," he said to us. "Have a nice night."

"See?" I said to Chloe, as they drove slowly on their way. "Does that make you feel better?"

"I guess so. But still, the murderer could be living in one of these houses. We have no idea." Then her eyes swept Mrs. Zhang's porch.

"No idea whatsoever," she said.

16

Just after lunch the next day, I was building my courage to approach Jack about the Jenny Ho's adventure when I got Alejandra's text:

> Can we put Jenny Ho's off for a night? Brian said he might bring Kyle for a "drive-by" visit after dinner. I hate that SOB so much!!!!!!!!!!

I didn't participate in the flurry of Brian-bashing in the text stream that followed, although I was tempted to send a "like" to Rachel's "manipulative asshole" comment. The postponement of our field trip was both a relief and a disappointment. Now my discussion with Jack could wait, but regrettably, another day would go by before the dishes were turned over to Thacker.

Another text came in, this one from Rachel:

> Wacko is home. Heard her calling the killer felines just now.

Chloe drove downtown to the florist and returned with a sunny bouquet of peonies and daisies. I told Jack of our impending errand and invited him to come along to see how our neighbor was holding up, considering last night's vandalism and chest pains, etc.

"To snoop, you mean," he sniffed. "I decline, thanks."

This from Mr. Nosy Nellie himself.

Chloe nudged me and giggled as we walked out the front door. Then her smile wilted, and she let out a nearly inaudible "Oh." I followed her suspicious eyes to where Mrs. Zhang and Wei were getting out of Wei's BMW in the driveway.

Wei smiled and called, "Hello, Marilyn." He and Mrs. Zhang waited politely in the driveway with their sacks of groceries until I found my manners.

"My daughter, Chloe," I said. "Chloe, this is Zhang Wei and his mother, Mrs. Zhang."

Mrs. Zhang nodded her approval. "This is correct. Zhang. Not Chang." While she didn't go so far as to smile at Chloe, she inclined her head and mumbled, "Pleased to meet you, I am certain," before walking inside with her small bag of groceries. All at once I remembered that the receipt I had captured in their driveway two nights before was still in the pocket of my jacket. I had an excuse to call on him later. On both of them, I corrected myself.

"I'm very glad to meet you, Chloe," said Wei with a warm smile. He turned and followed his mother inside.

The instant the door closed behind them, Chloe commented, "Something wrong there. Too smooth."

Annoyed, I defended Wei. "He's a doctor. And besides, Asians are culturally more polite."

She whispered, "Mom, my god."

As Alejandra, Rachel, Chloe, and I approached Lisa Cardwell's front door, her face appeared briefly in the living room window. She was on her phone, peering toward the opposite corner from us and turned away before she saw us. A moment later, we stood on her front steps, Rachel's finger hovering an inch from the bell when she suddenly hissed, "Shhhh," and leaned into the door.

Alejandra and I exchanged "Here we go again" glances, but the voice Rachel had detected was Lisa's as she argued in a shrill voice with someone over the phone.

"Stop trying to scare me … Look, it's not working, and I swear to God, I'll call the police again … whoever you are, they'll find you …"

As the four of us crowded in close, waiting for the conversation to continue, the door flew open and we lurched forward, nearly plowing into the unsuspecting Lisa. She stepped back just in time, clutching her white corduroy bathrobe tighter around her. Her bun was disheveled, and dark circles emphasized the prominent eyes, contrasting unfavorably with her pallid complexion and rendering her almost ghoulish.

"What on earth? How long have you been here?"

"Oh, we just now arrived," Chloe said. Alejandra and I nodded vehemently.

"Bullshit," said Rachel. "We heard you talking to someone on the phone. Sounded like you were being harassed."

"Jesus, Rachel," said Chloe.

"We're sorry," murmured Alejandra.

The two of them radiated chagrin, and I would've echoed Alejandra's apology, but Rachel snapped, "Look, there's a killer loose in our neighborhood. We need to work together here." She turned back to Lisa. "All of us. So what's up? If it has anything to do with the murder or what happened in your kitchen yesterday, you should tell us."

It was clear from Lisa's hesitation that she didn't trust us, and why should she? Her previous encounters with Rachel were enough to make her question that one's sanity, and here we all were, obviously a team, with Rachel as spokesperson.

I stepped in before Rachel could alienate her further. "Lisa, we're anxious, as I know you are, to see Michael Redding's murder solved. Alejandra has been harassed as well. If we work together, maybe we can help the detective get to the bottom of it all."

After a moment of uncertainty, she said, "Well, if you

think it might be useful.”

She led us through the living room, past a large-screen TV where I was surprised to see an affronted talking head decrying the “lame stream media’s” outright lies about our president. She pulled the remote from the pocket of her robe, aimed it, and the screen went dark, but not before I saw the unfamiliar word “Newsmax” on the banner across the bottom of the screen. I made a mental note to ask Jack if he knew about this possible alternative to Fox—not that he was looking for an alternative.

As we entered the kitchen, I noticed that the damage from the previous day’s vandalism had been erased. The house was smaller than most in the neighborhood but clean and tidy, at least the part of it we could see. There was a strong Lysol odor, perhaps the result of cleaning up the cat feces.

“You’ll have to excuse my appearance,” she said, smoothing the front of her robe. “The workers just finished replacing the pane in the back door and I was about to jump into the shower when the phone rang, and it was—” She inhaled deeply. “Would you all like some coffee?”

“I would love some,” I said at the same time the other three chorused, “No, thanks.”

I was fully caffeinated already: coffee for breakfast, Diet Coke for lunch. But bonding over a beverage might lead to revelations from Lisa, just as the iced tea in Alejandra’s backyard had resulted in a case of motor-mouth for Rachel.

As Lisa poured coffee for all of us, the others having decided to follow my lead after all, her slender hands began shaking to the point where she briefly put down the pot and wiped them on her robe. Which was startling but understandable, considering the home invasion and that intriguing snippet of phone conversation we had overheard from the other side of the front door.

So I was surprised when she said, “I should explain

that I have a medical condition. It's nothing serious. But when I'm under stress, it's more pronounced."

Parkinson's Disease, perhaps? It took down Molly, my poor foster mother, and considering her gradual, heartbreaking decline, I hoped for Lisa's sake it was something less debilitating.

We sat around Lisa's table, stirring cream into our coffee. I thought it prudent to be silent and let Lisa open up to us in her own time. But of course, Rachel couldn't wait for that.

"So," she said. "Do you know the person who was harassing you on the phone just now?"

Lisa shook her head. "His voice is familiar, but I've tried and can't put a face with it. I can't tell you how much sleep I've lost, trying to remember."

"That must be very difficult for you," I said. "You're probably exhausted."

My reward for demonstrating good listening skills was an annoyed glance from Rachel before she pressed on: "What's he threatening to do? Is he the one who decorated your kitchen with cat shit?"

"I'm almost certain he is, yes." She stared into space and sipped her coffee. Not one sip, but two, pausing in between to think. I could feel Rachel's impatience. I caught her eye and shook my head: *talking isn't listening.*

But when Lisa continued to sip coffee in silence, I said, "It's a terrible feeling, isn't it? Being so afraid? I assume you've told the police about the calls?"

She winced. "I guess I should, but ..." She trailed off with a sheepish smile.

"You mean you haven't?" Rachel looked around the table to see if we all were as astounded as she was. We were. "Your house was broken into and vandalized, and you haven't told the cops you're being harassed over the phone by someone whose voice is familiar?"

"Huh," said Chloe and Alejandra in unison.

"Maybe if you tell us what he's threatening to do?" Chloe prompted. "Or if you can think of any reason why he's out to get you?"

"It's embarrassing," she said.

More than embarrassment, what I detected was a reluctance to open up to us about what was obviously a private matter. This I understood from my own experience. But my secrets were nobody's business, while Lisa's might help to solve a murder.

"We're all adults here," I said. "You'll feel better if you don't hold this inside." I wasn't entirely sure this was true, but my own patience was wearing thin, and I feared Rachel was ready to grab Lisa by the lapels of her bathrobe and give her a good shake.

"It's that he—he wants money from me. Lots of money, more than I can afford to pay. He claims to know about my, um, my past and says he'll tell both my kids everything." Her eyes welled up. "He recites their addresses and phone numbers to me."

"Oh, no!" Alejandra moaned. Too close to home. Chloe reached out and squeezed her hand. A flicker of interest passed across Lisa's face, and she studied Alejandra for a moment. I thought she might comment, but instead she fell silent again.

Just as Rachel opened her mouth to say god-knows-what in the spirit of moving things along, Lisa closed her woeful eyes and took a long, deep breath. Then after a determined nod, she said, "You're right. I need to tell the police. But regardless, there's no point in getting you all involved."

"There is, though," Chloe said. "We're all trying to help the detective—"

"What's in your past that he could blackmail you about?" Rachel broke in. She sounded even nosier than I felt, and I thought Lisa would clam up for sure. Instead, she gave Rachel a sheepish smile.

"I was a nun once." She waited for us to absorb what she must have assumed was a shocker on its own, before adding, "Or at least, I was a novice. I was driven out of the program when I got pregnant. By a priest, but I never ratted him out." Her smile withered. "Son-of-a-bitch denied everything. Denounced me along with the others."

"Bastard," Rachel spat. "But getting pregnant, even for a nun, isn't a crime, is it? And it's nothing you shouldn't be able to tell your kids about." She looked at me for confirmation, me being the resident expert on motherly matters, evidently.

Before I could answer, Lisa said, "You have to understand that my daughter is deeply religious. She had planned to become a missionary. But then she fell in love with a fireman, married, and had a couple of adorable kids instead."

I feared she would whip out her phone and force us to waste time cooing over the latest photos of the little darlings, but she just allowed herself a brief, wistful smile.

"Then she should be willing to forgive you. Right? Christians are all about that." Rachel said. I wasn't sure it was sarcasm until she added, "Or maybe not, in the age of Trump."

Lisa raised her eyebrows. "Let's not get political, okay? I do happen to be a supporter of the president, for which I do not apologize."

Yes! Thank you, Jesus.

"Another thing is, Amanda was close to her dad—my husband, the man she believed to be her father. I met him when she was less than a year old. He persuaded me not to tell her the truth. He was a saint, such a good dad to her."

Rachel began, "But surely now you could—"

"She would be devastated." Lisa shook her head. "I just can't. There's no need."

"What a terrible burden you've carried all these years,"

I said. "It must have been so difficult."

She nodded, so I continued, "And this awful man who is threatening you, could he be connected to the church? Might he be the priest, your child's father?"

She shook her head firmly. "No, that man is long dead. And the church has its faults, but they're not known for shaking down the flock for money."

"How much money?" Rachel blurted, as though the answer mattered.

Lisa ignored her. "At any rate, I absolutely do not want my daughter, or my son either, to know about this."

She looked anxiously from one of us to the other. "Do you really think I should tell this to that detective? What if it makes the blackmailer angry?"

"It might," said Rachel. "But it'll increase your odds of finding the prick."

The rest of us chorused our agreement.

Lisa appeared to be considering her options. While we waited, a pleasant new possibility occurred to me. I'd started to warm up to Lisa after she proclaimed her political views. What if she joined our late-night gatherings? Maybe we could become friends. Coffee in the backyard. Shopping and lunch, that kind of thing.

Chloe asked, "Why did you call the police when you saw what had been done to your kitchen, if you didn't want them to know about the threats?"

The question surprised her. "Why, I was terrified. I thought whoever broke in might still be in the house somewhere. What if it was that drummer's killer? And I started to have those chest pains."

"You have to call Detective Thacker," Rachel repeated. "You're right. Maybe your blackmailer is the same person who killed Michael Redding. It's possible."

The rest of us nodded, and relief passed across Lisa's face, as if she had been hoping we would make the decision for her.

"I'll do it," she said. "I doubt there's a connection, but I'll tell him. Thank you."

She rose, letting us know the conversation was over.

On our way out, my eyes fell on a group of framed photographs on a table next to the door. Four or five smaller ones were of what I assumed to be Lisa's family in various combinations. I didn't look too closely at those, but my eye was drawn to the largest photo: an 11x14 of an attractive, celebratory, early middle-aged couple raising champagne glasses toward the camera. The petite, smiling woman wore a sleek, diagonal haircut, her make-up was subtle but effective, and her doe-like eyes sparkled.

Lisa caught all of us looking and said with a wistful smile, "That was a while ago, on our twentieth anniversary."

"Wow," Rachel blurted. "You look—"

"What?" said Lisa, with a hint of challenge in her voice. "Younger? Prettier?"

"Even prettier than now," Rachel said without missing a beat. "But that's understandable. None of us look our best when we're all stressed out. As we all are these days, myself included."

"Yes, well. You have youth on your side, at least."

Before I could offer a reassuring comment that might lead her to reveal her age—I judged her to be fifty-two or three, fifty-five tops, roughly ten years younger than me—she opened the door wide, and taking the hint, we trooped outside. On her way down the steps, Chloe froze, causing Rachel to bump into her from behind.

"Careful, honey," I admonished her. Then I followed her gaze into the street, just as Zhang Wei walked past us and raised his hand in a friendly salute. We waved back and watched until he turned the corner.

Chloe said. "He must have followed us over here. Do you think he was watching Lisa's house?"

"Hmm," said Rachel. "Maybe we need to report this to Detective Thacker."

"Report what?" was my response to that ridiculous suggestion. "That our friendly neighbor walked past Lisa's house and waved when we came through her door? He's keeping his eyes open, remember? Just like we are."

"Maybe they're doing it, the cat lady and him," Rachel offered with a snort. "Oh. Sorry, Mrs. M."

"And what if they are?" I was annoyed. "That's no concern of mine. Or yours, either."

Still, I hoped they weren't doing it. Nothing against Lisa, but I felt Wei could do better. Another doctor, maybe. Or at least a professional of some kind. But then it occurred to me that perhaps Lisa was a professional herself, or had once been.

"Did Lisa say what career path she took after the convent? We should have asked. It might have jogged her memory, helped her to place the man's voice."

"She didn't say, and we didn't ask. What's the matter with you, Marilyn?" Rachel elbowed me. "You should've thought of that."

"Why me?" I huffed, before I saw that she was teasing.

We agreed to press Lisa for more information. But when would we see her again?

"I'll get her phone number." Rachel had already turned back. "She's an insomniac like us. I'll see if she'll join us for the next meeting."

"Good idea," I said, pleased that I hadn't even had to suggest inviting her.

But Rachel had reversed course. "Oh, wait a minute."

Looking over her shoulder, said in a quiet voice, "We don't know this woman at all, really. What if she's the murderer? She certainly has no conscience where those killer cats are concerned. And her politics—"

My irate expression stopped her short.

"Politics have nothing to do with this investigation," I snapped, not bothering to keep my voice down. "Nor do the cats, who are only doing what nature has programmed them to do. Many people love cats. Even the Clintons had one or two living in the White House. Now get on over there and ask for her phone number. Or do I have to do it myself?"

After agreement from Alejandra and Chloe, she shrugged and turned back toward Lisa's house while the rest of us started home.

Despite the coffee I'd had at Lisa's, the sight of my bed solicited a wide yawn. As I sank down onto it, my eyes fell on the gray sweatshirt jacket that I had draped across the bedroom chair—my housekeeping had gone to hell, another casualty of insomnia and its accompanying exhaustion. I remembered again that the receipt I kept meaning to return to the Zhangs was still in the jacket pocket. Probably it was nothing important, but that wasn't my call. I would call on them after my nap, for sure.

But when I awoke, two hours had been lost. I had just enough time to shower before starting dinner. And I still hadn't asked Jack about tomorrow's Jenny Ho's adventure.

And anyway, shouldn't I have a peek at the receipt before returning it? Not that its origin was any of my business, but wouldn't I look silly returning a receipt for, say, $6.50 for a pack of cigarettes? Or something embarrassing, like a pharmacy receipt for Viagra for Wei or rectal suppositories for his mother?

Before I could have a look, the doorbell rang. I tossed the jacket back onto the chair before walking to the top of the stairs.

"Marilyn!" Jack called. "Detective Thacker is here."

When I joined them, he was telling Andy, "You're early. Dinner's not for another hour."

"Good one," the detective said amiably. "But I'm not here for dinner."

Chloe came bounding down the stairs, decked out in flattering black pants and a striped blouse covered with a smart gray blazer, eyes lit like Christmas.

"Hey there," she said, and Andy's smile grew wider.

She turned to Jack and me. "Oh. I meant to tell you. Andy is taking me to dinner. I got all caught up in our visit with Lisa and forgot to mention it."

Andy asked, "And how is Mrs. Cardwell doing today? I haven't spoken with her since her discharge from the hospital."

"I'll fill you in," said Chloe.

Of course you haven't followed up with her, I thought. *Because you're incompetent. Otherwise you'd be questioning the pants off that woman about who might have broken into her house. I mean, a man has been murdered, a woman's house has been vandalized, and what are you doing? Taking my daughter out to dinner.*

But then I realized it wasn't such a dumb idea, from his standpoint. He would no doubt get the details of our visit with Lisa from Chloe over a couple of glasses of Pinot Grigio. I wanted to pull Chloe aside and ask her to let Lisa approach the detective in her own way, but they were already out the door.

Jack's chin was nearly on the floor.

"Don't worry," I reassured him. "She's buttering him up to get all the info she can about the murder investigation. That's all."

"What do I care?" His petulant tone betrayed him. "White, black, red, yellow, we are all brothers under the skin. Never mind if their kids would be shunned by both black and white communities—"

"Jack, it's her business, and his. She's a smart girl. And she did say she meant to get as much out of him as she can. About the murder, I mean."

Then he surprised me with an abrupt but welcome change of subject.

"Can we get out of the house for a change? Go to dinner ourselves? I'm feeling housebound lately. Doors locked, blinds down all the time."

I didn't need to be asked twice. A distraction was in order, and not just from Michael Redding's murder. I liked Detective Andy Thacker just fine, but he was not my idea of the ideal son-in-law. Believe me, it was not his skin color that gave me pause. His handling of the murder investigation caused me to worry that he might not have much of a future as a detective. Parents are concerned about these things when it comes to potential mates for their children.

But as I had just reminded Jack, whatever Chloe's intentions were regarding Detective Thacker, that was her business. I dared to hope that no matter what she had in mind, she would manage to wrangle from him some tidbit or two that might help our investigation along.

"I'll run upstairs and change while you make a reservation," I said.

He still looked anxious, so I paused to give him a quick kiss. My own mood had lightened. "Date night! Great idea, honey. It's been a while."

"Mmmm," he said, reaching out to pat my butt as I walked away. "Too long."

When I glanced back, he waggled his eyebrows at me, and I giggled. There would be no discussion of the murder investigation over dinner, I promised myself. Unless maybe, after the wine took effect, I'd find the nerve to ask him about accompanying us to Jenny Ho's. It had to be done soon.

But I would not check my phone during the wee hours to see if I'd been summoned by Rachel. The Middle of the Night Club wasn't my only responsibility. Or my only need. I was feeling surprisingly open to the idea of intimacy.

17

Thanks to a relaxing dinner at Terra & Mare, and especially to the Chianti I had with my lasagna, topped off with three lip-puckering sips of the bitter *digestif* that I let Jack talk me into, I dozed straight through the night for the first time in weeks.

But when I did wake up, it was with knots in my stomach and an agitated swarm of possibilities buzzing in my head. Most worrisome was the unsolved murder of Michael Redding, a mystery compounded by other ominous events: the hateful, racist messages directed at Alejandra, the blackmailing of Lisa and vandalism of her kitchen, the Peeping Tom, and the envelope left on my doorstep. But none of these weighed on me more than the concealed evidence awaiting discovery beneath Alejandra's bed.

Well, tonight we would get the Jenny Ho's "field trip" out of the way. And even if we uncovered nothing new in the way of evidence, I would insist that those dishes be turned over to Andy, pronto.

As Jack snoozed on, I showered and started downstairs to see if Chloe was up and having breakfast. Perhaps she had wrangled some pertinent information last night from Mr. Some-Things-Are-Confidential.

I was usually so alert to the girls' comings and goings, even after they were too old for curfews, that a key in front door lock or the slightest creak of the stairway would strike my ear like a thunderclap. However, if Chloe had returned last night—*when,* not *if,* I admonished myself—I had slept through it. Maybe one glass of wine would suffice next time.

While passing her bedroom door, I stopped cold at the sound of Chloe's muffled giggle. As I paused and pressed my ear to the door, straining to make out her hushed words, my heart did a double flip-flop. *She wouldn't dare, would she? But what would I do if she did?* When I finally determined that I was listening to one side of a phone conversation, I was flooded with relief—although not exactly flattered by what I heard.

"... What matters is that I had a fun time. That's all I'm after for now ... yes, she'll be quizzing me for details. You know how she is ... Okay ... Love you, too, Natalie ... bye."

I skedaddled down the stairs, slipped on the bottom step, and fell on my tush. *Ouch,* but nothing injured except my dignity. I recovered it, put on a pot of coffee, and was seated at the table, eyes glued to the lead story in the *Las Oliviñas Weekly,* when Jack came down a few minutes later.

He poured himself a cup. "What's for breakfast?"

"Yes, it was indeed a nice evening. And 'Good morning' to you as well."

Surprised at the edge in my voice, he came over to kiss my forehead. "Sorry. I woke up famished. But wasn't it clear last night how much fun I was having?"

We exchanged smiles, but mine was strained. His comment had triggered a disconcerting thought: what if Chloe had come home while we were in the middle of—

Oh, stop. So what if she had? Surely, she didn't expect us to become celibate in retirement. Still, my face reddened at the possibility, just as she bounded down the stairs and flounced into the kitchen. If she noticed my discomfort, she didn't let on.

"What's for breakfast?"

The dance in her step and the satisfied, secretive smile annoyed me for no other reason than I currently possessed the energy and good humor of a snapping turtle.

"Whatever you're fixing," I said.

I'd meant it as a joke, hadn't I? So why was I irked when they chuckled in response? But then, what was so darn funny about the idea of someone else whipping up a meal for once? Although why should I be surprised? The kitchen had always been my domain and they knew how much pleasure I'd always gotten from cooking.

Lack of sleep was making me cranky and muddle-headed. And no wonder, right? One decent night's rest couldn't make up for weeks of sleep deprivation, especially when the sources of my nocturnal anxiety did not dissipate with the dawn but followed me out of bed each morning like the remnants of a persistent nightmare. Adding to my dark mood was the dread of approaching Jack about the upcoming trip to Jenny Ho's.

Chloe rose to the challenge. "No problem. How about scrambled eggs and bacon?"

"Sounds good. And I'll make pancakes," said Jack, every bit as chipper as Chloe.

And I, the sole sourpuss, put on a mask of serene gratitude. "Oh, that would be wonderful! Thank you."

Great. A thousand-calorie breakfast. I'd been steering all of us toward healthier options like whole grain cereal and a turkey sausage patty, yogurt with fruit, and the like. I looked Chloe over from behind while she was reaching into the refrigerator. Maybe she had lost a couple of pounds, but I wouldn't have bet on it.

I set the table and poured orange juice, and because Chloe was humming while she worked, I thought it reasonable to ask if she'd had a good time the night before.

She surprised us by launching into an enthusiastic review of the evening. The new downtown restaurant, El Cerrito, served the best margaritas she had ever had here in Las Oliviñas. The several appetizers she and Andy had sampled were so yummy they had indulged to the point where they almost weren't hungry for dinner. Andy had made great recommendations for entrees, and afterwards they had strolled down Main Street to that frozen yogurt store where you select your own toppings, such as chocolate or mint sprinkles, M&Ms, or whatever. She had loaded hers up, but Andy had settled for only peppermint sprinkles.

Throughout the monologue, her date was never referred to as Detective Thacker or even Detective Andy. It was "Andy this and Andy that." Just Andy. But surely that was meaningless. So what if they were becoming friends? That could be a good thing for our group's private investigation.

I waited until the recounting was finished and she began to hum again. Then I asked, "Did Andy give you an update on the case? Anything more about the Peeping Tom incidents?"

Jack chimed in: "What she means is, did he accidentally leak any information he was keeping from us before?"

"Oh. Hmm. let me think." It was as if the idea of prodding Andy for news about the investigation had never occurred to her. She delivered a platter of bacon to the table and returned for the eggs. "No, I guess not."

"I thought that was the whole idea of you going out to dinner with him." Jack threw me an accusatory glance. "That's what your mother said, anyway."

"I never said any such thing!" I huffed.

Jack's jaw dropped, and before he could find his tongue, I took the lie a step farther. "I said it would be nice if she did learn something new regarding the murder case, that's all."

After scowling at me for a moment, he must have decided my fabrication wasn't worth spoiling breakfast over. He muttered, "If you say so," and dug into his pancakes.

"It just didn't come up," said Chloe, whose serene smile had not faltered. "These pancakes are awesome, Dad."

We let the matter drop, but truth be told, I was even more annoyed than Jack. How had Chloe blown this opportunity? How hard could it be to wheedle a clue or two from a man as prone as Andy Thacker to self-important chatter about himself and his work?

She had already moved on. "Mom, when Andy walked me to the door last night, your buddy Mr. Wei was outside smoking on the porch again."

"Buddy?" Jack chuckled.

"He's no more my buddy than anyone else's," I was quick to say.

"He's always there, is all," Chloe commented as she began clearing the table. I stood up and waved her away.

"I'll get the dishes, since you two cooked. It was delicious, and I appreciate the break."

"Are you still up for a drive to the lake today, Marilyn?" Jack asked. "A short hike and a picnic lunch? Good day for a swim, too. What do you think, Chloe?"

She beamed. "Sounds fun!"

Darn. It had seemed like a wonderful idea last night after the second glass of Chianti.

To avoid disappointing Jack, I said "Sure, why not?" and started planning our lunch. Maybe the relaxed atmosphere at the lake would put him in a receptive mood for our Jenny Ho's discussion.

Jack was right; it was indeed a fine day for a swim, with temps in the nineties and so little humidity our suits dried completely between dips. At a picnic table in the shade, we feasted on roast beef sandwiches, carrot sticks, and potato salad. With Jack's help, Chloe finished off the half bag of Doritos she had tossed into the basket when my back was turned.

While Jack went for a short hike, Chloe and I relaxed on the blanket we'd spread in the shade of our beach umbrella.

"Have you asked him yet?" Chloe asked as soon as Jack was out of sight. "Jenny Ho's?"

"I wanted to do it last night, but we were having a fun time and I didn't want to spoil it. We so seldom go out for a relaxing dinner anymore." *You know, just like you didn't want to ruin your date by probing Andy about the Peeping Tom.*

"Well, we said it would happen tonight."

"I'll do it," I said. "The day is young."

After a short rest, I walked over to the bathroom, and when I came back, Jack had returned. He looked up at me with an incredulous expression as I settled into the lawn chair beside him.

"You've agreed to this?"

"What's that?" I asked, although I knew. Maybe I should have been angry that Chloe had taken matters into her own hands, but I chose to be relieved instead, since he seemed more baffled than irate.

"You want us to go with these girls to a strip club. In Oakland."

"I haven't committed," I said. "I think it's a crazy idea. But they seem determined to go with or without us, so I said I'd run it by you."

"Please, Dad," Chloe wheedled. "We would feel safer if you were with us. And it would be great if you could drive, too. We can take Alejandra's van, but—"

"Only if she empties it out first," I said.

Jack sniffed. "Well, I'm certainly not going to give my blessing to this harebrained scheme. I'm against it, whether we all go or just you girls. I'll agree to it only if we go early in the evening, and on a weeknight when it might not be so crowded."

"How does everyone know about strip clubs' slow times except for me?" I asked.

Jack ignored the question. "When is this escapade scheduled to take place?"

Chloe beamed at both of us. "We were hoping to go tonight, actually."

Jack said, "Might as well get it over with," and Chloe clapped her hands "Yay!"

On the way home, she asked if we could stop downtown for coffee. While I marveled at the fact that our daughter seemed more than willing to hang out with us, Jack drove around the block several times in search of a parking spot.

"You might not remember, Chloe," he said. "But it never used to be a problem finding a place to park."

He gestured toward a small cluster of four-story buildings as we cruised slowly past. "That's so-called affordable housing, right on Main Street. That's what the city council sees as progress."

"You should run for the council yourself, Dad. You have strong ideas, and plenty of people must agree with you. Plus, your financial background would be good for the budget."

Jack harrumphed.

"Good idea," I said, while thinking, *a snowball's chance, at best.*

Jack gave up on finding a spot and parked in the new pay garage, adding to his ill humor. Nonetheless, we had stimulating conversation (no politics) over coffee and were all in good spirits when we returned home in the late afternoon to find Detective Thacker's unmarked car on the street in front. The man himself was on Mrs. Zhang's front porch, talking to Wei.

"Oh," said Chloe when she caught sight of him.

"Another date so soon?" Jack pulled the car into the

driveway that had become its home now that the garage was filled with woodworking paraphernalia waiting to be experimented with.

Chloe's good humor went south in a hurry. Her icy voice challenged him from the back seat. "Would that be a problem? Is there some reason you don't want me to see Andy?"

I answered for him. "Of course it's not a problem. Your dad asked a simple question. You had dinner with Andy last night, and now here he is, standing on our neighbor's porch. I don't think it's an unreasonable assumption that he might have come here to see you."

"Except that he's in the middle of investigating a murder that happened right down the street. Jeez."

I let it drop. No need to spoil what had so far been a pleasant day. Who knew when Chloe might decide she'd had enough of our company?

Wei broke off his conversation with Andy and nodded in our direction, then looked away and waited in silence as we walked up our front steps. Andy offered his usual cheery smile, but turned quickly back to Wei, dismissing us without so much as a wave. Chloe hesitated, but I nudged her toward the door. "Let's not interrupt."

When I went downstairs after my shower, Chloe was forming hamburger into patties. "Another postponement on Jenny Ho's. Alejandra has a stomachache, she says. That's two nights in a row that she's bailed."

My momentary relief was quicky overridden by frustration. "Maybe she doesn't want the Jenny Ho's visit to happen, since we agreed to turn the dishes over to Andy after that."

Chloe nodded. "We can't put it off much longer. One more day, then we either go to Jenny Ho's without her or go ahead and give Andy the dishes. Or both."

After dinner, while she waited for Andy's text, she and I passed the time by wrangling with a 2,000-piece jigsaw puzzle that Jack and I had been torturing ourselves with for weeks, some sadistic designer's masterpiece: lemons in a yellow-orange bowl on a yellow-orange tablecloth against a yellow-orange wall. When the final piece refused to fit into the only remaining space, we both shouted "Noooo!"

Chloe jumped up and left the room, then returned with scissors. Before I could object, she had trimmed the edges of the recalcitrant piece. "Voila!" she said, jamming it into place. She chortled, I tittered, and there followed a long, cathartic, mutual giggling fit. Wiping my eyes, I said, "Wait until your dad sees this."

"Will he be pissed?"

"Of course not. He has a sense of humor, you know."

She turned serious. "I used to think so. I don't really get why he thinks it's funny to give people snide nicknames, though. I overheard him referring to Andy as 'Detective Mooch' the other day. What's that about?"

"Oh, that's only because he always visits around dessert time," I said, and then quickly swerved. "Anyway, sticking people with nicknames was just a thing he and his friends did for fun back in college. But it's true," I acknowledged, "that as he gets older, some of the monikers are more insulting than silly. Lately, I've asked him to back off some of that."

Having conquered the puzzle, we tuned into a recorded episode of "Downton Abbey." She checked her phone every few minutes, but there were no messages or calls from Andy. Our update on his talk with Wei would have to wait until morning. And we were on our third day of hanging onto the darn box of dishes. Our third day of concealing evidence in a murder investigation, when the killer might very well be living in our own neighborhood.

As we trudged upstairs to bed, I fought the urge to raise the question that had been bothering me since breakfast. Because overall, it had been a fun day for us as a family. Why risk a discussion of her failure the prior evening to grill Andy about the Peeping Tom? We were both tired, and prior experience told me that such a discussion was unlikely to end well. But I resolved to bring it up later. She owed our group an explanation for not carrying out her assignment, didn't she?

"He'll get in touch with you tomorrow," I reassured her, as we said good night at the top of the stairs.

"Sure." She checked her phone again. "Surprise. Alejandra says she feels better and would like to get together later, like around 3:30 after she's slept for a while."

"Imagine that."

"I think we should, don't you? Since Jenny Ho's keeps getting put off, we ought to put pressure on Rachel and Alejandra to go ahead and turn over the dishes."

Yes, and you'll have to give us your status report on the Peeping Tom assignment. But that jab went unspoken, of course.

"Yes, we should meet," I said. "You're right. We have a lot to talk about."

18

I awoke at 3:30 a.m. and went downstairs to find Chloe, clad in pj's and a light sweater, nibbling on a cookie at the kitchen table.

"Rachel just texted that the cat lady is joining us tonight," she said, "but we shouldn't tell her about our Jenny Ho's trip. Her being an ex-nun, she might think poorly of us."

"Most likely." As if the idea of our nosing around in a strip joint wouldn't raise the eyebrows of any sensible person, nun or otherwise.

As we left the house, I sneaked a glance at Mrs. Zhang's porch, but Wei was nowhere in sight. A brief, cordial encounter would've been reassuring, after his offhand dismissal earlier. What could he and Andy have been discussing so intently?

All thoughts of Wei scattered as Chloe and I walked into Alejandra's living room and were greeted by the sight of our fellow crime solvers, including our new recruit, Lisa, seated in a circle of metal folding chairs. The rocker that Rachel usually claimed was now home to a plastic container filled with sewing paraphernalia, while the sofa held several cardboard packing boxes of various sizes, all filled beyond capacity.

Boondoggles sat at attention near Lisa's feet, eyes

glued to this stranger as if expecting a Milk-bone.

"I've spoiled him," Alejandra apologized to Lisa, as she took the dog by the collar and led him to his usual spot in front of the sofa, where he lay with paws folded under his chin and continued to stare at Lisa with baleful eyes.

"You should feel honored," I said. "He growled at me, first time I came over."

"Me too," said Chloe who surveyed the circle of chairs and selected one between Alejandra and Rachel. "Goodness, this is different."

"I found these chairs just sitting out on the street marked 'Free,'" our hostess informed us. "What a bargain, huh? I figured they'd make us feel like we're in an official meeting."

"Make us feel like our butts hurt, you mean." Rachel shifted in her seat to make her point, miraculously managing not to tip her glass. While the rest of us sipped our tea, she got up and sauntered into the kitchen. Upon her return, she muttered, "Screw this" and sat the topped-off glass on the floor. She dragged her folding chair out of the semi-circle and replaced it with the Bentwood, the contents of which she unceremoniously dumped onto the metal chair—and then stepped backwards and kicked over the full glass of red wine.

"Dammit," she said. "How did I do that? Sorry, Alejandra. I'll clean it up."

"Never mind. I'll get it." Alejandra looked both miffed and concerned as she scurried to the kitchen for towels. Perhaps, like me, she suspected that Rachel was losing the battle with alcohol despite the efforts of the good people at Alkies Online.

As Alejandra and Chloe mopped up, Lisa's amused gaze followed Rachel as she retrieved her glass and returned to the kitchen for a refill. Her reaction troubled me until I reminded myself that Lisa was new to the party. A young, pretty woman under the influence could be entertaining enough, the first time you witnessed it.

Once we were all resettled, I said, "Let's get started. Maybe first order of business should be to find out how Thacker reacted when Lisa told him about the blackmail."

"She already talked about that before you ambled over here," Rachel complained.

"I beg your pardon," I said in an icy voice. "Ambled?"

Lisa ignored Rachel and turned to me. Her bun was brightened tonight by a wide purple scrunchie, the gray streaks covered by what I suspected was a do-it-yourself color job; any decent stylist would have guided her toward highlights or a lighter shade of brown. Maybe I could further motivate her: we could shop together at Nordstrom for clothes and makeup, as Sue Ellen and I used to do, followed by lunch at the cafe on the top floor.

"I don't mind repeating it," she said, bringing me back to reality. "Thacker says I was right to tell him about the blackmail. Since Alejandra and that old Chinese woman are also being harassed—all of us within a two-block area of where the murder took place, he thinks it's possible there's a connection."

"The old Chinese woman. Mrs. Chang. No, Zhang, not Chang," Rachel said, then repeated it louder, in a singsong voice. "Zhang, not Chang. Not Chang, but Zhang."

"What's this about Mrs. Zhang?" I hoped we were about to find out what the detective's meeting with Wei last night was all about.

"So what's next on the agenda?" Rachel demanded, as if I hadn't spoken. Completely schnockered. But then, she had never shown much in the way of manners even when sober.

As Lisa lifted her cup, some of the contents sloshed over the side. She sat it down and held her hands out with splayed, trembling fingers for us to see, then clasped them together in her lap.

"I should explain that I have a medical condition," she

said, repeating verbatim what she had told us at her house two days earlier. "It's nothing serious, but when I'm under stress, it's more pronounced." And just like before, she ended the explanation with a "woe is me" sigh.

"Bummer," said Rachel.

"Anyway, to answer your question, apparently the old Chinese lady is getting some anonymous postcards. Thacker wouldn't tell me any more than that." She sniffed. "Some things are confidential, he said. But he assures me he's on top of it."

I sensed Chloe bristling beside me. For my part, I was perplexed by the repetition of the whole "medical condition" explanation. Was it a sign of early dementia? Here was a woman within ten years of my own age with similar political views, who lived just a block over, in a clean, orderly house. All in all, a more likely replacement friend for Sue Ellen than the other two on whom I'd been pinning my hopes.

But while I approved of Lisa's outspoken manner, was it really necessary to deride the detective's efforts? Chloe thought not.

"Andy's doing everything he can. Just look at how much time he spends in the neighborhood. And both officers assigned to him are trainees who need constant direction. I think he's doing a fine job."

Rachel chuckled. "You Middleton girls and your crushes."

Chloe frowned at her and I gritted my teeth. "Nobody's got a crush on anybody. Let's not waste time on that nonsense."

Rachel teased, "Come now, Marilyn. I've seen you out talking to Zhang-not-Chang on his mom's porch at all hours. Chloe, you better keep an eye on your mother."

Chloe just grinned because, of course, the idea of her mother harboring a crush on anyone was beyond ridiculous. Instead of admonishing them to "grow up," I reminded them why we had asked Lisa to join us.

"Lisa, what kind of work did you do after you left the convent? Could there have been someone you worked with who has a grievance of some kind?"

"Angry enough to smear cat shit all over your countertops." Rachel laughed. "That's pretty damn pissed."

Lisa thought for a moment and then chuckled. "Well, I guess it's possible that some irate applicant at the DMV might hold a grudge."

"The DMV?" asked Chloe.

"Yes. Up until last year, when I lost Dale and developed this medical condition and decided to take a break from working, I was one of those crabby DMV clerks that people would dump their frustrations on after being told their wait might be an hour or more."

"Yep, "said Rachel. "I can see someone thinking up cat shit revenge over that."

"But not the extortion," I said. "That's way more serious. And it would require some knowledge of your past."

"It would seem so," Lisa agreed.

Chloe asked, "Lisa, did Andy collect your cell phone? So he could trace those calls?"

"Yes, he took it. He's supposedly doing whatever it is they do to track numbers that are blocked, which these were." She shook her head, annoyed. "He isn't in much of a hurry. So I've had to purchase a prepaid phone with a different number. Not exactly convenient."

"How did you happen to show up here, then? If you didn't get my texts?" Rachel's face had "Gotcha" written all over it.

Lisa smiled. "Goodness, honey. You don't remember ringing my doorbell at 3:00 a.m.?"

There followed a good ten seconds of silence, all eyes on Rachel.

"Sure, I remember. Just seeing if you did." As she put

down her glass and placed both hands beneath her thighs, a parade of emotions marched across her face: confusion, recognition, dismay. And a flicker of fright. A wake-up call? I hoped so.

"I'm sure he'll get it back to you as soon as he can," said Chloe. "He's just so busy."

Way to stand by your man, honey.

"Okay, now to bring Lisa up to date." Alejandra opened her notebook, and with our interspersed contributions, she reviewed what we knew so far. The strip clubs and porn sites, the 911 call, and the possibly related issue of the Peeping Tom, all of which had come from Detective Thacker. She then listed the index cards with their racist threats, the extortionist phone calls to Lisa, and the vandalism to her kitchen. None of this was news to Lisa, who seemed almost bored until Alejandra mentioned the anonymous envelope with its list of clues that had been left on my porch, addressed specifically to me.

"What envelope is this, now?" Lisa turned to me. "Dropped on your front doorstep, you say? Why would someone give such a list to you and not to the detective?"

"Damned if we know." Rachel was still sitting on her hands, probably to keep them from reaching for the glass in front of her. Her expression was somewhere between chagrined and surly.

"What were the items on the list?" Lisa asked. We had her full attention now.

Alejandra read them off: "Jenny Ho's, *getyerroxoff.com, chicksonchicks.com,* Twenty-four-Hour Fitness, Maple Avenue Elementary."

"Same as the original clues," Lisa observed. "Except that the school and the fitness center are new, right?"

"Yes," I said. "Although Jack and I both remember that he offhandedly asked about the school and the gym that first night he stopped by. And he didn't seem surprised that they were among the clues given to me."

"So then, it seems we should be looking for a person who's connected in some way to all these places." Lisa looked around for agreement. When we all nodded, she continued, "Was there anything else in the message?"

"Well," I said. "Just one other sentence. Or two. Two short sentences."

She waited. My reluctance came mostly from not wanting to rile or embarrass Chloe. But also, I was surprised to find myself feeling protective of Andy, as if it might be disloyal to repeat the note verbatim: *Help the fool to do his job. Someone needs to.*

Chloe saw my uncertainty and came to my rescue. "There was a note on the bottom of the page that said, 'Help the detective to do his job.'"

Since both Alejandra and Rachel pretended not to have noticed Chloe's paraphrasing, I decided it wasn't worth correcting.

Lisa was stroking her chin, and I noticed that her fingers had stopped shaking. *Parkinson's*, I thought again. Intermittent trembling was a common symptom.

"Interesting," she said. "Definitely a clue worth exploring."

So she was inclined to become one of us, then. I'd worried that she might find us lacking—she had been a nun, after all. Well, almost a nun. And here we were: a probable alcoholic, a budding hoarder, and a Nosy Nellie. And of course, Chloe, who was developing a frustrating blind spot where the detective assigned to the case was concerned.

Lisa cleared her throat, suddenly uncomfortable. "There's something I haven't told you. Thacker suggested I keep it to myself for now, but—well, I'm almost certain it's relevant."

"That's why we're here," Chloe encouraged her.

"I got a postcard in the mail just a few hours ago." Her eyes darted from one of us to the other, wary of taking us into her confidence. After a moment, she blurted out, "The postcard had a photo of Jenny Ho's on the front. The message said, 'Your body, your choice. I'm watching you always.'"

A collective chill settled over us with that last sentence, so I chose to focus on the first part of the message. "Your body, your choice? What do you think that means?"

"Duh," said Rachel. "'My body, my choice' is a slogan for pro-choice advocates."

Lisa's hands had commenced trembling again, so she tucked them between her tightly pressed thighs. "That's how it struck me as well. So I suggested to Thacker that he look for a connection between Jenny Ho's and, I don't know, abortion or the pro-choice movement. It seemed obvious to me"

"To me as well," I said. "Strippers probably get abortions on a regular basis."

"Mom, for god's sake," Chloe scolded.

Lisa sniffed. "Obvious to any clear-thinking person. But all he would say is 'maybe' it's related. He did agree that since the postcard shows a photo of the club, it clearly connects whoever sent it to the first anonymous clues the police got about Jenny Ho's."

Chloe was puzzled. "But if Andy agreed that there's a connection between your postcard and Jenny Ho's, I don't understand why you're upset with him. Did he say why he isn't sure there's a tie between the message on the postcard and the pro-choice movement?"

"He claimed that 'Your body, your choice' could just as easily be a physical threat to me, or maybe even a suggestion that I—that I was complicit in what happened to me in the convent."

The others were speechless, so I said, "That must have been so difficult for you to hear."

"Yes, and assuming that's true—and I hate to think it is, but who knows? —then his theory would tie the postcard to the blackmailer. So wouldn't that mean the blackmailer is the murderer? And regardless, shouldn't he be taking that pro-abortion message more seriously?"

Lisa continued to press her thighs together around her quaking hands. The insides of her thin legs must have been taking a pounding, judging by her level of agitation. "Oh, I'm just so confused and frustrated! And worried that the murder and all this harassment are connected and in the wrong hands."

Chloe's eyes darkened. I was prepared to play referee, but Rachel chimed in: "Time to move on, folks." She was now rocking gently with both hands grasping the arms of the Bentwood. More subdued than usual, but back in the game.

Lisa closed her eyes and took a deep breath. Sounding calmer, she said "Yes, please. Tell me what you've learned so far."

I said, "Alejandra, why don't you tell Lisa about our suspects."

Alejandra obediently listed the Peeping Tom, Daniela, and her husband, Eric, along with Brian, Alejandra's own ex. Rachel and I contributed their possible motives.

At the mention of Brian, Chloe asked, "By the way, did he show up with Kyle the other night like he promised?"

"Of course not." Alejandra pursed her lips. The inevitable skewering of Brian lasted for several minutes before she put an end to it by abruptly turning to Lisa. "As for this list, we don't really think any of them are guilty. Except for maybe the Peeping Tom."

Rachel waved her hand in a "maybe, maybe not" gesture that Alejandra ignored, choosing to change the subject. "I just remembered that both Rachel and Chloe were supposed to be looking for information about the Peeping Tom. Any luck, either of you? Rachel, you start."

When Rachel's response was a blank stare, Chloe prompted her. "You were supposed to contact neighbors on Nextdoor and find out what they knew. Did you do that?"

"Oh, right. No, because too much other stuff was going on. Lisa's cat shit business and all. I'll do it, though. It's only been, let's see ..." She tried to do the math on her fingers but gave up. "A few days." To counter our frowns, she declared, "Nextdoor sucks, anyway. People on there are so nosy and paranoid."

Alejandra let her off the hook. "What about you, Chloe? We know your dinner the other night got interrupted when Andy got called over to Lisa's house. Have you had a chance since then to ask him about the Peeping Tom?"

"Not really," said Chloe. "He's been pretty busy."

"Well, two nights ago you went out to dinner with him," I said as nonchalantly as possible, although my heart went flippity-flop in anticipation of the flaming eye-darts I knew would be coming my way. "No talk of the Peeping Tom?"

All eyes in the room swung from me to Chloe, who reddened. I felt a twinge of maternal guilt. But goodness, she had blown off an opportunity to squeeze information from Andy. Didn't we deserve an explanation?

Instead of eye darts, she merely frowned at me before saying, "Honestly, I tried. I complimented his handling of the case, said I was concerned about my parents' safety, told him the idea of a Peeping Tom gave me the heebie-jeebies. But he only repeated things we already knew." With a defiant look at me that was extended to include the others, she added, "I didn't want the evening to turn unpleasant and ruin the possibility of a chance to learn more."

"How romantic," Rachel said dismissively.

I said, "So to summarize, in addition to what we already knew, we now have the mysteries of Lisa's blackmail and the postcard threat she got today. And the postcards sent to Mrs. Zhang."

Chloe asked, "So, what's the connection between the

three of you who are being targeted?"

None of us could think of anything. Mrs. Zhang, Alejandra, and Lisa. They were neighbors, but essentially strangers to each other with little in common.

"We should all give that some thought and come back to it later. Right now," I said in a firm voice, anticipating resistance, "We need to talk about the dishes."

Alejandra winced. "I'm not sure we should discuss those tonight. We agreed to wait until after—" she broke off, no doubt remembering Rachel's preference to keep Lisa in the dark about the upcoming Jenny Ho's escapade.

Chloe said, "Alejandra, we've had them for three days now. It's time to turn them over to Andy." She looked from Rachel to me, seeking support. "Right?"

"You bet," I said.

"Nuh-uh," said Rachel. "We can't go to Andy yet for reasons of Alejandra's legal status as it relates to the fucking current deportation-happy administration.

Lisa was predictably startled. "What's this, now?" Her questioning eyes searched each of our faces. When no one spoke up, she asked, "What on earth are you talking about? You've found some dishes?"

While the rest of us clammed up like guilty middle-schoolers in the principal's office, Rachel was undaunted. "Go ahead and tell her," she instructed Alejandra. "She's one of us now. She won't tell Andy until we give her permission. Right, Lisa? Those are the rules."

"Well," Lisa cleared her throat. "Of course. I never repeat anything I'm told in confidence. I'm sure you wouldn't be—yes, I'll keep your secret. For now, anyway."

Alejandra's eyes sought my opinion, so I said, "Rachel's right. We invited Lisa to help us investigate, and the dishes are the biggest clue we've got so far."

In the three seconds it took Alejandra to reach a decision, Rachel grew tired of waiting. "A box of dishes showed up on Alejandra's dining room table. Origin unknown, probably garage sale or thrift store. One was missing—"

Alejandra cut her off. "I told you, I never bought those dishes. I never, ever buy anything without looking it over good first and making sure I really want it."

Lisa's grasshopper eyes darted around the room, taking in the clutter, but she was silent as Rachel continued, "Right. And since the rest of the dishes match the one in Andy's photo—the one Michael was eating from—we're trying to figure out how this box got here before we turn it over."

Lisa's response was exactly what I'd hoped for. "You can't be serious." She looked at each of us in turn until she found the most receptive pair of eyes—mine. "But this is withholding evidence. You mean to tell me you're still holding onto a box of dishes that are—I mean, it's obvious they're an important clue, if—"

"Now, don't get your panties all in a bundle," Rachel interrupted. "We have our reasons. If Alejandra gets arrested for murder, she could get deported, even if she's not convicted."

"Deported?" Lisa turned to Alejandra. "Do you mean you weren't born in America?"

Alejandra's briefly recited her immigration issues. As Lisa listened, I studied her face, which was largely unreadable since she had closed her eyes to concentrate. While I expected her to share my outlook on illegal immigration in general, I hoped she wouldn't be so strident in her views that she would hold Alejandra at fault for circumstances beyond her control.

When Alejandra had finished, Lisa got right to the point. "I see. So you're afraid that since the dishes are here on your premises, you'll be suspected of the murder."

"Sure she will," Rachel said. "She's got motive, too. Michael offered to haul off some of her possessions." She waved her arm to needlessly call our attention to the mess that surrounded us. "Made some nasty crack about it. Right, Alejandra?"

Alejandra lifted her chin. "He said I had so much junk I looked like a hoarder, and that the neighbors were disgusted."

Unnecessarily blunt, that Michael Redding. It was news to me that he had spoken those words to Alejandra. I probably should have reassured her that the neighbors thought no such thing, but the lie could not find its way onto my tongue.

It was Chloe who said, "Well, that was mean of him." She spoke directly to Alejandra. "Look, I know this is difficult, but it has to be done. Andy needs to know."

"Now, now. Don't let love get in the way of logic," Rachel smirked.

"But logic would lead us to turn over the plates," Lisa said. "To do otherwise is illegal."

"Fuck logic," Rachel muttered. "Other ideas?"

To my surprise, Lisa seemed resigned to postpone ratting us out, at least for the time being. "Well for one thing, have you tried searching the inside of the box for clues?"

Rachel said, "I unpacked all the dishes so we could count them. Probably left my fingerprints all over them, too. Another reason not to call this in." Her cackle told us it was a joke. Otherwise we wouldn't have known.

"So, you still have the dishes? Here in the house somewhere?" Lisa's expression had changed from judgmental to eager. "Maybe we should take them all out of the carton again—using gloves, of course—just to make sure there are no hidden clues. Even a loose hair might mean something."

I was impressed. I'd worried that Lisa might not be flexible enough to fit in with our group. But she showed a willingness to compromise, possibly bend a few rules. Fortunately, this flexibility was tempered by logic and caution.

As had become her habit, Alejandra looked at me for permission. I nodded. While the rest of us cleared a space on the dining room table by moving some cartons and loose items onto the floor, Alejandra retrieved the box of dishes along with a pair of gardening gloves.

Lisa's enthusiasm was contagious. She was practically rubbing her hands together. "Go ahead, Alejandra. Open it and take the dishes out, one by one. We'll all be searching for clues. Hairs, smudges that might be fingerprints. Anything."

We all crowded around while Alejandra retrieved the first plate and held it up for our scrutiny. She waited until we signaled that we'd seen nothing, then carefully set the dish aside. She repeated this until each of the five plates, six saucers, and six cups had been examined.

"Nada." Rachel voiced the disappointment we all felt.

Alejandra picked up a plate and was about to repack it when Lisa leaned over and peered into the box. "Wait," she said.

We all looked. Covering the bottom of the empty box was a swatch of white material that must have been placed there as padding for the dishes. Alejandra pulled it aside to reveal a rectangular strip of bubble wrap. On top of the bubble wrap was a small square of white paper. Alejandra left the scrap of paper in place while she lifted the cloth out of the box with two gloved fingers, unfolded it and held it toward us.

"Huh," she said. "A plain white t-shirt."

The rest of us gawked.

"What?" she asked, then turned the shirt around to find out what had struck us dumb.

"Holy shit." Rachel murmured.

The t-shirt was indeed plain white except for the startling design on the front: a stylized sketch of a topless woman in a red thong straddling a stripper pole. And scrawled in black script on the rainbow-colored stage floor beneath the woman's stiletto heels:

Jenny Ho's
Oakland, CA

Alejandra draped the t-shirt across a kitchen chair and reached for the piece of paper. "It's a receipt. From a place called Good as New. And there's an address!"

"Sounds like a second-hand store. Can you read the address?" Chloe asked.

"2107 Clancy Blvd." Alejandra held it up triumphantly, her voice taking on a "ta-da" tone as she finished, "Oakland, California! Oh my god."

We each repeated the "Oh my god" except for Rachel.

"Hold on a sec," she said, sounding more sober than she had a right to. "Alejandra, do you ever shop in Oakland?"

"No way! Ever since I moved here, I've avoided Oakland." She looked at me, suddenly alarmed. "Andy will believe me, won't he?"

"Of course," said Chloe, and I nodded. It seemed the right thing to do.

Rachel said, "If he doesn't, we'll just have to convince him."

"Well then," Lisa said. "Finally we're making progress. We need to call Thacker right away so he can trace the receipt if that's possible. What's the date on it, Alejandra?"

Alejandra squinted at the narrow slip of paper. "I think it says April 11."

She thrust the receipt toward Chloe, who verified, "Yes, April 11. About two months ago—and look: the price has been crossed off and changed by hand, with a note that says 'damaged'." The price went from $29.00 to $14.50."

"Damaged!" Rachel repeated. "Didn't that plate in the photo Thacker was showing around have chips in it?"

"Definitely," I said. "And there are also chips in one or two of the saucers. Anything else, Chloe?"

"It says, 'cash transaction.' So it may be hard to trace,

unless some clerk has an amazing memory."

"Well you never know," said Lisa. "This is a start, anyway. If Thacker can just figure out what to do with it."

Alexandra's eyes welled up. "Will he arrest me, do you think?"

We all spoke up at once to reassure her, but Lisa cut us off. She seemed almost irritated. "Of course he won't arrest you. That t-shirt ties the dishes and the murderer to that sleazy strip joint, to which you have no connection, I assume. And more importantly, you've no motive except that Redding made snide remarks about your hoard—about your accumulations." She nodded in agreement with herself. "Weak motive, to say the least. No motive, no arrest."

At our bemused expressions, she chuckled. "I read a lot of murder mysteries. And I'm hooked on those BBC mystery series."

Even Alejandra and Rachel agreed that we had no choice but to return everything to the box and call Andy. Which was easy, since Chloe had his private number programmed into her cell. She didn't even bother to identify herself, which gave me pause.

"You'd better come over to Alejandra's house." She walked away from us, into the dining room, and we heard only snatches of their brief conversation, the words "box of dishes" and "plate missing" being the only ones that mattered.

We all sat back down to await his arrival, except for Alejandra who wiped her eyes on her sleeve as she went to the kitchen to prepare more tea. Rachel raised her eyebrows at me, and I gestured that she should be the one to follow. Sloshed or not, she was the best friend Alejandra had in the room.

Alone with Lisa and me, Chloe whispered, "He won't arrest her, will he, Mom?"

"I don't think so. Lisa's right: Alejandra had no motive

to kill Redding and no connection to Jenny Ho's, which is clearly at the center of all this."

"Well," said Lisa with a cheerful smile, "at any rate, this has been an unexpectedly productive meeting."

The only rainbow was the excitement in her voice. And now that she was one of us, the opportunity for real friendship presented itself. I would have her over for coffee on the back porch soon, just the two of us, like it used to be with Sue Ellen. And she loved mystery novels! The possibility of a new book club was looking more promising all the time. Since I would no longer be the sole conservative, maybe we could even delve lightly into politics—next year would be an election year and things were already heating up. Together, Lisa and I might steer the others toward a more reasonable, unbiased outlook. It could happen.

Then Lisa's smile became conspiratorial as she surveyed the room and said in whisper, "I just don't see how anyone can live in a mess like this, do you?"

I exchanged startled looks with Chloe, who pressed her lips together as she got up without a word and went to join the others in the kitchen. I uneasily reminded myself that Lisa's response mirrored my own initial reaction to Alejandra's premises. It was a perfectly normal, if admittedly snide, response.

I opened my mouth to remind Lisa that Alejandra was under a lot of stress, what with the divorce, losing custody of her son, no family left in the country, the threatening notes, the box of dishes. The hoarding problem might solve itself once those issues were addressed. Meanwhile, we should cut the poor girl some slack.

Instead, with a weary smile, I murmured. "Yes. Well."

As Chloe and I crossed the street on our way home, she whispered, "I'm glad we didn't invite her to come along tomorrow. She'd probably pass out from horror."

19

Over breakfast the next morning, Chloe and I filled Jack in on our breakthrough: the discovery of evidence that might identify the purchaser of the dishes. But he was unwilling to give us credit.

"Breakthrough, huh? A sleazy t-shirt and a 'cash transaction' receipt? If you say so. How did Thacker take it when you told him about the dishes?"

I guess we had all expected—unrealistically, in retrospect—that Andy would maintain his usual friendly, upbeat attitude. To his credit, he had been professional throughout the terse interrogation we endured upon his arrival. Aloof, bordering on icy, even with Chloe, but professional. To our relief, he had not arrested Alejandra, but had instructed her to be at the police station the next day at 9:30 sharp to give a statement. Probably that's where she and Rachel had been headed when I watched them drive away a few minutes earlier.

Chloe defended my position. "Come on, Dad. Those dishes, along with the t-shirt as another tie-in to Jenny Ho's, ought to be a big boost to Andy's investigation. How can you not agree?"

"He already knew about the strip club, thanks to the anonymous phone tips. He should've been all over it already."

"Right," I said. "But now he has something tangible to trace. Dishes and a t-shirt. We even know where the dishes were purchased. All he has to do is find out who bought them, and he'll have the murderer."

"Right," said Chloe.

Jack said, "Maybe."

"And it gives us all the more reason to check out the club ourselves." Chloe refilled all our coffee cups. "Thank God Lisa suggested we reopen the box and look for clues. It made it easier to convince Alejandra to turn the dishes over to Andy."

Jack grumbled, "Better late than never."

Chloe's phone buzzed and after a quick glance, she excused herself and hurried upstairs to her room. No explanation given, none needed. Her relieved expression said it all.

Jack went out back to replace another broken sprinkler head, leaving me alone in the kitchen. Maybe it was the second dose of caffeine, but I found myself pacing from kitchen to living room to den to dining room, repeat, repeat.

Something about that t-shirt was nagging at me. It had been new, the $16.00 tag still on it. As cheap as it was tawdry. Who would use such a thing to line a box of dishes? Who would've bought such an offensive piece of apparel in the first place? The woman depicted on front was topless and for all practical purposes, bottomless. Okay, she was just a cartoon, but still. No one would wear such a thing in public, would they? Where might one wear it, then? At the strip club itself? Certainly not stripper attire, I should think. Too much coverage.

Who did that leave? A server or a bartender? I wished we had checked the size—it might hint at the gender. But if it had belonged to a server or bartender, why did it still have its tags?

No, more likely an enthusiastic patron—under the

influence, probably—had bought it as a souvenir and experienced buyer's remorse when the booze wore off. But why use it for packing dishes? Why not shove it into a dark closet or pawn it off on Goodwill?

I abruptly stopped pacing and sloshed coffee on my blouse.

If the dishes belonged to the killer, as seemed evident since one of the plates was used to serve Michael the Thai curry, couldn't that mean that the murderer purchased the t-shirt specifically to place in the box, yet another clue that pointed the investigation towards Jenny Ho's—and away from himself?

Intrigued by this possibility, I wanted to run it by Andy, to see if his thinking synched up with mine. Despite Chloe's faith in him, and the surprising sense of loyalty I had felt toward him in the face of Lisa's criticism, I was not bubbling over with confidence.

But Andy was probably still on the phone with Chloe. To avoid interrupting, I had best listen outside her door to find out. My plan was to walk away immediately if I heard her voice, but her words froze me in place.

"... yes, I know, but he spends a suspicious amount of time out on the porch, just watching the street. And the day we were all at Lisa's, he just happened to be walking by as we left. You don't think that's odd? ... I know, but ... Okay, but ... All right, then ... I can't tonight, I'm sorry. I've made plans with my parents ... No, I promise. I said I won't, and I won't."

I hurried back to my own room. A moment later there came a soft tap at the door.

"Mom?"

"Yes?" I faked a surprised smile as she let herself in, but she wasn't fooled.

"Did you need something?" she asked.

"What do you mean?" I braced myself for a scolding, but to my relief, she wasn't angry.

"Look, I know you just overheard me suggesting that Andy investigate Zhang Wei. I can tell you like him, and maybe I'm off base. But I think we all owe it to Andy to share our suspicions, don't you?"

"Certainly. I just think we should agree as a group before making accusations, that's all. I don't think either Alejandra or Rachel distrusts Dr. Zhang. Nor do I."

"So what? I wouldn't be at all upset if you told Andy that you had doubts about Alejandra's friend Daniela, for example. So what's with your protective attitude about Dr. Zhang?"

Good question. *His good manners and intelligence, his kind eyes and warm smile. Stimulating conversation.*

"I only know that he's a retired doctor, a nice man who moved in with his mom to make her feel safer after a neighbor was murdered. It seems a real stretch to accuse him, just because he's keeping an eye on the street, looking after his mother."

"But again, so what if it is a stretch? Any clues whatsoever should be—"

"May I ask how Andy responded to your suspicions about Zhang Wei?'

"Hmm. Well, pretty much like you did," she admitted. "So there's probably nothing for you to be concerned about. He said he's getting close to solving the case, and he basically asked me—all of us, actually—to be patient and let him handle it."

I raised my eyebrows. "So you mentioned tonight's planned excursion to him?"

She sighed. "No. Was that wrong? I was afraid he'd try to talk me out of it."

"Understandably so," I said. But I knew this wasn't the response she had wanted, so I added, "I don't see any harm in keeping it secret. Probably nothing will come of it anyway, but if it does, you can fill him in after the fact and just accept the consequences."

Her relieved eyes thanked me as she turned to go. "That's what I thought, too."

I called after her: "Is it possible you don't trust Zhang Wei because he's Chinese?" When she whirled to glare at me, I grinned. "Gotcha."

Relieved that Andy shared my viewpoint—Wei was behaving like a devoted son and nothing more—I picked up my phone, thinking I'd call him to share my thoughts about the disgusting t-shirt. But seeing as how he had asked Chloe—and all of us, according to her—to butt out because he was close to solving the case, I would respect that. For now, anyway.

Before dinner that evening, Jack suggested a walk. We went on a fifteen-minute jaunt that included a tour of the immediate neighborhood. Returning, as we approached our house, Jack remarked, "There he is. Mr. Eagle-eye. Guardian of the neighborhood."

How annoying.

"Has Chloe been talking to you?"

He looked surprised. "No. Why?"

When Wei called out "Good evening," Jack responded in kind. I smiled and waved, then followed him into the house.

"Rachel wants us to leave for Oakland by 7:15," I reminded him.

He went upstairs to shower, and as I prepared the salmon with rice and asparagus, a nutritious meal I had planned with Chloe in mind, I kept puzzling over why she and Jack had such burrs up their behinds about Zhang Wei. In Jack's case, maybe it really was because Wei was Chinese. I hoped not.

Maybe I felt differently about Wei because I'd spent more time with him—although not all that much, really. There had been only a couple of chats, but each time we spoke I had gained insight into his character. They hadn't had the exposure I'd had to his easy manner, the soothing voice, the engaging warmth and good humor.

I found myself searching for an excuse to pay him another front-porch visit. Then I remembered the receipt I'd snagged as it blew across Mrs. Zhang's front yard on that windy night last week. It would still be in the pocket of the jacket I'd tossed onto the bedroom chair.

The clock on the microwave told me there was no time for a social call this evening. I sighed. Oh well, there was really no hurry, was there? With the rice already simmering, salmon in the oven, and asparagus set to steam, I hurried upstairs for a quick shower of my own.

On my way up, I crossed paths with Chloe, who was pocketing her phone as she giggled to herself about something. I guessed it was probably some witty text message from Andy, but she patted my shoulder and said, "You can relax, Mom. Rachel helped Alejandra empty her van and they took it to the carwash." She paused, still smiling. "For your benefit. How about that?"

I sniffed. "Unnecessary," I said. "But much appreciated."

20

"Twenty bucks a head just to walk through the door?" Jack grumbled as the leather-clad hostess led us through a room whose walls and stainless-steel furnishings were awash in revolving colors: garish red to shocking blue to electric pink to neon green. The recorded music, which I assumed would be classified as hard rock or heavy metal—I'd never really figured out the difference, having lost interest in rock music when it took a turn for the worse back in the mid-seventies—was so loud that Jack had to shout to be heard.

"What are you complaining about?" Chloe admonished him. "Rachel paid for all of us."

The hostess led us to a table against the back wall, either because she read my eyes or because we weren't the kind of party they wanted anywhere near the revolving center stage—which was currently empty, as Rachel had predicted it would be so early in the evening, except for what I assumed were two dancers in loose, sheer kimonos who were stretching their limbs, warming up. I hoped we would be gone before they got around to entertaining us and the other early-bird patrons who had yet to arrive.

A server in a nude-colored spandex bikini that changed colors every few seconds along with the rest of her, including the green (or possibly blue) spiky hair and the unnaturally long fake black lashes, approached our table with a reluctance that suggested it had been assigned to her as punishment. Perhaps she had pegged us as an unlikely source of generous tips.

"Hey there," she said with a lack of enthusiasm that bordered on rudeness. "My name is Marty and I'll be taking care of you tonight. Can I get you started with some drinks?"

Rachel, who had put herself in charge of our adventure with no argument from the rest of us, ordered a round of beers and—to my dismay—shots of tequila. I threw Jack a warning look, and he held up both hands. "Just the beer for me, please." He grinned uncomfortably at the server, whose expression had warmed somewhat as she reevaluated the tip potential. "Designated driver," he explained.

"Bring his shot anyway," said Rachel. "We won't let it go to waste. And we'll run a tab."

"Sure thing." She was downright perky now. "I'll be back in a sec with your drinks."

When she was out of earshot, Rachel said, "See how it's done? You have to get them on your side."

"More make-up than clothes," I observed.

Jack had held onto the cocktail menu. "Fourteen dollars for a glass of beer?"

"You don't get out much, do you, Mr. M.?" Rachel leaned forward and motioned for us to come closer. "Like I said before, just let me handle the Q and A, okay? I'm not bragging, but I think I might relate to these people better than you all do."

"No argument there," said Jack.

Rachel chose to believe he was agreeing to keep his mouth shut, and she looked at the rest of us in turn, soliciting nods from each of us. Chloe and Alejandra complied.

"But what if we have a valid question that might move things along?" I asked.

She shook her head. "Too dangerous. You might arouse suspicion. I know what I'm doing, okay? Trust me."

As Marty placed our drinks on the table, Rachel went right to work. "Not too busy tonight," she commented. "Is this typical for a Thursday?"

I looked around. A few customers had trickled in behind us. There was a table of three men who should have been playing with their grandkids somewhere, another table with a solitary young man in business attire who was nursing a cocktail while ogling the dancers warming up on stage, and yet another table with a steamy couple who should have gotten a room, and probably soon would, judging by the way the man was stroking the woman's thigh beneath her short skirt.

Marty chirped, "Yes, weekends are a lot busier. It gets crazy sometimes."

Rachel nodded knowingly. "I guess it's the same everywhere." When Marty looked at her curiously, she added, "I tend bar at a club in Las Oliviñas."

"Las Oliviñas?" Her smile broadened at this unexpected opportunity to work the tips. "I knew someone from out there. He was planning to move here when—" As she broke off with a suspicious abruptness, I followed her eyes to the bar, where a tall, well-dressed man, middle-aged, with slicked-back dark hair and an air of authority stood conversing with the bartender.

Marty dropped her eyes as she set the last glass of beer on the table in front of Alejandra. "Will there be anything else right now?"

"What's your friend's name?" Rachel asked with casual interest, ignoring the server's abrupt change of subject. "Las Oliviñas is like a small town in some ways. Maybe one of us knows him."

The distracting wash of revolving colors didn't conceal Marty's discomfort.

"Maybe it wasn't Las Oliviñas. In fact, it wasn't. I

remember now." She gave us a "silly me" smile. "It was Los Gatos he was from."

Rachel, who had shown impressive restraint up to this point, fell victim to her own impatience.

"Your friend's name wouldn't happen to be Michael Redding, would it?" she asked in a conversational tone. She sampled her beer while holding Marty's eyes. The rest of us exchanged bemused glances: so much for not arousing suspicion.

But Rachel's brash move paid off: at the mention of Michael's name, Marty visibly flinched. She recovered quickly, but not before we saw fright pass across her (currently yellow) features.

"No. As I said, my friend was from Los Gatos." Her eyes shifted again toward the imposing man at the bar, who was surveying the room, possibly estimating tonight's profits. I thought his eyes locked briefly with Marty's just before she added, "My mistake."

"Oh," said Rachel. "Too bad. I was hoping maybe it was Michael. He was our neighbor and a good friend of mine. His band used to play at the Coal Bin, the bar in Los Oliviñas where I worked." She paused. "He passed recently."

"I'm sorry for your loss," said Marty. "I didn't know him, though."

"Are you sure? The band played here sometimes, too," Rachel persisted. "Crocodile Lips? Great band, but I can't really imagine them without Michael on percussion. He was awesome."

Marty chewed her lower lip. She clearly wanted to escape but didn't want to risk losing her tip by being rude. "Oh, sure. I do remember that band. They haven't played here for a while now."

"Probably fell apart after Michael was murdered," Rachel said. "Such a shame."

With another surreptitious glance at the bar, Marty said nervously, "Murdered? I heard he died from an allergic reaction. He had a peanut allergy, someone told me."

"So you did know him, then?" Rachel persisted.

"Not really, no. I just knew the band's drummer had died, that's all. A reaction to something he ate, they said."

"Possibly," Rachel said. "But there were mysterious circumstances, so the police are investigating his death as a homicide."

"Oh," was Marty's quiet response. I studied her face and thought I saw traces of several possible emotions: Fear? Mistrust? Sadness? One thing was certain: she was not surprised at what should have been a shocking revelation—not until Rachel's next comment, which startled the rest of us as much as the server, since it was an outright lie.

"I'm surprised the police haven't been in here to interview you all. Because they seem to have narrowed the investigation down to this place, and we heard they were getting ready to make an arrest." She downed her shot of tequila and looked around the table. "Are we ready for another round?"

Beside me, Jack muttered, "What the *hell*?"

"I think that means yes, don't you?" Rachel grinned at Marty.

The server hurried away, but a few minutes later, it was the slick, black-haired man from the bar who came over and stood behind Alejandra while directing his fake, toothy smile at Jack. He leaned across the table and extended his hand. "Art Doherty, owner of this establishment. You're here to watch the dancing, are you?"

"What else?" Jack said with a nervous smile.

He glanced around the table. "These your beautiful wife and daughters, Mr. ...?"

"Jack Middleton, and yes, this is my family." He cleared his throat and tried for a laugh, an effort thwarted by his obvious discomfort. "This is a family establishment, I gather?"

The practiced smile wavered, and the man's tone became a tad less friendly. "Jack, if you're here for the dancing and you continue to buy drinks, you can bring your grandma for all I care. But I'll have to ask you not to upset my servers. Marty says one of you was asking about a friend of ours who passed recently." He looked at each of us in turn, trying to suss out the guilty party. When we didn't rat Rachel out, he continued, "We're like a family here, and still wrapping our heads around Redding's death."

"We're sorry for your loss, sir," Rachel said. "Michael was our friend, too. We were just trying to—"

"To find out what we know about his murder?" Having identified the agitator, he turned his stony gaze upon her, his voice calm but mildly threatening. "We've already told the police anything we thought might help them find his killer. You don't look like detectives to me, so how about if you enjoy the show tonight and leave off upsetting my staff? Can we agree to that?"

Rachel reached for Jack's untouched tequila and downed it. "This is not a good way to make your customers happy. Happy customers drink more and tip better. I know because I worked in a bar for nine years."

"You know what, Mr. Doherty?" I hurried to interject, fearing a scathing rebuttal to Rachel's critique. "Would you mind cancelling that round she just ordered? I think some of us have had enough."

Art Doherty's eyes never left Rachel's as he answered, "I think that might be for the best." Before walking away, he said to Jack, who was reaching for his wallet, "Your drinks are on me. But I'm sure you'll want to be generous with Marty's tip to make up for upsetting her."

As Alejandra and Chloe downed their tequila shots, Rachel reached for mine, which was untouched. "I'm not leaving this behind."

As we made our way to the exit, I heard Jack mumble,

"Jesus," as we passed the table where the lone business-man was being visited by one of the dancers, who had shed her kimono and was gyrating her thong-covered privates within inches of his smiling face.

I nudged him. "Eyes straight ahead, Mr. Middleton."

Just inside the front door, we waited for Alejandra, who had claimed she couldn't hold her bladder a minute more and opted to take a chance on the ladies' room.

"Yuck," I said, and Chloe giggled.

"You can't catch anything from a toilet seat, Mom."

"Except for a bad case of crabs." Rachel jabbed me with her elbow.

Jack said, "Well, this trip was entertaining, but I'm not sure how productive it was."

"You're wrong," said Rachel in typically blunt fashion. "They definitely do not want to talk about Michael Redding's murder, and there must be a reason for that."

"I agree," I said, and shared an observation of my own. "Did you see that on the wall behind the bar they have t-shirts for sale just like the one we found in the box?"

Rachel exclaimed, "Good eye, Marilyn. I didn't notice that."

Just then, Marty, our reluctant server, hurried out of the ladies' room, ignoring us on her way back to work. She was followed by Alejandra, who wore a baffled expression. "Let's go," she said. As we walked out, she looked behind her as if she feared being followed. And as we started toward the car, she thrust a piece of paper at me.

"Marty followed me into the bathroom and handed me this flyer. There was a whole stack of them in there."

I unfolded the paper, and we stopped to huddle and read it despite Jack's nervous plea to "Keep moving."

I scanned it without bothering with the small print. All that mattered were the first few lines, which made my discovery of souvenir t-shirts seem trivial in comparison.

Reject Defunding of Planned Parenthood!
Join our Rally
July 6, 1:00 p.m. at Oakland Civic Center Plaza
Your Body, Your Choice!

"And look at this." Alejandra pointed to the bottom right corner of the flyer, where the name Marty Clement had been scrawled, followed by a phone number and the words "Call me."

"She ran out of the bathroom before I could ask any questions."

Rachel crowed, "Still think it wasn't a productive night, Mr. M.?" And as we settled into Alejandra's spotless van for the ride home, she inquired, "Anyone but me want to stop by the Coal Bin for another round?"

21

Chloe was out having pizza with Andy. On our drive home the previous evening (which had not included a stopover at the Coal Bin, despite Rachel's whining), we had agreed as a group that Andy should be given the flyer with Marty's phone number along with other details of our trip. After Rachel had failed to wrestle the flyer from my hands, insisting that she should contact Marty before getting Andy involved, she settled down and agreed with us that Chloe was the best candidate to represent, and if necessary, defend us. Chloe was understandably nervous, seeing as how Andy had requested that we butt out of the investigation.

As Jack and I finished our leftovers out on the patio, he pointed out that nothing had been said by our server or her boss that stood out as incriminating evidence. True, Marty had first said she didn't know Michael, although her response upon hearing his name had suggested otherwise. But it could also be true, as Mr. Doherty had claimed, that she had been upset by his death and simply didn't want to discuss it—especially since a murder investigation was in progress.

I said, "Still, that flyer with the pro-abortion reference clearly echoes the message on the postcard sent to Lisa with a photo of Jenny Ho's on the front. And Marty suggested that Alejandra take it, and offered up her phone number, so that must mean something. We'll see what Andy thinks."

As he loaded the dishwasher, Jack suggested we watch another episode of "Longmire" to distract ourselves. I begged off as I remembered the receipt I had been meaning to return to the Zhangs.

I hurried upstairs, where I pulled the receipt from the pocket of the jacket I'd worn the night I'd found it. It was faded and smeared as if dampened by rain, but by holding it under the lamp and squinting, I finally made out the familiar name of the establishment just as Jack called from downstairs, "Marilyn? You in bed already? I can't find the darn remote."

When I didn't respond, he came upstairs and found me sitting on the bed, eyes glued to the receipt. Nothing was readable except the date and the name of the strip joint.

"Oh, god," I murmured.

"What's up? What is it, Marilyn?"

Silently, I handed it over and fell backwards onto the bed. *How could I have been so naïve?* While I gazed at the ceiling, silently chastising myself, he adjusted his glasses and turned the receipt this way and that until he grunted in recognition.

"Where the hell did you get this?"

"Mrs. Zhang's driveway," I said. "Last week. I was meaning to return it in case it was important. But I haven't worn the jacket since then, and I forgot."

He extended a hand to help me up and we went downstairs, where I paced the living room floor while Jack made the call to Andy. As I listened to him explain our latest discovery, I started to shiver.

I had refused to see what Chloe and even Jack had pointed out to me. Even now, I couldn't picture the refined Zhang Wei patronizing a strip club. I tried to imagine him hammered, telling the waitress in a slurred voice to add one of those sleazy t-shirts to his tab. But my disappointment in Wei was overshadowed by fright. Had I unknowingly befriended a killer?

That anonymous tip Andy had shared with us that first night: "Check out Jenny Ho's. Dope deal gone wrong ..." Gynecologists had access to drugs, didn't they?

When Jack was finished breaking the latest news to Andy, he hurried through the house, checking the locks on doors and windows. "Jesus Christ," he said to me in passing. "Mr. Chang, a murderer. A dope dealer, maybe. Who would've thought it?

"Not Chang, Zhang," I mumbled. "Zhang, not Chang. Zhang Wei." Rachel would've been proud.

While Jack made the rounds, I put on a pot of decaf. Then we sat down at the dining room table to await the detective's arrival.

Chloe and Andy cut short their date and arrived less than twenty minutes later. They declined the coffee, and we stood in the foyer while Jack presented Andy with the receipt. Chloe laid her hand on my shoulder. "You all right, Mom?"

"Sure," I said, keeping my voice light. "Just a little alarmed at the prospect of a murderer living next door."

Andy was all business. "Now let's not get ahead of ourselves. We have only the establishment name, not the customer's identity, although we might be able to trace that by the credit card info." He scanned it again. "Although only the last four digits are printed out, and they're all smudged and hard to read. But it's something to go on. I'll run it through the lab."

"You can read the date, at least," I said, sounding snippier than I was aiming for. "It's May something, not long before Michael's death. Shouldn't that help?" It didn't seem all that difficult to me. *Call Jenny Ho's and confiscate their books, amateur.*

"It's a little more complicated than that, Marilyn." Then he lost the condescending smile and went into interrogation mode. "I understood Jack to say you found this in your own privet. Is that correct?"

"Yes, but it's the hedge that separates our yard from Mrs. Zhang's. The wind blew it loose, and I grabbed it as I was headed over to Alejandra's house."

"I see. So technically," he said, "that could mean the receipt belongs to you or Jack."

"You've got to be kidding me!" Jack exploded. "Why in hell would we call you to report finding a receipt that belonged to us?"

Unruffled, Andy turned to me. "So this is not your receipt, Marilyn? Look carefully before answering." With infuriating politeness, he held the slip of paper within a foot of my eyes. I slapped it away. Of all the insults.

"Of course not! Like Jack said—"

"And it's not your receipt either, Jack?"

"Hell no, it's not mine. And I resent the implication. This is so obvious that even—even Marilyn's little band of amateur detectives could see it."

I let that pass. Chloe glared at him.

"Maybe that's true, Jack," Andy said, maintaining his professional demeanor. "But these are questions I have to ask. It's procedural, no offense intended." He glanced again at the receipt before tucking it into his jacket pocket.

How did it get all smeared like that?" Jack asked suddenly. "It hasn't rained in over a month."

Andy nodded. "I was wondering the same thing. The privet takes water from a dripline, I assume. No watering?"

"None," Jack and I said together.

"Who knows, then? Dew, maybe. Anyway, I'll go call on Dr. Zhang now. But even if the receipt does belong to him, the fact that he might've visited Jenny Ho's doesn't prove that he's Michael Redding's killer."

Chloe voiced what we were all thinking. "But Andy, in

view of the text tips you got and the thrift store receipt and the t-shirt in the box with the dishes, plus that flyer from last night, if this is his receipt, then—"

"It would mean that Dr. Zhang visited a strip club in Oakland at least once and lost the receipt for the evening's purchases. That's all. And as of right now, we don't even know that the receipt is his."

"Will you stop by again after you've talked with him?" Chloe asked. "We'd feel better knowing if you—I mean, how it went and all."

"Sure," he said, his eyes softening as he patted her arm. "I'll do that. And listen, try not to worry, okay?"

"Sure thing," Jack growled as he bolted the door behind Andy. "A killer is probably sitting on the porch next door, taking in the night air, but there's nothing to be concerned about." His grumble grew into a rant. "No sir, no need to worry. Why, that receipt probably belongs to us, Marilyn. We just forgot all about it, is all!" The words trailed after him as he stalked off to fume in front of the TV. "Detective Hambrain is on the job. No fear."

Chloe was seething, but she knew this wasn't the time to object to the latest insulting epithet. As for me, after the conversation we'd just had with Andy, I wasn't in the mood to defend him.

Half an hour later, Andy was back, and we all took our seats at the dining room table. Our anxiety was so obvious that he got straight to the point instead of hinting for dessert as he might have done.

"Look," he said. "The details of my conversation with Dr. Zhang are confidential. But I will tell you enough to hopefully give you peace of mind."

Peace of mind? Hah. If the receipt belonged to Wei, which seemed more likely than not, I'd be disappointed and sickened. I might even throw up the dinner that was already threatening to mutiny. If the receipt wasn't his, then a killer was still at large. A no-win scenario.

"Dr. Zhang professes to know nothing about the receipt, and as incredible as you might consider this to be, I believe him."

"That's such a relief!" Not exactly peace of mind, but at least my dinner would stay down.

With Chloe's and Jack's quizzical eyes on me, I hurried to add, "I mean, if it's true, then we're not living next door to a murderer. That's good to know."

Jack turned to Andy. "But if it's not Zhang's receipt— although we have only his word to go on there, right? — and it's not ours, then how did it get in the privet between the two houses?"

Andy swallowed the last of his coffee. "That mystery remains to be solved," he said. "By me." His eyes met mine. "That is, if your neighborhood detective agency is willing to trust me to do my job." He looked at Jack. "And did I hear that you've recently become a member, Jack?"

Jack scoffed. "Designated driver, is all. And I promise you there won't be any more of that nonsense. I told them it was a harebrained idea."

Andy hesitated. "Actually, your field trip was helpful," he admitted, "in that it strengthened a connection I had already made."

Sure you had. "That's good to know," I said. "The flyer Alejandra found in the bathroom, right? And Marty the waitress?"

Caught off-guard by my direct inquiry, he nodded. "Yes, but unfortunately, Ms. Marty Clement has had to take a few days off for a family emergency and isn't answering her phone." Then he remembered protocol. "I'm not at liberty to tell you anything more right now.

"Of course you're not," said Jack. "Some things are confidential."

"Anyhow, I encourage you all to keep putting your heads together. But please don't put yourselves in danger. If you uncover something that requires an investigative visit, come to me and let me handle it. And let me know immediately when you find something as important as those dishes." He waggled his finger at me, then at Chloe. "That box is a key piece of evidence."

"Sorry about that," Chloe said. "As I've told you several times tonight."

They exchanged smiles. All was forgiven.

"Well then," Jack said, as Chloe walked Andy to his car. "I guess there's nothing for us to worry about." His voice dripped disgust as he checked the time and started upstairs. "You coming to bed?"

"Soon," I said. The decaf in my cup was cold and stale, so I tossed it and poured myself half a glass of Merlot. It wasn't my habit to drink after dinner, but these were not normal times. The first sip went down easy, and I sat down at the table to think.

When Chloe came back inside, she said, "Whew, huh?" She poured herself a full glass of wine and went to watch TV.

I thought about joining her, but I was in no mood to be distracted by dark misadventures of adolescents trapped in the Upside Down. Relief about the receipt, along with the detective's faint praise of our group's participation in the investigation, had energized me.

I should've been disappointed that the receipt I'd found in Mrs. Zhang's yard hadn't led to the arrest of Michael Redding's murderer, since it meant that the killer was still free—possibly somewhere in the neighborhood. Instead, I was relieved and happy that Andy believed Wei to be innocent—isn't that what he implied? Inexperienced though the detective was, his title alone lent him some credibility, didn't it? So there was no reason why Wei and I shouldn't resume our neighborly front porch chats.

But what if Andy had told Wei that Jack and I had jumped to the conclusion that the receipt belonged to him? That could certainly make our next encounter awkward.

But he should understand that we only went to Thacker as a precaution: we had all been encouraged to turn over any possible piece of evidence. Even Andy had said we did the right thing.

I would try to get some sleep in case a meeting was called later. Maybe Wei would be on the porch smoking as I left the house, and we could chat briefly.

But then a text came in from Alejandra:

```
No meeting tonight. Sinus headache. Sorry.
(sad-face emoji)
```

Darn. I wasn't sure if my disappointment stemmed from the cancelled meeting or from the missed opportunity to see Wei. The possibility that Andy might have said something to embarrass me ("You know those two, Nosy Nellies that they are ....") began to feel like a certainty.

I called to Chloe, "No meeting tonight. Alejandra's got a headache. I'm going up to bed." Then I asked myself, *what for*? It wasn't as if I expected to sleep, so why waste time kicking the sheets and punching my pillow?"

Would Wei be outside on the porch now, brooding about Andy's visit? There was no way I'd be able to sleep without making sure he wasn't angry with me. Before going upstairs, I would peek outside, and if I saw the glow of his cigarette, I would get this over with sooner rather than later.

Quiet as a housecat on the prowl, I opened the front door and stepped outside. There was no cigarette glow, but Wei was indeed on the porch. And he was speaking to someone standing at the bottom of his steps.

"Go home, now," he said in a firm, fatherly voice. "Sleep it off, okay, dear?"

"Bullshit," Rachel slurred. "Not until you admit the truth!"

22

I was as flabbergasted as Wei when Rachel let out a wail and started to bawl at the sight of me. His worried eyes followed as I hurried over and placed my hands on her shoulders. "Now, now, Rachel. What's this?"

"Mom?" Chloe had come outside and stood watching us from the other side of the privet.

"Come and help me, honey."

I turned Rachel toward her own house, but she pulled away and gestured at Wei, shouting between sobs. "He's lying, Marilyn! It was so loud, coming out of his yard. You could hear it all over the street!" Her eyes were so pathetically hopeful that my throat tightened when she asked me, "Did you hear it from your house, maybe?"

Chloe joined me at her side. "Hear what, Rachel? Mom, what's going on?"

"I'll explain later," I said. "Let's get her home and put her to bed."

But Rachel jerked her arm free again. "That voice!" she answered Chloe. "It's a fucking CB radio, that's what it is!" Her sobs had subsided and now she turned to glare at Wei. "What's your problem, asshole? You were right here on the porch. You would've heard it as well as I did! Why can't you admit it?"

Understandably perplexed, Wei seemed about to address Rachel, then looked at me instead. His eyes changed instantly—kindness and concern replaced by an aloofness that felt like a reprimand, and when he spoke the chill in his voice was undeniable.

"I trust you two will see the young lady home." With a dismissive nod, he turned and went into the house, closing the door behind him. Almost certainly, Andy had told him of Jack's and my suspicions. Nosy Nellies. I felt a little ill.

With Wei out of her reach, Rachel let herself be led home and did not object when we sat her down between us on the sofa. She leaned her head back and let out an angry "Aargg! I am so fucking wasted!"

"Yes," I said. "That seems to be the case. What were you thinking, confronting Dr. Zhang that way? What was that all about?"

Knowing how much she loved talking about herself, I feared a replay of the unnecessary details: Deb's cheating, Rachel's own vindictive mistreatment of her dying spouse, blah blah. Before she got to the point, Jack might wake up and wonder why I hadn't come up to bed.

On the other hand, other than some gibberish about a CB radio, Rachel had never revealed specifics to me about the mysterious voice she claimed to hear sometimes. I knew only the details Alejandra had confided.

If Jack woke up worried, he could text me, as we had agreed.

"Earlier, you mentioned the voice," I prodded, after making sure my phone hadn't been silenced. "You've heard it again?"

"Oh yes. Every few days it happens." With a defiant glance, she waggled her finger at Chloe. "I'm not making this up. Nobody believes me, but I'm not."

"I believe you," Chloe reassured her. "I see no reason you would lie about such a thing. Will you tell us more?"

"Yes," I said. "Maybe if we know what the voice is

saying, we can help."

"It's that bitch Liliana, the slut Deb had an affair with," she said. She turned to Chloe. "Deb admitted everything to me when she was first diagnosed with cancer."

Oh boy. Would we have to listen to the entire tawdry tale before she got to the important part?

"I hated her. Both of them. I made Deb's life miserable. Even after I knew she had cancer. I was in shock, I think."

Yes, we know all this, I wanted to say. *Tell us about the voice.* But my improved listening skills kicked in, and I held my tongue.

"Big surprise I should take to alcohol, after what she did to me. I was just coping the best I could."

Then, as if she too had grown tired of the "poor me" routine, she suddenly segued to a new, disturbing chapter in her story.

"The first time it happened was two weeks after the funeral. I'd been to Trader Joe's and was putting my groceries away when I heard a woman's voice coming from the living room. I was hungover but sober, hadn't had a drink since the night before." She looked from Chloe to me, measuring our responses. "I swear."

"We believe you," Chloe assured her. "Go on."

"I thought I was losing it. From what she was saying, it was obviously Liliana talking to Deb, although I couldn't hear Deb's side of the conversation—it was like something from a horror movie. The dead wife and her lover haunting the widow. Trying to drive her nuts."

Having heard this much from Alejandra, I was better prepared than Chloe, whose eyes widened into cartoonish circles. Welcome to Crazyville, honey.

"They were flirting with each other, except I could only hear Liliana, not Deb." Rachel's voice grew even more bitter. "They were talking about me. And about their—their hookups on the road."

Reading Chloe's blank stare, she explained, "Long-haul truck drivers. Overnights in cheap motels and parking lots of all-night truck stops. How romantic, right?"

In the interest of hurrying things along, I contributed something Alejandra had told me. "So when you hear the woman's voice, is she encouraging Deb to leave you?"

"Oh you bet. Ridiculing my job, as if there's shame in bartending. That's the first conversation I overheard, actually."

She rested her head on the back of the sofa again. "I went into the bathroom and threw up. Just thinking about it now makes me want to vomit."

"Oh goodness. Should we get you to the bathroom?"

She patted the hand I had laid on her arm. "Nah, I'm good. Thanks, though. You're a real bud."

Chloe asked, "Did you go into the room where the voice was coming from?"

"Yep. Then it moved into the bedroom. And when I went in there, it started blaring from the kitchen. She was playing games with me, the slut."

While we pondered this, she continued, "The second time, though, a few days later, her voice came through my computer. Scared the shit out of me. Another time it blared out of the TV. Right in the middle of a 'Seinfeld' rerun."

"Does it always happen inside the house?" Chloe asked.

"Nope. I've heard it in the backyard more than once. In the front yard only once, and then tonight was the first time it came from across the street." She pointed her finger at me. "From your boyfriend's yard."

"And the voice never speaks directly to you?" Chloe's quiet, sympathetic interrogation style was having a calming effect on Rachel.

"No, they just yammer at each other. And it's only her talking, then a pause, then her answering whatever Deb had said to her. I never get to hear Deb's voice," she added wistfully, as if that wouldn't be even more hair-raising.

"How many times has it happened?" I asked.

She rubbed her forehead. "I'm not sure. Maybe fifteen or twenty."

"That must be terrifying," Chloe said, which should have been my line.

"Indeed," I contributed.

"No shit. But anyway, I remembered this time when I was a kid, my aunt complained about how her TV would pick up transmissions from her neighbor's CB radio in his garage. So I decided that was the only explanation that makes sense." She looked from Chloe to me, soliciting agreement.

Chloe's eyes met mine: *What the hell?*

"Well now," I said. "I guess a CB radio is one possible explanation. But your aunt had this experience—what, twenty years ago or more? I mean, do truckers even use CB radios to communicate these days?"

Rachel's eyes welled up, and I regretted my words. "Not that it couldn't happen," I added.

"Mom has a point though, Rachel." Chloe said. "Surely truck drivers have upgraded their communications technology along with the rest of the world."

"You would think so, wouldn't you? But Deb certainly used her CB. And anyway, I googled it and most truckers still have them because they've been the norm for a thousand years, and it's almost like a fraternity or something. They really get into all that corny trucker lingo. All that 'breaker one-nine' shit. They still think it's cool." She sniffed. "Whatever."

"But Rachel," Chloe asked carefully, "do you really think Liliana would be so vindictive as to go to all this trouble? She would have to be—I don't know—criminally insane or something. Right, Mom?"

"I should think so."

Rachel said, "Well if it's not Liliana, then who in the hell is it? I've tried to convince myself it's just two unknown truckers flirting with each other to stay awake on the road. And I was almost convinced, but the comments were just too personal."

"Are you sure? You already told us she made fun of your job," I said. "But that could have been a coincidence. Many women work as bartenders these days."

"Sure. Even when their chatting progressed from dissing my chosen occupation to discussing plans to meet up for coffee, one last face-to-face before heading into town, and even when she said the name of the place, Rhoda's, I told myself 'so what?' Lots of truck drivers know the place. So what if it happened to be Deb's favorite breakfast spot? But then it got so much more personal, the things she said."

"There must be another explanation," Chloe insisted.

"I'm telling you, it has to be Liliana. Otherwise, it's some weird psychic phenomenon kind of thing." She gave me a defiant look. "Karma, or God or somebody, making me listen to how they used to talk about me behind my back before Deb died. Either that or I'm just batshit crazy."

Bingo! I thought. *We have got to get this woman into analysis.* At best, she was delusional. At worst, psychotic. Another troubling possibility occurred to me: while Rachel was still bartending, in those days following Deb's funeral when she had admittedly drunk too much on the job, had she confided in Michael Redding during one of his gigs at the bar? Told him her tale of betrayal and woe, confessed to hearing voices? What if instead of offering sympathy, he had laughed at her?

Rachel blew her nose and repeated, "It has to be Liliana."

Chloe persisted, "Did the speaker ever actually say Deb's name? Or yours? Or hers? If not, how can you be a hundred percent sure it's not two other drivers? It could be that—"

Rachel interrupted her. "You've no idea. I've had to

listen to that bitch flirting with Deb. Not just flirting. She knows things. Both our names and yes, she uses them. She even brings up one specific sex act that Deb could never talk me into trying. I mean, who does that stuff? I'm not a prude, but damned if I'm gonna—"

I cut her off. "Does this only happen when you're drinking?" Good listening skills be damned. Some roads are better left untraveled.

"I told you, I was sober that first time." She thought for a moment. "I guess I was shitfaced some of the times. I mean, I was miserable and lonely, so why not drink?"

Chloe asked, "Have you thought of getting in touch with Liliana, having a conversation with her? You might be able to tell by talking to her whether or not she's hiding something."

"I'd rather sleep with Mitch McConnell than talk to that bitch." She teared up again.

"Maybe you could try therapy again," I suggested. "A good psychologist could help you to cope with the stress, if nothing else."

"With drugs, sure. But I've already got Zoloft for the depression and Valium to help me sleep." She closed her eyes again. "I guess I'll have to learn to live with it. But sometimes when it's especially loud, it just seems unreal to me that someone—like that Zhang over there, and the cat lady—I just need to know that other people can hear it, too—that it's not just me. And then I get desperate. I just lose it when they claim not to hear anything. That's sick, I guess."

She would get no argument about that.

"So what's the point in throwing more bucks at a therapist? Not that I don't have lots of money, because I do," she said for Chloe's benefit, since I had been informed of her inheritance more than once already. "Deb left me enough money to live on forever. Guilt money."

"Well, that's something, anyway," said Chloe. "But you

know, I think Mom's right. Since you've got the money, what's the harm in trying again?" Her voice brightened. "I mean, what if it's the medication that's causing you to hear voices? I've heard of that happening."

"I knew you wouldn't believe me. Nobody does."

"Of course we believe you!" I said. "It's the source of the voices that we're questioning."

She cradled her head in her hands. "I don't know. Maybe I am crazy. I probably am."

"No, I'm sure you're not crazy," Chloe said. "I'm betting you need your medication adjusted. Maybe the Valium on top of the Zoloft is too much."

"And the wine can't be helping," I said. "The combination might not be the best thing for you right now, with all the stress you're under. The stress we're all under."

"Fuck it," she said. "I need to crash now. I just—I just—it's so scary. I never know when it might happen again. Maybe if I have a little more wine, I can fall asleep—"

"I'll stay here," Chloe said unexpectedly. "Just give me a blanket and a pillow. I'll be right here on the sofa. If you hear the voice again, wake me up and we'll face it together, okay?"

"Really?" Rachel took Chloe's hand and brought it to her lips for a quick kiss. "Oh my god. You'd do that for me? You're so awesome. Marilyn, your baby girl is so awesome." She let her head fall onto Chloe's shoulder.

"On one condition," said Chloe.

"Anything you say, my new bestie." She twisted her head to look at me. "She's my new bestie, Marilyn."

"I'll stay here tonight, and tomorrow morning you'll call that therapist and ask for a phone conference about this voice you're hearing. If she wants you to come into her office, you'll make an appointment. Deal?"

"Dammit. I knew there was a catch." But she sounded relieved. As for me, I was not so sure I wanted my daughter to spend the night on the sofa of a delusional person who heard voices and flew into a rage when others claimed not to hear them. I hoped Rachel would reconsider and decline Chloe's offer.

"Whatever," she said. "You don't have to sleep on the sofa. There's a futon in Deb's office—my office now. Blankets and pillows in the closet."

"Well then," I said. "I guess I'll go home now."

Chloe walked me to the door. As I hugged her, I whispered "I'll leave my phone on. Call if she gets out of hand. Or call Andy. Or just 911."

My concern seemed to annoy her. "Come on, Mom. Rachel isn't dangerous."

"I know," I lied. Then I added, "I'm proud of you, sweetie. If you can get her to call the therapist—"

"What are you two conspiring about?" Rachel mumbled, rubbing her eyes with the backs of her hands. "Go home, Marilyn. We've got this."

As I hurried across the street, I peered into the shadows on Mrs. Zhang's porch, but there was no sign of Wei. The memory of his cool dismissal brought back my guilt and chagrin. I would have to find a way to apologize.

But wouldn't he have done the same—contacted Thacker if he'd suspected Jack or me? Still, why had we jumped to conclusions with no more evidence than a receipt blowing across his yard? A receipt that could have belonged to anyone on the street—or even a neighbor around the corner. Maybe it had ridden the high wind of that evening from two blocks away or more, come to a temporary stop in the privet, and dislodged itself just as I was preparing to cross the street.

But I pushed thoughts of Wei aside. Why did his opinion of me matter so much? And after all, we were not yet a hundred percent sure of his innocence. Maybe I would be vindicated after Andy checked the credit card info on the receipt.

Still, it would be the neighborly thing to do, apologize

for any misunderstanding. I would ring his doorbell tomorrow, should he not appear on the porch at a reasonable time. "I hope you understand why we called Andy about the receipt instead of coming to you directly," I would say, or something to that effect. "And I hope we're still friends. I so enjoy chatting with you." Worst case, he would say "I don't think so, Nellie," and slam the door in my face.

But tonight I had bigger worries than Wei. I climbed into bed with my phone under my pillow, unmuted, and checked it randomly throughout the night, but Chloe did not reach out. I lay awake pondering her theory about the medication causing Rachel to hear voices. Of all the possible explanations, that was the one I found most appealing. My final thought before falling asleep was that tomorrow we would get Rachel started on the road to recovery.

But what morning brought was the scream of sirens approaching our neighborhood just after dawn, growing ever closer and shutting down with an abrupt "whoop whoop" across the street.

Still in my robe, I ran outside. And although Wei was standing in his mother's front yard, gazing intently at the action in front of Rachel's house, I didn't give one thought to my mussed hair and overall disheveled appearance. Jack followed a step or two behind, urging me to "Wait up, don't get too close." But of course, he didn't yet know that Chloe had spent the night with Rachel.

23

"My daughter's in that house!" I shrieked at the two uniformed officers who blocked our way. Jack drew back as if I'd struck him. When he made a move to push past them, the burlier of the two grasped his arm.

"Sorry, sir. We have to let the paramedics do their job."

"If she has done something to Chloe, I'll—" I collapsed against Jack, sobbing.

"Marilyn, what the hell? What is Chloe doing in Rachel's house?" He was angry, and who could blame him?

I told him how Chloe and I had found Rachel berating Wei on his mother's porch, and how we had taken her home to calm her down. How she was furious because he had claimed not to have heard the voices she insisted were coming from his front yard.

"Jesus Christ! And you let Chloe spend the night after hearing that?"

I couldn't defend myself. All along, my instincts had told me Rachel was insane. She was on my private murder suspect list, for crying out loud. Consumed with fear and guilt, I alternated between monitoring Rachel's front door and sobbing into Jack's shirt. He continued to hold me, although to say his embrace was warm would be a stretch.

Over Jack's shoulder, I saw Wei still standing in his

mother's front yard, arms folded across his chest. He appeared concerned but was probably simply curious. Why should he care about the well-being of either Rachel or Chloe? One had screamed in his face about nonexistent voices, and the other was the daughter of two Nosy Nellies who had sicced a murder investigator on him over a piece of paper found blowing on the breeze. I followed his eyes to where Andy's car was rolling into place behind the emergency vehicle.

I rushed over, but before I could plead with Andy to tell me that Chloe was okay, he raised his cell phone toward me. "I tried to call you. It's Rachel. Chloe's fine, Marilyn."

Oh, thank you, God. Just then Rachel's door opened. Another police officer emerged, followed by paramedics carrying a body on a stretcher. An oxygen mask hid most of Rachel's face, the only part of her not covered by a white sheet. Another sob escaped me at the pitiful sight, and Jack emitted a soft murmur of concern.

He cleared his throat. "Andy must figure that whatever happened has some connection with the Redding case. If not, why is he even here?"

Just then Chloe rushed through the door and down the steps. She flung herself into Andy's arms.

"Question answered," Jack muttered.

Close on Chloe's heels came Alejandra. She hurried over to Jack and me. "Oh god, Marilyn. Who knew this would happen?"

"What exactly did happen?" Jack asked. "Somebody tried to do her in, or what?"

"Oh no, no. Not that." She dabbed at her eyes. "They're not sure, but it looks like she tried to—I mean—oh, I can't even say it!"

Jack had no problem saying it. "Suicide attempt?"

Chloe nodded. "Pills. Who would've thought she might do such a thing?"

"I would've," Jack said. "Anybody would've. You

middle-of-the-night people, with all your nosing into everyone and everything, I can't believe you wouldn't have seen it."

"That's enough, Jack." I patted Alejandra's shoulder. At least someone was grateful for our presence. Then I followed Jack's eyes. The hurt in them as he watched Andy whisper reassurance to our daughter moved me to try to comfort him.

"Chloe's okay, Jack. That's the main thing."

"I know that," he snapped.

When Andy saw us watching, he whispered something to Chloe and gave her a little push toward us before walking over to converse with the police officers. The paramedics had loaded Rachel into the back of the ambulance, and now they slammed the doors shut and departed, followed by one of the cop cars. A few seconds later, we covered our ears against the deafening blare of the sirens.

Chloe leaned into me for a hug. "I was going to call you right after I talked to Andy, but he said he'd let you know what was happening. He wanted me to focus on trying to wake up Rachel until the paramedics arrived. I hope you weren't too worried."

"Only for a minute. We ran over here as soon as we heard the sirens. No time to grab our phones." I hugged her again. "Oh honey, I'm so glad you're okay. I was afraid—I mean, Rachel seems so unstable, I thought for certain—"

Chloe pulled away from me. "Mom, really? You thought Rachel might—what? Kill me?"

Alejandra, too, looked surprised. "Not Rachel. She wouldn't hurt anybody."

Andy's approach saved me from having to mount a self-defense. "You ladies are going to the hospital? I'd offer you a ride, but I need to pick up my mom and drive her to a treatment."

Chloe's disbelieving eyes refused to let go of mine. "Really, Mom?" she asked again. I thought it best to save the response for a moment that had less of an audience.

Abruptly, she turned to Andy. "Yes, we'll go now. Take care of your mother." She looked at Alejandra. "Can you drive? I'm low on gas."

"Take my car, Chloe," I said. "Or hey, why don't I just drive you? I'd like to—to make sure she's okay and all."

"I'll just grab the key if that's okay. I wouldn't want you to be in danger in case she goes berserk at the hospital and decides to attack someone."

As she stalked toward the house, Andy made a silent whistling motion with his lips and departed in a hurry. Jack followed Chloe, muttering something about respect, or lack of it. I looked at Alejandra to see if she was miffed at me too, but she avoided my eyes.

Chloe backed the car out of the driveway, and as Alejandra climbed in on the passenger side, Chloe said something to her that I couldn't hear. Alejandra glanced at me and nodded.

Okay, so those two were disappointed in me. Wei was offended. Jack would be in a snit when I got home, ready to further chastise me for allowing Chloe to sleep on Rachel's sofa.

Alone in the street, I looked across and saw that Wei had relocated to his usual post on the front porch. He immediately averted his eyes, making a point, it seemed to me, of raising his cigarette to his lips. A snub? Or was he being polite, pretending not to notice my disheveled appearance? Elegant or not, a robe was a robe. And bedhead was simply indefensible outside of a person's own home.

"Marilyn? What in God's name?" Lisa had approached from behind me as I was making up my mind to confront Wei. "I was driving home and had to pull over for the ambulance."

When I had finished filling her in, she said, "Well, to be honest, it's not surprising, is it? It was obvious she had a drinking problem and was holding onto some issues about her dead girlfriend. Or wife, whatever she was." She saw that my eyes had welled up again. "Oh dear, Marilyn. Are you okay?"

Her nonchalant response had hit me wrong. "I'm fine. It's just—I'm worried, is all."

"I'm so sorry," she murmured. "I've been insensitive. You're closer to her than I am, so of course you're troubled."

I nodded. But truth be told, my tears were not for Rachel. And the knowledge that I was crying out of self-pity only made me feel worse. Chloe was right to be mad at me. What kind of a friend was I to Rachel?

"It's not just that," I said. *Shut up, Marilyn. You'll come across as self-absorbed and disloyal. Your sole concern right now should be for Rachel.*

Sensing my uncertainty, Lisa said, "Why don't you come over to my house? I'll make coffee, and you can tell me what's troubling you. That is, if you feel like sharing." She smiled. "Otherwise, we'll just have coffee."

While the timing was imperfect, I welcomed the chance to chat with Lisa alone. To get to know her better and discover if my instincts about the potential for a closer friendship were on target. And after offending nearly everyone else on the block, I could use a sympathetic ear.

I'd like that," I said. "Let me run inside and change. You go on ahead. I'll be right over."

As I turned toward the house, I saw that Wei was watching us and making no attempt to hide his frown. Well, fine. Let him worry that I would further sully his reputation by gossiping with Lisa about the incriminating receipt—after all, he had not been cleared of guilt just yet. And if he had only returned my gaze a minute earlier with a warm smile or even a nod, instead of snubbing me yet again, I'd be on his front porch right now, explaining why I'd impulsively assumed the receipt was his. It was his own fault that it hadn't happened.

24

I could have interrupted Jack's shower to explain that I was on my way over to Lisa's. He would be expecting breakfast, but how hard was it to pour a bowl of cereal or scramble an egg? He wasn't asked to fend for himself very often. I dressed quickly, brushed my teeth, and grabbed a banana to eat on my walk over.

While Lisa poured us coffee, I texted Jack my whereabouts and then scoped out Lisa's small but pleasant kitchen, with its painted wood cabinets. Blue was never a decorating choice for me, but it seemed to work in this house, with its Early American furnishings; again, not my style, but to each her own. Lisa's cargo pants and striped J.C. Penney's tank top were also not my style, although I would give her points for the beige and black color combination.

"By the way," she said, as she placed the cups on the table. "Thacker finally traced those blackmail threats. No surprise: the calls were made from a stolen phone. The owner has been cleared. Some teenage girl got distracted and left it in a Starbucks in Oakland. So we still don't know who was calling me."

"That's too bad. Have you received any calls on your new number?"

"No. And just the one postcard, so far. 'Your body, your choice.'" She gave her head a derisive shake. "Which our friend Thacker refuses to properly investigate."

Startled, I realized that with all the turmoil around the strip club receipt and Rachel's meltdown, none of us had thought to share with Lisa the results of our excursion to Jenny Ho's. Not only did she not know we had gone there two nights ago without inviting her, but she was still in the dark about the flyer that Marty, our server, had thrust upon Alejandra: an invitation to a rally in support of Planned Parenthood. How could I have neglected to tell Lisa something of such importance to her? My friendship skills really did need sharpening.

As I was wondering how to save face while assuring her that Andy now had an unmistakable lead that tied her postcard threat to the pro-choice movement, she rinsed a bowl of strawberries and placed them on the table.

"Those look delicious," I said, buying some time.

Just as I had decided my best bet was to simply blurt it out with an apology for my tardiness, she resumed her complaint. "I wish I had more faith in Thacker. I haven't slept well in weeks." Unhealthy circles under her eyes gave her claim credibility. "I just don't feel safe. You know?"

"I do know. I'm not sleeping so well myself."

When her nose wrinkled briefly, followed by a noncommittal sniff, I sensed that I'd fallen into the deadly "all about me" trap, a sure way to avoid making new friends. So I qualified, "Of course, Jack and I haven't been harassed like you and Alejandra. And Mrs. Zhang. But someone did put that envelope with the clues in it on my porch. And after all, a man was killed in his own home. How can any of us sleep at night?"

Something passed through her eyes so quickly that I almost missed it. At first, I thought it was anger, but then she said, "At least you have Jack."

Before I could acknowledge that her situation was worse

than mine, of course, since she was alone and all, she continued. "But I have my faith, and that's worth a fortune. I find myself in almost a constant state of prayer these days, Marilyn. Not just about the murder, or the blackmail, but just … everything, to be honest."

"I pray at lot too," I told her with a reassuring smile. "Let's face it, there's so much to pray about these days."

I wondered if we were about to embark on a political discussion. I would've welcomed the chance to assure her that our views were compatible. But with a little wave of her hand, she said, "Well, that's a conversation for another day, I hope. Now, speaking of Thacker, has he done anything about that box of dishes Alejandra turned over to him?"

"If he has, he hasn't said so. But it's been less than a week."

She changed course, flashing a toothy smile that caught me off-guard. "So, would you like to tell me what's bothering you? Other than Rachel's well-being, I mean."

Rachel was right about Lisa's oversized eyes, and Jack had nailed her fragile build with the "Bird Legs" moniker. But her attractive smile made up for a lot. When the blackmail threats and the Michael Redding business were behind us, no doubt we would see that smile more often. As we became friendlier, I could guide her toward an updated hairstyle, more flattering clothes, and better makeup choices.

But at the moment, she was awaiting my response.

"It's just that—oh, it's nothing that won't pass. At least I hope not. But I'm afraid Chloe is miffed at me. And maybe Alejandra, too."

I told her of Chloe's irate response to my expression of concern for her safety because of Rachel's instability.

"But my goodness. How can she not see that you had every reason to expect the worst? Any parent would've felt the same." She gave me a sly sideways look while stirring a second lump of sugar into her coffee. "Although, maybe I wouldn't have shared my thoughts with Chloe just as they brought Rachel out on a stretcher."

We both smiled. She was starting to remind me of Sue Ellen. Supportive, yet willing to gently chastise me when I'd earned it. Exactly the kind of friend I needed. Alejandra was sweet but struggling with her own issues and lacking the maturity and experience of a woman my age, or Lisa's. And as for Rachel, although her disdain and mistrust of me had been less obvious lately, any remaining doubt as to her stability had been shattered by the wail of the siren this morning.

"And then there's Dr. Zhang," I blurted out, after a short debate with myself. Did I really want to share my unhappiness about his disapproval? Why did it bother me so much, anyway? Reporting the receipt had been the right thing to do. Not my fault I caught it as it blew across his yard. I would see if she agreed.

"Zhang, did you say? Oh yes, the old lady's son, right? What about him?"

"Nothing important. At least Andy doesn't think so. But I found a receipt in his mom's front yard that came from that strip club in Oakland. The place where Michael Redding's band used to play sometimes."

Her eyes widened. "It was in his yard?"

"Well, between our two yards, actually," I conceded. "It blew out of the hedge in between. But I knew it wasn't ours, so ..."

"So you told the detective?"

"Yes, Andy went to talk to Dr. Zhang about it, and he denies that it's his. Andy must have told him that Jack and I had suggested it made him a suspect in Redding's murder, and now he isn't speaking to me."

"Is that a problem?"

Taken aback, I stammered, "Well, no. I mean not especially, but—it's just that I hate to think—we were on friendly terms before, is all."

"This bothers you, that he isn't your pal anymore?"

Was she making fun of me? She was looking away as she reached for the sugar dish and stirred yet another lump into her coffee. Both her hands were trembling quite noticeably. I averted my eyes, hoping to avoid another explanation of her "medical condition." While it had been interesting enough the first time, it was beginning to rival Rachel's "Poor me" saga for biggest conversational time waste.

"It's this medical condition," she said. "Makes it hard to hold the coffee cup steady, but it helps if I use both hands."

"I see," I replied, while wondering how two spastic hands could not work against each other. "That must be so difficult for you."

She shrugged. "We must take whatever hand the good Lord deals us." If the pun was intentional, she didn't claim it, so I withdrew my smile.

Now then," she continued. "Back to this Chang fellow—or Zhang, is it?"

"Yes, Zhang Wei. Wei is actually his first name." I paused, momentarily confused. "I think so anyway."

"Are you really feeling guilty about reporting him to Thacker? I mean, what else could a responsible person do?"

"So you don't think we overreacted?"

"Not at all. In fact, I wouldn't let this matter drop, if I were you. Besides, you have an 'in' with Thacker, right?"

"Well, I don't know that you'd call it an 'in.' He seems to be dating my daughter, which I find baffling, but ..."

"But there's no accounting for taste, right?" She chuckled. I wasn't sure whether it was Andy or Chloe who had been insulted. She sensed my confusion and hurried to add, "Chloe is so pretty and smart and all."

"So you think I should push Andy to further investigate any connection between the receipt and Wei?"

In mock surprise, she said, "Oh, it's Wei now, is it? No

more Dr. Zhang? Are you holding out on me, Marilyn?"

While it was nice to see her in a breezier mood, the teasing made me uncomfortable. It was annoying enough that I had to put up with it from Rachel.

"Hardly. He's a neighbor, that's all. He seems nice, but then again, I've never spoken to him for more than a few minutes."

"Relax, I'm kidding." She took another sip of coffee, then gave me a teasing sidelong look. "I'm curious, though. A bit of a crush, maybe? We all get them, you know."

"Not me," I said, possibly too quickly. "Happily married for thirty-five years."

"Congratulations." Wistfully, she added, "Dale and I were married for just short of thirty when he was murdered last year."

Murdered! It hadn't seemed relevant, so none of us had asked her anything about her husband's death. Or his life either, for that matter.

"I'm so sorry. I was under the impression he died of a heart attack. I thought someone told me that was the case." Better to lie and save face than to appear self-absorbed and shallow.

Perhaps suspecting the falsehood, she looked down at her coffee. "Oh no, hon. No. Dale was shot in the chest when he tried to stop a bank robbery in process."

Stunned, I finally said, "That must have been horrible for you."

"Oh yes. You bet." She added coffee to both our cups, and I didn't stop her, although I was already feeling over-caffeinated.

Her voice grew increasingly bitter. "And to make it even more nightmarish, the illegal bastard who killed him got off with a slap on the wrist. Nine years in jail." She gauged my reaction as she added, "Should've been given the chair."

I didn't disappoint her. "Of course! And why wasn't he?"

"He claimed the gun went off accidentally, although there was a roomful of terrified witnesses who said otherwise." She raised her cup to her lips, watching my eyes as she repeated, "Nine years."

"Oh my god, that's terrible. I'm so sorry." Anger rose in me on her behalf. "There's no excuse for that kind of leniency."

"Well, tell that to our liberal courts and Assembly. And the pretty boy Governor."

"I know what you mean."

She turned wistful again. "Dale had just retired and we had planned a cruise that summer to celebrate. Then he took a part-time job as a security guard at Wells Fargo."

"I'm so sorry," I said again. "How tragic."

"Yes." She tried to smile. "Thanks for listening to my tale of woe, Marilyn. But enough of that. Tell me about your daughter. Is she an only child? No grandkids?"

Clearly, the subject of her husband's death was still too painful for her to talk about, so I honored her request to move on. I delivered the scoop on Natalie and Chloe: their time-consuming careers, their infrequent visits, their nonchalant attitude about long-term romance. I finished with, "So no grandkids, unfortunately. You said your daughter has—what? Two, is it?"

One thing I had learned from my book club year was that nothing lights up a woman's eyes like the subject of grandkids. If I had to endure a series of iPhone photos, then so be it. That's what friends are for. But she did not reach for her phone.

"Yes, Amanda's family is in Reno. My son, Martin, has been in Chicago for the past two years. He's single, a policeman like his dad." A proud smile came and went in a heartbeat.

"Do they call often, at least? I usually hear from the girls on Sunday afternoons, but in between I'm lucky if they respond to a text. Especially during the school year."

"I know what you mean. And sometimes when Amanda or Martin visit, we get into these ridiculous spats over politics, of all things." She smiled self-consciously. "I'm a proud conservative, and so was Dale, but both my kids somehow ended up somewhere to the left of Jane Fonda, politically." She hurried to add, "But I shouldn't say such things. I hope you're not offended."

I laughed. "Not at all. In fact, Jack and I are in that exact situation with our girls! And honestly, it's nice to make the acquaintance of another Bay Area Republican."

"Yes, we're a rare breed." She smiled and sipped her coffee before taking a surprising detour. "And all is okay between you and Jack?"

Caught off-guard, I answered, "Oh yes. We get along well. He's a good man."

She nodded. "Maybe that's all we can wish for, at our age. The fire goes out for every couple, eventually."

Okay, so I wanted a new friend to chat with, even about private matters. And yes, I was hopeful about our budding friendship. But this was a bit premature.

"Well anyway, I need to get going before Jack starts to worry." I carried my cup over to her sink, which was spotless and otherwise clear of dishes.

"I'm sorry, Marilyn. Did I cross a line? My curiosity gets the better of me sometimes, I'm afraid."

"I've been accused of the same," I admitted. "No problem, but I do have to get home."

She walked me to the door. "I hope I haven't annoyed you. To be honest, it felt so good just to sit and chat. My best friend died of cancer two years ago, and I haven't been in town long enough to develop new attachments. It's been a while since I've had a coffee date with a girlfriend. Sorry if I got carried away."

We had even more in common than I'd realized.

"I lost my best friend recently, too, so I understand. By the way, I know you're—or you were—Catholic, but Jack and I have attended Fifth Street Methodist for twenty-five years. Nice people, and visitors are always welcome."

She smiled. "I've tried dozens of different churches since my nightmare experience in the convent. Nothing seems to fit. But if you and Jack are members, maybe I'll give the Methodists another try. Anyway, it was fun chatting, Marilyn. I wish you could stay longer."

"I'm happy to visit with you, but right now I need to get home so Jack can give me hell for letting Chloe sleep on Rachel's sofa."

She frowned. "Stand up for yourself, Marilyn. You allowed Chloe to stay overnight because Rachel needed her. You had no way of knowing she would swallow a bottle of pills."

"Thank you," I said. "I appreciate your saying that." And I did. It was exactly what Sue Ellen would've told me.

"And Marilyn, I should not have made light of your feelings about Dr. Zhang, whatever they are. But to be honest, I should think you'd want to avoid him until you know for sure he's not a killer."

"That's what everyone seems to think," I said, hoping she wouldn't sense my disappointment. "And you're probably right."

And then I remembered that I still hadn't filled her in on our Jenny Ho's trip.

"Listen, Lisa. Regarding the murder case, I need to tell you something."

So I apologized in advance for the delayed report, and then explained that we had gone to Jenny Ho's on an investigative field trip. And that she hadn't been invited because we didn't know her well enough to predict how she would respond to the idea. That we had questioned a waitress named Marty about Michael Redding. That Marty had seemed hesitant to talk to us, and we were sure she was hiding something. And that the owner had rudely asked us to leave.

Lisa listened without comment, her expression growing ever more incredulous as I related how Marty had followed Alejandra into the restroom and handed her the invitation to a Planned Parenthood rally with Marty's name and phone number scrawled on the bottom. By the time I had finished, all color had drained from her face. She moaned, closed her eyes, and pressed both quivering hands to her cheeks.

Alarmed, I fumbled in my pocket for my phone. My experience with my foster mother had taught me that with Parkinson's, anything could happen. A seizure? A stroke? I mentally slapped myself for not first sitting Lisa down in a chair and warning her that what I had to say might disturb her.

I babbled: "Lisa, do you need to lie down? I've upset you. I'm so sorry. Can I do something? A wet washcloth? A glass of water?"

After a few seconds, she lowered her hands. When I saw that her eyes were glazed and her forehead damp with perspiration, I pulled my phone out of my pocket. But then she spoke in a voice calm enough that I relaxed a little.

"No, I'm okay. It's just that—just that this is such a shock, Marilyn. I mean, I had assumed the threat was connected to Redding's murder somehow, but this—this makes it so real."

"Let's sit for a bit," I said, taking her arm. She didn't resist as I led her over to the sofa. I went to the kitchen, found a towel, and dampened it with cold water to place over her eyes and on her forehead. "I'm sorry," I said again.

After a minute, she removed the towel and gave me a weak smile. "Marilyn, I'm the one who should apologize. This was unexpected, that's all. I'm fine, but I'm afraid I'm not at my best right now." She stood up and took a second or two to regain her balance. "I'll take my medication and lie down while I absorb this. I'll give you a call later if that's all right."

"Of course." I followed as she led the way to the door. "And if I don't hear from you, I'll give you a ring to make sure you're okay." Relieved that she was speaking normally and had regained some color, I ended my account of our field trip on a reassuring note.

"Andy is trying to reach that server who gave us the flyer. He seems hopeful that she can tell him something useful."

Lisa was skeptical. "This happened two days ago, and he still hasn't managed to contact her?

"Apparently, she's had to take some time off work. A family emergency, her boss said. And Andy says she isn't returning his calls."

Lisa's expression darkened. "The mysteries keep on coming, don't they? Let's just pray the poor girl is still alive."

"Lisa!" I stopped in my tracks. "That had honestly not occurred to me."

My worried response brought a smile as she opened the door for me. "Let's not borrow trouble. It's in God's hands, right? I'm afraid I've become a bit paranoid."

"We all have," I assured her.

On the way home, I told myself there was no basis for Lisa's dire speculation where Marty was concerned. Andy had seemed to buy the "family emergency" story, for what that was worth. But what *was* that worth, exactly?

When I turned the corner, there was Wei on his front porch, peering in my direction. As if he had been waiting. And he did not look away as I approached.

Despite Lisa's advice and that of my family, I was torn. Still, I met his eyes just long enough to offer a tepid smile and a "good morning" in response to his before climbing my own steps. Was I imagining his disappointment as his eyes followed me? Hadn't he looked as though he was about to initiate a conversation?

But Lisa was right. And Chloe. And Jack. That darn

receipt almost surely belonged to Zhang Wei, whether Andy wanted to believe it or not.

Still, I hesitated to accept Wei's guilt, and I took some comfort in the fact that Andy, at least, shared my doubt. But if not Wei, and certainly not Jack—I refused to go down that fruitless, destructive path again; what had I been thinking? —then who? The theory I'd recently tried to sell myself on, that the receipt had blown into the privet from another neighbor's house and dislodged itself just as I walked into the street that night, now seemed like the half-baked result of wishful thinking.

I tried calling Chloe for news of Rachel, but she didn't answer. Jack was eating a late breakfast at the kitchen table, a bowl of cereal and coffee. I poured myself some Bran Flakes and joined him.

"I'm sorry," I said, preemptively. "It was an error in judgment. I should have talked Chloe out of staying over."

"She's okay. That's all that matters."

Relieved, I changed topics. "You got my text? Lisa showed up and asked me over for a chat. We have a lot in common, so I want to get to know her better. I'm afraid I upset her by telling her about our Jenny Ho's experience. But I do think there's friendship potential there."

"Bird Legs? Sure, why not?" He shrugged. "By the way, Chloe texted about a half hour ago. Rachel's awake but can't have visitors. They want to evaluate her in the psych ward for a day or two."

"Chloe texted you? I just tried to call, and she didn't answer. Did she say when she might be home?"

On cue, the door opened. Chloe entered and tossed the car key onto the counter in the general direction of my purse. Unable to avoid my questioning eyes, she said only, "She'll live. After an evaluation, they'll decide when she can come home."

"But do they know if she—what do they think happened?"

"They wouldn't tell us anything and wouldn't let us see her. Her mom and stepdad came in as we were leaving, but they hadn't yet been told anything either."

"Her family lives in the area, then? I don't believe she ever mentioned them."

Then I remembered a self-pitying remark Rachel had made in Alejandra's backyard that afternoon of our first get-together. *I gave up my family for that woman.* So maybe she and her mother were still estranged. But if her mom had come to the hospital, perhaps a reconciliation was on the horizon. After all, what mother wouldn't give herself an attitude check after a child's attempted suicide?

"Her mom seems nice enough," said Chloe, as if reading my mind. "The stepdad, not so much. Just a first impression, though."

As she headed for the stairs, she turned to look at me. "Really, Mom?" She shook her head in a way that seemed a bit less incredulous than earlier, which I took as a positive sign.

"Will you be home for dinner tonight?" I asked. "I thought I'd make a tuna casserole."

She smiled a little at my joking reference to her least favorite meal. "Oh yummy. But Andy asked me out again. He needs to talk. It's rough on him, the stress of the investigation along with his mom's illness."

As she disappeared up the stairs, I called after her. "Ask him if he's had any luck tracing that box of dishes, okay? And if he was ever able to reach Marty, our secretive server."

Her response was barely audible, "Yeah, sure."

I turned to Jack "How about you? Tuna casserole for dinner?" It was his least favorite as well. The question brought just the response I was hoping for.

"Let's get take-out."

I passed the afternoon with a two-hour nap, the *New York Times* crossword, forty minutes on the elliptical machine, and chapters one through seven of Louise Penny's latest novel. Through it all, my concentration was assaulted by questions—questions prompted by Lisa's response to learning that Andy was trying to reach our Jenny Ho's server. Was Marty's "family emergency" that had resulted in her sudden absence from the strip club a reason for worry? Why hadn't she returned Andy's calls? Hadn't she seemed intimidated by the club's owner, Art Doherty? Had Andy thought of all this already?

After a dinner of Thai food (no peanut curry for either of us), I brought out my laptop and rearranged my suspect list. Wei had been moved to the number one spot after I realized the receipt was his. But shouldn't I trust my gut to some extent? And Andy seemed convinced of his innocence, so that must mean something, right? Still, the instincts of Jack, Chloe, and Lisa deserved consideration. Wei would remain at the top of the list for now.

My remorse about having immediately assumed that Rachel had harmed Chloe instead of herself did not prevent me from moving her up to the middle of the list. Yes, I did consider her a friend—an unstable, lonely, alcoholic, pill-popping friend, estranged from her family, conflicted about the death of her cheating spouse, guilty about her own mistreatment of the dying woman. Possibly delusional. But still, a friend.

And then there were the other suspects, all but forgotten during my recent preoccupation with Zhang Wei's potential guilt. But maybe this was an oversight. Take Alejandra's friend Daniela, for instance, a woman of questionable morals. What about Brian, Alejandra's bullying ex, a conniving, dishonest immigration attorney?

I moved Daniela to the number two spot, followed by Brian Stevens, the Peeping Tom, and Daniela's husband, Eric. I added Art Doherty to the list, placing him briefly at the top. Then I shuffled all the names around before finally admitting to myself that I had no idea which of them was a more likely suspect than the others.

Suddenly, I felt woefully incompetent. Who was I kidding? Jack was right: my friends and I were no more than wannabe Miss Marples—amateurs who dared to question the competence of Andy Thacker, a trained investigator.

Spontaneously, I added to the list: "Someone previously unsuspected."

Alejandra's name I erased completely.

25

Bluish rings around Rachel's eyes accentuated the pallor of her skin, which was devoid of makeup. But her hair was clean and combed, and she was wearing the yoga pants and t-shirt Alejandra had dropped off the day before. She looked pretty in a fragile, bruised sort of way.

"Come on, guys. You can't think I did this on purpose. We all know how much I love myself. Right, Marilyn?"

Two days after what we had been assuming was Rachel's suicide attempt, the four of us sat around a square table in the visiting area of the hospital psych ward, amid a scattering of ashen-faced patients and an attendant in green medical garb with a no-nonsense air of authority. She sat at a desk in the corner with her back to the wall, her eyes flickering upward from her computer at frequent intervals to assess the room and let us know she was in charge. Alejandra, Chloe, and I had just delivered our hugs along with such inanities as "How are you?" (me), "I'm speechless," (Chloe), and "Oh my god. Oh my god," (A wet-eyed Alejandra). Shrewd creature that Rachel was, she had read the question in our eyes.

"I'm sure that's what they told you. But I know what I did and what I didn't do." She reconsidered. "I mean, well,

I don't remember everything, exactly. But it's not what you think."

"What is it then?" Chloe asked, injecting a touch of humor. "Do set our thinking straight. And they didn't tell us much, by the way. Only that we're not family, which we already knew."

"So they called your mom," said Alejandra. "But I assume you know that?"

Her response was between a snicker and a cough. As if she wanted to laugh but it hurt too much. She waved off the question, and we waited while she collected her thoughts.

"So best I remember, here's how it came down. Chloe and me talked until ten o'clock or so, and after that—"

"Twelve-thirty," Chloe corrected. "But go ahead."

"Anyway, I was half sober by that time because Chloe the Enforcer had cut me off and hidden the wine. I couldn't sleep so I went to look for a meeting online, but nothing was happening."

"That AA site you told us about?" Chloe asked. "The one for nonbelievers?"

"Yeah. Quadruple A, it's called: Alcoholics Anonymous for Atheists and Agnostics. I've been trying it for a couple of months, but I can't get past steps 8 and 9. See, you're supposed to make a list of everyone your drinking has harmed, and you have to go and apologize and shit. Believe me, I know only too well who I've harmed." She gave each of us a meaningful glance. "But as you know, it's not like I don't have my reasons."

"Sure," said Alejandra, and we all murmured agreement.

The familiar "pitiful me" tone had crept into Rachel's voice. I steeled myself for a recap, but she spared us.

"So it's too late to apologize to Deb, obviously." Her voice was hard. "And I'll be goddamned if I owe that bitch homewrecker an apology. Am I right?"

"Well," said Chloe, "did you actually have interactions with her because of your drinking?"

"Hell yes. Wouldn't you? There's no way I'll ever forgive her for breaking up my marriage. Fucking forget it."

"So you have confronted her? In person?" Chloe pressed.

"Not in person, no. The slut won't come anywhere near me. All she did was whine to Deb, try to convince her to grab onto 'the few months of happiness you have left,'" she mimicked. Her eyes flashed fire as she finished in a matter-of-fact voice, "What a cunt."

I flinched, then recovered enough to ask, "So if you didn't confront her in person, what did you do?" Her answer made Chloe and me wince, but Alejandra looked like she had heard it all before. And I'm sure she had.

"Lots of stuff. I went on Deb's computer and found her contact info. Email, Facebook, Instagram, Twitter. I let her have it."

She read my reaction and gave me a defiant look. "I know you're shocked, Marilyn. You can't relate, can you? You've never been betrayed by someone you gave up your family for. My mom won't even speak to me. Or at least, she wouldn't, until the hospital lied and told her I tried to do myself in."

"Is she speaking to you now?" Chloe asked.

"She's supposedly coming today. But she'll probably bring the Reverend with her. Mr. Conversion Therapy himself."

"Your dad is a minister?" Chloe asked.

"Stepfather. And not just any kind of preacher. He's got a mega-church in San Jose filled with Evangelical types. Until they gave up on saving my soul, the son-of-a-bitch used to send me emails every Sunday with Bible verses condemning sodomy and reminding me that if I changed my ways, God would forgive me, and so would he and my mother."

"And what did your mom have to say about this?" I tried to withhold judgement, but honestly, what kind of mother would tolerate a man who sought to drive a wedge between her and her child?

"Not a hell of a lot. At first, she would meet me for lunch on the sly. Then he found out, and him and his church convinced her she was sinning by disobeying her husband. Then the fucker wrote a book promoting that conversion therapy bullshit."

"Ugh," said Chloe. "I thought most churches had agreed that it was nothing more than temporary brainwashing. I've even heard it referred to as psychological torture."

"This new therapist agrees—and the old one, too, to give her a little bit of credit for being not just a pill pusher. Anyway, you should check out this prick's book. The best part is the chapter about how I continue to willfully break his and my mother's heart—and Christ's—by refusing to let that program 'fix' me."

"I didn't know conversion therapy had been discredited," I said.

Chloe gave me the "of course you didn't" look, a combination glare and eyeroll.

"Anyway. Long story short, Mom drank the Kool-Aid, and I hadn't seen her for three years." Rachel chuckled. "But now, here she is, with Mr. Poker-up-the-ass in tow. They're supposed to visit in"—her eyes went to a large round clock on the wall—"in about half an hour, I guess. I asked her to come without him, but you can bet that won't happen." She crossed her arms and shrugged. "Anyway, why am I blabbering about this crap? You're probably tired of hearing about my problems all the time."

Alejandra reached for her hand and held it. "You can always talk to us about anything, Rachel. Even if we've heard it before, we don't care. Right, Marilyn and Chloe?"

I assumed it was Alejandra's guilty conscience speaking,

atoning for the times she had made up lame excuses to leave the room during a replay. I nodded agreement while hoping it wouldn't unleash the familiar blow-by-blow of Deb's adulterous behavior.

"So you've seen the therapist already?" Chloe asked. "Do you feel you've made progress?"

"Oh yeah. I've met with her twice. You know how I feel about therapists. Pill pushers, the lot of them. Although this one did say she might back me off the Zoloft altogether, which is fine with me."

Alejandra prompted, "So can you remember what happened after you and Chloe went to bed that night?"

"Oh yeah. Most of it, anyway. So Chloe was in bed, and I was trying to find a meeting to log into. Then, that voice—the bitch's voice—came blaring out of the computer. Talking to Deb, not to me."

She put her head in her hands as if to avoid seeing our reactions. "Believe me, I know how bizarre this sounds. I swear to you, I hear them—I mean her; Deb's response never comes through—and it just—I can hardly stand it, it's so awful to hear her flirting and—" She tried and failed to swallow a sob, and the result was so startling that the attendant got up and marched over to our table.

"I'm okay," Rachel tearfully assured her.

"Are you sure about that?" Her stern face gave us to understand that if she decided Rachel was not okay, we would be out the door faster than you could say "cuckoo's nest."

"I'm fine." Rachel had collected herself. "Just let me finish telling them this story, okay?"

The attendant looked at me, my age identifying me as most likely to be in charge. "A few more minutes, okay? An hour is all they're allowed the first few days, and she's expecting another visitor soon."

As she walked away, Chloe said, "The first few days, huh? How long do you suppose they'll keep you in here?"

"Let's not get off track," I said. "Let Rachel tell us what happened that night after she started hearing the—the CB transmissions."

Rachel's voice was a whisper. "The slut just wouldn't shut up. I turned off the computer, but her voice followed me into the kitchen and was coming out of the microwave, and then—oh, I don't know. It's like it was just in the air, all around me."

"You were supposed to wake me up," Chloe scolded. "That's why I was spending the night, remember?"

"Honestly? I temporarily forgot you were there." Lest Chloe should feel insulted, she added, "No offense."

"Go on," I said. "The voice wouldn't go away, so then what?"

"So sometimes the Valium helps. I take a few more than I'm supposed to, and an extra Zoloft, and then I can fall asleep. So that's what I did."

"How many did you take?" Chloe asked in a hushed voice. We were all aware of the attendant's gaze. She had stopped within earshot, probably as curious as we were to hear the story play out.

"A handful," Rachel admitted. "And I had forgotten that I'd already taken some earlier, when I heard the voice coming from Mrs. Zhang's yard. So altogether—" She shook her head. "I really couldn't say."

"Well, the Valium bottle was completely empty," Chloe interjected. "If that helps."

"Huh. Well anyway, I didn't mean to put an end to myself. I swear it's the truth."

"So what did the therapist say when you told her all this? About the voices, I mean?" I pressed on, aware that the guard-nurse had one eye on us and the other on the clock.

"She said something about drug and alcohol interaction and abuse and withdrawal, or something."

"I knew it! So she thinks this is something fixable?"

Chloe asked. "With therapy or a medication change, maybe?"

"She didn't say that, no. She also mentioned stress and bottled-up resentment and PTSD and a lot of other psychobabble. Bottom line, I could be loony-tunes." She shrugged. "Or not."

"I think not," said Alejandra firmly.

With that, we said our goodbyes and Rachel walked us to the door. "You'll be back, right? I mean, I think we should have a meeting, don't you? I need you to catch me up on what Chloe's boyfriend has uncovered in the past couple of days."

Chloe said, "There's not much to tell yet, but who knows? By tomorrow, he may have solved the case."

I kept my doubts to myself. Andy had seen Chloe both nights since Rachel's overdose but had shared no news with her about the harassment of Alejandra, Lisa, and Mrs. Zhang, the origin of the Jenny Ho's receipt, or even the box of dishes, which Chloe had dutifully asked him about at my request. When she had asked about Marty the waitress, he had gotten testy, reminded her that some things were confidential, and asked if they could please talk about anything other than the murder.

"We'll meet here. You can bring the bug-eyed cat lady, too, if you want," Rachel called after us.

The attendant followed us into the corridor. "No meetings," she said.

As we walked past the cafeteria, I glanced inside. A sad-looking woman about my age was staring into her coffee cup. From her attractive facial structure and ash-blond hair I guessed who she was even before Alejandra nudged me and whispered, "Rachel's mother." I wondered where the evil stepdad had gone off to.

"Mom!" Chloe hissed, as I veered off course and headed into the coffee room. "What are you doing?"

"Just saying hello," I said in a normal voice. Why

whisper? We were not doing anything wrong. The woman looked up, surprised. Then she recognized Chloe and Alejandra from two days earlier, when Rachel was first admitted.

"Oh, hello," she said. Neither her tone nor her expression was welcoming, but neither were they disdainful—although she did draw back in surprise when I pulled up a chair.

"You're Rachel's mother?" I asked.

"Mom, we should be going," said Chloe, clearly appalled.

"I'll meet you in the parking lot. I'd just like a minute with Mrs.—uh—Mrs.—"

"Daily," she said. "Veronica Daily. Her wary eyes lingered on the two younger women as if to beg their intercession. But Chloe, pink-cheeked and wordless, nudged Alejandra and they scurried away.

"I'm Rachel's friend, Marilyn Middleton. My husband and I live across the street from her. She's a lovely young woman."

"Well, yes. Thank you. Pleased to meet you."

"I just wanted to say that I'm relieved you're here. I know it means a lot to Rachel." I continued, writing the dialogue as I went. "She has mentioned that she misses having you in her life."

That last part wasn't exactly true, since Rachel's comments about her mom, at least the ones I had heard, had been a hundred percent disdainful, heavy with resentment. When her mother's eyes welled up, I forgave myself the fib.

"She has told you, then? About how we—Brad and I— how our religion required us to—to—"

"To reject your own child?" I kept my voice low and calm. "To be honest, that doesn't sound very Christian to me."

Predictably, she went on the defensive. "The Bible

clearly says that homosexuality is an abomination. If you're a Christian, you know that."

"Sure," I said, to her obvious surprise. "It also says we women shouldn't cut our hair, that if our husband should die, we're to marry his brother. And I believe slavery is given the thumbs up. Among a host of other rules we've abandoned through the ages."

As I spoke, her face had flushed crimson and her gaze had shifted. I guessed the reason even before I followed her eyes to the doorway. The man standing there was tall and gaunt, slightly stooped. From behind rectangular wire-rimmed glasses, he peered at me with icy blue eyes. Icy enough to produce a surge of fright that I felt from my head down to my knees. But I had traveled this far, and darned if I wouldn't finish what I'd come to say.

I ignored the man as I stood up and spoke to Mrs. Daily. "Your daughter told me she hopes to visit with you alone. She misses you. That's all I really wanted to tell you."

As I drove the car out of the hospital parking lot, Chloe and Alejandra waited for me to explain myself. Instead, I clutched the wheel to steady my hands, took a deep breath, and said, "Rachel seems to be doing okay, under the circumstances."

"Mom? Tell us what you said to Rachel's mother. And we saw her stepdad out here on his phone. It looked like he went back inside. Did you—"

"I just said hi and introduced myself. And I told her she's a lousy excuse for a mother."

"Oh my god," they said in unison. "Mom, you didn't!" Chloe cried.

"Of course not." They giggled, and I changed topics. "So Chloe, why don't you invite Andy to dinner tonight? We can pick his brain together and later share with the others what we've learned."

She sighed. "I feel kind of guilty."

Oh brother.

"It's all for a good cause," I said cheerfully. "Anyway, it's not like that's the only reason you're seeing him. Right?" I wasn't sure what I wanted her answer to be.

"Of course not. I like Andy." She turned away from me to look out the window. "I like him quite a lot, actually."

A second later, she glanced at me surreptitiously. I kept my eyes on the road and my expression noncommittal. It was too early in the game for me to express my doubts about Andy's suitability as a son-in-law. Racial differences aside, police work was dangerous, and the internet had told me that cops have the highest infidelity rate of all the professions. But it's not as if she and Andy were engaged or anything, I reminded myself.

In the back seat, Alejandra sighed. "It must feel nice to be in love. I've never had the experience."

I waited for Chloe to remind Alejandra that she and Andy were still getting acquainted. Sure, they were having fun, but "love?" Too soon to tell.

But Chloe said only, "Aw, that's so sad, Alejandra. But you'll fall in love someday. When the right guy comes along."

And that was all she had to say about that.

26

At 2:00 a.m. on the morning following our visit to the psych ward, Alejandra called a meeting.

"It feels strange doing this without Rachel," Chloe lamented.

Alejandra poured tea for all of us as I murmured agreement and Lisa, last to arrive, settled into the Bentwood rocker that had been Rachel's territory. Chloe and I had returned to our former seats on the sofa; in the few days following our last meeting, the folding chairs had disappeared along with several cardboard boxes, bags, and miscellaneous yard sale treasures. While the room was far from tidy, the reduced chaos was welcome. Not only was our meeting space more pleasant, but Alejandra's efforts suggested that she hadn't given up on regaining visitation with her son.

Lisa's response to Chloe's remark was a tepid smile. The stress and insomnia of the past month had taken its toll on us all, but Lisa's face was a sad portrait of exhaustion and discouragement. Two days earlier, when I had told her about the flyer from Jenny Ho's, my intent had been to give her hope that Andy would soon solve both the murder and her harassment case. But her reaction had been contrary to my expectations. And tonight, she was certainly not radiating hope.

Boondoggles, who had been observing her from his spot on the floor in front of Alejandra, got up and lumbered over to Lisa. He parked himself at her feet, thumped his tail on the rug, and gave a single hopeful yip.

"Boonie, no! You don't beg treats from anyone but me." Alejandra took hold of his collar and led him back to the sofa. "I'm sorry, Lisa. He must really like you."

"So it seems," said Lisa, pursing her lips and patting her bun in a way that suggested the feeling wasn't mutual. But then, she was a cat lover.

"I think we should get started," Chloe said. "Do we have an agenda tonight, Alejandra?'

Alejandra picked up her notebook. "First thing on the list is 'new news.' So, is there any?"

Lisa spoke up first. "I heard from Thacker again today."

She lost another battle with her cup and the tea swam over into the saucer. Alejandra hurried to hand her a napkin from the center of the coffee table, where a bowl of Doritos sat next to a dish of guacamole. Without taking her eyes from Lisa, Chloe reached for a chip—her fourth so far—and I made a mental note to bring apple slices and a peanut butter dip to the next meeting.

After wiping up the spilled tea, Lisa stilled her hands by clasping them together in her lap. I waited for her to tell us yet again about her medical condition. Might as well get it over with.

"I'm so sorry," she said. "Did I explain that I have this medical condition? It's much worse when I'm under stress."

"Yes, you told us," I said. "So what did Thacker have to say?"

"Nothing relevant. He nosed into my personal life some more and claimed again that he was close to solving all the harassment cases as well as the murder." She sniffed. "Believe it, and I'll sell you a bridge in Brooklyn."

Chloe ignored the jab at Andy. "He said the same thing to me when he called earlier tonight. He also told me he had called on that thrift store in Oakland, Good as New, and questioned the employees. No one there remembers the sale of the dishes, but they've had some staff turnover." She glanced at Alejandra, whose crestfallen expression reminded us how much was at stake for her.

"The receipt didn't tell them anything?" I asked.

"Nothing we hadn't already figured out. The dishes were discounted at the register, probably because the purchaser had noticed damage of some kind. Andy assumes it was those chips on the one plate. Also, the box of dishes was the only item purchased and it was a cash sale."

"That's disappointing," I said, and Alejandra sighed. Lisa was silent, her eyes expressing barely a trace of polite interest.

"Well, it wasn't me who bought them," Alejandra said. "I never go to thrift stores or any other places in Oakland."

Her anxious voice moved me to reassure her. "We know, Alejandra. No one except Rachel thought you might have bought those dishes and forgotten about them. And I don't think she really believed it either."

Two little white lies told with the best of intentions. Alejandra's relieved smile justified the fibs.

Lisa wasn't impressed with Chloe's news. "Well, this isn't much help. We knew from the address that the store is near Jenny Ho's, but unless the person who purchased the dishes can be identified, it'll be hard to trace the path from the thrift store to Alejandra's dining room."

She was right. We sat in disappointed silence for a moment, and then Chloe turned to me. "Mom, you had a question for Alejandra?"

"Right," I said. Chloe and I had agreed on the way over that there was no point in bringing up the sore topic of Brian, who was still refusing to bring the boy, Kyle, to visit.

So I asked if Daniela had ever come clean with Andy about her barroom visits.

"Oh." Alejandra looked down at her notes, underlining what I suspected were random words. "I thought I told you. Yes, they got together last week." She looked up at our expectant faces. "That's all I know. So, is that all for tonight?"

She was holding out on us. I had been stifling yawns for the past ten minutes and was tempted to shrug it off and head home to my beckoning bed. But tiredness was making me cranky.

"So, I assume she told Andy about how she used to hang out with Michael down at the bar when her husband was out of town? Lying to her mother to get her to babysit?"

"Mom, for God's sake. What she told her mother is none of our business." Nonetheless, Chloe's frown was for Alejandra, not me, as we all waited for her response.

"Okay, look. Daniela wouldn't tell me what all she said to him. And now, for some reason, she's avoiding me. Except for a couple of texts, I haven't heard from her." She closed her notebook, the discussion apparently over.

Chloe took the cue and segued. "I've invited Andy over for dinner tomorrow night. Mom and I can press him about the link between Lisa's postcard and the flyer Marty gave us. Maybe he will have questioned Marty by then."

"Don't count on it," Lisa muttered between clenched teeth. We all pretended not to hear.

Chloe's dinner invitation to Andy was news to me.

"Wonderful," I said. "I assume you've decided on the meal you'll be preparing."

She laughed. "I know you're teasing, but I actually was planning to cook something myself. Something simple. But would you please handle dessert? You know how Andy loves your baking."

"Yes, I'm aware."

"Well, then." Chloe checked her phone. "Four-thirty.

We should call it a night, don't you think?"

As Alejandra closed the door behind us, Lisa touched my arm and asked in a quiet voice, "Would you all mind walking me to the corner?"

I was practically sleepwalking by that time, so yes, I did mind. But my annoyance dissolved as I considered her circumstances. As spooked as we all were over the murder and the various harassment incidents, at least Chloe and I had each other and Jack. Lisa was in the same boat as Alejandra and, before her hospitalization, Rachel. All of them alone at the end of the day.

As we approached the sidewalk, Lisa's eyes traveled across the street to Mrs. Zhang's porch, and mine followed. There was no sign of Wei, and I was surprised when Lisa exhaled in obvious relief. So now she was spooked by him, too. I regretted having shared with her my suspicions about the Jenny Ho's receipt I'd found in the hedge, dumping yet another pile of fear and uncertainty on her shoulders. And pointing another pair of accusing eyes at Wei.

Chloe insisted we walk Lisa all the way home, since it was just a block over and we all had our cell phone flashlights. It was the right thing to do, so we carefully made our way through the shadows. With Lisa's gloom feeding on the darkness, threatening to infect Chloe and me, I broke the silence with an observation: "I think that was our shortest meeting to date."

Chloe murmured agreement. There was no response from Lisa. But as we left her at her doorstep, she scanned the street both ways before cautioning, "Be careful, you two. Remember what that postcard said: he's always watching."

And on that cheery note, she went inside.

Was it a mistake to leave her in such an anxious state? A real friend would offer to spend the night on her sofa, as Chloe had done for Rachel. But we were already on our way home, and to now reverse course, ring the doorbell, explain my intentions, borrow pajamas, make up the sofa, and go to bed without brushing, flossing, or properly cleansing my face—well, to be honest, the idea was exhausting and not at all appealing.

"Whoa. She was quite the ray of sunshine tonight," Chloe commented as we walked home.

"And no wonder," I said. "Those threats, especially that pro-abortion postcard, were downright terrifying. I hope she has a gun under her pillow and knows how to use it."

She clicked her tongue in typical knee-jerk liberal disdain. "That's a scary thought, Lisa with a gun."

"Scary?"

"Oh, come on, Mom! Would you want to be in the same room with a flustered Lisa trying to aim a pistol?"

A titter escaped me, the product of exhaustion and nerves, and she laughed, too. I elbowed her and said, "Be nice, now."

A mother must always strive to set a good example.

27

"Any plans for the Fourth?" Andy wanted to know.

He was seated on the patio with Chloe and Jack, waiting for me to serve dessert.

"Not yet," I replied on my way to the kitchen, where I spooned blackberry crumble onto dessert plates and topped each serving with a dollop of whipped cream. A full pot of coffee waited on the counter, and I was reaching for cups when I spontaneously decided in favor of the cool Sauvignon Blanc we had served with dinner. So what if it wasn't considered a proper dessert wine?

Whose idea was it to have dinner on the patio during a heat wave? Chloe's, of course. And somehow, she was oblivious not only to the damp foreheads of the rest of us but also to the dots of perspiration above her own upper lip. The temperature had dropped to a nearly tolerable 89 degrees as the sun dropped behind the neighbors' rooftops, but the air conditioning was so soothing that I took my time uncorking the new bottle and loading the dessert dishes onto a serving tray.

As a result of my dawdling, I missed whatever ideas were being tossed around for tomorrow's Independence Day festivities. If the heat wave continued, I planned to celebrate at home with the thermostat set at 70 degrees while Old Glory proclaimed my patriotism from above the front steps.

When I rejoined them on the patio, Chloe was saying, "The parade starts at nine in the morning. Maybe we could drive down to watch for a while."

"If we can find a parking spot," Jack complained.

"Yes, the new downtown is really coming along," Andy said. "All those new ethnic restaurants and shops. But I can see where parking might get tricky if you're opposed to using the new free parking garage." This was uttered without a hint of sarcasm, but I saw Chloe suppress a giggle.

I set their desserts in front of them and took my seat at the end of the table across from Jack. "Will you be celebrating the Fourth, Andy?"

"I was just telling Chloe and Jack that I'll be on duty all day. I'll try to stop by for a stretch of the parade, though."

Near the start of the meal, Chloe had asked if he had anything to share with us about the murder or the harassment cases, but he had respectfully asked if we might engage in more palatable conversation while enjoying the delicious spaghetti and meatballs.

So we had talked of his mother's health: her prognosis had improved; it looked like she might beat this thing after all. We had learned that Andy's assistants, Baumgartner and Navarro, were starting to get the hang of their duties. Chloe had reminisced about high school hijinks, giggling about sneaking out of the bedroom window to go get wasted, as if that were a normal activity for any teenager; Andy was the only one who laughed along with her.

But there was no reason to put it off any longer. After all, discussing Michael Redding's murder and related events over dessert had been standard procedure since the onset of the investigation. *A month ago today*, I silently lamented, *and the killer is still free.*

"This looks delicious," Andy said. "It's amazing how many excellent dessert ideas you have, Marilyn. I should ask you to give my mom some baking lessons once she feels up to it." He caught Chloe's eye and they exchanged smiles. "And it goes without saying that the spaghetti was a culinary delight as well."

"Why, thank you," said Chloe. "Now, unless it's still confidential, would you mind telling us what's going on with the pro-choice message on Lisa's postcard and that flyer we got from the strip club? Is there a connection?"

"You mean, as it pertains to the Michael Redding case?" Andy said. "Well, yes and no."

Chloe and I exchanged "did I miss something?" glances.

"It's not exactly a Yes or No question, babe," Chloe said.

Jack's eyes shot me a large, bold exclamation point. But nothing in Andy's response indicated that the term of endearment was anything he hadn't heard before. He leaned back in his chair.

"What I mean is: yes, of course, the message is a clue that we need to take seriously. Lisa's postcard came from Jenny Ho's, and while at the club you were given a flyer with the same message, so possibly the postcard and the flyer are connected." He paused. "Possibly."

Jack was even more impatient than Chloe and me. "So 'yes,' there's a possible link. Where does the 'no' come in?"

"No, I'm not convinced that 'Your body, your choice' is a reference to the pro-choice movement, where Mrs. Cardwell's postcard is concerned. As I told her, the message could be a bodily threat to her, personally—pay up or else—or it might refer to—" He cut himself off, not sure how much we knew. "It may have something to do with events in Mrs. Cardwell's past."

"That baby she had out of wedlock?" Jack asked.

Oh, why had I felt compelled to share that private part of Lisa's past with him? Chloe must have wondered the same thing. She made a distinct "Tsk" sound, but I avoided her eyes.

"Exactly" said Andy. It was unclear whether he was agreeing with Jack or with Chloe.

"What about that server, Marty?" I asked. "Have you been able to reach her? It must mean something that she pressed that flyer on Alejandra, along with her phone number."

"Ms. Clement and I will be meeting later tonight."

"She's alive, then?"

Their astonished faces made me feel silly, but only for a moment. After all, was it really being paranoid to worry that ill might have befallen a potential witness in a murder case? The possibility should have occurred to all of us, especially to Andy. Lisa deserved credit for being the only one among us to consider it. But Lisa wasn't present, so why bring her name into it?

"Well," I said, "it was quite a coincidence that she disappeared from the club soon after giving us the flyer, don't you think? You must have wondered about that yourself, Andy."

He rewarded my plagiarized logic with a smile. "Good thinking, Marilyn. Unfortunately, we can't tell our dads when to have a heart attack. But listen, I do have some information regarding the receipt from Jenny Ho's that you found in your yard."

"In Zhang's yard, you mean," said Jack.

"It blew out of the hedge between the two yards," Chloe reminded him.

My Sauvignon Blanc suddenly tasted vinegary. Were we about to learn that the receipt belonged to Wei, thereby connecting him to Michael Redding's murder? At best, it would identify him as a patron of sleazy strip clubs.

"The lab was able to trace the receipt based on date

and time, along with a few of the digits in the account number which were still readable. The receipt did not belong to Zhang Wei, which I know might be disappointing news." He grinned. "But possibly not to you, Marilyn."

So that my suddenly flushed cheeks might be interpreted as a reaction to the heat, I dabbed my forehead with the end of my napkin. Was my regard for Wei that obvious? I ventured a glance at Jack, but he was homed in on getting to the bottom of the matter.

"So who did it belong to then?" he demanded. "It's not ours and it's not Zhang Wei's, you say. So whose was it?"

"In fact, Jack," said Andy, "it belonged to Michael Redding."

While Chloe and I digested this stunning bit of news, Jack plowed ahead, so exuberant he nearly toppled his wine glass.

"So that ties Zhang to Redding's murder for sure," he said.

"How so?" Andy asked.

Jack's incredulous eyes went from Chloe to me, then back to Andy. "The dead man's receipt is found in his yard, and that doesn't make him look guilty? What the hell? What am I missing?"

"Well, for one thing, we don't know how the receipt got into the privet. At least, I don't. Do you?"

His smile hadn't wavered, but there was just enough reproach in his voice that Chloe hurried to say "Of course we don't, but ..."

"So you need more evidence, is that it?" Jack pressed.

Andy said only, "I'm going to have to ask you again to trust me. We're almost there."

And for this we had prepared and served him dinner. Still, it was a relief to know he seemed to doubt Wei's guilt.

We thought he would clam up, then. But after a pause during which we all gazed at him with disappointed eyes—actually, Jack's were more disapproving than disappointed—he must have decided he owed us something more in exchange for the meal that had inspired his rave review only minutes before.

"All right then, I'll tell you this. Just between the four of us, Marty Clement is very eager to meet with me. I suspect she knows something relevant to the case."

Jack said, "Presumably something that connects the mysterious Dr. Zhang with the strip club. Maybe she can explain why the receipt was on his lawn."

Andy chuckled. "Sure thing, Jack. But since the wind blew the receipt out of the hedge between the two yards, I suppose I'll need to ask what she knows about you and Marilyn as well."

That set Jack's head to swinging from side to side, a barely audible "Ffft" escaping his lips.

Chloe moved on. "So okay, Andy. But regarding Lisa, she's a mess. Right, Mom?" I nodded, and she continued, "That postcard, especially, really got to her. I think she might appreciate a bodyguard until you have enough evidence to arrest Mr. Zhang—" at this, both Andy and I frowned at her—"or whoever it is you suspect. Would that be possible?"

"I sure can't argue that she's a mess." Andy shook his head with a grin as if we were all having a joke at Lisa's expense. When not even Chloe smiled back, he turned serious.

"I've been in regular contact with Mrs. Cardwell. More than regular. She's nothing if not communicative. And we're patrolling her street around the clock." He laid his napkin on his plate, correctly assuming that seconds were not in the offing. Impatience crept into his voice. "We're watching your street as well, along with the rest of the neighborhood. As we've been doing ever since Mr. Redding's murder."

"Yet someone is finding ways to place threats or other clues in our mailboxes and on our doorsteps," Jack pointed out. "Alejandra, Mrs. Zhang, Marilyn, Bird Legs."

"Lisa," I reminded him. "Let's call her by her name, shall we?"

Chloe rewarded me with a short nod of approval and Jack scowled at both of us.

"Whatever you say. The point is, Detective, have any neighbors outside of the ladies' investigative clique been targeted?"

It's always advisable to follow a reprimand with a compliment. "Good question, Jack," I said. "I've been wondering that myself."

Andy nodded. "Yes indeed, that is an excellent question. And the answer is 'no'." He turned to me. "Any thoughts on the matter, Marilyn?"

I took a moment to process an idea that had just occurred to me. "The others are getting threats of one kind or another. Alejandra's are racist hints about her boy and deportation. Lisa's is harassment and blackmail. You haven't shared whatever delightful messages Mrs. Zhang is getting, but presumably they're threatening as well?"

He nodded. "Go on."

"But the note left on my porch wasn't a threat. It was a request for us—or for me at least—to help you find the murderer. Should we assume that the person making all the threats was not the person who left me the note?"

Andy smiled. "Good thinking, Marilyn. But there is one thing that your note and Mrs. Cardwell's postcard have in common."

"The reference to Jenny Ho's," said Chloe.

"Bingo!" Andy beamed at her. "Lisa was threatened like Alejandra and Mrs. Zhang, connecting her harassment with theirs. But only she and Marilyn received messages that mentioned the strip club, which we suspect is connected somehow to Michael Redding's murder. So that links Lisa's postcard to Marilyn's note, which is thereby tied to all the other harassment." He paused for dramatic effect. "And very likely, therefore, to the murder.

I was impressed, and Chloe beamed her approval. Even Jack could not find an argument with Andy's conclusion.

"Makes sense," he acknowledged. "But why do you think some of the girls are being targeted and not others? What about Chloe and Rachel?"

"Good question, Jack." Andy's condescending tone suggested that he already knew all the answers and was merely testing us: "What do you think, ladies? Chloe's new to the group and doesn't live on the street, which could explain why they haven't bothered with her. But what about Rachel? She hasn't been harassed at all."

"Unless," Chloe said, her eyes lit by a new possibility, "unless there really is a CB radio somewhere in the neighborhood, and someone is using it to terrorize Rachel."

"Too far-fetched," Jack pronounced. "Her doctor already said it's all in her mind, brought on by drugs and booze."

Chloe frowned at him. "That's not how she put it, exactly."

Andy surprised us by saying, "Let's assume for a moment that Rachel's therapist is wrong. That the voices are real and not in Rachel's head. And that all the threats and Marilyn's note came from the same person who is responsible for what Rachel is hearing. What conclusions would that lead us to?"

Chloe giggled. "I feel like we're in detective school, and you're the instructor." She had refilled all our wine glasses some minutes ago, not bothering to ask who was interested. We all continued to sip as our brains churned away in overdrive.

Chloe offered up a theory: "Since the voice Rachel hears is female, would one conclusion be that a woman is behind all of the harassment? This Liliana person Rachel keeps accusing? Deb's former lover."

"Not necessarily a woman," said Andy. "Electronic

voice manipulation is easy enough for anyone with the right skill set.”

My turn: “Maybe someone is trying to distract us because we’re onto something?” Even as I spoke, I knew it made little sense. “But we’re all working together. Why would he harass the others and encourage me?”

“Maybe he likes you,” Andy said, “and doesn’t care much for your friends.”

Naturally, Wei was the first person I thought of—as Andy must have anticipated, although his noncommittal smile could have meant anything.

“Let’s focus on Rachel for a minute.” Andy turned to me. “What do you think, Marilyn? Could her therapist be wrong? Could those CB radio transmissions, or whatever they are, could they be real and not just in Rachel’s head?”

It was a tempting theory: Rachel wasn’t delusional but was being harassed like Alejandra, Lisa, and Mrs. Zhang. But as much as I wanted to latch onto the idea, I couldn’t get past the fact that no one else had heard the woman’s voice, not even when standing beside Rachel when she claimed to be listening to the one-sided conversations.

Andy read my mind. “Weren’t you both with her in Mr. Zhang’s yard the other night when she accused him of lying about not hearing the transmission? And you didn’t hear anything, right?”

“What if he was lying?” I heard myself say—that on-again, off-again suspicion of Wei refusing to stay in the closet I kept shoving it into. “The voices had stopped by the time Chloe and I arrived. What if Wei had some kind of transmitter inside his house, recorded the voices, and then—” But Andy was shaking his head.

“What about the other times? You told me once that she heard the voice when you and Alejandra were with her in Alejandra’s backyard. Mr. Zhang was nowhere around, right?”

"Right. Not that I know of."

"And then again when you were standing in her own front yard with her?"

"Yes. We heard nothing, even when she shushed us and told us to listen. Then another time, we came upon her berating Lisa—this was back when we only knew her as the woman with the cats who killed Rachel's birds—she was ranting at Lisa about not admitting she could hear the voices, just as she later accused Wei. Dr. Zhang, I mean."

Andy drained his glass, and Chloe refilled it, oblivious to my frown. He would have to drive home, after all. Then again, there was always Uber.

"Speaking of Rachel," Andy said, "I stopped by to see her today."

"Any idea yet when she can come home?" Jack's concern seemed real enough. Maybe he missed the view from his office window.

"Well, there's good news and bad news about that, I'm afraid."

"Why haven't you told me?" Chloe was visibly annoyed. "Tell us now, for god's sake."

"Mostly good news," he assured her. "They're dismissing her from the psych ward in two days. They've decided she's no longer a threat to herself."

"If she ever was," said Chloe. "She claimed she took too many pills after losing track of the count."

"And the bad news?" Jack asked.

"She won't be home for a few weeks. They've convinced her to check into a rehab center up in Marin County."

"Oh, thank God," I said. My obvious relief surprised all of them, so I felt the need to defend my remark. "She so clearly needs help." Then off my tongue rolled words that had nothing to do with the situation. "My mother was an alcoholic. If she had gotten assistance in time—" I broke off. I hadn't meant to say it, and I didn't want to continue. But they were all waiting, and I heard myself finish: "She would never have met that man."

Damn that second glass of Sauvignon Blanc.

They waited until it was clear that I had no intention of elaborating, and then Chloe did me the favor of leading the conversation back to Rachel.

"So it'll be a few weeks before she gets to come home," Chloe lamented.

"Drying out takes a while," Jack said.

"I sure hope she sticks with it." Embarrassed by my previous outburst, I stood and began collecting dessert plates and wine glasses.

What was I thinking, blurting out my mother's mistakes? She and her problems were none of their business and had nothing to do with Rachel's situation.

With Andy on his way to meet with Marty, Chloe made a fresh pot of decaf. We sat at the table and rehashed what we had learned at dinner.

Andy had said he was closing in on the killer. And to my relief, everything he had told us suggested that whoever he was closing in on was not Zhang Wei. Still, there was no denying the relief on Lisa's face when she had peered anxiously at Wei's doorstep and found it empty. Maybe Wei wasn't a suspect in Andy's eyes, but for some reason, Lisa was afraid of him.

My own back-and-forth guilty/not guilty judgment of Wei was eating at me as well, but of course I could not discuss that with Chloe or Jack. I needed to talk to Lisa. Alone with her, I could find out why she was afraid of Wei— if in fact her fear was real and not a product of my skittish imagination.

"We can't have a meeting tonight," Chloe said with a wide yawn. "I need catch-up sleep. And Lisa's jitters are contagious. Let's have a night off."

"I'll text the others," I said.

So the meeting was cancelled, which was fine with me.

"Would you come up to my room for a minute, Mom? I

need to talk to you about something."

After closing her bedroom door behind us, she sat down and patted the bed beside her. "Sit down."

Uh-oh.

She took my hand and gave it a squeeze before she began. "Mom, you were obviously upset tonight at dinner when you mentioned your birth mother. You almost never talked about her when Nat and I were kids. We don't even know her name." I reflexively pulled my hand away, and she hesitated before adding, "I wish you would confide in me, Mom. You can trust me."

I did trust her. These past few weeks had brought us closer, allowing me to see just what a responsible, thoughtful, loving adult she had become. But did I trust those memories? Would letting them out of the closet be cathartic? Or would they turn on me, flogging me into another panic attack?

I did my three deep breaths routine and began.

"Her name was Shirley McElroy. A single parent, living on government assistance, addicted to alcohol and rough men. She took up with one loser after another, and one despicable bastard in particular."

Despite this accurate, unflattering depiction of her character, my heart ached with the parade of memories that marched across my vision like scenes from a movie trailer: the two of us snuggled on the sofa watching cartoons together, her belting out "Hit the Road, Jack" while braiding my hair. The way she always called me "Bunny." That last, long, desperate hug.

"When I was five years old, she would leave me alone in the apartment to go hang out in taverns with this horrible man, Lee Houston. They'd come home plastered. He would slap her around, and—and—sometimes he would force himself on her."

"Oh, Mom, no." Chloe reached for my hand and held it tightly.

"I'd hear everything through my bedroom wall. But she always came to my room later to reassure me she was okay." I sat for a few moments with my eyes closed, gathering my thoughts. "One night they stayed out until nearly daylight. Came home wasted, of course. That night, he—they screamed at each other, and he was threatening her. I forced myself to go into the living room and—and he had her pressed against the wall with his hands on her throat."

"Oh god, Mom ..."

"He let go of her when he saw me, but I ran across the hall and hammered on the neighbor's door."

Chloe squeezed my hand harder. "You poor thing."

"Yes, that's what Mrs. Channing said. And the police. And the social workers who decided enough was enough, and that I should go into foster care."

"That must have been so traumatic for you, to be taken from your mom at that age. Even if she wasn't the best parent."

"I do think she loved me." I paused. "Once I was born, anyway."

Chloe looked at me curiously, so I explained, "When I was a teenager, I learned from Molly that Shirley had wanted to get an abortion, but her family talked her out of it."

"Grandma Anderson told you that?" Chloe frowned. "Maybe it was a lie. How did she know what your mom wanted?"

"Molly and Shirley were friends in high school. Stayed friends until Shirley's behavior got out of control."

Chloe pursed her lips. "I loved Grandma Anderson, but that was just so wrong of her to tell you that."

"Anyway, my dear, that's the end of that story."

She wasn't ready to go yet. "That explains a lot, Mom. Not just about your reaction to aggressive behavior, but also your views on abortion."

No surprise that she would make that assumption. But irritating, all the same.

"Not at all," I insisted. "I just know it's wrong to kill innocent babies, and I would feel that way regardless." Then I saw that I was missing an opportunity. "But it's true that I thank God every day for allowing me to live." I held her eyes. "Every day, Chloe."

I steeled myself for her argument that everyone's circumstances were different, blah, blah, blah. But she only said, "Thanks for telling me, Mom," and hugged me.

Downstairs, Jack was watching TV. He looked up and asked if I wanted to find a movie on Netflix. I had planned to call Lisa to check on her anxiety level and arrange a coffee date for the next day, but the wistful nature of his request, along with an exhaustion that was due in part to my impromptu therapy session with Chloe, propelled me to the sofa.

"Comedy? Thriller? The latest Avengers?" He waved the remote.

"Comedy, please. Make me laugh out loud."

As I drifted off to sleep later, Andy's grinning countenance floated into view. He waggled a finger at me as he pulled his notepad out of my sight.

Maybe he likes you, he said. *And doesn't care much for your friends.*

28

On the morning of the Fourth, I awoke rested and with a more positive outlook. Not only had Andy promised to have news for us soon regarding the murder, but my mood had been lightened by my talk with Chloe the night before. Her extended visit with us had been a true gift—a rainbow amidst the storm that had engulfed us for weeks.

Instead of driving downtown for the parade, Jack suggested we just take a walk around the neighborhood. "Too damn hot," he said. "By noon, it'll be 105 out there. And there's something I want to run by you."

I had been looking forward to the parade, especially since Chloe was in town to accompany us. With its floats, flags, marching bands, and familiar faces in the streets and in the crowd, it was always a spectacle of hometown pride and good old American patriotism at its best. But Jack had piqued my curiosity, and he was right about the heat.

Wei wasn't on his mother's front porch as we set out, which was fine with me. My conflicted feelings about him would be sorted out soon enough, and until then, I was inclined to avoid awkward encounters.

As we crossed the street, a mournful bray caused Jack

to jump back. But Boondoggles was separated from us by Alejandra's front windowpane.

"Hey Boonie," I called.

Jack sniffed. "So the hound's your pal now, too?"

"He's not a bad fellow," I said, ignoring the sarcasm. "Alejandra has trained him to behave." This last part was a stretch to be sure. But it was true that Boonie wasn't a bad fellow.

"We don't do this enough anymore," Jack grumbled. "You're hardly ever up before eleven or twelve, and you nap in the afternoons most days. Later, you're too tired."

Torn between guilt and annoyance, I chose the middle ground. "Jack, I know I said I'd try to move some of our get-togethers to daytime hours. Things have just been so crazy." He grunted, and I continued, "And soon, our group won't have any reason to meet. According to Andy, at least."

"You bet."

"You don't really believe he's close to solving the case?"

"Who knows? I sure as hell hope so. It's been a month now."

He stopped and squinted toward Butte County in the north, where smoke from a thousand-acre forest fire was blocking our view of the distant hills. "Another day in paradise," he muttered. "I hope we're not in for another season where we have to mask up to go outdoors."

I stopped too, but not because of the air. We had turned the corner, and two houses down from us, Andy was driving away from Lisa's house accompanied by Officer Baumgartner, one of his two assistants. Lisa stood in the doorway, shooting eye daggers at their retreating vehicle. Ten o'clock in the morning, Jack pointed out, and she was still in her robe. Her bun was covered by a red handkerchief-print bandana that was straight out of the 1950s.

"What's this?" Jack mumbled. "More trouble for that

woman? She sure has her share.”

I raised my arm in a greeting, but as soon as our eyes met, Lisa backed into the house and closed the door behind her.

“Well then.” Apparently, I wasn’t the only one with rusty friendship skills. “What do you suppose? More blackmail?”

“God knows. We’ll have to let Chloe sweet-talk it out of him.”

Since Jack was in a peevish mood and inclined to stay there, I spent the remaining two blocks of our walk silently pondering the purpose of Andy’s most recent visit to Lisa. We were approaching our house when I remembered Jack’s earlier comment.

“You wanted to run something by me,” I reminded him.

“Oh yeah.” He cleared his throat. “It’s probably a crazy idea, but I’ve been thinking about Chloe’s suggestion.”

By the silence that followed, I gathered I should have remembered said suggestion, but I searched my brain and came up with nothing.

“You remember,” he prompted. “She said maybe I should run for city council.”

“Oh, that.” And without giving it enough thought, I added, “I thought she was kidding.”

He bristled. “Why did you assume that? Is it such a far-fetched idea?”

“Not at all. It’s just that—” *It’s just that you’re well known for your inflammatory letters to the local newspaper, in which you disagree with most everything the popular mayor and the equally esteemed current council has promoted*—”It’s just that you’ve never shown any interest before,” I said. “Not far-fetched at all.”

“And a lot of people agree with me, as Chloe pointed out. Those people who don’t kiss the mayor’s behind deserve representation, too.”

Although I figured his odds were about as good as

being struck by a falling airplane or catching the plague, I said, "Well, if you want to do it, you'll have my full support."

"The next election is a year off yet. We'd have to lay the groundwork, build a support base," he said. "Do some fundraising, social media and all that."

I cringed, imagining myself glad-handing strangers and sucking up to potential donors.

"Whatever it takes," I said. Maybe I could distract him somehow, perhaps prod him to get serious about the woodworking. I could whip up some projects on his behalf.

The morning and early afternoon passed without the news Andy had promised. But at three o'clock, my phone rang. It was Lisa, calling to apologize.

"I guess you saw that imbecile leaving my house this morning. I'm sorry if I was rude. I wasn't in the mood to talk."

The insult was a bit much, I thought. Borderline incompetent, perhaps, but an imbecile? Then it occurred to me that maybe I could use her disdain to my advantage.

"Believe me, I share your lack of faith in Detective Thacker. Jack and I both do. We give him the benefit of the doubt to keep Chloe happy."

I felt safe telling this half-lie since Chloe was well out of earshot, having left for a grocery run with Jack only minutes before.

"I sensed that," she said. "What we put up with for our kids, huh? Anyway, I was wondering if you might come over for coffee. I could really use some company, and there are things I want to tell you." To my surprise she added, "You're such a good listener, Marilyn."

Chloe and Jack had gone to buy steaks for the grill, along with ingredients for coleslaw and potato salad, our nod toward the otherwise unobserved holiday—that and the limp American flag above the front steps. So why not grab the chance to chat with Lisa?

"I'll be right over."

As I walked down the front steps, I reflexively glanced over at Mrs. Zhang's porch.

Wei did not put out his cigarette, and I interpreted this to mean that I was not to be invited onto the porch for a chat. But while we might never again have the friendly rapport I'd enjoyed before, I would take the high road and resume being neighborly. His response would be up to him.

"Good afternoon, Wei. Happy Fourth of July."

"Yes," he said. "Let us hope so." There was uncertainty in his voice, and sadness.

Before I could decide whether it was appropriate to ask what he meant, he said, "I suspect it will be." He inclined his head with a smile so slight and fleeting that I might have imagined it.

"Well," I said. Then watching his face closely, I added, "I'm off for a coffee date with Lisa. You know—Mrs. Cardwell who lives around the corner?"

I remembered how he had watched Lisa and me talking on the morning Rachel was taken away in the ambulance. I had wondered then if his frown meant he was concerned that I might tarnish his reputation by spreading my suspicion of him around the neighborhood. But now his expression moved from startled to concerned to bored so quickly that I wondered if I'd imagined the startled and concerned segments.

"I see. You two are friends, then?"

"Sort of. We're just getting to know one another."

"I see," he said again. "Well, have a nice time."

Thus dismissed, I mumbled "Thanks" and crossed the street. Before turning the corner, I stole a look over my shoulder. He was speaking into his phone, and as our eyes met, he turned his back to the street. Well, then. What did I care? If Jack, Chloe—and possibly Lisa—were right, he was most likely a cold-blooded killer—or at best, an immoral man who frequented strip clubs.

Then I reminded myself again that Andy seemed to share my gut feeling about Wei's innocence. The others were condemning him without proof—and I had done the same, jumping to conclusions about that receipt—but that was not how it was done in America. Not how it was meant to be done, anyway.

From now on, no matter what my conversation with Lisa revealed, "innocent until proven guilty" would be my stance regarding Zhang Wei. As I approached her house, I was hoping she wouldn't give me reason to rethink my decision.

29

After ushering me inside, Lisa thrust her head through the door for some sharp-eyed, left-to-right street surveillance. As she latched the deadbolt behind us, I began to wish I'd declined her invitation. My own stress was causing me enough problems. Why was I encouraging this fearful, distraught woman to unburden herself on me, potential new friend or not?

But she had already locked us both inside, so I might as well find out what Andy had been doing at her house this morning, and if she had any other pertinent information to share.

Motioning me to follow, she hurried into the kitchen. The hunch of her back and a slight limp were new and probably attributable to her medical problem.

Thank goodness, she had ditched the stained robe and Lucy Ricardo bandana we had glimpsed earlier as she stood in her doorway glaring at Andy's departing vehicle. The familiar tan cargo shorts were back, along with a sleeveless top in patriotic color blocks, and the severity of her bun was softened by a stars and stripes headband. The clothes were clean and unwrinkled, and she had brushed color onto her cheeks, positive indicators regarding her emotional state.

Still, if we ever did get to the point of shopping together, I would have to tactfully discourage so much exposure of those twig-like limbs. Even on a day like this, 101 degrees and climbing, there were other options.

I took a seat at her small kitchen table while she poured coffee at the counter. I would've preferred iced tea or ice water, Diet Coke on ice, anything with ice on a day like this. But she hadn't asked.

Her tremor was the worst I'd seen it, and the cup she was holding in her right hand lost about a fourth of its steaming contents on its way to the table. "Darn," she said. But thank God, she spared me the mention of her mysterious medical condition. She had other things on her mind.

"The incompetent, bumbling fool," she grumbled as she sat down across from me. "He's on the wrong track for sure now."

She paused to concentrate on her coffee. As she clutched the cup with both hands and lifted it slowly to her mouth, I was startled to see that her entire head was bobbing ever so slightly. Was her condition deteriorating, or had I been so focused on her hands that I'd failed to notice that the trembling didn't stop there? But it was rude to stare, and this didn't seem the time to ask about her health.

"You mean Andy, right? But are you talking about the murder case? Or your harassment? Or both?"

Her phone was on the table in front of her, and since my arrival she had looked at it twice despite the absence of any chiming, beeping, or buzzing. Now she picked it up again, and it bounced out of her twitching hands into the pooled coffee she had spilled onto the table earlier.

Muttering the f-word as effortlessly as Rachel often did, she got up again to retrieve a sponge and went after the mess with a vengeance, scrubbing first the phone and then the tablecloth, her teeth clenched in frustration. Despite her tidy appearance and the immaculate state of her home—a reassuring whiff of lemon-scented Lysol still lingered—she was clearly overwrought, and while I wanted to ask about the incessant checking of the phone, I didn't want to add to her aggravation.

But without my asking, she spoke up.

"My son sometimes calls at this time of day. On Sundays. Or holidays like this."

"That's nice," I said, and of course I meant it. But I couldn't allow us to get sidetracked. While exploring familial relationships might be an effective bonding experience, such chitchat could wait for another day. "You asked me over because you wanted to talk. Was there something specific?"

She sat back down, and as her eyes locked onto mine, she clasped her hands, prayer-like, and rested her chin on her fingertips. "Oh Lord, there's so much to say, I don't know where to begin."

"You said that Andy was on the wrong track," I reminded her again, striving to sound helpful rather than impatient. "You could start by telling me what you meant by that."

"Do you know how many babies are aborted every day in the United States, Marilyn?"

Caught off-guard by the unexpected detour, I swallowed a painful amount of coffee. When I had finished coughing, I said, "Too many. But no, I can't recall the number, although I'm sure I've read it."

"Three thousand," she said. "Every day, Marilyn."

"A travesty," I said.

Your body, your choice, the postcard mailed to Lisa had read. If the sender had meant to shake her up, he had certainly succeeded.

"It's murder," she corrected, emphasizing with her imposing eyes as well as her voice.

"Agreed," I said. "Except maybe in the most extreme cases."

She frowned. "What do you mean? When is it ever okay?"

"Well, for example, my friend Sue Ellen's niece was about to give birth to a baby whose brain was mostly unformed. She had two other small kids, and—"

"Only God has the right to decide who lives and who dies."

What was this about? She was angry, but there was a deep sadness there as well, and no wonder. Such a depressing matter to be dwelling on. Especially for a former nun, who would of course have strong feelings on the subject, which explained the postcard with its pro-abortion slogan, meant to antagonize her.

"In most cases, I agree that it's wrong," I said, sensing that she was in no mood for a discussion of the finer points. "And too easily accessed in this country, certainly."

She pressed both her hands against the damp tablecloth, forcing them to be still. "You agree with me that abortion is murder, Marilyn?" Her eyes held mine, and before I could answer, she continued, "And still you befriend that man?"

With that question, a missing puzzle piece swam toward me. But instead of snatching it, trimming it to size, and jamming it into place as Chloe had done with the ornery jigsaw puzzle, I slapped it away.

"I don't understand. Are you talking about Zhang Wei?"

"Duh," she said.

It was the kind of response I would've expected from Rachel, not from an articulate woman in her fifth decade.

"The way he's always watching. Standing there on the old lady's front porch, puffing on his cigarette like some cool detective from a noir novel." She leaned forward in a menacing manner that caused me to draw back. "And he's always walking past my house." She shuddered.

"I'm confused," I said. "Do you think Wei is blackmailing you? That he sent you the postcard with the threatening message?" Part of me wanted to stop there. But why had I come, if not to press her for the truth? "He's the connection with 'Your body, your choice.' Is that what you're saying?"

And as I spoke, the missing puzzle piece plunked itself into place. Instead of shouting "Voila!" like Chloe, I uttered my own silent, frustrated "Duh."

Because who performs abortions, if not gynecologists? How had I been blind to this obvious connection between Wei's profession and the "Your body, your choice," threat? And none of the others had grasped the significance either—not even Andy Thacker, apparently, whose job it was to connect the dots. Or maybe he was aware of the link and had deemed it unimportant. I hoped that was the case.

"Is that what you're saying?" I repeated. "That Zhang Wei is your blackmailer? Because Andy thinks the photo of Jenny Ho's on your postcard ties it to Michael Redding's murder, and with the mention of abortion, then ..." I almost didn't dare to continue. "Are you saying Zhang Wei killed Michael Redding?"

Lisa's smile was contemptuous. "I'm saying you should think twice about nursing a crush on a murderer. If you believe abortion is sinful, as I do, how can you stand to even look at the man, much less indulge in romantic fantasies about him?"

"Whoa, now," I protested. "I do not fantasize about Zhang Wei."

So what if I had done so on occasion? What business was that of hers? Anyway, it was unlikely to happen again if Lisa's accusations turned out to be true. But surely her claims were unfounded, or at least exaggerated. If Wei's work included abortions, perhaps there were special circumstances, like in the instance of Sue Ellen's niece. And murder? On what grounds was she accusing him?

"So when you looked over at his front porch the other night like you were afraid you might see him there, your fear was based solely on the fact that he used to be a gynecologist? I mean, even if he did perform an occasional abortion, maybe it was only—"

She cut me off. "Only when 'necessary'?" Her attempt to put quotation marks around the word with her fingers were foiled by their trembling. "Like in the case of your friend's brain-dead baby, who was not given the chance to be healed by God's mercy? No, no, no. No, Zhang was a nondiscriminating baby killer, my dear. This is the man you're sweet on."

"But Lisa, do you and Wei have a—a history of some kind? Why would he blackmail you? And why would he kill Redding? Maybe that's what Andy's missing: a motive."

Lisa checked her phone again and then laid it on the table, face down, before again turning her intense gaze on me.

"You're not listening, Marilyn. I'm trying to tell you that Zhang did something much worse than blackmail. Worse than killing Redding, who was no prince himself."

I ignored her disrespectful jab at the deceased. "Lisa, do you know for sure that Wei performed abortions? Not all gynecologists do. It's a—a specialty, I would imagine."

"Oh yes. I know everything there is to know about Zhang." Then she added, pointedly, "And so did Michael Redding." She stood up and walked to the counter. "Anyway, there's more to be said. I'll have to hurry. Would you like more coffee?"

"No thanks. Have you told Andy everything you know?"

She splashed coffee into both our cups anyway. "Forget all that for a minute. There's something you're going to learn about, and I wanted you to hear it from me."

When she returned to her chair, she reached over and laid her quivering hand on mine. I hid my distaste so as not to discourage her from confiding in me.

"Oh, this is so difficult." She withdrew her hand, thankfully, and began to smooth the fabric of her shorts, looking down to avoid my eyes. "Andy and his cohort have taken my computer. Also some notebooks and software."

She looked up to check my reaction. When I failed to find an appropriate response to this bombshell, she continued, "Thacker has come to suspect, you see—I mean to say that he's getting to the bottom of this whole—" She waved her hands in the air as if trying to capture the right words—"this whole blackmail thing I had him investigating."

Having gotten that off her chest, she picked up her coffee cup and then set it back down without drinking. "Oh well, it was inevitable. Once you all pointed him at poor Marty."

"Marty? Marty from the strip club? You know Marty?"

"I thought I did," was her odd response.

"Do you know what Marty has told Andy? He hasn't shared that with the rest of us."

"He'll figure it out now. Probably has already. All about the blackmail and the other harassment," she said. The bitterness in her voice surprised me.

"Well, isn't that a good thing?" I asked, although everything in her manner suggested otherwise. "You've been complaining that he should've solved it long ago."

She was shaking her head. "You don't understand. And why would you? Which is why I invited you over here. To explain myself."

She grasped my arm and spoke deliberately, as if delivering sad but important news to a child. "It was me, Marilyn. I broke through my own back door, ransacked my kitchen, and faked the phone calls I told Thacker about."

Despite the doubts I had already been harboring about her mental stability, I was astonished. "But why would you do such a thing? You're telling me you spread cat poop on your own kitchen countertops?"

Her smile was rueful. "Yes, I'm afraid I did."

Instead of trying to justify this outlandish behavior, she took another unexpected turn. "There's more I want to say about your choice of friends." She gestured toward the window that looked out on Rachel's backyard, and her eyes hardened. "That alcoholic lesbian over there—"

"Now, hold on a minute. Rachel is indeed my friend. Homosexuality is—"

"Sin," she finished for me. "What's happening to our country, Marilyn? No morals anymore. Homosexuals marrying and adopting innocent children to corrupt? Illegals swarming across the border and popping out babies for us to support with our tax money."

"That's not always the motive," I said, still absorbing her malice toward Rachel while feeling compelled to defend immigrants on behalf of Alejandra. "And anyway, it's not the children's fault. If they're hungry, we still need to feed them."

"And send them to school. Pay their medical bills. And the liberals with their open border baloney don't bother to think about whether there might be a limit to how many we can support. Too many foreigners, too much perversion. I'm sick and tired of it all. This is my country and it's being warped into a place I barely recognize."

While I could see her point about open borders and our nation's declining values, Lisa's slurs and overall hateful attitude were disturbingly unchristian. Anyway, I hadn't come here to talk politics. Or to be lectured about my choice of companions.

"It's a difficult situation," I conceded. "But nevertheless, Alejandra is still my friend. As is Rachel."

She waved a quivering hand in a gesture of impatience.

"I know you're a Christian like me, Marilyn. That's why I want you to hear my motives from me and not from that dimwit detective." She spat out his name: "Thacker, your daughter's boyfriend. Talk about your affirmative action taken a step too far."

Stunned to hear a thought I'd once entertained spewed back at me with such malice, I could only offer a lame rebuttal. "That's a bit mean, Lisa."

"What's wrong? she asked. "You said earlier you agreed with me that he was incompetent."

"It's just—Lisa, all this venom towards the neighbors and Andy. I don't think it's healthy. I thought we were all working together."

"Who is 'we'?" She asked disdainfully. "Do you mean our little middle-of-the-night gang? You, chubby-pants Chloe, the dyke, the chalupa, and me?" She chuckled. "What a motley crew."

For a moment, I felt immersed in the kind of semi-nightmare I associated with having consumed a spicy dinner too close to bedtime. Certainly, this was not the woman with whom I had hoped to go shopping for clothes and makeup at Nordstrom.

When I had recovered my voice, I laid into her.

"How dare you insult my daughter? And my friends, too—yes, they are my friends and what business is that of yours? You—" And then the echo of her remark silenced me.

She watched awareness settle over me, and not knowing how to interpret it, gazed at me with a mixture of curiosity and contempt.

"Chalupa," I said. "You just called Alejandra 'Chalupa.'"

She shrugged. "So I did. But maybe Messalina would be more appropriate. Or Thrift Store Sally." She chuckled at her own wit.

"Chalupa," I repeated.

She gave her head an impatient "whatever" shake and checked her phone again.

Anger propelled me to my feet. "*You* left those hateful notes for Alejandra. You threatened her! You—so was it also you who sent the postcard to Mrs. Zhang and left the envelope with clues on my porch?"

"Oh dear," she said. "I've upset you. I do wish you'd sit back down."

Despite her startling confessions and the disturbing insight into her character, I sensed there was more to be learned—some of it possibly relevant to Michael Redding's murder—so I swallowed my reservations and returned to my chair.

"Those are hate crimes you've committed," I informed her. "You must know that."

She sighed. "I didn't expect to get caught. Yes, I might get a few years behind bars for harassing Alejandra and old lady Zhang. They'll get me for hacking into Rachel's security system and harassing her, too. And of course, there's a penalty for wasting police time on a crime I committed myself."

I was a step behind. "You hacked into Rachel's security system? What on earth, Lisa?" It struck me that she might be delusional. "You were a nun and later a clerk at the DMV. How would you know how to hack a security system?"

She gave me a sly smile. "You should have asked more questions, Marilyn. You would've learned about a whole other chapter in my life. But I'll let Thacker fill you in about that. It's all in my records, which he has no doubt nosed his way through by now, thanks to Marty."

"What does Marty have to do with this? How do you know her, anyway?"

She shook her head. "Again, you'll need to wait for Thacker. We need to talk about Zhang Wei."

"Okay," I said. "You're accusing him of killing Michael Redding. Based on what? Just because he was a gynecologist? That doesn't mean he's a murderer."

She swiped invisible crumbs off the tablecloth with her palm. "Zhang was an abortionist. Which is another word for 'murderer'," she insisted, her voice rising. "If Dumbass would investigate him properly, he'd learn about the women who died from botched abortions done in his clinic. Not to mention the hundreds of babies."

The coffee soured in my stomach. Botched abortions. Dead women. Murderer. I could not reconcile the words with the gentle, soft-spoken Zhang Wei.

"And of course he killed Redding," she added. "Redding knew everything. Sure, abortion is legal, sadly. But carelessness resulting in death is not. Nor are certain drug transactions."

Her phone lit up, but she merely glanced at it and laid it back down. We surveyed each other in silence until it brightened again to announce the arrival of a new text. She turned the phone face down on the table and her anxious eyes bore into mine.

"Thacker's trying to reach me. That's why I had to tell you all this now. He'll try to pin Michael Redding's murder on me because of what he found in my records." She grasped my arm again. "I swear to you, Marilyn. It wasn't me who killed Redding."

"But how would Andy—"

She leaned toward me, her words pouring forth in a torrent. "Zhang is the guilty one. He murdered Redding. But more important—listen to me, Marilyn. Zhang and his partner, Dr. George Abelman, they—" She swallowed, then forced the words out: "They killed my daughter."

"Your daughter! But you said your daughter lives in Reno—"

"Zhang deserves to die for the deaths of my Amanda and the others—at least one more that I know of. And all the innocent babies. Not to mention Michael Redding."

My heart was alternately galloping and skipping. I experienced a wave of vertigo. *Breathe, Marilyn. This is no time for a panic attack.*

Her words were still tumbling over each other. "I hope you'll forgive me for any worry I caused you, Marilyn. I like you, and I had really hoped we could be friends. I didn't know you would get suspicious of Jack over the Jenny Ho and porn site clues I gave Thacker. I had to steer him toward those places, so he would find the killer.”

“So those clues pointed to Zhang Wei—how exactly?”

“I don’t have time to get into that,” she said again. “Thacker will lay it all out for you.”

“But why didn’t you just tell Andy—wait a second! How did you know I was suspicious of Jack? I never told you that.”

She got up and walked to the window again. When I rose to confront her, she turned and leaned against the sink.

“Lisa, did you bug my house? Or Alejandra’s? Otherwise, you could not have known about my suspicions. Or about Alejandra’s legal status, which you mentioned in those awful notes you wrote to her.”

“I wired Alejandra’s house, not yours,” she said defensively. “I wouldn’t do that to you.”

She braced herself against the edge of the sink. She was ashen and her trembling had worsened. I knew she needed to sit down, but I was too angry to suggest it.

“Lisa, why did you join our group if you’re so disdainful of us? And why the clues on my doorstep? If you suspected the killer was Wei, why not just go to Andy?”

“I’m not disdainful of you, Marilyn.” Her desperate eyes begged me to understand. “Listen, if I had accused Zhang directly, Thacker would’ve assumed I had it in for the bastard because of my daughter. He needed help, and you all seemed eager to lend a hand. I gave you the clues and joined your meetings so I could give you a push now and then, that’s all.”

It was all so incredible. Could it really be true? Maybe she was insane or suffering extreme paranoia brought on by anxiety. Or maybe she was on medication for the Parkinson’s and having an adverse reaction.

Her voice grew wistful. “At first I was kind of glad you were suspicious of Jack. I was jealous when I’d see you out walking together, sharing a private joke, settling into your retirement. You two had what Dale and I would've had if that illegal son-of-a-bitch hadn't killed him and robbed us of the chance." She blinked away tears. "I didn't mean to hurt you, Marilyn. That was before I got to know you."

While she waited for me to do the Christian thing and forgive her, I pondered my next move. She had just confessed to harassing my neighbors, eavesdropping on our private conversations, bugging Alejandra's house, even blackmailing herself and vandalizing her own home. No mentally stable person would be capable of such behavior. So why was I still standing in her kitchen instead of sprinting for the door, dialing Andy on my phone as I went?

But oddly, I didn't feel threatened. Her claim that she liked me and had hoped to be friends seemed genuine. It could never happen now, of course, but this wasn't the time to let her know that. And while leaving was the logical thing for me to do, curiosity trumped common sense, and I sat back down.

Dragging one of her spindly legs, she walked over to join me. She grasped the table edge and lowered herself halfway before collapsing into the chair. Our conversation might have been easing her conscience, but it was certainly not doing her medical condition any good.

I was about to press for details about her eavesdropping, but she guessed my intention and waved me off. "I'll let Thacker fill you in. I thought he'd never catch on. But—" she raised her shoulders in a 'who knew?' gesture. "I never thought he'd get to Marty."

No point asking about Marty again, so I backtracked.

"Why did you lie about the blackmail, Lisa? And vandalizing your own kitchen? Why call attention to yourself?"

"I needed contact with Thacker so I could keep an eye on his progress, or lack of it, in the murder case. Because I know I could be the next victim. As I said, Marilyn, I know all about Dr. Zhang Wei. And he knows that I know, which is why he's always watching my house."

"But why not just tell Andy—"

"I told you why! He wouldn't believe me because of certain things he's found out by now." She clutched my arm tighter. "Please, Marilyn, help me. You have Thacker's ear—tell him about those murdered girls and their babies. It was Wei who killed them—Wei and his butcher partner. He deserves to die for that alone, not to mention what he did to Redding."

The doorbell chimed, loud and unexpected, startling both of us. Lisa pushed herself up from the table and shuffled into the dining room to a cabinet where she jerked open a drawer.

And to my horror, she pulled out a handgun.

30

I screamed and sprang from my chair as Chloe's half-joking question rang in my ears: *"Would you really want to be in the same room with Lisa and a loaded gun?"*

It had to be Andy at the door, didn't it? *Please God, let it be Andy.* I wanted to call out a warning, but the shout died in my throat as I became mesmerized by the sight of Lisa struggling to hold onto the gun as she staggered like a drunk toward the front door.

I found my voice. "Lisa, please. Put the gun away. It's only Andy—"

"Wait here! It's too soon for Thacker. Stay back." The pistol wobbled dangerously in her hands.

After peering through the eyehole, she cried "Oh!" and weaved her way back to the French door in the kitchen, where she yanked down the shade, stepped back and stood clutching the gun with both hands, aiming it in the general direction of the back door.

"It's him, Marilyn! He killed Redding and now he wants to silence me. He knows Thacker's getting close."

I lunged for my purse and fumbled through it, panic growing as I remembered laying my phone on the kitchen counter after texting Jack that I was leaving to visit with Lisa. Her own phone was on the dining room table, and I would have to go around her to reach it. Instead of risking it, I pleaded in a whisper, "Lisa, please. Let's call Andy and let him handle this."

She dropped the pistol, but it wasn't my plea that was her undoing. The gun danced off her fumbling fingers and fell a few feet away. She bent over to reach for it, grasping the table's edge to steady herself, but my foot got there first and sent it flying into a corner of the dining room. From her bent position, she latched onto my leg for support, but I shrieked and pulled away.

And then we both screamed as one of the panes in the French door shattered, filling the room with the sound of splintering glass. *It's Andy. It has to be Andy!*

"It's him!" Lisa shrieked. "Marilyn, it's Zhang. The gun—pick up the gun!"

She collapsed onto the kitchen floor and struggled into a sitting position, her arms flailing wildly despite her efforts to wrap them around herself. She had lost control of both arms and, I assumed, both legs. Her terror amplified my own, and I ran to collect the gun, thanking God for Jack's insistence that we both complete a firearms training course when we'd bought the pistol for his bedside table. *God, don't make me have to do this. Let it be Andy. Please let it be Andy.*

I pointed the pistol at the door, willing my hands to stop trembling. "I have a loaded gun," I screeched. "I've called the police." *Please let it be Andy.*

I watched in horror as a bare arm slipped through a jagged opening in the shattered pane, pushed aside the shade, and unlocked the door in one deft motion. The door inched open.

As Wei's eyes met mine, I moaned and took a step back. Lisa shrieked, "Marilyn! He'll kill us both! Pull the trigger!"

Lisa's terror was real, I was sure of it. I had no choice but to accept the truth: Zhang Wei, who was standing in the doorway wielding a long-handled hammer, had murdered Michael Redding. Jack, Chloe, and Lisa had tried to warn me. And I, blinded by a stupid childish crush, had refused to see the evidence.

Wei slowly raised the hammer out to his side and held it there at arm's length as he took a step toward me.

"Put that down," I squeaked. "Drop it. I know how to use this gun."

"Marilyn," he said, in a soft, steady voice, "I'm not going to hurt you."

"Pull the trigger!" Lisa was sobbing in terror.

Wei glanced at her, then back at me. "Your friend needs an ambulance, Marilyn. I'll call—"

"No!" I shrieked as he started to reach into the back pocket of his pants. "I'll do it myself."

But I had no phone. And Lisa's phone was on the table, too close to where Wei was standing. My heart thudded erratically in my chest and a soft moan escaped me as my bladder spasmed, threatening to let go. Both my hands were slippery with sweat as I clutched the gun, one finger dangerously close to the trigger. A flicker of fright passed through Wei's eyes.

The front doorbell chimed.

Lisa pleaded, "Marilyn! For God's sake."

Wei said, "Answer the door, Marilyn."

"No!" Lisa croaked. "He might have an accomplice."

"Don't move," I instructed Wei, who slowly let the hammer drop to his side, but did not let go of it. My legs threatened to collapse under me as I began inching my way backwards toward the front door. "Who's there?"

"Police," said Andy's familiar voice." Open up, please."

With a relieved "Oh!" I threw open the door.

Andy said, "Whoa" at the sight of the pistol I was pointing at his chest. I spun around to aim it at Wei again and screamed when I saw that he was bending over Lisa's helpless figure.

"No!" I shouted. "Andy, he's got a hammer!!"

Instead of drawing his own weapon, Andy pried the pistol from my hands while Officers Baumgartner and Navarro stood behind him looking on curiously—instead of rushing into the kitchen to arrest Zhang Wei. Or Lisa. Or both.

"Relax, now," Andy said. "You're not in any danger. We're here." He put an arm around my shoulders.

"But he—Lisa says he killed Redding because Redding knew about his abortion practice and something— something about careless practices and drugs. She says he's been watching her house and—"

"We've got this, Marilyn. You need to relax. Why not sit down for a minute?"

Ignoring his advice, I babbled on: "And Lisa! She—I tried to be friends with her! All this time, she was blackmailing herself and harassing Rachel and Alejandra. It was her all along, and we had her helping us—oh my god!"

"You couldn't have known," he said, as the two officers walked past us into the kitchen.

I pulled away from Andy to watch as they knelt to examine Lisa, who was still convulsing, although she had fallen silent except for an occasional gasping intake of air.

"She needs an ambulance," said Wei in an authoritative voice. "Now. Or you'll lose her."

The officers looked up, and Navarro obediently whipped out his phone—while Wei watched in silence, still dangling the hammer at his side.

"And she might have some medication in the house somewhere that you should bring with her, in case she loses consciousness and can't talk to the doctors," Wei continued in that same calm, instructive tone.

Baumgartner hurried off to search for the meds and returned empty handed. "Nothing in the bathroom or bedroom."

"But she mentioned medication the last time I was here," I managed to say.

Baumgartner dutifully mounted a search of the kitchen. "No medication except for this." He handed the bottle to Andy. "Prescribed by a vet. Same stuff I give my Lab to calm him down when the fireworks start."

"She has cats," I murmured. Who would care for the little bird-slashers now? Certainly not Rachel. Perhaps Alejandra would step up.

Andy perused the label and tucked the medication into his satchel. He was visibly annoyed. "Don't touch anything else without your gloves, okay? Now put them on and start shutting down the house."

"Sure," said Baumgartner. "What do I need to do besides lock the doors and windows?"

Chloe was right about these two assistants needing constant supervision. Poor Andy.

"That'll do for now," Andy said curtly and turned to Wei. "Dr. Zhang, I'll need you to come down to the station." He looked at me. "You too, Marilyn. We'll want your statement. I'll call Jack and ask him to drive you. It won't take long."

When Jack arrived, we stood on the sidewalk watching Andy drive away with Zhang Wei beside him in the front seat. A minute later, we heard the sirens of an emergency vehicle coming to collect Lisa Cardwell, who was still being watched over by Officer Navarro. Officer Baumgartner stepped outside and was just about to lock Lisa's front door when his earlier comment came back to me wrapped in an exclamation point: *"Same stuff I give my Lab to calm him down ..."*

"Wait," I said to Jack. "I've left something inside."

Almost certain of what I'd find, I opened the cabinet from which Baumgartner had retrieved the bottle of pet tranquilizers. There on the shelf, along with six cans of Fancy Feast and a packet of treats for the felines, were two boxes of Milk-Bones and three packets of something called "Beggin' Strips," with a cartoon figure of an ecstatic dog on the cover.

So even before Officer Navarro climbed into the ambulance behind Lisa's stretcher, I knew.

Maybe he likes you and doesn't care much for your friends.

Except for the pronoun, Andy had nailed it.

31

As Chloe placed a slice of Key lime pie in front of him, Andy's eyes lit up like Fourth of July fireworks, the racket of which we had moved inside to escape. But just as he picked up his fork, she burst out, "Did Lisa really kill Michael Redding, Andy? Why? Why did she do it?"

We were seated around the dining room table, where Andy had just wasted several minutes apologizing for having missed dinner. He had opted for a sandwich at his desk while piecing together testimonies, filing reports— and making stops at three different hospitals, which he promised to explain later.

He waggled a finger. "All will become clear soon. But first let me share some of the discoveries we made while examining Lisa Cardwell's personal effects, along with some information she provided at the hospital. There are things you all need to know."

If there was a "staying cool under pressure" class in detective school, he must have aced it. There was no indication that the hectic pace or the dramatic events of the day had jangled his nerves in the slightest.

Following Jack's and my return from the station, I'd revealed to Chloe and Jack the terrifying events of the afternoon. Chloe had given me several backrubs I barely registered and Jack had asked multiple times if I didn't want a glass of wine. My stomach had rebelled at the thought of alcohol, so Chloe had brewed me an herbal tea—not ginger, thank goodness.

With Jack too agitated to manage the grill, Chloe had ordered pizzas, pointing out that the steaks would keep until tomorrow. It had belatedly occurred to me that with Rachel still in rehab, Alejandra might be spending the holiday alone, pining over the ongoing separation from her boy. I'd invited her over to eat pizza with us while we waited for Andy's arrival. She now sat next to Chloe, watching Andy with expectant eyes like the rest of us.

Andy took a few seconds to savor his first bite of the chilled pie. "Delicious." Prompted by Jack's scowl, he hurried on. "Okay, then. As she confessed to Marilyn, it was Mrs. Cardwell who left those threatening notes for you, Alejandra."

Alejandra nodded. "I could tell she didn't like me—or any of us—that much, but I had no idea. I would not have guessed."

She liked me, I thought. But then, that was nothing to brag about, was it?

"For several months, she'd been gleaning information about several of the neighbors from the internet." He paused. "By the way, you all need to change your passwords for Facebook—for everything else, too. I don't think she'll be using them now, but better not to take a chance."

"Great," Jack said. "That's just great."

"She listened in on your back-patio conversations as well," Andy told Alejandra. "At first, she was only curious about what you all were up to over there. A Nosy Nellie, as it were." He grinned at Jack and me. I grimaced and Jack scowled at him.

"As you know, the back of her property is separated by a fence from both Alejandra's and Rachel's backyards. She spent a lot of time out there, eavesdropping on Alejandra's chats with Daniela or Marilyn or Rachel, and with Brian, Alejandra's ex-husband. That's where she learned about Alejandra's immigration status and Rachel's bitterness toward her deceased partner—although Rachel vented a lot about that on Facebook, too, I understand."

Jack said, "So Lisa was offended because the country was falling apart, as she told Marilyn? That's why she harassed Alejandra and old lady Chang?"

"Zhang," I mumbled reflexively.

Andy nodded. "Racism was her sole motive for that, yes. Plain old hate crimes, nothing to do with Michael Redding's murder. And just wait. It gets even better."

Despite the dark subject matter, he seemed to be having a good time. But if he thought his relaxed, cheerful delivery of the appalling details would soothe our anxiety, he was mistaken. The faces of the others mirrored my own dread as we waited to find out what he meant by "even better."

"One day she overheard you all talking about working together to explore the murder."

He swished his wine around in the glass, took a sip, and savored it while we waited in silence except for a noisy yawn from Boondoggles, who was curled up next to Alejandra's chair. As an afterthought, I'd suggested that Alejandra bring the creature along. Why punish the neighborhood by leaving him alone to bray and howl through hours of fireworks racket—as Michael Redding had done the previous year?

"And then you all started meeting after midnight, so she wasn't picking up much from the backyard anymore. That's when she bugged the light fixture in Alejandra's dining room."

Alejandra's hands flew to her mouth. I tried to imagine a bug-eyed, nervous Lisa bent over her computer, deviously mining our private information. Sneaking into Alejandra's home through an open window or unlocked back door. Climbing onto—what? A chair? A kitchen stool? A stack of clutter? —and with those frail, quaking arms, attaching a listening device to the ceiling fan light fixture. When? While Alejandra slept? While she was out? I shuddered.

"But how did she get into my house?" Alejandra wanted to know. "I lock my doors and windows, like everyone does now."

"It seems she had keys to both your front and back door."

"But that's not possible! Where would she have gotten them?"

"She was out in her backyard on the afternoon your ex-husband came to visit without your son. She peered over the fence and noticed your set of keys protruding from the lock on that shed in your yard. While you were occupied with Mr. Stevens out front, she climbed the fence, snagged the keys, and ran out to Home Depot to have the housekeys duplicated."

"But it was only a couple of hours before I found them in the shed door!"

He shrugged. "She used the do-it-yourself key duplication machine. Doesn't take long."

Alejandra had turned pale. "She's had my housekey this entire time?"

"Yes. So once your house was wired, she was able to overhear your discussions about such things as Jenny Ho's and the porn sites. And the concerns it may have caused some of you."

His eyes swung my direction and I glanced at Jack. Would he guess that I'd blabbed my disloyal thoughts to Rachel and Alejandra? But he merely looked puzzled, not suspicious.

"This is so creepy," Chloe said. "She has to be insane, right?"

"I'm not a psychiatrist. I do know she had a calculated

reason for everything she did. Marilyn, she told you part of it."

I nodded. "Not enough, though. She confessed to the harassment but insisted that Wei killed Redding. She claimed that Wei was an abortionist." I waited for Andy's confirmation or rebuttal, hoping for the latter. But he just said, "Go on."

"She said that Redding knew things Zhang might go to prison for. Things having to do with careless practices at his abortion clinic. And something about illegal drugs. But she didn't explain how they knew each other, or what the Jenny Ho's connection was."

"Before we get into that," Andy said, continuing to take the long way around, "let's talk about Rachel and that CB radio."

"Right. The psycho told Marilyn she was behind that, too." Jack was incredulous. "How'd she pull that off?"

"Rachel's home security system," Andy said. "An easy hack, for those who know how. And once you're in, you can speak or play a recording through the speakers located throughout the house." He chuckled at our shocked expressions. "It's been known to cause a nightmare or two, and in at least one case, a heart attack."

"I've read about that," Chloe said. "There are cases of perverts scaring the crap out of little kids, even threatening them."

"So, through eavesdropping and Facebook hacking, she knew the circumstances of Rachel's divorce and her partner's death. And so she pretended to be Deb's lover, flirting with Deb over a CB radio." He chuckled. "Pretty creative, I'll give her that." When Chloe frowned at him, he added, "Sick, but creative."

I still couldn't grasp it. "But how did Lisa know how to hack someone's security system? Or even Facebook, for that matter? She told us she was a clerk at the DMV. Was that a lie?"

"Not a lie, just a half-truth. A couple years after she left the convent and had her baby, she married Mr. Cardwell. With his support, she went back to school and got herself a degree in computer science and a master's in electrical engineering."

We were all speechless until Alejandra said, "Wow. That's impressive."

Andy nodded. "She was an IT specialist at the DMV for fifteen years, until after her husband's murder. Then because her nerves were shot, she started making lots of errors, so they moved her to a desk out on the floor."

"A tech whiz," Jack mused. "Who would've suspected?"

"Well also, after her husband retired, he did some P.I. work, pretty common for ex-cops. Most likely, she learned a lot from him about eavesdropping technology and the like."

Alejandra's suddenly slapped both cheeks with her palms. "Andy, does Rachel know about this?"

"Yes, I've filled her in. That was one of my hospital stops today. I thought it was unkind to let her go on wondering if she was insane."

"I knew she wasn't! I never doubted it for a second." Alejandra's face flooded with relief. "Oh, I am so happy to hear this!"

"Wait," said Chloe. "What about those times she heard the voices outside in her yard, and other people standing nearby didn't hear anything? Including Dr. Zhang and you two." She looked at Alejandra and me.

Andy explained, "Her therapist was present when I talked with Rachel. She suggested that once the idea had been planted in Rachel's mind, the combination of stress, alcohol, antidepressants, and the Valium she took at irregular times in varying amounts could have led to her hearing subsequent voices without help from Mrs. Cardwell. She could also be confused about what she heard at which time. But this is something the therapist and Rachel will delve into together."

"That would explain how Rachel thought she heard the woman talking about personal matters that only she and Deb knew about," Chloe observed.

"This is all fascinating, as promised," Jack said. "But isn't there something else you wanted to tell us? For example, how did she get Redding to eat that Thai curry?"

"I'll get to that," said Andy. "But first let's talk about your neighbor, Dr. Zhang."

My stomach flipflopped as Wei's face swam before me, concerned but reassuring as I pointed the pistol at him with sweaty, jittery hands, my finger tapdancing nervously with the trigger. *I'm not going to hurt you, Marilyn.* But he had refused to lay down the hammer with which he had shattered the pane of Lisa's back door. Could I be blamed for fearing him?

"The first clue we got on this case," Andy began, "wasn't the reference to the strip club and porn sites. If you recall, I told you that some things would have to remain confidential."

"I believe you did say that once or twice, yes," Chloe said with a trace of impatience. So what were you keeping from us?"

"Only a few hours after we found Mr. Redding's body, a text message was sent to my office from a stolen phone— not the one that was later used to send the other clues. This message said straight out, "Dr. Zhang Wei murdered Michael Redding.""

Jack spoke for all of us. "So let me get this straight. You got a tip first thing that Zhang Wei was the killer. You were sitting on it all this time, refusing to consider that it might be true because—because why, now?"

Andy laughed out loud. "Sitting on it? Jack, Jack." He shook his head as if to say *good one.* "Of course we investigated thoroughly. We cleared Dr. Zhang on the same day we got that message. Now, may I continue?"

"Unreal," Jack muttered. "Why didn't you tell us about

that when we were all in a tangle over the damn receipt Marilyn found in the yard?"

"Let him finish, Jack, for God's sake," I snapped.

I hid my trembling hands in my lap, twisting and untwisting my linen napkin as I waited for Andy to continue assuring us of Wei's innocence. *What if I had shot him?*

"Dr. Zhang was an ob-gyn, as you know." He watched my face as he added, "And yes, he sometimes performed legal abortions in his clinic, he and his partner."

Disappointment put an end to what was left of my appetite. I put down my fork. "She said he killed her daughter. I suppose that was true, then?"

Andy's appetite was still intact, and he swallowed another bite of pie before answering. "Amanda died a year ago last March, only two months after her father was killed. Mrs. Cardwell blamed her death on depression and guilt connected with the abortion Dr. Zhang performed. But Dr. Zhang didn't kill Amanda. She committed suicide."

Alejandra was the first to find her voice. "Suicide! And she told us Amanda was living in Reno, married with a couple of kids. Oh this is just too sad!"

"Yes," Andy agreed. "Mother and daughter had been estranged over Amanda's career choice and other behavior, but soon after the abortion, Amanda reached out to her mom. She was experiencing guilt and regrets and claimed that the baby's father had convinced her to have the abortion against her wishes."

"Poor Lisa," Alejandra repeated, as if speaking of someone other than the woman who had terrorized her over a period of weeks, even threatening her son in one of the notes. "No wonder she despises Dr. Zhang. In her mind, he killed her daughter."

"She does indeed harbor a great deal of malice," Andy said. "So much so that she has repeatedly sought revenge. She filed a complaint with the state medical board, but that got her nowhere. She lawyered up and tried to press charges, pointing out that Amanda had been on anti-depressants for three years, which in Mrs. Cardwell's mind should have been reason for Dr. Zhang to refuse her the abortion."

"I should think so," I said.

Andy continued, "But the attorney convinced her she didn't have a case. She then turned to stalking and, after he retired, tracking Dr. Zhang through creative use of the internet. She learned he had retired to Las Oliviñas. It was no coincidence that Michael Redding, the other person she held responsible for Amanda's death, was also a resident of our town."

"So Zhang and Redding did know each other?"

"Right. In fact, Wei had moved his mom, and later himself, to Las Oliviñas because Redding had sold him on how affordable and safe your neighborhood is."

"So Lisa moved here to be near Michael and Zhang Wei, to make harassing them easier," Chloe guessed.

Andy nodded. "Yep."

"What about the other woman who died? Lisa called it a botched abortion." I experienced a wave of nausea just from speaking those words.

"Botched? Well, there was a rupture and some hemorrhaging that couldn't be contained. It's rare, but it happens, usually in middle-aged women. The woman's family sued Dr. Zhang, unsuccessfully, but Lisa found out through her stalking."

When he decided we could handle more, Andy continued, "So as to how Mr. Redding and Dr. Zhang knew each other—" He paused and turned to Chloe. "Could I please have just a little more wine?"

Chloe complied, and there was a grunt from Jack that I interpreted as an urge to crack the bottle of Sancerre over Andy's head.

"So," Andy went on, "Art Doherty, the owner of Jenny

Ho's, where Mrs. Cardwell's daughter, Amanda, worked—"

"Oh, Jesus." Jack shook his head. "This can't get any crazier."

"Yes, that's right. Amanda was an exotic dancer." The silent *So what?* he directed at Jack was unmistakable, and I prayed Jack would hold his tongue.

"Good God," he said. "No wonder they'd been estranged." Chloe's sharp glance prompted him to add, "Lisa being a former nun and all."

"Anyway," Andy continued, "Mr. Doherty had for the past four years been referring customers to Dr. Zhang— young women who worked at the club. He would give the doctor's card to the pregnant lady, and if she was hesitant to make the appointment, he would ask Michael Redding to encourage her. It seems Michael knew all the women, one way or another."

"No surprise," said Jack. "Sort of a pimp, you would call him?"

"Dad, my god," said Chloe between clenched teeth.

Andy frowned. "No, I would not call him a pimp. Sometimes Michael would drive the young ladies to their appointments and consult with the doctor afterward to get instructions for follow-up, etc. For all these services Doherty would pay him a fee."

"Disgusting," Jack muttered.

"Another way to look at it," said Andy, "is that Doherty was concerned about the women's well-being. If they couldn't afford the fee, he paid it himself. Keep in mind, these ladies chose to get the abortion. No one was forced."

At this typical liberal defense of a morally repre-hensible procedure, my anger flared, and I didn't try to hide it. "Their babies had no say in the decision. None whatsoever."

"Mom," said Chloe. "Those women no doubt had their reasons. No one gets an abortion lightly. It would be—"

"I disagree," I cut her off. My nerves were shot, my voice

razor sharp. Any leftover regard for Zhang Wei lay in shreds on the dining room floor. "What liberals won't admit is that some women use abortion as birth control. Isn't that what these women were doing? And it should all be legal, according to the pro-abortion faction. It's sinful, just as Lisa pointed out."

"But still," Jack said.

All our heads swung toward him. Looking sheepish, he cleared his throat. "What if they didn't know who the father was? Or maybe they were raped." He shrugged. "It happens. Maybe it's for the best, sometimes, to—you know—stop the process."

Astonished, I turned my anger on Jack. "Oh sure. You really think all those girls were raped? And you heard Andy: if they were hesitant, Redding talked them into it."

Andy cleared his throat. "In any case, regarding Mrs. Cardwell's daughter—"

"And Zhang Wei. He performed abortions for a living! My god, Jack. Don't defend him."

"That's not what I was doing," he said, irritated but correctly intuiting that I was in no mood for a debate. "At any rate, Marilyn, Andy has the floor right now."

After a moment, Andy decided it was safe to continue. "Regarding Mrs. Cardwell's daughter, Michael Redding had a vested interest in putting her in touch with Dr. Zhang."

He looked around the table, waiting for us to put it together. He was met with four faces frozen in anticipation but not a smidgeon of recognition. So much information to process. All those frightening details about Lisa's hate crimes, and on top of that, Andy's verification that Wei had performed abortions—one of them on Lisa's daughter, no less. And out of guilt, the poor girl had committed suicide.

"As it happens," Andy said, his eyes flitting from one of us to the other, anticipating our responses, "Mr. Redding was the father of Amanda Cardwell's baby."

After a chorus of "Oh my god," (and one "Should've

guessed," contributed by Jack), Andy continued, "So Mrs. Cardwell had lost both her husband and daughter within two months of each other. She was estranged from her son, who came out as gay several years ago."

"Of course he did," said Jack.

"Around the time of her daughter's death, Mrs. Cardwell began noticing a trembling in her hands, and sometimes in her arms and legs. She would shake uncontrollably at times—"

"Yes, we know," I said, inexplicably irritated by this mention of Lisa's mysterious condition. "She brought it up at every opportunity. It's Parkinson's, right?"

"Perhaps. But she was afraid to see a doctor, so it's never been diagnosed, except by Mrs. Cardwell's friend the internet. According to the physician who gave her an initial exam at the hospital earlier today, it might be a treatable condition—there are several possible causes—but she had decided it was either Parkinson's or worse, a brain tumor."

While we digested this, he continued. "So anyway, the deaths of Amanda and Mr. Cardwell, the estrangement from her son, and her own medical situation all contributed to her misery." He shook his head. "Her reasoning ability went all to hell."

"So sad," said Alejandra.

Thacker continued, "Her religious beliefs conflicted with murderous thoughts toward Redding and Zhang. The sad thing is, she had finally convinced herself that although they were evildoers who deserved to die, she should leave the vengeance to God. She would settle for confronting Redding and Dr. Zhang in person, venting her anger, calling them both out as killers. They would be given a chance to repent. Her goal was to find some closure before she died."

Since previous attempts to hurry him along had been fruitless, we waited in silence. But his next words sent a shiver through me.

"So that was Mrs. Cardwell's plan when she visited Michael Redding that afternoon. Closure through confrontation, nothing more."

We all leaned towards Andy, dessert and wine forgotten.

32

ndy spoke as if filing a verbal police report: "Around noon on the day of the murder, Mrs. Cardwell walked to Mr. Redding's house and rang the doorbell. When she told him who she was and why she'd come, he blocked his doorway and told her that he had absolutely no regrets about Amanda's abortion. They'd both known they had no future together, neither of them had wanted the baby."

"That must have been so hard for Lisa to hear," Alejandra sympathized.

Andy nodded. "Michael told her he had been sorry to learn of Amanda's suicide. She had seemed like a nice girl, but he hadn't really known her all that well. And then he shut the door in Mrs. Cardwell's face."

"Sounds like the Redding we all knew and loved," said Jack.

"Mrs. Cardwell, at that point, forgot about finding closure through confrontation. She was so poisoned by hatred—and her growing mental instability was a contributing factor—that she began making plans as soon as the door slammed in her face. She walked home and then drove to the grocery store, where she purchased ingredients for Thai peanut curry."

A soft moan escaped me, and my bitterness toward

Zhang Wei was forgotten as I contemplated the horror of what Andy was about to reveal.

I was alone with Michael Redding's killer. I drank coffee at her kitchen table. I held a gun on Zhang Wei and almost let her convince me to pull the trigger.

Chloe asked, "How did she know about his allergy? From stalking him?"

"Worse than stalking, actually. He wasn't one to lock his door, so she had entered his house more than once during the past year, gathering contact information on his family and friends. Medical records, insurance forms—she probably knew more about him than his own mother did."

"So scary," Alejandra whispered.

"You're sure that woman was never in our house?" Jack asked. He squinted up at the light fixture with its innocent soft glow. I suspected he would give it a close-up examination later, with my encouragement.

"She says not," Andy replied. "I think she would've admitted it along with everything else. Anyway, she whipped up a batch of curry. And then she went to call on Mr. Redding again."

Chloe said, "But surely she didn't expect him to willingly eat it. She must have—do you mean ...?"

Andy nodded. "Yes, she took her Glock with her. And she let herself in through the back door, which was of course unlocked. Redding was in the shower, so she sat in the kitchen and waited."

"But what about Boonie?" Alejandra asked. "Didn't he warn Michael? Or try to attack Lisa?"

"Oh, she was already pals with Boondoggles. On previous visits, she had brought him treats. This time, she had a tranquilizer slathered in peanut butter and a pound of ground beef with her, half of which she used to quiet him on her way in. The other half she threw to him as she made her exit."

For the first time, Alejandra seemed angry at Lisa. "So

that's the reason Boonie always begged her for treats. He only did that with me, normally."

"But why didn't Redding just refuse to eat the curry?" Jack asked. "He must've known it would kill him. Looks like he would've chosen a bullet to the brain. I would've."

"She threatened to visit his mother," Andy said matter-of-factly. He drained his glass and pushed it toward Chloe, who ignored it. "She recited Mrs. Redding's address, phone number, the whole bit. It was either eat the curry and die, or refuse and she would shoot him and then go after his mom. That was the threat, anyway. She claims she had no intention of following through."

"Why the curry?" Jack pressed. "Seems unnecessary since she had the gun."

"Because she had planned to make his death look like suicide. She was prepared to force him to write a note, but then she spotted an open box of dishes on the edge of the kitchen table. Until then, she had been focused solely on killing Mr. Redding, but the dishes gave her an idea."

"So it was Michael who purchased those dishes from the thrift store?" Chloe asked.

"Uh, no." Andy seemed suddenly uncomfortable. "Technically, the dishes belonged to Alejandra."

Alejandra drew in her breath as we all turned our eyes on her. She started to protest, but Andy held up a hand to stop her.

"I never saw those dishes before," she said anyway.

"We'll come back to that. So anyhow, Mrs. Cardwell moved the curry from the plate she had brought it on to one of the plates from the box. According to her, Mr. Redding took his own sweet time ingesting the curry despite her prodding. He seemed to be mocking her."

"Easy to believe," Jack said.

"When she pressed him to hurry, he answered with a smirk and a 'What are you gonna do about it?' according to her. She said, 'You'll be in hell soon. And I intend to send your baby-killer doctor friend straight to death row. He'll pay for your sins, and his.'"

Chloe hugged her arms, which were crawling with goosebumps.

Andy continued, "Mr. Redding's response was 'Knock yourself out, bitch.' By this time, his eyes and lips had nearly swollen shut and his face was masked with splotches, according to Mrs. Cardwell. He began to wheeze, and he let his head fall onto his plate." He paused. "Are you okay, Marilyn?"

I had buried my face in my hands, and I left it there as I mumbled through my fingers, "Go on."

"This is where Mrs. Cardwell made a crucial mistake. She was sure Mr. Redding was close to death. His eyes had rolled back in his head, and he was salivating. She couldn't find a pulse, but that was probably because she was shaking badly—partly from nerves, along with her condition—so she knew there wasn't much time before she'd lose control of her limbs and be unable to walk, much less carry the carton of dishes."

"She left before making sure he was dead?" Jack was incredulous.

"Yes. But it was either leave at once or risk ending up in a crumpled heap on the floor, like you saw this afternoon, Marilyn. Anyway, she figured the odds were in her favor, based on his condition. And if she turned out to be wrong, she planned to use the gun on herself. Her will to live had pretty much died with Amanda."

He continued, "She believed he was either dead or would be within minutes, so she grabbed the dishes, along with a receipt from Jenny Ho's that she later smeared with water to make most of the information unreadable before inserting it into the hedge between your yards for Marilyn to find—and she exited through the back door, taking an out-of-the-way route back home so as not to be recognized by anyone on the street."

"But he revived enough to call 911," Chloe murmured.

"He'd been faking to a certain extent, and he rallied enough to locate one of his Epi-pens, which he kept stashed in various locations—we found two others in the house—and to make the call, but he couldn't remember Mrs. Cardwell's name, having only met her that once. And for the past few years, Amanda had gone by her stage name: Cindi Lockhart."

"So he just said, 'neighbor knows …' and then he died." Chloe finished for Andy, her eyes welling up as she spoke.

We sat for a moment, contemplating Michael Redding's tragic final moments.

Chloe spoke again. "And Lisa sneaked the dishes onto Alejandra's dining room table after it was over?"

"He returned the dishes to Alejandra, yes."

Alejandra's voice quivered. "I never saw those dishes before."

Andy spoke gently. "I'm sorry, Alejandra. When I met with your friend Daniela, I showed her the dishes. She remembers being with you when you purchased them at a yard sale across town after the lady who picked them up at the Oakland thrift store had a change of heart about keeping them."

"Daniela! She told you that? I can't believe …" As her voice trailed off, I studied her face and was reminded of Rachel's reaction when realizing she had forgotten that she had called Lisa at 3:00 a.m. to invite her to the meeting. Another wake-up call?

Chloe asked, "But how did Michael end up with the dishes?"

"It seems Mr. Redding had a habit of helping himself to items from Alexandra's front porch and yard when she was away. Or at night, he'd walk over with a flashlight and pick up whatever caught his eye. Nothing of any value, or so he claimed to Daniela. It was just a lark."

"Daniela knew this? And she never told me?"

Alejandra's face was crimson.

He looked at her thoughtfully. "It's likely she didn't want you to know she was having these kinds of conversation with Mr. Redding. Anyway, on the night he took the dishes from your porch—which was two days before the murder—he bragged to Daniela about it down at the Coal Bin. Told her he planned to give them to his mom, and he figured you wouldn't miss them anyway."

Jack marveled, "So Redding stole Alejandra's dishes from the driveway, and then Cardwell stole them from Redding after she made him eat the curry, and then she sneaked them into Alejandra's dining room." Jack marveled. "Whoa."

"Yep," said Andy. "But first, she hid the dishes in her shed for several days while figuring out how to connect them with Dr. Zhang. He hadn't moved in with his mom yet."

"Surely she had sleuthed out his address across town," Jack said. "Or why not just put them at his mom's house? Wouldn't that still have led you to Zhang?"

"She considered that, of course. But Ms. Zhang rarely left the house except in broad daylight, and her neighbors were known to be vigilant." He winked at Jack. "Finally, Mrs. Cardwell overheard you all planning to do your own investigative research, and soon the copy of Alejandra's housekey was in her possession. So she decided that since I'd already searched all the houses on the street, she would plant the box on Alejandra's premises and then infiltrate your group to move things along in case you all didn't eventually uncover the box among Alejandra's—um—stuff."

He continued, "But since the dishes wouldn't be found on Zhang's premises, she needed another way to tie them to him. So she added the Jenny Ho's t-shirt, which was among some swag from the club that had ended up with her when Amanda died. And she left the thrift store receipt that was already in the box. Since the store was near the strip club, it was another way to point me in that direction."

He went on to explain that Lisa's new plan was to further focus the investigation on Jenny Ho's, where she hoped the manager, Mr. Doherty, when interrogated, would confess his dealings with Michael Redding, which in turn would reveal Redding's connection to Zhang Wei.

"And that part of her plan succeeded," he continued. "The other clues, the porn sites, the gym, and Maple Avenue Elementary took longer for us to unravel, but they eventually connected Mr. Redding with Dr. Zhang as well."

"How so?" I wondered. The porn site seemed predictable enough—no surprise if a porn star got an abortion. But an elementary school teacher? Of course, I did not say this aloud.

"Mr. Redding had quite a love life. While dating Amanda, he admitted to her that he was also seeing at least three other women. One was a porn actress, and another worked at the school on Maple Avenue. Amanda told this to her mom while unburdening herself about the abortion."

"A schoolteacher? Doesn't sound like his type," Jack commented.

"Not a teacher, no. She worked in the front office. But to help pay the rent, she waited tables at Jenny Ho's on weekends. And yes, she had visited Dr. Zhang's clinic as well, referred by Michael Redding."

"So," said Chloe. "I'm guessing the third girlfriend worked at Twenty-four Hour Fitness?"

Andy nodded. "You got it. In fact, she was the forty-five-year-old woman who died from hemorrhaging during her abortion."

Jack broke the ensuing silence. "So Redding boasted to his pregnant girlfriend—Lisa's daughter—about boning the other women. What a guy." I could tell he was feeling vindicated for his animosity toward the victim. The scene with the rosebush confrontation had probably been running through his head for months, to the soundtrack of Michael's taunt: "Get a life, old man."

"Long story short," said Andy, which of course was a lie. "Once she had decided to frame Dr. Zhang, Mrs. Cardwell began planting clues. She had stalked him enough to know that he was a creature of habit: on Sunday afternoons he always cleaned his house and read for a while before driving to his mom's house for dinner. So she knew there was a good chance he would have no alibi."

"He did have one, though?" Alejandra asked.

"Airtight," said Andy. "Helping his elderly neighbor clean out his attic."

"But what about a motive?" Jack asked. "You were supposed to think Zhang killed Redding because he knew too much? But all those abortions were legal, right?"

"One of the first clues that came in from the stolen phone said, 'A drug deal gone bad,' remember?"

We all nodded.

"Dr. Zhang—who is still a licensed practitioner, by the way—was regularly prescribing OxyContin for Mr. Redding, who for several years suffered chronic neck and back pain because of a car accident, aggravated by his aggressive drumming. Redding's regular doctor had cut him off when he saw he was addicted."

"But Zhang thought it was fine to keep prescribing pills to an addict? Disgusting," Jack pronounced.

"Another way to look at it is that Mr. Redding was indeed in pain, at least for a while, and he seemed to function okay on the medication." Andy replied. "And it wasn't illegal. But Zhang had, in fact, cut Michael off just two weeks before the murder when he learned that Michael had weaned himself off the Oxy months earlier and was now making a profit off the pills, which cost him nothing with the insurance his mom paid for, by selling them to a custodian at Jenny Ho's."

"And Zhang found that out—how?" Jack asked.

Andy smiled. "A concerned employee at Jenny Ho's, our friend Marty Clement, clued the owner in. In turn, Mr. Doherty contacted Dr. Zhang and asked him to stop prescribing the stuff. Which he did."

"So Redding was pissed, and there's your motive," said Jack. "They might have argued over it."

"Or so Mrs. Cardwell wanted us to believe. Along with the dishes and other clues pointing to him, there might have been a case, except that Dr. Zhang had an alibi."

Chloe said, "But how did Lisa know about the narcotics? Or that Michael was angry about Dr. Zhang cutting him off?"

Andy grinned. "Here is where I have to thank you folks for leading me to Ms. Clement. When I finally got hold of her, I found her more than willing to talk, as long as it was outside of her workplace. Turns out she had been good friends with Mrs. Cardwell's daughter, Amanda."

"We all knew she was acting suspicious that night," said Jack, the man with 20-20 hindsight.

"Anyway," said Andy, "she had contacted Lisa after Amanda's death to express condolences. Lisa befriended her, hiding her disapproval of Marty's profession, and this led to Marty telling Lisa everything she knew about Mr. Redding, which was quite a bit. She had dated him briefly herself before deciding he was a 'douche,' or so she told Mrs. Cardwell."

"Lisa said you would figure everything out after talking to Marty," I said. "So Marty knew that Lisa killed Michael?"

"No, it was Dr Zhang she suspected, based on some brainwashing by Mrs. Cardwell. She had bought Lisa's theory that the murder was the result of the two men arguing—she herself had overhead Michael ranting over the phone to a person she believed was Dr. Zhang, clearly furious about having his Oxy cut off. But when I told her that Dr. Zhang had been cleared as a suspect and asked her if she knew anyone else with reason to kill Mr. Redding, it took her about two seconds to come up with a name: Lisa Cardwell."

"But the two had become friendly," Chloe pointed out. "Marty ratted her out anyway?"

"Yes. Not long before you all met her at Jenny Ho's, Marty had cut off contact with Mrs. Cardwell. She said the extreme hatred of Dr. Zhang and Michael Redding made her uncomfortable. And then Marty told me she had been turned off by Mrs. Cardwell's racism and other prejudices, and Bingo!" He tapped the side of his head in a self-congratulatory gesture. "I knew that Lisa was connected to both the murder and the harassment cases."

"Hold on," said Jack. And then he asked a question I should've thought of myself. "Why did Zhang show up at Lisa's house today with a hammer if he didn't intend to harm her?"

"Oh, right," said Andy. "Now that is another darn good question, Jack. I'm going to have to put you on the payroll if you keep this up."

His compliment added to my sense of inadequacy. Why had I thought myself capable of helping to track down a psycho killer? For that's clearly what Lisa was, and far from suspecting her, I had invited her into our group where she could not only keep track of how the investigation was progressing but manipulate it as well. I pushed my self-flagellation aside and waited for Andy's response—which, when it came, totally floored me.

"Dr. Zhang was concerned about Marilyn's safely."

My cheeks grew warm, and yes, I felt a twinge of regret for the uncharitable remarks I had made regarding Wei's unfortunate career history. Only a twinge. It passed quickly, as Andy turned to me and continued, "When you mentioned to him that you were off to visit Lisa Cardwell, the name struck an unpleasant chord."

"So he called you?" I remembered Wei turning his back to me and speaking into his phone as I walked toward Lisa's house.

"Not right away." He was offended. "Or of course, I would've appeared at the door much sooner. Instead, he called the office of his former partner, Dr. Abelman. It took Abelman's admin about fifteen minutes to go through their records to uncover communication from the state medical board about the complaints Lisa Cardwell had raised against their practice the year before. Then the whole thing fell into place—he remembered her email rants, letters to the newspaper, her connection with Michael Redding through Amanda."

"So he called you then?" Chloe asked.

"Yes, but I was in a meeting with the chief. So he kept calling back, and meanwhile started pacing the street in front of Mrs. Cardwell's house."

"Admirable," said Chloe, in a weak attempt at humor. "Maybe you should hire Dr. Zhang instead of Dad."

In response to this unexpected praise of someone other than himself, Andy quickly added, "Of course, I already knew of Dr. Zhang's connection with Mr. Redding from previous statements I took from him immediately after the murder and from conversations we had at various other times."

"So Zhang rode in on a white horse to save Marilyn?" Jack asked. "What a guy."

Andy ignored the snide comment. "Meanwhile, I'd finished examining the evidence we found on Mrs. Cardwell's computer, and I was trying to reach her to let her know I'd be by soon to discuss it. When I finally picked up Dr. Zhang's call, expressing his concern for Marilyn's safety, he was already on the street in front of Mrs. Cardwell's house." He looked at Jack. "But not on a white horse. He just ran over there on foot. And instead of a sword, he carried a hammer."

Perhaps due to shock— I must've still been in denial—I had an inexplicable urge to defend Lisa. "But I never felt like—I mean, she never threatened me. She just wanted to recruit me against Dr. Zhang, to help her convince you he was the one who killed Michael Redding."

"You probably weren't in danger," Andy reassured me. "She told me she thought of you as a friend. As you say, she only wanted your help."

"So he rang the doorbell, and when she didn't answer, he panicked and took a hammer to the back door," Jack concluded. "Is that the gist of it?"

"He didn't panic until he heard a scream followed by Marilyn begging Mrs. Cardwell to put down the gun," said Andy. "Of course, I arrived shortly thereafter to arrest Mrs. Cardwell."

"Just in time to prevent me from shooting Zhang Wei." That horrible scenario had been running through my head all evening. "And Andy, she seemed genuinely terrified that he was about to kill her. Is she that good an actress?"

"Not at all. Even at the hospital, after confessing everything, she insisted that Dr. Zhang had been coming for her because he knew she had killed Mr. Redding." He shrugged. "Guilty conscience, maybe? But her reasoning was a bit warped all the way around, as we've seen."

Chloe changed the subject. "What about the Peeping Tom? Was he connected to the murder at all?"

"Oh yes. I mean, no." He thought for a moment. "Only peripherally, is what I mean."

Jack's growl was more audible this time. But it was Chloe who said, "Get to the point, babe."

"The Peeping Tom," Andy said, "or at least one of the sightings of him, was shall we say, a bit of manipulative fabrication on the part of Mrs. Zhang." He grinned. "I guess mothers sometimes go to great lengths to convince their grown children to move back into the house."

"You mean she made that whole thing up about seeing

him run across my lawn after Brian left that afternoon?" Alejandra put down the glass she had just picked up. "But what about the other sightings?"

"Those were real. Yesterday we picked up a young man, a student at the community college. He admitted to the other offenses, but swore he was never on this street. At my request, Dr. Zhang pressed his mother, and she admitted her claim was a ploy." He smiled. "She was spooked by the murder and the reports of a Peeping Tom, just like the rest of you. Bottom line, she wanted her son at home to protect her."

"Well, it's good the real Peeping Tom is off the streets, anyway," said Chloe. Then she moved on. "So Rachel was one of your hospital visits. Who were the other two?"

"Oh, well. Mrs. Cardwell, of course. Who I was allowed to see long enough to get a statement, read her the rights, and put her under hospital arrest." He paused for effect, and we complied with respectful nods all around. "She had recovered almost completely with the help of sedatives and was able to confess everything regarding the murder— which she was willing to do only after I convinced her that there were absolutely no grounds for us to arrest Dr. Zhang."

"And she admitted to all the harassment and eavesdropping, too?" Alejandra asked.

"Yep. But I had already put it together from info we gleaned from her computer, not just the spying technology but also document files in which she had gleefully recorded the results of her efforts." He took a sip of wine. "She was pretty proud of herself."

"And who else got a hospital visit?" Chloe said, suddenly worried. "Was it your mom?"

"Yes, I stopped by to sit with her through her treatment, as usual. Her last one."

"You're a good son," Alejandra said. All of us, even Jack, expressed agreement.

Andy leaned back in his chair with a satisfied smile and looked from one of us to the other. "So, have I answered all your questions?"

It seemed he had. Other than a few astonished murmurs, we were unusually quiet for a group of friends seated around a table sharing dessert. Then Andy said, "Oh, speaking of Rachel," (although we hadn't been), "she asked me to give you something, Alejandra."

He retrieved his briefcase and removed a letter-sized envelope. "No idea," he said in response to her questioning eyes.

And so we said our goodbyes, Alejandra coaxing the meandering Boondoggles across the street, Chloe and Andy standing on the front steps watching them go. A wave of sadness washed over me. Now that the investigation was over, would Chloe head back to Portland to prepare for fall classes? She was still outside on the steps, conversing with Andy in a low voice, when Jack turned me toward the staircase and gave me a gentle push.

"Bedtime," he said. "And no middle-of-the-night meeting for you. Doctor's orders."

I managed a weak smile. "Okay, doc. But don't you wonder what will happen now? With those two, I mean?"

"It's none of our business," he reminded me. "Now upstairs you go."

Before I could comply, Chloe stepped inside. "Alejandra just texted me. You won't believe what was in that envelope Rachel sent by Andy." Without pausing, she continued, "It's a check for a huge chunk of money. Rachel's note said it's meant to pay Alejandra for watching her house, but she wants the money used for therapy and a lawyer, so Alejandra can get her son back and tackle her shopping issues. Isn't that just so generous? So sweet?" She laughed. "And it's just like Rachel to end the note with 'I may have mentioned a time or two that Deb left me a buttload of dough.'"

We murmured our approval of Rachel's generosity and waited to see if Chloe would mention her plans for the rest of the summer, but all she said was, "See you at breakfast" before she headed upstairs.

We followed, and just before I fell asleep, an unexpectedly painful image invaded my vision: Wei was standing on his mother's front porch in the light of the nearby streetlamp, and his smile was warm as he put out his cigarette and waved me onto the porch.

"I'm not going to hurt you, Marilyn," he said.

Beside me, Jack was already snoring. I rolled over and kissed his cheek.

"Good night, Mr. Meddleson. Sweet dreams."

About the Author

Peggy Schimmelman lives with her husband and a neurotic cat in Livermore, California. Her work includes the poetry chapbooks *Crazytown* and *Tick-Tock* and the novel *Whippoorwills*. She is co-author of two Wild Vine Writers' anthologies, *Long Stories Short* and *Two Truths and a Lie*. Her work has appeared in *North American Review, Pacific Review, Haight-Ashbury Journal, Comstock Review, Wild Musette Journal, Flash Fiction Magazine, 100wordstories.org,* and others.

If you enjoy *Insomniacs, Inc.,* Peggy would appreciate your review on Amazon.com and/or Goodreads.com.

Book club questions for *Insomniacs, Inc.* and *Whippoorwills* can be found at
https://peggyschimmelman.com.